IN THE
WANING
LIGHT

ALSO BY LORETH ANNE WHITE

A Dark Lure
The Slow Burn of Silence

Wild Country
Manhunter
Cold Case Affair

Shadow Soldiers
The Heart of a Mercenary
A Sultan's Ransom
Rules of Engagement
Seducing the Mercenary
The Heart of a Renegade

Sahara Kings
The Sheik's Command
Sheik's Revenge
Surgeon Sheik's Rescue
Guarding the Princess
"Sheik's Captive" in *Desert Knights* with Linda Conrad

More by Loreth Anne White
Melting the Ice
Safe Passage
The Sheik Who Loved Me
Breaking Free
Her 24-Hour Protector
The Missing Colton
The Perfect Outsider
"Saving Christmas" in the *Covert Christmas* anthology
"Letters to Ellie" a novella in the *SEAL of My Dreams* anthology

LORETH ANNE WHITE

IN THE WANING LIGHT

 Montlake
Romance

F
WHI

Published by Montlake Romance, Seattle

www.apub.com

Amazon, the Amazon logo, and Montlake Romance are trademarks of Amazon.com, Inc., or its affiliates.

ISBN-13: 9781503949669
ISBN-10: 1503949664

Cover design by Jason Blackburn

Printed in the United States of America

This one is for the folk

at Kelly's Brighton Marina.

MEGGIE

"We are not dispassionate viewers of the world. Witnesses and detectives are heavily influenced by what they expect to see, what they want to see, and what they actually see. The more ambiguous the latter, the more influential the first two. Similarly, what we remember depends upon what we believe—the human mind is not an objective recorder of information . . ."

~ MJ Brogan, *Sins Not Forgotten*

The white bookshelf in the living room was where my sister kept her goldfish in a little aquarium with a plastic coral reef under which they could hide, silvery bubbles trailing gently to the surface, perfectly regulated temperature and oxygen content. It worried me, as a child, those little orange fish trapped in their box, mouths gasping, eyes beseeching through the glass for a way to swim free. *Don't be stupid, Meggie,* my sister would say. *They live in a perfect world. There are no predators in their water, like the poor wild fish have to deal with in the sea.* But Sherry didn't know that sometimes the predator lives right there. Among us. In that perfectly regulated world. And he looks just like all the other fish in the bowl . . .

Meg lifted her hands from the keyboard and tried to rub blood back into her fingers. She was cold to the bone, working in fingerless gloves at the tiny camper table. Wind off the Pacific buffeted her rig, and rain thick with slush *thucked* against the windows. Outside the sky was black and thunder growled. The docks groaned and heaved against moorings as the waters in the bay crept insidiously higher, waves slapping and chuckling over the lip of the deck, over the sandbags, slinking toward the marina buildings that she and Noah had vacated an hour ago. The phone lines were down. Power was out all the way up the coast. The storm and tsunami surge moving in.

She was writing to keep her mind off waiting, as a way of moving forward. Writing this story because it's what she'd set out to do—the sole reason she'd returned to Shelter Bay.

But she'd not known how much it would take out of her, and it still was not done exacting its toll.

Every now and then, the faint beam of the lighthouse managed to penetrate the fog in its Cyclopean sweep, an omniscient, mythological giant that loomed high on the black rocks at Shelter Head—warning sailors of the jagged maw below. The foghorn put out its haunting moan—a sad, sonorous sound that tugged at Meg's soul, full with the mystery and lore of shipwrecks and sailors lost at sea.

Her camper was packed and ready to move to higher ground if the surge rose any higher. Noah was finally sleeping—she could hear from the deep, steady rhythm of his breathing as he lay tucked up in her sleeping bag. The child was exhausted, and Meg wanted to remain with him at the marina as long as she could because his father was still out there. On the water, alone, searching for his brother.

The Coast Guard was no help. They were deluged with distress calls from boaters up and down the coast caught by the dramatic shift in weather and the sudden tsunami warning, and there was a

Japanese tanker adrift farther north, pushing dangerously toward the rocks near Cannon Beach.

Meg scrubbed her gloved hands over her face, a greasy sickness bubbling in her stomach at the thought of Blake. Of what had happened between them. The secrets those Sutton brothers had kept from her all those years.

Secrets that had killed her family.

If it wasn't for Noah, she wouldn't be here now. She'd be back in Seattle. But as much as she hated Blake at this moment, she was not about to abandon his young son. She'd wait until she got a call from him on her cell, or until he returned.

If he returned . . .

She forced her focus back to her laptop. Not much time left until her battery died. She'd been writing her book out of sequence, puzzle chunks coming together bit by bit as she'd interviewed the principals involved with Sherry's murder.

> The fish in Sherry's bowl died before the end of that summer. My parents forgot to feed them. And then they forgot me.
>
> I died, too, that summer. In a different way.
>
> So did the town.
>
> Before Sherry's murder, Shelter Bay was a picture-perfect postcard town. A place where tourists flocked for holidays and ate ice cream and rode horses on the beach and laughed around campfires in the state park. Where kids left bikes in the road and those bikes would still be there come morning. Where neighbors never locked doors and shared hot apple pies over fences. Sherry's death tore open a community, exposing a shocking black gut. It made enemies of friends and turned justice gray. Our innocence was stolen that day. And it didn't stop there—like a pane of glass that had been smashed, the cracks from the first violent stroke feathered insidiously out over the ensuing months to create a web of even

deeper, more dangerous fissures that ended up swallowing two families whole. And taking yet more life.

That hot August day started like one hundred others, with the rise of the sun and the screech of gulls as the salmon boats went out. With the soft clunk of wood on wood as small crab boats jostled for space, nudging each other playfully along the docks of Bull Sutton's Marina. With a crisp wind lifting spindrift from the crests of rolling breakers, and bending the dune grasses that grew in white sand along the miles of spit. With sandpipers and black oystercatchers scuttling along the foam scallops left on hard-packed beaches by waves withdrawing from the shore only to rise up and pound back down again.

It had been a summer full of watermelons and sunblock and backyard barbecues, of purple blackberry smiles, of sea salt tingling on sun-warmed skin, of burning knees skinned raw in pursuit of tree houses and yet higher boughs. Of brightly painted buoys, and crab pots, and driftwood art. Of fresh local cheese from Chillmook farms, and the briny scent of pink crabs being boiled fresh from the bay.

A summer to be lived, full throttle, with the ferocity of youth. And skateboard wind in your hair.

But this day was going to be different. Before the sun set on this last day of innocence, Sherry Brogan would be dead. And I would be found unconscious in the shore break, lolling in the waves like a dead seal, my skin fishbelly white. Blue lips. Slimy seaweed tangled in long hair slicked back from a gaping gash across my brow.

That was almost a quarter century ago . . .

Meg paused. Then she scrolled quickly up to the top of her document and typed in a title. *Stolen Innocence*. She stared at it a while, the cursor winking in her dark camper. Thunder clapped and she flinched, her blood electric. A jagged streak of lightning cut into the black bay. It was closing in. Almost right above. Sleet pelted down harder. Noah moaned in his sleep. She glanced in his direction, then reached across the table and opened the blinds a crack with her fingers. It was hard to see how high the water was now, through the sleet, blackness, and mist. A few more minutes and she'd go outside with her flashlight to check again.

Deleting the title, she retyped: *The Stranger Among Us*. She chewed her lip.

This was not how she usually worked.

In all her other books, before she even started, Meg knew exactly who the perpetrator was. Don't pick an unsolved case. This was almost a cardinal rule in true crime. Before you started to write, you had to know the ending. You had to know who your villain was, that he'd been captured, charged, tried, and convicted. Certainly, she followed cases, trials, saved newspaper clippings, took notes in anticipation, but readers of true crime expected to see justice prevail. That was the appeal of the genre. It made people feel a little more in control of a world where bad things happened to good people. They gravitated to the genre because it gave them real-life heroes—cops, prosecutors, judges who helped bring closure to victims. Who righted the natural order of things. It showed there was recourse. It restored faith.

But this time Meg was unsure who the villain was.

She'd thought she'd known. The sheriff, deputies, DA—the whole town had been one hundred percent certain that twenty-two years ago Tyson Mack had raped and strangled Sherry Brogan, and that he'd been punished for what he'd done.

Until a few weeks ago.

Until Meg had returned to Shelter Bay to write Sherry's story.

Until she'd started peeling back layers to reveal a dark web of lies and misdirection and eyes turned blind to the fact that someone else could have done it.

And that *he* could still be out there. Among them.

She returned her attention to her words. The battery would need to be charged soon. Maybe twenty minutes left. Meg considered technique for a moment. Perhaps a more omniscient, almost Dickensian approach, zooming down into the story with an all-seeing eye, might help her distance herself from the case, and ease the flow. *Just get it down. However it comes. You can refine later. Don't think of Blake and Geoff out there . . .*

She resumed typing:

> If you were to fly over this section of the Oregon coast, you'd see the village of Shelter Bay snugging up against a large body of water protected from the ocean by a spit of white sand four miles long. Man-made reefs guide the tidal waters in and out of the bay mouth, and it's here where fishermen often push their luck just a little too far, bringing out the search-and-rescue Jet Skis and ambulance. The north end of the spit is state park. It's covered with coastal pines and scrub, and networked with trails, a popular spot for camping with horses.
>
> Looking back twenty-two years ago you'd note two key residential areas bisected by the coast highway that curves around the town's waterfront commercial hub— one subdivision to the west, up a rise that afforded vistas of the sea, and a smaller one to the southwest, over the Hobson River, which feeds into the bay. The southern subdivision is where the Brogans' double-story stands. Behind the house, state forest rolls thick and wild up into mountains and covers thousands of acres. Because of the diverse terrain and climate in this county—over seventy miles of scenic coastline, five bays, nine major rivers—it's not unusual for people to go missing.
>
> But murder—now, this is something Sheriff Ike Kovacs and his deputies are not accustomed to dealing with.
>
> Let's zoom the camera in closer, pan over Front Street with its quaint little stores, past the town hall and fire hall and elementary school, over the Catholic church and tidy

cemetery, the Lighthouse Diner with its mini replica of the lighthouse that stands proud at Shelter Head. Now, zoom in on Bull Sutton's Marina.

Telescope the camera in yet closer; come right down to the marina. See the bobbing boats? The buoys? The little turquoise shed at the far end of the dock that houses the life jackets and crab pots? The one with the orange life ring on the wall? Focus on the girl in denim shorts running down the gangway. Her long hair is deep red—the same color as the wood of ancient cedars that grow up the coast. And she's not a girl, really. She's in that tricky window between childhood and womanhood. She'll be fourteen in a week.

Her cheeks are pinked and her eyes sharp with intent as she races in her sneakers along the far dock. A boy, Blake Sutton—sixteen—towhead and tan, with fierce green eyes under a deep, strong brow, stops hauling in a crab net and watches her lean, pale legs.

"Where are you going, Meg?" he calls.

"None of your business!"

"Why no crab pots?"

She doesn't answer. She reaches the end of the dock and scrambles into a boat: tin hull, green paint, Johnson two-stroke outboard motor. Not wasting a second, she unties and casts free the mooring line, and pushes her craft away from the dock. She yanks the starter cord. In a puff of blue smoke the engine coughs to life.

"You should take a life vest!"

She ignores him. She turns the tiller handle, increasing engine power. Slipping out of the marina, she ramps up speed across the bay, leaving a wake of white foam on dark green. The tide is coming in, and all about her the sea is aflicker and murmur and illusion. She's not worried. She imagines the carpet of Dungeness crabs underneath, crawling atop one another, sea spiders moving along the sand floor with the ebb and surge.

As she reaches the center of the bay, wind smacks her full in the face, salty and cold off the point. She lifts her face to it, a pennant of coppery hair snapping behind her. She owns the summer. This bay. This town. This is her world. She knows the water's moods as surely as she knows the contents of tidal puddles in rocks, where to find purple periwinkles, where to pick the best mussels and dig the fattest butter clams. It's her territory. Her own little aquarium. Safe from predators that don't hunt in perfect sunny American-apple-pie towns like Shelter Bay.

But in the play of light and shadow among the shore pines and swaying dune grasses on that late September afternoon awaits a fate, a horror she cannot imagine because it's not even remotely in the realm of her experience, so terrible she will not be able to remember it for twenty-two years. So terrible it will fracture this town, and shatter lives within. It will cost Meg her family. Life as she loves and knows it.

Blake watches her go.

She's moving fast and with purpose toward the white sands of the opposite shore.

He wants to follow, to play on the ocean with her. To kiss her mouth. But summer has kept him chained to the marina, working for his dad. Anger slices through him. His older brother has shirked his duties again, sneaking out before dawn with his sack to collect flotsam for his "art." Blake saw him from the upstairs window, his boat skimming like a bug on the predawn, glassy stillness of the bay. Also headed for the spit.

"Blake!" his father calls from the marina up top. "Got a customer waiting!"

He slams down the empty crab pot and stomps in his rubber boots up the gangway.

Unaware of what awaits her on the shore, just over the dune crest with its cluster of shore pines, the girl nudges the snout of her green boat onto the beach with a soft scrape of sand beneath. She steps into water, and pulls her craft up the slope of hard-packed sand, careful to avoid sharp oyster shells—

Meg stilled at a soft clunk outside her camper, a sound out of synch with the other storm noise. She listened carefully, trying to identify it below the moan of the foghorn and the distant crash of waves and wind. A scratching came at the camper door, and the handle moved. Her pulse quickened. She heard another clunk and felt a sense of motion, as if something had bumped her truck upon which the camper shell was secured. The door handle jiggled, louder. But the door was locked. She stared at the handle as she reached quietly over to the drawer below the fridge. She slid it open. Mouth dry, she closed her fingers around the hilt of a carving knife. Thunder crashed, and her heart kicked. Slowly, she got to her feet, knife fisted in her hand. She reached for the blind over the table, edged it open a crack. Lightning streaked into the bay, and in the freeze-frame, she saw glistening black water, silhouettes of gnarled shore pines bending into wind and silvery slush. Debris cartwheeled across the parking lot. A rope snapped in the wind. But nothing more.

Carefully, she moved to the blind on the opposite side of her camper, but as she did, she got a whiff of smoke. Then stronger. *Fire.* Panic licked into her stomach. She had two gas cylinders, one open, feeding into her heater and powering her fridge. A full tank of diesel fuel in her truck. The whole rig could blow sky-high in seconds.

"Noah! Wake up—quick!"

She lunged to unlock the door, then halted. Panic squeezed her brain. What if someone was trying to flush them out? She had to chance it.

"What's happening?" Noah sat up, confused and thick with sleep.

"Grab your jacket, get over here!" She twisted the door lock free, swung down the handle, pushed. But the door held fast. She shouldered it. Nothing happened. She rammed harder. But it was stuck dead. The scent of smoke thickened. It was seeping in from below

9

the bed. She caught a flickering glow of orange through the small window that looked into the back of her truck cab. Flames. Noah started to cough.

Someone had locked them in. They were trapped—human meat in a tin can about to explode.

Focus. Panic kills. Think. Logic . . .

Hands trembling, Meg yanked up the blind and struggled to slide open the window. It was stuck. She lunged for the opposite window, breaking nails as she scrabbled to open it. It had been jammed shut, too. Her gaze shot around the interior. Fire extinguisher. She snapped it free and rammed the back of it into the glass of the biggest window over the table. Cracks feathered through the glass. She rammed it twice more, and pieces crumbled outward. Rain, wind, slush blew in, saturating her face.

"Noah, over here." She smashed the extinguisher along the bottom rim of the window, eliminating sharp edges. Wrapping a blanket around Noah, she helped him onto the bench seat. "I'm going to lower you out, okay? When you hit the ground, run. As far as you can, up to the coast road before this blows. I will find you up there. Go!"

Rain drenched through her sweater as she helped Noah out. His feet hit gravel. He glanced up, white-faced, wide-eyed.

"Go! Run!"

He turned and raced away, a little form on skinny legs into the wet, black storm.

Meg struggled to squeeze herself sideways through the window. Her legs swung down, feet hitting gravel. She reached back inside to get the knife. But as she did, she felt a hard crack at the back of her skull. Her body juddered, went still. Pain exploded through her head and radiated down her spine, to her fingertips. Her vision blurred. She tried to turn around, to put a foot forward, to run, but her knees buckled and she slumped to the ground.

Another blow came sharp at her ribs. She felt a bone crack. Gasping for air, she tried to roll away, to get onto her hands and knees. To crawl. In the periphery of her mind she was aware of flames licking out of her truck, fed by the tearing wind. Smoke roiled, acrid, thickening. Slush beat down. Meg staggered up onto all fours. Her vision was blackening. She had to get away before the gas cylinders exploded. But as she moved one hand forward, someone yanked her up by the hair, spinning her around.

Lightning split the sky. And in that instant she saw.

Him.

His eyes met hers. And in that moment, suspended in time and pain, she saw in his features an expression of utter equanimity. And she knew.

She knew with bilious, oily certainty. She finally had *The End* of her book—and she'd never get to write it. Because now that she knew it was him, she also knew with certainty . . . she was dead.

CHAPTER 1

Four weeks earlier. Seattle.

"And tonight we have in the studio with us renowned true crime writer Meg Brogan." Stamos Stathakis, *The Evening Show* host, stretched out his legs and hooked one cowboy boot over the other, reclining at an odd sideways angle in a boxy, lurid orange chair. Meg faced him in a matching chair that was too low, too close, and made her wish she'd worn pants instead of having to now carefully press her knees to the side in order to look half respectable in her tailored skirt.

On the table to his side was a copy of her latest hardback, *Sins Not Forgotten*. Behind them, a floor-to-ceiling screen displayed the bleak and snowy image of her cover. The artist had reworked it several times in an attempt to capture a grim "Nordic noir" tone. In front of them, beyond the starkly lit dais upon which she and Stathakis were positioned, the eyes of the studio audience glistened in the dark. And into that darkness, Stamos threw his trademark, conspiratorial smile, a look that said, *this woman is about to be skewered.*

Sorry, not happening, Stathakis.

Nevertheless her pulse quickened. She became aware of Jonah, her fiancé, observing from the wings, alongside her publicist. The studio felt hot. An irrational sense of unease feathered softly into her chest. She was good in front of a camera, but never comfortable.

"Before turning to true crime writing, Meg was most well-known for her brief and controversial stint as crime editor for the *Seattle Times*. Prior to taking over the *Times*'s crime desk, she clawed her way up from the trenches as a junior reporter to pen award-winning and unflinching features on matters of crime and punishment. Then came her popular blog, and the guest television appearances where she's increasingly asked to offer commentary on high-profile cases. Her debut book, *You Are Mine: A Story of Obsession*, first hit the shelves and the *New York Times* list five years ago, and Meg's been soaring up charts since, showing herself as a force to be reckoned with in the competitive genre of true crime. Now, in her latest hardcover, *Sins Not Forgotten*—on sale tomorrow"—he held up the book. The camera zoomed in—"Meg takes us on a gothic trip into the dubious territory of memory, and its unreliability, effectively shining a light onto an old and very cold case that was all but forgotten. Thank you for being with us, tonight, Meg. Can you tell us a bit about your latest book?"

Restraining the urge to push back her hair, she smiled. "*Sins* is the story of Gloria Lulofs, who, as a young girl, was being sexually abused by her father in a barn on the family's Minnesota ranch when two boys from a neighboring reservation intervened in an attempt to save her. Gloria's father murdered both boys with a pitchfork and buried their bodies in the barn while seven-year-old Gloria watched. The crime went unreported for fifty-six years. Gloria, traumatized by what she'd seen, repressed all memories of the horrific event, as well as memories of the ongoing sexual abuse. Until she was in her sixties, when she came forward to report what she'd begun to believe she was remembering."

"But police found no record of two boys missing from the reservation," Stathakis added.

"Correct. And Gloria's father denied all allegations. The police did not believe her credible, either. She was in fairly advanced stages of pancreatic cancer, had been an alcoholic most of her life, and she was on medication, showing signs of early-onset dementia. The investigation was dropped."

"Until a newspaper picked up her story."

"Yes. The paper brought in ground-penetrating radar equipment. Shapes were detected in the frozen ground below where the Lulofs' barn had once stood. Permission was granted by the current landowners to dig up the area. Human remains were found— two boys who had slipped through the cracks at their reservation over half a century ago. Forensics confirmed Gloria's account, and Hans Lulofs, in his late eighties, was charged and convicted on two counts of murder and sexual assault last year."

"A huge catharsis for Gloria, who died only three months ago, holding your book, I believe. As if she was waiting to have this resolved before she could peacefully pass."

"I'd sent her an early copy." Meg's voice caught slightly. She cleared her throat. "Closure can have profound psychological and physiological effects."

"Why is it, do you think, that closure is so vital to the victim or the victims' families? Is it a form of revenge, to see the criminal caught and punished, that gives satisfaction?"

"I don't think so. In my experience speaking with victims, hearing the guilty verdict is often a hollow-feeling victory. It's more a case of being released. During an investigation into a crime, throughout the arrest process, the trial, the victim, and loved ones are gripped in a stasis. Their lives are on hold. Once a case has been adjudicated, and the bad guy put away, once they've gotten the truth of what happened, they're finally free to grieve. To allow the old self to die, and to be able to begin again."

He allowed this to hang a moment, then leaned forward.

Meg tensed.

The host had a formula. He liked to come out of left field with a backhanded question, usually delivered right toward the end of an interview, the camera panning out before a guest could fully extricate herself. Meg glanced at the clock on the studio wall. It would be coming any second now.

"You interviewed Hans Lulofs for the book."

"I won't do a story unless I have access to the perpetrator—he's the antihero of my books. I always pick a case based on him. Or her."

"You've mentioned before that ideally you want an antihero, or villain if you will, who appears to have everything: good looks, charisma, charm, success, love, wealth, brilliance, respect, talent— the kind of traits we'd all love to have—the *least* likely person in the world you'd expect to be arrested for murder. Because this is good for sales?"

Meg smiled. "Because it has the most universal and commercial appeal, and it lends itself to story structure. I learned from the best in the business, Day Rigby—she's become something of a mentor to me."

"But Hans Lulofs doesn't quite fit this bill, does he? He's a crippled old man, a chronic alcoholic at the end of a miserable existence scraping a life from a barren ranch. Not exactly commercial appeal." He leaned further forward, right into her space, his eyes suddenly boring into Meg's. "So why? Why *this* case? What was it about Hans and Gloria that got to *you*?"

Meg cleared her throat. She could feel Jonah's gaze from the wings, feel his judgment. She felt Stathakis's *coup de grace* lurking in his next words.

"It was . . . I think the fallibility of memory has always intrigued me. How it works, its role in criminal investigations, identification, prosecution, trials. How our own minds can deceive, and protect us from pain. And here was a perfect case in point. A forgotten crime. But not entirely erased. In some ways it had been oozing just under Gloria's consciousness her entire life. It fueled her drinking,

her self-destructive behaviors, her inability to form proper relationships." She forced a smile. "I do think Gloria's story will reso-
nate with something in all of us."

Stathakis eyed her, allowing two full seconds of silence.

"So it's not about *your* memory loss—your own deep-seated
need to recall a murder—that drew you into this story?"

Wham.

"Excuse me?"

"Your own sister, Sherry Brogan, was brutally raped and strangled twenty-two years ago. You yourself were attacked and left for
dead, concussed, no memory of the actual assault. Your own father
died in prison serving time for murder, did he not? Perhaps *this*
is the subterranean driver that sucked you into Gloria Lulofs's
case? Is this what drew you into a lifetime of writing about crime,
seeking to understand minds of the monsters who live among us,
and kill? Digging deep for the 'why.' Because it's closure *you* want.
Deep down here"—he thumped his sternum softly with his fist,
eyes steadily boring into hers—"it's all about you. Your past. Your
need to understand *why.*"

"My past," she said slowly, darkly, holding his gaze, "has nothing to do with my work. I fell into crime writing in college while
studying for an English lit and psychology degree. A student riot
erupted on campus. I was on the spot. I wrote it up for the univer-
sity paper. I kept on the story as it continued to unfold, both for
the campus paper and stringing for the *Times*. Then I did more
freelancing while a student. After I graduated, the *Times* offered
me a job."

"Ah." He leaned back. That smile. "But there's no denying we
are all products of our pasts, are we not, Meg? No matter how we
try to pave it over, those subconscious drivers shape us. Will you
write it one day—the Sherry Brogan story?" He paused. "Or is this
the one story you cannot write?"

Out of the corner of Meg's eye, her publicist made a panicked rolling movement with her hand: *go with it, roll with it, almost over.* Jonah stood stiff.

Meg smiled, folded her hands neatly on her lap. And sat silent. Television, radio hosts hated dead space. Her eyes locked with his, warning him that her line in the sand lay right here.

"It certainly has all the commercial elements you look for," he prompted. "The darkly seductive, devastatingly handsome young antihero from the wrong side of the tracks. A man who volunteered at the local animal shelter. He rapes and murders Shelter Bay's golden girl, homecoming queen, forever tearing apart and changing a town. All-American values, innocence lost. Telling your story might be as cathartic for you as it was for Gloria Lulofs. Do you ever fear, Meg, that what is locked in your memory might have changed the outcome, that your father might not have ended up in prison?"

She lurched to her feet and reached for the mic pinned to her blouse.

His hands shot up in surrender. "No worries." He smiled at his audience. *See? I rattled the big-name crime author. See her vulnerabilities exposed now?*

He held up her book again. "*Sins Not Forgotten*. On sale from tomorrow. Thank you, Meg Brogan, for joining us on *The Evening Show*."

Applause sounded. There were shuffles in the shadows. A cough.

Meg unclipped the mic and dumped it on the chair. She spun around, stepped off the dais, strode toward Jonah and her publicist, her high heels clicking on wood, face hot. Stathakis came rapidly after her. He placed his hand on her arm. Meg spun back at him, anger stomping through her chest. "We had an agreement," she said, very quietly. "My sister's murder was off-limits tonight. I refuse to be pigeonholed by something that happened to my family twenty-two years ago."

"I'm sorry—"

"Like hell you are," she ground out through her teeth. "You intended using Sherry's story from the moment you first mentioned it backstage. I should have—" She felt Jonah's arm sliding around her waist.

"Relax, Megan," Jonah said softly in her ear as he drew her away. Her publicist stepped in front of Stathakis to run interference.

"Not worth it," Jonah whispered, leading her out of the studio.

But Stathakis's words dogged her into the chill winter night.

What is locked in your memory might have changed the outcome . . . or is this the one story you cannot write . . .

———

"Let it go. You did fine," Jonah said as he escorted Meg along the waterfront to the restaurant for a late, celebratory dinner. Icy wind whipped about them, carrying the briny scent of ocean. The halyards of yachts chinked against masts, float planes straining against moorings as waves slapped pontoons. Tiny snowflakes had begun to crystallize in the January night and they pricked Meg's cheeks. The radio in the cab on the way over had reported heavy snow already falling in the Cascades.

"Besides, you looked great. That's what *really* matters."

Meg cast him a sardonic glance. He grinned at her and she felt a familiar punch of attraction. Jonah was dark and handsome in his wool coat—a sleek and powerful jaguar in an urban jungle. He carried authority in the set of his shoulders, in the athletic grace of his stride. His was a command presence born out of a supreme confidence in his own intellect and genetic good fortune. A forensic psychiatrist with a private consultancy in demand by law enforcement agencies around the globe, Jonah was Meg's on-tap resource with the psychopathology of the real-life villains in her books, often sitting in with her on much-coveted pre- and post-trial interviews. The package came with an impeccable sartorial sense, a faint British accent, and the financial resources with which to indulge his love of all things fine.

Meg was seized by an urge to just lean into him, let herself go, let their relationship swallow her wholly and properly. Be the woman he wanted her to be. Yet always, there was this tug of restraint she could never quite rid herself of. A tension. Like a wire stretched too taut, humming just under audible range, ready to snap at any moment.

"He's an asshole," she quipped, as they started up a gangway strung with white fairy lights. Wind gusted and hair blew across her face. "I told him backstage—Sherry's murder was off-limits."

He opened the restaurant door for her.

"Why?"

She stalled. "Why what?"

"I mean, why is it off-limits? Maybe it would be good to just put it out there, talk about it. He did have a point, you know, with his question about your memories in relation to Lulofs's."

"Oh . . . no. No. Don't *you* go pulling out the old victimology tricks and profiling *me*, Doctor Lawson. Sometimes people just do things, okay? Doesn't all have to be traced back to childhood trauma."

But by the time they were seated at a table in front of tall glass windows, cocooned with candlelight and looking out over the bay, snow starting to fall in fat gauzy flakes under the halos of lamps, Meg's mood had soured further. She picked at her napkin while Jonah perused the wine list and ordered a Burgundy from the slopes of the Saône River.

Once the waiter had poured the wine and left, he said, "Maybe you *should* write it, Meg. Go back and put the past finally, properly, to bed. Get closure."

She stared at him. "I have closure. Tyson Mack is dead. Why are you even pushing this?" She reached for her glass and took a fierce slug of wine.

He crooked a brow, watching her intently. "Stathakis was right about the commercial potential." He raised his glass, gently swirled the liquid. "The ending is poignant, too. Your father going to prison. Your mother—"

"Stop," she said, her voice low, quiet. "Stop right there." Something in her tone must have brooked no argument, because he went very still, his dark blue eyes holding hers. Her cheeks burned and she took another heavy pull of the damn fine Burgundy she knew he'd ordered because they'd visited the vineyard. It was where he'd proposed. Over two years ago. And by the price it was a wine to be savored.

"You of *all* people should get why I don't want to tackle it, Jonah. It's personal. It's *mine*—not for public consumption, not for money. And it's over. Christ, it's almost a quarter of a century ago. I don't want to talk about it anymore. I *have* put it to bed. And there are more cases. Tons. Sick killers—monsters out there who'd make excellent antiheroes, more subject material than I'll ever be able to tackle, so why in the hell worry about Sherry's story? I moved on years ago." She reached again for her glass.

"Except, you haven't."

She stilled, glass midair. She held his eyes. "Shall we just eat? Order? Call the waiter—" She raised her arm to summon somebody. "Anybody! Some service here, please?"

He reached for her raised hand, lowered it slowly back to the table.

"Prove it," he said quietly.

A whispering chill of foreboding sunk into her chest.

"What do you mean? Prove what?"

He removed the wineglass from her grip, set it down gently,

and took both her hands in his across the white linen tablecloth. Candlelight sparkled in his eyes, but they were cool and sharp with an intensity that scared her. He swiveled the diamond cluster around her finger as he held her gaze. The ring they'd bought together in Paris.

"Marry me, Meg. Let's set a date. Tonight."

Her mouth opened. On some level she'd known this was coming tonight, that it was the root of her tension. The whispering, rising panic. The tightening claustrophobia.

"I . . . wow." She tore her gaze from his, but he cupped the side of her face, forcing her to look back into his eyes.

"We've been together three years now. It's over two years that you've worn this ring, since we made each other this promise in France. The first time I suggested a wedding date, it was that you needed to finish your book, the research. Then it was conflict of interest in the coming trial. There was travel. Time. Then it was financial." He paused. The silence in the restaurant felt loud—pressed against her ears. The air thickened, tightening her throat. "You have it all now. Your books are all bestsellers. Offers to do more. You're independently well-off. You've checked it all off the list. So, let's just do it. Tomorrow. This weekend. Next month."

Blood drained from her head. She felt dizzy. She opened her mouth to speak, but the waiter came. Frustration sparked through Jonah's striking face.

"Are you ready to order, sir?"

"What're you having, Meg?" Jonah said, not bothering to look at the menu, nor the waiter.

"Uh . . . I'll have . . . the special."

"Same." He handed his menu back to the server, his attention fixed solely on her.

"Everything all right for drinks?" the server said.

"Yeah." Still, his gaze didn't leave her or waver for a second.

As the server left, Jonah said, slowly, quietly, "You can't do it, can you? You cannot commit. Look at you . . . you live in my house, sleep in my bed, but you park your truck and camper and Jetta in my driveway. You keep a supply of clothes in there, a backup laptop. Ready for what? Emergency escape?"

"The camper is my office."

"You could get a real office, you know, with foundations and walls and a roof."

"I like the mobility."

"You can't put down roots." His eyes challenged hers. "It's just a matter of time before one of the monsters you write about will be released from prison. You should consider security. A proper house, a condo—"

"I have a house."

Compassion entered his features. "Yes, a house in Shelter Bay that now stands empty and borderline condemned. A house covered in graffiti, and tempting squatters, that is now earning you warning notices from the city."

"I've been meaning to list it, but it's in a bad state of repair—no one will buy it as it stands."

"Then tear it down, for God's sake. It's not like you don't have the money. It's sitting there sheltering ghosts."

"My aunt might want to move back—"

"*Listen* to yourself, Meg. Irene is in an assisted living facility. The prognosis is not good. You'll be forty in a few years. I'm forty already. It's a fair time for us to enter a new stage."

"What are you trying to tell me, Jonah? That it's time to grow up? Because maybe I like—"

"I'm trying to tell you that there are only so many growing seasons to a life, Meg. Only so many years to have children. We spoke about this—kids. A family."

Tick tock bio clock.

She inhaled deeply, drawing on anger now, using it to beat back the biting edge of truth in his words.

"You haven't even been to see Irene since she went into that home. You haven't returned in eighteen years. You can't put roots down here, yet you can't go back, either. See? You have *not* put it behind you. This is not about your work. It's about your problem with intimacy, with letting people in. You want connection, yet you push people away. You push *me* away."

The server brought food. Meg stared, unseeing, at her plate. Throat tight. Unable to breathe. Skin hot.

"If you ask me—"

"I'm not asking you."

He continued anyway. "It's the same thing that cost you the crime desk at the *Times*."

Heat flushed up her chest, neck, and into her face. The curse of a redhead. An anomaly of genetics that embarrassed her into wearing her emotions on her sleeve.

"Why tonight, Jonah? Why push this tonight?"

"Because it's time. The end of the line. I want to marry you. Either we cross this line and go forward. Tonight. Together. Or we face up to the fact that it's never going to work." He paused for several beats. His voice went quiet. "I want to be with you, Meg. I want to make a life, a family with you. I'm tired of being kept on hold. In stasis. Isn't that what you told Stathakis about lives in limbo, lives without closure? Well, that's how I feel about us. If that means you going back to Shelter Bay and writing this, then let me help you do it."

"Sometimes," she whispered, "I really hate you, you know that? When you drag out all the psychobabble and metaphysical shit— sometimes . . . sometimes I think you're with me because you see me as some live-in test case. The 'fiancée in the petri dish.'" She made angry air quotes. "The damaged rescue puppy that you think you can rehabilitate, and 'save' because it serves the so-called altruist in you, the Dr. Lawson of the realm of fractured minds and souls." She leaned forward. "But you know as well as I do—there's no such thing as pure altruism, is there, Jonah? You do it because it makes *you* feel good, and self-righteous. The Messiah."

He leaned back, rubbed his brow. She'd cut him, and she loved him, and she couldn't stop jabbing in and twisting the knife. And an indefinable kind of terror and panic was rising up her throat. A self-destructive craving for annihilation. She was whirling into a tunnel, and just gaining speed, unable to stop.

"Maybe," she said darkly, "I'm having a bit of trouble *committing* since you went and fucked Jan Mascioni."

He flinched, glanced out the window, blew out a long, controlled breath. Always so damn controlled. He reached for his glass. Holding it by the stem, he took a sip of wine. When he spoke, his voice was soft, defeated.

"We've been through that. You know why that happened."

Hurt flushed through her. So easy for him, just to fill his bed with another woman.

"Jonah—" She reached for his hand.

He moved it away. "No, Meg. Don't do this. Not this time."

"Do what?"

"Obfuscate like this. Touch me like this. Try to connect with sex when you're really using it to shut me out." A glimmer of anger finally. In his eyes. In that face, that body that attracted her, this man she loved, but couldn't truly connect with. It was like she had a type of autism or something. As much as she needed him she had an intense need to be alone. And she couldn't the hell find a way to combine those two drives at war inside herself. Pain balled in her throat. She held her mouth tight against it.

"Give me a date."

"I . . . I can't. Just not tonight. I—"

His jaw set in a fierce line. "If not tonight, then, when?"

"I . . . I think I need some air." She got up. Dizziness swirled. She braced her hand on the table to steady herself.

"Meg." He grasped her wrist, tight. "Walk away now, leave this restaurant, and it's over. You know that. This time it's over for good."

She stared at his hand on her wrist.

He released her slowly. She turned, hesitated. She walked.

Legs like columns of water, she made it past the reception area, pushed out of the door, and was hit square in the face with a bracing icy wind and biting crystal flakes off the black sea.

She grasped the railing for balance, the wind drawing water from her eyes, because she didn't cry. She hadn't cried since the day her father was charged. Since her mother took her own life. With her bare hands she gripped that frozen railing. And she waited. She waited for the door to fling open behind her, for Jonah to come out. To take her home.

Where they would make fierce love until she hurt. Because that's what usually happened when this—or any other prickly subject—came up. When she was trying to avoid hearing the possible subterranean truths, that she was fucked up in her head and unable to allow anyone to love her. Refusing to need—truly need—anyone again.

But the door remained shut.

He didn't come.

And she knew, this time he wouldn't. This time, it really was over.

CHAPTER 2

Three days later. Oregon coast.

Meg peered through the wipers slashing arcs across her truck's windshield. Rain slanted silver in her headlights. The road was lonely, dark, a sepulchral mist sifting through trees. Strangler vines snaked around coastal pines, cutting off lifeblood, creeping over everything, as if at war with Himalayan blackberry—the place being slowly consumed by alien invasive species and populous sprawl.

The signs had flashed by in the night. GEARHART. SEASIDE, CANNON BEACH, MANZANITA . . .

Tension tightened her stomach.

Are you happy?

Jonah had asked this question in the fall, during a visit to the pumpkin patch, as they'd chased his two nieces through the corn maze. He'd grasped her hand, swung her around to face him, kissed her full on the mouth in the rustling privacy of the corn walls. Eyes bright. Hands cold.

"Of course I'm happy," she'd told him.

Why wouldn't she be? She had literary acclaim, financial success. Her health. Strength. She was busting with career energy. She'd snagged the man the *Seattle Times* had dubbed the most eligible bachelor in the Northwest. A man with the looks of a dark and broody Heathcliff on high misty moors. A man who was ridiculously independently wealthy in his own right, and who, without question, loved her deeply.

Or had.

She'd met him over three years ago while interviewing him for one of her books. He'd been the consultant for the police on the case, and had presented evidence in court on the state of mind of a serial sexual sadist.

But if anything, her Jonah was an acute observer of human nature, a perpetual delver into the psyche. An obsessive watcher, and he'd been watching her that chill October day. He'd seen in her eyes something deeper, a shadow, as she'd chased his nieces through the husks of corn. They were sisters with the same four-year gap between them as Sherry and herself—the older one remarkably beautiful and full of grace. The younger one gawkish and tomboyish and slavishly loyal to her sibling. An awkward little shadow.

Sherry's shadow, they'd once dubbed Meg. The redheaded little hoyden who'd chased continually in the wake of Sherry's golden light. The kid sister who'd idolized Sherry's feminine magic, the way her big sister could smile with the apparent naiveté of a child while simultaneously wrapping people around her little finger.

"Come. Let's find the girls!" Meg had pulled away, the husky corn walls suddenly too close, a prison labyrinth she needed to escape.

But Jonah had held on a moment longer. "What do you want out of life—children?"

"When we're ready." She'd left him alone in the maze. She'd run after the girls, chasing perhaps a memory through the dead growth, chasing something in herself, or perhaps, as Jonah would have said, running again. From allowing him—anyone—in.

Hot irritation flushed through her, and her hands tightened around the wheel of her Ford F-350. On the back of irritation rode self-reproach, a kind of shame. She reached over to the passenger seat, jabbed the record button of her digital recorder, and took a breath. *The beginning, just start at the beginning* . . .

"I should never have lied for Sherry that day," she said softly into the mic of her hands-free headset, peering into darkness, headlights cutting narrow tunnels into mist. She passed a brooding monkey puzzle tree choked with ivy. "Should never have covered for her—" A sign caught her headlights, white paint bouncing back the gleam of her beams. SHELTER BAY. FIVE MILES.

Something ran across the road. She hit the brakes, skidded to a stop on the gravel shoulder. Her heart thudded. All around her camper and truck, bushes waved in the wind. The skirts of conifers swirled.

She stared at the sign, an unspecified dread mounting in her, forgotten neurons reawakening with fear, drawing her mind down the stairs into the cobwebby murk of her own subconscious. Once the happy hamlet of her youth, Shelter Bay was now a Stephen King-ish town in her memory, a place where blackness lurked below a cracked tourist facade.

And we all know what happens to heroines who go down the stairs into the basement, candle quavering . . .

"That's where it first went wrong," she said softly into the mic. "If I'd told Mom and Dad right away that Sherry had gone with him to the spit, instead of going to find her myself, to warn her to hurry home. Save her bacon—" She cleared her throat, beating back tension by speaking louder into the darkness, against the squeak and slap of her wipers. "I don't know what in me was always trying to save Sherry. Protect her. What did I know at age thirteen, fourteen—was it premonition? Was I beginning to see, subconsciously, as my own sexual awareness dawned, that my sister was tripping a sort of dangerous light fantastic? Dancing just a little too close to the sun that final summer before college, before

29

what was supposed to be the rest of her life? Because in the end, by lying for her, I failed her. Even after her death I failed her, by not remembering. In many ways everything that happened that late August day, and after it, was my fault . . . It should have been *me*, not Sherry, who died."

Meg shifted her truck back into gear and pulled out into the empty road. Hands firm on the wheel, she fought the mounting urge to pull a U-turn, and just call it quits. Because if she was going to write Sherry's story, she *had* to go back. She always visited the key locations when she wrote a book—she wanted to take her readers there, too. Wanted them to see, feel, what she'd seen. And, just as she was doing now, she verbally recorded her thoughts and impressions as she went, capturing her own knee-jerk reactions that she would later refine, interpret, and weave into the cold facts of the case.

Just another job, another book. Do it all the same way, and you'll be fine . . .

"You could argue it every way to Sunday, but there was no escaping the fact that Sherry was the special daughter. The first-born. The blessed one. She had everything. Tall, lithe. A golden girl to my shorter, dark-red looks. Honey tan to my pale complexion and freckles that made me look like a boiled lobster in the sun. An open smile and easy laugh that could ignite a crowd. She made people feel good. She'd just graduated—had a scholarship lined up for Stanford. Homecoming queen. Had been dating Tommy Kessinger since the eighth grade, a star quarterback. A gold, Greek god himself. A college football scholarship in hand, his sights set on the NFL. Shelter Bay's young royalty and the world was their oyster . . ."

Meg cleared her throat, negotiating a sharp bend down the twisting road. Steep now. Water running in a sheen down the hill. Her camper buffeted by gusts of wind.

"Until Tyson Mack had growled into town on his custom chrome cruiser, with muscled biceps and rippling tats . . . oozing dark sex appeal, danger, thrill . . . until Sherry had mounted Ty's bike and gone with him to the make-out spot on the dune spit near the state park boundary. And I'd covered for her while Tyson raped and strangled and left her dead in the dunes." Meg tapped her brakes before another sharp turn.

"After her death, I used to see the question in my mother's eyes—*why Sherry?* I used to feel that question in town. I felt blame. And I wore it like a hair shirt, craving the discomfort as a form of self-flagellation. An attempt at redemption I'd never find."

Jonah's words sifted into her mind . . .

You need to go back, Meg, and forgive yourself for not having been able to save your sister. You need to see it was not your fault . . .

Bitterness filled her mouth. She peered lower through the arcs of the wipers as she drove along the twisting coast road. The drop-off to her right was sheer.

Close now.

She inhaled deeply, taking another stab at it, memories cloaking about her like the mist and darkness enveloping her rig.

"The brutal sexual assault and murder of Sherry was a sin, a violation against this small town of Shelter Bay . . ." Fog was dense at the bottom of the pass. The road leveled. And suddenly there it was. The fork in the road. The wooden sign swinging in the wind and rain. SHELTER BAY, home of white dunes and Dungeness crab.

Her chest cramped and she slowed, skin growing hot as she focused on the road hemmed by dune grasses. Then came lights. First, the old diner. She slowed to a crawl. It was still there—with its mini replica of the Shelter Head lighthouse, a landmark that had once defined home. She and Sherry had played in that small lighthouse, like a dollhouse at the bottom of the lawn, while her dad ate breakfast in the diner.

She passed the old motel. Crooked sign. Peeling paint. It was in an even worse state of repair now. *Bates Motel,* they'd called it as kids. Didn't look much different from the old black-and-white Hitchcock movie version. She wondered if crows still roosted in the old cottonwoods at the back and beaded the telephone lines out front at dusk, black menacing shapes watching the cars go by.

Never catch me staying there. I'd rather be dead than caught staying in a place like that . . . Sherry's chuckle. Meg jumped at the memory, so vivid that she glanced over at the passenger seat, as if she might see the spectral form of her sister sitting there, conjured from micromolecules of memory.

. . . Crazy that they haven't spruced it up yet. Or demolished and rebuilt it . . . You going to stay at the old house tonight, Meg?

Meg dragged her hand down hard over her mouth.

She drove past the elementary school, the rec center where she used to swim, the township offices, fire hall, and she turned into Front Street. It was empty, rain glistening on the pavement, signs swaying in the wind. The old buildings had been gussied up, given rugged frontier facades. Quaint. Pseudo-artsy.

It was the same and it wasn't, she thought as she cruised slowly through, tires crackling on the wet street. The old town, a palimpsest with the past scraped off, rewritten with bolder, brasher strokes of tourism and commerce, a bigger community. But whenever spaces are rebuilt or remodeled, whenever the vellum is scraped down to be reused, evidence of its former use always remains, the ghosts of the past perpetually whispering just below the skin of the present.

"In those early days, right after her murder, I used to imagine Sherry up in heaven, watching our lives unravel like skeins pulled from carefully knitted sweaters—some rows collapsing faster, others thick and slow—as we all struggled with the aftermath. Mom, Dad. Tommy and his family. Sherry's best friend, Emma. Blake.

Sheriff Kovacs trying to do right by the town. I'd go down to the beach, hunker in the lee of some dune, and watch the heave and pull of the sea, and I'd try to make my body so still, like an empty vessel, in an effort to hear the whisper of Sherry's spirit, to let her in, to listen for some desperate message she might be trying to impart from the other side. A nudge perhaps. A clue to my missing chunk of memory that would tell us all what had really happened. *How* it had happened. Why. But I couldn't recall. Either because of the concussion, or because it was so terrible that I'd repressed it. And it's still down there inside me somewhere—a dark, festering, inky thing.

"Sometimes I actually felt her sitting beside me there on the dune, watching the waves . . . and she'd walk partway home with me, too, but always dematerializing as we got too close.

"Until the day my father hunted down Tyson Mack, and killed him. Until the day my mother, forgetting I was even there, took her own life in grief. Until the day I became an orphan and gave up the stupid notion of Sherry in heaven. And God. Because God and heaven and Sherry and everyone had given up on me."

Seriously, when did you ever give up on anything, Meggie-Peg . . . you, the little fighter for lost causes and animals . . . when did you once back down on a challenge . . . prove it to me, prove it . . . A chill shivered down the nape of Meg's neck. Again, quickly, she glanced at the passenger seat. For a nanosecond she almost caught the sense of Sherry's smile.

Shit.

This was not going to be easy.

She drew to a stop at a red traffic light, right in front of The Mystery Bookstore. A quiver of recognition shot through her. It was still there, with its bay windows and little panes that reminded her of something out of Dickens. And as she peered through the rain-streaked window at the storefront display, her heart kicked.

Her book. Her new hardcover, *Sins Not Forgotten,* was front and center, along with a promo poster of her. Her own face staring back out at her through little rain-smeared windowpanes. A distorted fun-house mirror.

She'd tried so hard to forget this town, but it had not forgotten her. Part of her was still here. Right in her favorite store.

Had her earlier books been stocked, too? Had the people of Shelter Bay read her words? She sat for a while, feeling a strange sense of dislocated identity. And guilt. And a sudden stab of longing for something long gone. Her mother, father. Sister. Family. A time when she'd been happy. A time when she used to come here to peruse the new books.

The light turned green. Meg drew in a deep breath and took the road to Forest End, her old subdivision. Her intention was to park the camper outside the family house while she fixed it up, and then to move in while she researched and worked on her book. It was darker here, near the forest, sparsely lit. Trees swished behind the last row of houses. She turned into the old driveway, headlights illuminating a chained gate. Meg removed her headset and stared at the lurid graffiti that covered the walls and boarded-up windows.

Pulling up her rain hood, she got out to open the gates. Rain beat down on her back. The chain was wet and icy cold in her hands, securely padlocked. Rusty. She jiggled the gate, but it held fast. Climbing back into her truck, she scrubbed her hands hard over her wet face, refusing to allow any more memories in.

This was dumb. You're wrong, Jonah. Sometimes you don't need to go back to go forward . . . the hell with this!

Angrily she keyed her ignition. She swung her truck around, wheels spitting up gravel on the sidewalk. She headed for the coast road, a half-baked purpose forming in her head to go someplace warm. Far away from this town. This stupid winter. Jonah. Her life. When she got too tired, she'd pull over and sleep. California.

Mexico. She could drive all the freaking way through South America. To Tierra del Fuego. Until she ran out of land.

So what if she was running . . .

But as she neared the town exit, the rain pummeled down even harder, wind gusting fierce off the Pacific, and a light on her dash began to flash orange. Fuel gauge. She swore bitterly and slowed, keeping her eyes peeled for a gas station.

———

Meg drew into Millar's Gas and Motor Shop and pulled up alongside a diesel pump. An attendant came running out. She asked him to fill her tank while she ducked into the convenience store in search of something hot to drink.

The doorbell chimed as she stepped into the fluorescent brightness. Meg shook off her hood, picked a few things off the shelves, and poured a self-serve coffee. She went to pay at the counter, where a plumpish, blonde woman with smooth, creamy-looking skin and apple-dumpling cheeks was serving a giant of a man. Meg stood behind the man, taking in his stained pants, muddy construction boots, ink-black hair.

He snagged his smokes and six-pack off the counter, turned, and stalled dead as his gaze lit upon Meg. His mouth opened, then closed. His features hardened.

Meg swallowed at the full-bore intensity and hot energy radiating off him. She nodded, smiled. But his eyes narrowed sharply as he pushed past her and out the door. Through the window she saw him climb into a black van with a circular logo on the side. His brake lights flared red before he pulled out onto the coast road.

A memory, a voice, came through her. Faint, so faint, it was almost the sound of sand scraping in the wind outside.

Wait. Stop! Don't run, Meggie, don't run!

She froze, trapped suddenly in a loop of time. She felt a hand grabbing at her arm, fingers digging into bare skin, terror rising in her throat . . .

"That be all?"

The woman's words jerked her back to the present. Shaken, she placed her items on the counter—a wrapped sandwich, a packet of potato chips, the coffee. Newspaper. A packaged cream-filled snack cake that she planned to inhale whole before she was out of the lot.

"Terrible night to be out and about. You just traveling through?"

Meg hesitated, suddenly drained. "Actually," she said, trying to force a smile, "I'm hoping to find a clean motel for the night. Or somewhere to camp my rig."

The woman glanced at Meg's rig parked outside, her Washington plates clearly visible.

"No fun camping in this storm," she said as she placed the items in a bag. Meg handed over her credit card. "State park is closed for the season, anyways. There's the One Pine Motel at the north end of town. It's a low-budget place."

Bates Motel . . . never catch me staying there . . . rather be dead than caught staying in a place like that, Meg.

You are *dead, Sherry.*

"There's also a new boutique hotel in Whakami Cove, one town over, if you're looking for something more upmarket. Pretty ritzy, though." She passed the card back to Meg along with the slip to sign. "It opened this past summer as part of a big new Kessinger-Sproatt waterfront development. And there's Bull's Marina, down on the bay."

Meg glanced up sharply.

"They have some cabins, but I don't know if they still stay open during the winter," the woman said.

"Bull Sutton's place? It's still there?"

"You know it?"

"I, uh . . . from years ago." Meg picked up her bag of goods, but hesitated. "That guy who was just in here—do you know him?"

Suspicion flitted into the woman's eyes and a frown tilted her brows inward as she weighed Meg's question.

"No worries. He . . . looked familiar, is all. " Meg nodded to her bag. "Thanks."

But as she reached the door, the woman called out behind her. "Name's Mason Mack."

Meg stalled. Swallowed. A chill trickled down her spine. Trying to keep her voice level, she said, "Guess I don't know him, then."

She pushed through the door and into cool mist. Her skin was hot, her blood electric. Rain clattered loudly on the tin roof, and shimmered in a bead curtain beyond the covered area. She climbed into her truck and glanced uneasily in the direction the man's van had disappeared. A nearly inaudible whine, like a wet finger tracing around the rim of a crystal glass, began circling in her brain.

Mason Mack.

The uncle of the young man who'd raped and strangled her sister. The young man her father had shot and kicked to a pulp. The reason her dad had died in prison.

She reached down, keyed the ignition. Her big diesel truck rumbled to life, and she let it idle a moment as heat blew into the cab and she ripped open the snack cake packet, and ate the awful thing in two bites, welcoming the instant sugar rush. She sipped her coffee, feeling vaguely human again as the whining sound slowly dulled in her head. But as she pulled out of the gas station, in her rearview mirror she saw the woman come up to the store window and stare out at her.

The image of the woman, her encounter with Mason Mack, filled Meg with unease as she arrived at a T-junction intersection with the coast highway. A sign pointed south to Whakami Cove. Another sign pointed north, back into town.

Another bolt of memory sliced through her, the voice louder this time, oddly familiar . . .

Wait. Stop! Don't run, Meggie, don't run!

Hot panic flicked through her stomach. Then came a memory of Sherry's voice . . .

Cover for me, Meg. You won't regret it . . . just tell Mom and Dad we went to see that new movie . . . do it for me . . . look, here's some cash . . .

Then *wham*. Yet another image. A flicker of black shapes against blinding white. It came with a sharp slice of pain up the back of her head. Then it was gone. Trees in her headlights bent suddenly in the wind, the gust tearing debris free that hurtled across the road and smacked into her windshield. She jumped, pulse racing, past slamming into present—a dark, wet, black horror trying to rise out of the abyss of her mind and crawl into her consciousness. With it came a raw instinct to flee. South. On the back of it rode a compulsion to stand ground, fight it. Make it show itself—this horror.

Prove it. Prove you can go all the way and get the life you deserve.

You haven't been back to see your aunt since she went into that home . . .

She gripped the wheel tight. *Fine, you damn town. You don't want to let go, then you got me.* Gritting her teeth, she turned north, to Shelter Bay, clamping down on all her reasons for coming back. A mile in she took another turn, this time toward the ocean, negotiating the zigzagging road down to the bay.

And there it was. Through the mist and whipping rain, the faint pulse of the lighthouse beam on the dark rocks of Shelter Head. A guide. A warning. A Janus message being sent out over the black sea.

And as she rounded the point, snugged along the bay, she saw the marina. Above the buildings a neon sign smeared by rain flickered in dull pink: BULL'S MARINA AND CRABBY JACK'S CAFE.

Another memory reared sharp and hungry, clawing open her chest. Blake kissing her on the dock. Her telling him that she was leaving. The desperation, the ferocity in his eyes, the emotion in his voice as he'd pleaded with her to stay, to just try. He'd enlisted the day after she left. Went straight into the army. Became a medic. She hadn't seen nor heard from him since.

His older brother, Geoff, had also left town, along with so many other of Sherry's contemporaries. Her murder had come at a time of change in the lives of her fellow graduates, but to Meg it felt as if her sister's brutal death had precipitated a more seismic shift in this town, and the lives within it.

She wondered if either of the Sutton men ever came home to see their dad. Did Bull manage this marina on his own? He had to be about seventy now—the same age her dad would be, if he were alive.

She rounded another curve dense with brush.

A small VACANCY sign beckoned at the top of the long gravel driveway. Meg tapped her brakes, hesitating a moment, before quickly swinging her wheel and taking her rig bouncing down the steep, rutted track to the water.

And she knew she'd just done it—taken her first solid step back into the past, into writing Sherry's story. Into the murk of her own memory. Because now she would have to speak to Bull Sutton. He'd ask why she was here, and she'd ask him what he remembered about that day that she and Sherry went missing. She'd ask after his boys. And he'd give her their addresses.

There was no turning back now . . .

CHAPTER 3

Meg hoicked up her rain hood, exited her truck, and jogged through the lashing rain to the office. There was a small light on inside. She tried the door. Locked. Cupping her hand against cold glass, she peered in. It looked much the same as it had when she'd left Shelter Bay—a store counter, some crab nets, and other gear on the walls. Life jackets. A vintage postcard display rack. Touristy knickknacks on a few shelves. Stairs at the back climbed up to the residence. Pop fridges flanked an archway that led into what was once Crabby Jack's Cafe, but now appeared to be a vacant room in the throes of renovation, shrouds of drop cloths on the floor, a ladder in the center of the room.

Meg stepped out from under the covered deck area and, holding her hood against the whipping rain and wind, she squinted up at the top floor where the Sutton men had all lived. There were some lights on up there. She could smell wood smoke from the chimney. Someone was home.

A dog barked.

She hesitated, the sound of the foghorn moaning in the mist. Thunder clapped, and rain redoubled its assault. She ran carefully back to her truck, avoiding the black puddles. She'd check in come morning.

Back inside the camper, she shook out of her wet gear, pulled on

a fleece jacket, and turned on the gas heater. It clunked and grumbled to life, blowing air with a noisy fan. The interior started to
warm as Meg made her bed, shaking out her down sleeping bag. The
camper rocked in the wind, rain drumming on the roof. Eager to
ease the chill, Meg poured a small glass of brandy, sipped, then took
out her phone. She debated for a moment whether to make the call.

Then, wrapping a throw around her shoulders, she bit the bullet and hit speed dial.

Jonah answered on the fourth ring, voice thick, as if with sleep.

She checked her watch, frowned. "It's me," she said.

"Meg. Where . . . where on earth are you? I've been trying to
reach you for two days."

"Shelter Bay." She inhaled. "I came home."

Silence. Then a ruffling sound, the kind sheets might make.
Her pulse quickened. When he spoke again, he sounded different,
as if he'd moved location.

"Are you okay, Meg?"

"I—" She worried her engagement ring around her finger,
thinking of Jonah's final words after she'd tried to talk to him
again.

*Keep it. I don't want it back . . . it's just a reminder of what didn't
work. I don't need a trophy for that.*

"I will be."

"What're you doing there?"

"I'm going to prove it," she said quietly. "I'm going to write the
story that everyone says I can't. I'm going to go back into the past,
to work through it all, and put it to bed. *The End.*"

A long beat of silence.

"Can you?"

"Yes. No . . . I don't know. But I'm going to try. And, Jonah . . ."
She closed her eyes, taking a moment to corral her emotions. "When
I'm done, when I've written *The End*, I'm coming back to Seattle,

IN THE WANING LIGHT

and—" Thickness caught in her throat. She took another beat to marshal herself. "—I . . . hope you'll still be there."

A soft curse.

She closed her eyes.

"Meg—"

"Who's with you?"

"I . . . listen, Meg . . . you were the one who walked out on me. On us. You chose to end it."

She scrunched her eyes tighter, a hot burn rising in her chest.

He's been patient, so patient, and I just blew through it all . . .

"I came to Shelter Bay because I want to win you back," she said softly. "I want the things we spoke about. Children. A family. A proper home—walls and a roof. I *want* to find a way forward, and I want it to be with you."

"Meg, I . . . I'll always love you. You know that?"

She killed the call, hands shaking.

Shit. She scrubbed her hands hard over her face.

What have I done . . .

———

"Whoa, Lucy, what's up, girl?" Blake Sutton came running down the stairs in socked feet at the sound of excited barking. He ruffled his black Lab's fur as he entered the dimly lit office. Cupping his hand against the glass he peered into the dark. He'd thought he'd heard knocking, but the thunder was loud. Rain hammered a din on the tin roof—the old wooden structure creaking like an ancient mariner's ship in the storm. The buoys tied to the rafters outside beat a steady *thump thump thump* in the wind, accompanied by the low, metronomic moan of the foghorns.

As lightning cracked out over the bay, he caught sight of a hooded figure in a glistening wet coat running along the fence above the small harbor, and ducking into a camper fitted onto a dark truck. A light went on inside the camper, but the blinds were drawn.

Blake watched for a few moments longer. No one in their right mind would be out on a camping trip now. Had to be a traveler passing through.

"Dad!" Noah's voice came from the top of the stairs. "You coming to read to me, already? You *promised*!"

Lucy bounded back up the stairs at the sound of his son's voice.

Blake hesitated, watching as a shadow moved behind the camper blinds. Lightning cracked again and thunder boomed, the sound rumbling like a giant off into the dark night. He wondered if that rig would even be there come morning, or if the occupants might decamp before paying. It didn't matter. His priority right this minute was Noah. He'd learned this the hard way. Way too hard—and reading bedtime stories was one of the few real connections he had with his eight-year-old son at the moment.

"Sure, kid," he called up. "You better be all tucked in by the time I get up there!"

The thumping of socked feet sounded on the upstairs landing, followed by a skittering of dog claws. Blake clicked off the lights downstairs. He'd check in the newcomers tomorrow, *if* the rig was still there.

Once he was upstairs and had snugged back into pillows propped against the headboard, Noah cuddled under the covers next to him, Lucy lying like a heavy log on their feet, Blake cleared his throat theatrically, and began, "Once upon a time—"

"Oh jeeze, that's for *babies*, Dad. Read the proper story."

Blake smiled, just a little. It was rare to tease fun out of Noah. He began to read from their latest boys' adventure series while outside lightning lashed over the bay and thunder growled. As he read, a part of Blake's mind wondered again who was huddled outside in that camper, and if they would be there come dawn.

Jonah snagged a fresh, white towel from the pile his housekeeper maintained daily. Naked, he made for the floor-to-ceiling sliding glass doors. Beyond the glass, the black surface of his infinity pool shimmered with pockmarks of rain. Mist obscured the ocean view, making eerie halos of lights on the opposite shore. He reached for the door handle.

"What're you doing?"

He stilled, glanced over his shoulder. Jan Mascioni propped herself up onto her elbow, her breasts small and pale in the dim candlelight. Her hair was blonde, again. It fell in a mussed tangle over her shoulder.

She was beautiful. A good fuck. And not interested in any sort of relationship beyond a hot tumble in the sack. His head pounded. He wished he hadn't taken Meg's call. She couldn't comprehend this side of him—his need for tactile comfort in the face of hurt. She was unable to wrap her head around the idea that he could sleep with a woman, and it didn't have to mean anything more than that. Besides, *she* was the one who'd made it crystal clear that it was over—three years of their life together. And now this bombshell— he'd had no hint that she was spiraling in this direction. He wasn't sure how to process the fact she'd returned to Shelter Bay. And why.

"Going for a swim," he said, coolly. "Coming?"

Jan gave a throaty chuckle as she flopped back onto the pillows, flinging her arms out wide as if in sated bliss. She was comfortable in her own skin, this woman, and had reason to be. She ran at least forty miles a week, held a black belt in karate, taught Krav Maga classes, practiced mindful meditation, and only ate plants. Her physique was faultless. Her mind formidable. Jonah had yet to unearth whatever vulnerability it was that she worked so hard to hide behind her carapace of so-called perfection.

"I'll keep the bed warm for when you're done." She raised a knee to afford him a view of the Brazilian-waxed delta between her thighs.

He felt his groin stir, and he yanked the door open too hard. Chill air gushed in from the night. His hot body braced to meet it.

Cold rain pecked at his bare back as he swam laps until his muscles burned. But when he reentered the house he felt no less relieved.

Toweling his hair, he walked up to the bed. Jan sat up, dropped her feet over the side, and opened her thighs wide, reaching out for his fingertips. She drew him toward her, and lowered her head, teasing his cock with the tip of her warm tongue as he stood there. He felt a moan building in his chest as blood rushed south and his erection rose. Conflict tightened.

He halted her abruptly, hands clamping down firmly on her shoulders.

With heavy-lidded eyes, she looked up. "Not good enough for you tonight, Doc?" she whispered.

"You're always good, Detective."

She sat back. "Ah, but not good enough to get *her* out of your system." She reached for the sheet, wrapped it around her torso, held his gaze for several beats. "I think you love her. I mean, really love her."

He snorted. "Want a drink?"

"Make mine a double."

He tucked a towel around his waist, and poured two glasses of Balvenie thirty-year-old whiskey that had been matured in a mixture of traditional oak and sherry casks, his favorite at the moment. He added a small block of ice to hers. He took the crystal glasses to the low table in front of the fire where she joined him, propping her feet up onto the ottoman and warming her toes to the fire. She sipped, and sighed with pleasure as she put her head back, turning to catch his eyes. "You live in the equivalent of a luxury hotel, you know that?"

He pulled a wry mouth.

Outside the rain was turning to snow.

"So, why *did* you let her go, Jonah?" Always the assessing, questioning cop. This was not a woman who rested. She was one of the city's top homicide detectives with a doctorate in psychology and a scary-ass solve rate. Jonah pitied the poor punk who got on the wrong side of Detective Sergeant Jan Mascioni.

He met her eyes. She was also a good friend of his, and respect he had for her in spades. He shouldn't have gone back to bed with her like this. The shrink in him knew why he had, though.

"Because she wasn't going to stay," he said after a while. He took a big pull on his drink, letting the warmth of alcohol blossom through his chest. "I suppose I knew it from the start. Maybe I was just hoping I was wrong. Tell me," he said, steering the topic onto safer ground. "Any leads on the floating feet thing?"

"Expect a call from brass in the morning. They want to bring your team on board with this one." She finished the last of her drink, got up, and dropped her sheet to the floor. She padded over to her pile of clothes, pulled on her skirt and blouse, holster. Adjusting her jacket over her weapon, she slicked her hair back into a ponytail with a deft flick of her hands.

She came over, kissed him full on the mouth. And in his ear, she whispered, "You can have any woman you want, Lawson, and you know it. Time is a healer of all things. Let her go."

Trouble was, he didn't want any woman. He wanted the crazy redhead who wrote books in her camper, who didn't give a shit about his wealth. Who didn't really fit into his lifestyle at all. Was that *why* he wanted her?

Whatever the reason, he was seized by a dark and pressing

sixth sense that maybe he'd made a fatal mistake in forcing her back home, and into the past.

He sipped his drink, wondering if he should have preempted this, her returning to Shelter Bay. Meg Brogan was not one to shy away from a challenge. *If* she wanted something.

He hadn't realized she truly wanted him.

CHAPTER 4

Meg woke abruptly and listened for a moment, trying to determine what had roused her. The wind had died. All had gone quiet. She could still hear the plaintive moan of the foghorn, but now she could also discern the distant crunch of waves against the man-made breakers at the mouth of the bay. She climbed down from her bed. The clock above the stove read 3:00 a.m.

Wrapping a sweater around her shoulders, she peered through the camper blinds. Clouds scudded up high, revealing glimpses of a gibbous moon that silvered the water and cast a ghostly glow on the sand dunes along the opposite shore. The spit. The dunes behind which they'd found Sherry. She shivered and rubbed her arms, caught for a moment between past and present, snared between the horror of that memory and the beauty of this bay that was once her home. This little marina that appeared to have been trapped in time. Returning here was like stepping right back into it all.

It made her think of Blake. He'd defined this bay for her.

She turned up the thermostat, lit the stove, and put the kettle on to brew tea. If she couldn't sleep, she might as well get started with an action plan. Better than lying here thinking. And in the morning, she'd visit her aunt's assisted care facility first thing. From Irene she'd get the keys to the chain across the gate, and the keys to the house. She'd check out the old place, get cracking on a list of repairs. She'd also drop by a real estate office. All this she could juggle while working on the story, setting up interviews, obtaining police, court, and autopsy records.

Meg seated herself at her small camper table. Sipping her tea, she opened her laptop and began to type a list of "primaries"—people who'd been directly involved with her sister's case. Her goal was to find out which of them still resided in Shelter Bay. If they no longer lived here, she'd get contact details and chase them down further afield. But right now, this was ground zero. And while emotionally challenging, the story itself should be simple—she knew it, had lived it. All she had to do was tell it in the voices of all the players.

Top of her list was Sheriff Ike Kovacs, who'd handled the investigation. The medical examiner. The old DA. Tyson Mack's defense attorney. She'd also love to score an interview with Keevan Mack, Tyson Mack's father. The image of Mason Mack from the convenience store suddenly filled her mind. The hostility in his eyes. A chill whispered over her skin. The words of her old mentor filled her mind.

. . . *make no mistake, if you want to write true crime, you are going to have to talk to people who have suffered something awful.*

She typed in both Keevan and Mason's names.

She'd also want to interview Bull Sutton, who'd led the initial search for the Brogan girls that fateful day. And Dave Kovacs, Ike's son, the young deputy who was among the first on the scene of the murder. Plus someone from the sheriff's search and rescue team, plus the doctor who'd treated her concussion. The female cop who'd interviewed her in the hospital. And Father John McKinnon, who'd tried to help her devoutly Catholic parents navigate the aftermath, to no avail, because an *eye for an eye, a tooth for a tooth* had clearly trumped *thou shalt not kill* . . . She paused, then typed in Blake's name. She'd get his army contact details from Bull. She didn't really want to speak to Blake, but on another level she knew she had to, if she wanted to do this properly. Blake was the one who'd found her. Saved her life. In more ways than one.

She reached for her mug of tea and sipped as she watched her blinking cursor, listening to the familiar crunch of waves. Emma Williams, Sherry's best friend, went down next on the list. Sherry had told Emma on the phone that day that she was going with Tyson Mack to the spit for an "illicit" liaison. Tommy Kessinger, of course. Her sister's boyfriend at the time had also been a close family friend. The whole Kessinger family had been close with the Brogan bunch. Everyone had believed the Kessingers would eventually become in-laws. Meg inhaled deeply at the possibility of seeing Tommy again. She rubbed her brow. This was going to be hard. But she'd started down this path now. She would not turn back until she was done.

She began to type notes in rough, from memory, starting with things she'd learned from Blake about that fateful day she and Sherry went missing.

THE STRANGER AMONG US

By Meg Brogan

BLAKE

Two hours pass and Meg is still not back. The marina guests return in their boat with a bucket full of fair-sized male Dungeness crabs. Blake keeps casting an eye out over the bay as he helps them moor and disembark, all smiles and sunburned faces. It's turning cool on the water, a band of thick fog blowing slowly across the spit, where Meg had headed. Dusk begins to steal insidiously out of the shadows, and the light wanes.

Blake's curiosity edges into worry. He's been not-so-secretly in love with Meg Brogan all summer, and probably long before that in a kid-soulmate-friendship kind of way. Young love is complex. It's fervent and fierce and spins on a dime. To Blake, Meg *is* summer. She's the ocean. She's crabbing. She's the heartbeat of this bay. She gives him the zest to bite into life with full-bore zeal, to throw back his head and laugh with a mouthful of purple berries. She makes him lie awake in his bed at night, watching the arc of the moon, listening to the electric beat of his own heart.

He's sixteen. She's almost fourteen. And their relationship is headed into trickier, headier, darker territory. This summer has been complicated by a kiss that tasted of salt, and watermelon. By a touch of his hand to bare breasts.

Back on the mainland, across the coast road, in a subdivision abutting the forest, stands the Brogan residence, a classic vinyl-sided double-story that speaks of love and detailed attention. Mowed lawn. Happy little flower beds. A birdbath cloaked in moss and homemade birdhouses hammered into a giant chestnut that offers shade in hot summers, and a twisted monkey bar of a climb up to a second-story bedroom window.

Smoke wafts from the BBQ out back. Meg's father, Jack Brogan, has a ginger beer at his side in a mug frosted from the freezer. He tends the flames, sips his drink, relishes the sweet scent of freshly mowed grass. A sprinkler throws staccato arcs at the end of the garden near the woods. It's a last summer get-together. In just over one week he and Tara, Meg's mother, will be driving Sherry down to Stanford.

Tara Brogan is busy making burger patties. She glances up at any sound; the crackle of tires on the street, a call out front, laughter . . . she's beginning to wonder where her daughters are. They'd gone to see that new movie at the cinema in town. The sky clouds over, and rain begins to spit. A sudden wind teases, tests, swirls, calling in a wall of dense sea fog that fingers with dark glee up from the marina and along the streets and into the village and subdivision. The fickle vagaries of coast weather.

Jack pulls the BBQ in under the eaves. It's getting dark. Rain comes down more insistently.

Tara begins to make a few phone calls, checking in first with Sherry's best friend, Emma. She's not home. Tara finds someone who was at the movies. No one saw Sherry or her little sister, Megan. Worry edges into anxiety. A storm starts to lash against the Oregon seaside town. The foghorn begins to sound from Shelter Head. The radio says it's supposed to get worse.

The phone circle widens, friends calling friends. Panic blackens Tara's eyes and chalks her face. Neighbors come around. The kettle is boiled and tea is poured. Voices are low murmurs as Jack Brogan finally calls his good friend, Sheriff Kovacs.

Kovacs immediately activates Search and Rescue. They start to put a search party together, but have no clues yet where to start. The woods? Town? Around the movie theater? The beaches? This place is between ocean, miles of dunes, and a state forest that reaches all the way into the mountains. And there is no "point last seen."

It's almost full dark when a call comes from Bull Sutton's Marina. Sutton's son, Blake, saw Meg Brogan taking the Brogan family crab boat out late that afternoon. The boat is still not back.

"Where? Which way? Did you see?" Jack Brogan demands when he gets down to the marina, grabbing Blake's collar, shaking the boy, wind, rain lashing at his face. His eyes are wild and his words hard, angry, full with a father's fear. "Why in the hell didn't you tell someone!"

"I didn't know she was missing! I was busy with the crab boil."

"What direction?"

"There. Across the bay, to the spit." Blake points. "I . . . I didn't think it was a problem. Meg knows this water—"

"She's only thirteen, goddammit!"

Blake doesn't remind her father Meg will be fourteen next week. He doesn't tell Jack Brogan how sweet his daughter's mouth tastes, and how he'd like to do things with her, like he does in his dreams.

"How could you not know there was a storm blowing in!"

"Jack." Sheriff Kovacs places his big hand on Jack's arm. "Easy now. Let me talk to Blake."

The fire engine arrives, and an ambulance, and a SAR incident van. More cops. Lights pulse red and blue in the storm. Men and women in heavy weather gear gather around the SAR van. A klieg light spits on. A rescue boat starts across the bay.

The sheriff takes Blake aside. The big cop's face is now white with worry.

"Was Sherry with her?"

"No."

"Did she talk to you before she left?"

Blake swallows. Looks at his feet. His face, too, is bloodless, his jaw tight, his arm and neck muscles corded wire. He should have done something, told someone earlier, left the tourists and gone to see for himself . . .

The sheriff's eyes darken and a frown begins to cut across his brow as the questions enter his mind.

"Were you the last one who saw her, Blake? Anyone else see her leaving the marina?"

"How would I know if someone else saw her after I did?" he snaps. "She took the boat, and she was being weird. I asked her where she was headed and she told me it was none of my business."

"She take crab bait? Was she going fishing?"

"No. It didn't look like she was going fishing. She . . . she appeared to be on a . . . mission. She looked worried. Was moving fast. Went right across the bay to Sunny Beach."

"You like the Brogan girl, don't you, Blake? Pretty little redhead. You know her well." A beat of silence. The foghorn blares. "Very well."

Blake Sutton's eyes flash up to meet the sheriff's. "What's that supposed to mean?"

"Nothing, son, nothing. Just trying to figure out whether we should be looking for those Brogan girls in two separate places, or one."

Search beams dance in the mist over the black water. Calls carry in snatches of wind. Bull Sutton marches fast down the gangplank in heavy rubber boots, a strident figure in his sou'wester. He climbs into his boat with the big engines.

The sheriff moves fast down the gangway to join him. The engines rumble to life. A powerful spotlight flares on, turning rain into a silvery sideways sheet.

"I'm coming!" Blake charges down the gangway and along the wobbling wooden dock after the sheriff and his dad.

"You stay right there." Bull Sutton tosses free the lines, and the boat churns backward, away from the dock.

"What do you think I am?! *A kid*? I can handle this water, this bay, the storm better than half the men out there!"

"Stay there," his father calls. "Man the fort, Blake. Keep the radio on. Need you on communications."

Blake clenches his jaw, hands fisting at his sides. Rain drenches him. The horns moan. Wind slaps waves against the dock and he can hear the thunder of surf against rocks at the mouth. His dad's boat is swallowed by dark and mist. Adrenaline thumps through him, as does the image of Meg, heading off in her little boat, bare legs, hair snapping in the wind. Small against the world.

You know her well . . . Very well . . .

CHAPTER 5

Blake watched Noah scrambling up the sandy trail behind the house, little red backpack bobbing, his towhead tousling in the breeze. When his son reached the road up top, he hesitated, but did not look back.

"Later, champ!" Blake called from the bottom, taking the gap before his kid vanished without a good-bye. "Don't forget, it's bus home today!"

Noah turned, gave a quick wave, then disappeared between the scrub, heading down the road to join the other kids waiting for the school bus.

Blake stuffed his hands in his pockets. He felt strange, a hollowness as he stood there in the wet grass in his gum boots. The morning was chilly, but the wind had died and the skies were clearing. In a few minutes the sun would crest above the east ridge and spool some warmth into the bay. Yet everything was dead. The tail end of winter was always the ugliest time of year, a time when it seemed that summer might never come. But he had work to do if he was to ready the marina and campsites and cabins before the annual influx of tourists. He also wanted to have Crabby Jack's Cafe renovated in time for a grand spring opening. He sucked in a deep breath and made for the office, boots crunching over gravel.

Who'd have thought he'd be like his dad, running this marina alone? A single father. After trying so hard to go another way, to find another route, just to circle all the way back as if destiny ordained it.

Focus on the routine. Check off the chores. Open the marina up. Even in winter there was the odd diehard fisherman who still wanted to go crabbing. Soon it would be spring—then the summer holidays, the busy season. His kid might grow to love it yet. Blake was forming a vision of the way it could be—Noah helping him with the campsite, and the boats, and the tourists, and the more serious crabbers and clammers and fisher folk.

While the marina life had not been for his older brother, Geoff, Blake had deep down always loved it, living by the push and pull of the tides, the seasons, the sea. If it hadn't been for Meg, for what had happened to her and Sherry . . . he probably would have stayed, taken over from his dad. Married Meg if she'd have had him. Instead she'd cut them all out of her life, excised this place like a cancerous tumor in order to survive. And he'd been too close to the lesion she'd needed to separate out. Collateral damage.

Sherry's murder had pitched some serious curveballs.

Blake unlocked the office, put on coffee. He glanced out the window at the camper. Still there. Last night, from his upstairs window, he'd seen the light go on inside, around 3:00 a.m. He couldn't say what had roused him and made him look. Perhaps the sudden quiet of the storm.

He ran through his list of chores, setting things up for the day, then checked his watch again before making his way over to the camper, Lucy in tow.

Blake knocked lightly on the camper door. "Hello? Anyone home?"

———

Peggy Millar cracked an egg and dropped it into the pan. It hit with a sizzle, the white lacing into a crisp curl along the edges.

"You'll never guess who came into the gas station last night," she said, reaching for another egg. She raised her voice to be heard over the stove fan. The scent of coffee mingled with the aroma of a loaf fresh from the bread maker that had been working its magic during the night. Outside, the day was clear, heavy conifers bejeweled with droplets shimmering in the early morning sun. The sound of traffic on the coast road grew steadily as the day got started.

Her husband, Ryan, just back from dropping Jamie and Alex at school, grunted at the breakfast table, reading his newspaper.

"Meg Brogan."

He glanced up sharply. "What?"

"Meg Brogan is back in town."

He stared at his wife. "Where? When?"

"I just told you. She came in to fill up her truck last night. She had a camper shell on top. Washington plates. She bought some food in the store."

"Meg Brogan is *back*? What in the hell is she doing back here? Did you ask her?"

"Just passing through, I think. Looking for a place to stay the night. I only registered it was her *after* she'd left the store. Her face was familiar, but I couldn't place it. Then as she got back into her truck, I suddenly remembered the poster in Rose's bookstore. Meg Brogan's book is right there in the front window. Her face plastered on the jackets."

She popped up the toast, placed a slice on each plate. Taking bacon off the paper towel on which it had been draining, she positioned two pieces neatly beside each slice of toast, then flipped the eggs before sliding them atop the toast. She brought the plates to the table, set one in front of Ryan. His attention remained fixed on her face.

"She wouldn't have remembered me," Peggy said. "I was in a grade above her. Didn't really have anything to do with either her or Sherry. Besides, I look different than I did back then." She went back into the kitchen, fetched the coffeepot. "Did you know Rose's book club is reading that latest novel of hers? Something about an old woman who remembered a crime from like fifty years ago." She held up the pot. "Top up?"

But Ryan just stared.

"You okay?" She set the pot down, slowly seating herself in front of her plate.

Ryan cleared his throat. "Yeah. Yeah, I'm good." He lifted his knife and fork, ate distractedly.

She sliced into her egg. Yolk spilled onto the plate. "I've been meaning to read that book," she said, delivering a forkful to her mouth. "I wonder if she'd ever write about the Shelter Bay murder."

"You mean her own sister's killing?" He stared, bloodless. "Why would she do that?"

"Maybe her memory might come back if she did, like that woman in her latest book."

He drained his mug, plunked it hard on the table, reached for his napkin, and wiped his mouth. "Got to get to work." He pushed himself to his feet.

"I think I'll join that book club."

"What about the gas station?"

Irritation flushed hot through her chest. "I could get Brady to work an extra hour or two a week. I think we owe ourselves some time off now and then. Now that the business is finally taking off in this new location. You could do with some downtime, too."

Ryan regarded his wife a moment. "We're only as good as the Kessinger-Sproatt contract. If we lose that, we're back to square one. Tommy saved our asses."

"Book club is not going to kill us, for Pete's sake, Ryan." She lurched to her feet, snagged her half-eaten plate, and angrily scraped the contents into the trash.

"We'll talk later." He exited the kitchen door.

"Later," she muttered to herself. "Always 'later.' Like I can't do a damn thing without *permission*." Peggy went to the window, dirty dish still in hand. She watched her husband lumbering over to his mechanic shop, where he spent seven days a week tinkering with vehicles. And most nights, too, a couple of beers at his side. He was getting heavy. What had once made him a handsome, square-jawed football force to be reckoned with in high school was now turning him into a shambling giant of a man. He carried his beer and her cooking in his paunch. Taking some time off, getting some exercise, maybe going fishing again, camping, was not only a dream, it was going to become a health necessity. If she could put it to him that way . . .

Maybe she should make oatmeal for breakfast tomorrow, instead of dishing up the cholesterol and fat in eggs and bacon. She could lose about twenty pounds herself, the doctor had said. As she stacked the dishwasher, a memory snaked up . . . Meg Brogan returning to school for the first time after the murder. It had been a cold January. Over twenty years ago.

Peggy stilled. Poor kid. She'd been a mere shadow of herself. Skin so pale and translucent her freckles had stood out like floating stars. In the following months she'd begun to cover her freckles with chalky makeup, and she'd cut her hair brutally short, dyed it punk black. As if somehow needing to wear her own aura of death. Or stamp it out, or something.

Peggy had ached to say something to Meg in the school hallway—her locker had been just near Meg's—but she'd never known what to say. And as the months wore on, Meg had begun to project a keep-the-shit-away-from-me hostility. So Peggy had just looked away. Like all the other kids had. Leaving Meg Brogan to walk and sit and eat in the cafeteria alongside them all like a silent specter, a shadow somehow removed from their own real, comfortable world, untouched by what had touched her.

Blake Sutton was the only person who'd persevered long enough to ever get through to her. Just about every girl in her class had at one time or another crushed on Blake. He'd wasted it all on Meg.

And then she'd gone and broken the boy's heart clean in two when she left. He'd never have married Allison if he could've had his Meg. And now look at him, a single father with a son he never wanted.

Peggy inhaled, glanced at the kitchen clock. This stuff was drawing her back. She needed to get ready, go help in the store.

———

With the base of his fist, Blake banged louder on the camper door. "Hello? Anyone home?"

No answer. He noted the Washington plates. Either the occupant was dead asleep, or out on a morning walk or . . . fishing? He frowned, turned slowly around, taking in the bay, and then he caught sight of a lone figure in the distance, on the Crabby Jack deck.

A woman.

She stood at the railing cradling a travel mug, looking out over the bay. Hair long and wild in the breeze. Chestnut-red, the color catching the gold in the dawn sun. Something snared like a bramble in his chest. With it came a hot rush of adrenaline. He shook it off. Disarmed by the coincidence, he crossed the vacant camper sites and made his way through the covered area in front of his office, and around the building to the front deck of the cafe. As he turned the corner, Lucy bounded ahead and nudged the woman's jeans in search of a greeting. The woman stiffened in surprise at the dog's touch, then she laughed when she saw it was a black Lab. She set her mug on the railing and crouched down to pet Lucy, revealing her profile. Blake's heart stilled. His breath, his whole body stopped dead in his tracks.

"Oh, hello, girl, who are you?" she said to his wiggly Lab as she examined the tag on her collar. "Lucy? Aren't you a pretty thing." She glanced up and froze. Paled. Her mouth opened, but words seemed to elude her. Slowly, she rose to her feet, reached for the railing, as if to steady herself.

Blake felt as though he was seeing a ghost. His world spun and tilted in a dizzying distortion of time. She'd matured—the lines of her features had refined. She was slender under that bulky brown coat. Almost a little too thin. Wan complexion. Same soft brush of freckles. Wide mouth. Light honey-brown eyes, almost amber in this light. Big eyes, dark lashes. Those eyes that had always sucked him in with their mystery, into the depths where Meggie's imagination lurked, the place he knew she hid the real girl, the vulnerable teen, the maturing woman. The place he knew hurt. And how he'd tried to help her out, but never could fully lure her into his light. Yes, for selfish reasons of his own, he'd tried. Meg had been his first love. Real love. The kind of feeling that went beyond sexual lust and attempts at gratification. The kind of feeling that delved deep into the realm of friendship, kinship. Soul mate, as trite as that might seem to some.

The woman who'd left this town, and him, because he reminded her of bad shit.

He knew what she'd become. He'd read her books. In tabloid rags at supermarket checkouts he'd glimpsed photos of her with that filthy-rich, celebrity-shrink fiancé of hers, him with his James Bond looks. He'd known every moment what Meg Brogan was making of her life.

And not for one of those moments had he ever expected to see her back here. Home. Standing on the deck of his marina. Petting his dog. And in the distance behind her, across the water, the spit where he'd found her lying unconscious and close to dead.

"Meg?" His voice came out hoarse.

Her gaze shot up to the sign on top of the building. BULL'S
MARINA.

"I know." He came forward. "I should get around to changing
that one day, huh. Only been mine for two-plus years now. Still,
it's been a lot of work to fix up. Damned Pacific Northwest, you
know—everything tends toward entropy. Even the buildings are
biodegradable. Salt wind doesn't help. Just feeds it. And then there
was that super tide that flooded Crabby Jack's. I'd like to get it
shined up before spring . . ."

Shut the fuck up, Blake, you asshole.

She stared, confusion chasing across her features. Her thin-
ness, paleness, made her eyes seem even bigger than he remembered, and they swallowed him whole. She held her thick hair back
off her face as wind gusted. The sun crested the top of the building
and caught her features. She blinked. An ethereal thing of beauty—
like some shining piece of a dream plucked out of his past and
plunked down into this soggy, decaying, paint-peeling reality that
was his present. He swallowed. Unsure. Feeling somehow less. As
if in approaching any further, speaking another stupid word, he
might spook her off. Shatter the illusion.

Jesus Christ, he was still totally messed up over this woman . . .

"Is . . . your dad?"

"Bull passed away. Two and a half years ago now. The old
ticker"—he tapped his chest lightly with the front of his fist—"finally
packed it in."

The news seemed to physically punch her in the gut. She lowered herself slowly onto a wet log bench. He hesitated, then moved
closer to her. Close enough to touch. Her eyes dipped over him,
taking in what had become of him over the past sixteen years. His
pulse raced. He shoved his hands into his pockets. "That your rig
back there?" he said with a jerk of his head.

She nodded.

He bent down, gave her a quick kiss on her cheek, stealing her scent. "God, it's good to see you again, Meg."

She swallowed.

He turned on the gas that fed into the concrete fire pit, and set it aflame. Fire whooshed to life in the cold air, the warmth almost instant; then he seated himself on the rough-hewn cedar bench opposite her. He leaned forward, forearms on his thighs.

"What on earth brings you back, Meg?"

———

Ryan Millar waited until his wife had disappeared through the back door of the convenience store. He reached for his cell phone, dialed, pressed his cell to his ear. As the phone rang, he ran his palm gently along the body of the tricked-out monster truck he'd jacked up on one of the garage hoists. The chrome, the studs—*this* was his true passion. This was how he liked to spend his time off, when he could sneak it.

His call clicked over to voice mail on the third ring.

"Hey," he said quietly, leaving a message. "It's Millar. I heard Meg Brogan was seen back in town—thought you might like the heads-up." He hesitated, debating whether to say more, then killed the call instead. He stood for a moment, phone in hand, staring at his own caricatural reflection in the chrome hubcap, thinking of dreams versus reality. How you made big shiny goals when you were young, and how life turns out misshapen in the end. How people settled. Found a comfort zone. Or a rut that just kept on getting deeper, and harder to climb out of.

Wind gusted, sending water drops spattering down from the brooding cedar onto the garage door. He started at the sudden noise. The weather was turning. . . . something foul carrying on the shift of the wind.

CHAPTER 6

Blake had changed. Rougher and more rugged, he'd filled out, muscled up. Fine creases fanned from the corners of his deep green eyes, and lines bracketed his wide mouth. He was sun browned, windblown. He looked like he'd seen and done things. War. Foreign skies. A man of the sea and wild places. Yet there was something beneath his powerful exterior that seemed somehow . . . fractured. This man who knew her probably better than anyone left in this world did—or could—appeared to have hidden wounds of his own.

The onslaught of feelings—guilt, remorse, affection, kinship— was so contradictory, so sudden and powerful, it slammed the guts right out of Meg, forcing her to slowly seat herself on the wet log, not quite trusting her legs. A memory simmered to the surface— racing down the gangplank and onto the dock, making for her family's little tin boat . . .

Where are you going, Meg?

None of your business . . .

If she'd made it his business, would everything be different? Time stretched. Gulls wheeled and screeched.

She found her voice. "I'm sorry about Bull," she said softly. "I . . . I had no idea you were back. The last I heard was that you'd enlisted."

"I did. Day after you left. Served as an army medic. Several tours. Long, long tours." A smile creased his face, putting dimples into his cheeks. He opened his hands, palms up. "And look at me now—here I am. Back home on the bay."

Wind swirled, sending the old weather vane above Crabby Jack's squeaking against rust. The deck down in the water below groaned under a tidal surge. Lucy the Lab sighed in resignation and lay down at Blake's boots in front of the fire. Then, his words almost a whisper, he said, "God, you look good, Meg." He cleared his throat quickly. "I saw you on TV a couple of weeks back, on that *Evening Show*. And Rose Thibodeau has your new book in her storefront window. She's going to want you to come and do a signing or something now that you're here." His smile deepened. It put light into his eyes. But it was surface. Because in those eyes Meg read deeper currents. Old hurts.

It twisted her gut.

Her gaze dipped to his forearms. They were tan, the hair on them gold. They rested on thighs thick as her waist. His legs were splayed apart, his big hands clasped together. The sight and shape of him so familiar, yet not. A strange sensation rippled hot through her, like an ache. For home, lost things. And it came with something trickier. Darker. Sexual. She swallowed, slowly lifting her gaze to meet his eyes.

"So, what *does* bring you home?" he prompted.

Home. What in the hell was home, anyway? "I came to write Sherry's story."

"Sherry's story? As in a *book*?"

"Yeah."

"So, it's work that brings you here?" A hint of derision, disappointment, glinted in his eyes.

She looked away, out over the bay. An osprey hit the water with a smack, surfacing with a writhing fish, droplets glittering in the sky as the bird rose with its silvery catch. "To tell you the truth, Blake," she said slowly, watching the osprey flap off, "I don't really know what brings me here. I just needed to come back for a while. I need to see my aunt, sort out the house. The city has been sending warnings. They've threatened to take action if I don't do something."

"It *is* an eyesore."

"I know. I drove by last night. In the dark it looked bad enough. I can only imagine what it looks like in broad daylight."

"And what's with the camper?"

"It's sort of my office. The plan is to park it at the old house while I fix things up: power wash the walls, put in new windows, see what the interior looks like." She met the intensity in his eyes, and heat flushed into her cheeks. "I didn't want to stay there alone last night. The gate is locked anyway. So . . . I came here."

He weighed her carefully with his gaze, taking a measure of her intent.

"I don't get it," he said suddenly. "Why come back and dig up all that shit, just for a *story*? Seriously, Meg—" He looked away for a moment. "So . . . how do you go about this, then? You interview everyone involved? Rehash every little sordid detail?"

"I'll try to speak with everyone who might still be in town: Ike Kovacs, Emma, Tommy, Dave. Keevan Mack, Ty Mack's lawyer, the ME. " She paused. "You."

He cursed, eyes narrowing. "No one wants to go through all that again."

"I need to do it, Blake. I need to walk in my own tracks, so to speak. Just driving back into town last night, into the mist, past the old landmarks, after all these years, I started to feel things. Bits of memory. Maybe something will return—more pieces."

"And those pieces are going to tell you what, exactly? Nothing new. We know who did it. We know who suffered."

"I don't expect you to understand—"

"The hell I don't. Is it for the money? The additional fame or notoriety this will bring you? You want to cash in on a tragedy that was this town's, paint yourself as some heroic little victim who pulled through all on your own? Some kid who grew out of her own tragedy and family violence to tackle crime and justice head-on, and now, wow, look at you, all grown up, fabulous and famous and self-indulgent?"

Anger thumped into her chest. "Bitter, is that what you've become, Blake? Because I can tell you now, it doesn't become you."

He gave a harsh snort. "So what *does* it feel like—to profit from the pain of others?"

"This was *my* pain—"

"No, Meg. Not just yours."

Silence thickened between them. Her blood pounded. The pulse at his neck pumped. His hands knitted tightly together and his eyes flicked briefly to her engagement ring. Something darker, more primal, tightened his mouth.

"I need to do it, Blake, for me," she said coolly, quietly. "I'm going to write it and might never publish it, but I'm going to damn well write it to *The End*." Anger firmed her resolve. It drove the guilt down deep, pushing back all the complicated things she was feeling for Blake right now. Her jaw tensed and her voice lowered. "What I saw on the spit that day is still inside me. I *know* it's there, repressed. And it's like a sick black cancer that has never stopped growing. It festers. It circles my dreams. I wake up nights, hot and . . . it's messing with me." She took a beat, marshaling herself. "Forgive me if I need to try and heal it."

He blew out air, got up, went to the railing. He fisted his hands around the wood banister, neck muscles taut as he glared out over the bay, toward the lighthouse, toward the point where he'd found her unconscious all those years ago. Where he'd saved her life. Sun glinted on his wedding band.

Meg's stomach folded softly into itself as she noticed it.

"*The End*," he repeated, quietly. He turned to face her, the rays catching the gold streaks in his dense brown hair.

"*The End* happened eighteen years ago, the day you left, when you ran away—"

"I didn't 'run' away. I went to start a new life, to study—"

"You just cut us all out, not even a damn Christmas card. Not even a note for my father. Or for Kovacs, or Emma and Tommy. And yeah, I did ask them. I did wonder if they got luckier than me. And what about Irene? You never came home to see her."

"I used to see her at the prison, when I went to visit my—"

"Listen to yourself."

She lifted her chin. "We've been through this, Blake. I've put it all behind me."

"Clearly, Meg, you haven't, because look, here you are, needing to resolve something unresolved."

She glowered at him, her skin going hotter, her pulse jackhammering. He held her gaze like that for several long beats.

"I just need to tell it, Blake." Her voice caught, and it startled her. She cleared her throat, looked down at her hands. "I didn't think I did, but I do."

He seated himself beside her, his muscled thigh almost touching hers. He sat silent a while. "I'm sorry." He paused. "I . . . just missed you."

Her attention returned to his wedding band. She thought of that last kiss, and her insides turned hot and twisty.

"You know it's not going to go down well, your being here, doing this?" he said quietly. "No one is going to welcome it. Or you, because of it."

She looked up and met his eyes. His lips were so close. She recalled the scent, the taste of him like it was yesterday. "I imagine there will be questions like yours, Blake, people wanting to know why." She cleared her throat again. "And there will probably be an initial reluctance to speak. But in my experience, from the cases I've done, it's been positive for people to tell their stories. Cathartic. It's not like anyone has anything to hide."

A darkness darted through his eyes, and Meg felt a sudden tremor of unease. He rubbed the stubble on his jaw, glanced out over the bay, as if struggling with something, then he smiled. But this time it seemed forced. He reached over, took her hand.

"Welcome back, Meg. Whatever the reason—it's good to see you." He hesitated. "Can I fix you some breakfast, coffee?"

She withdrew her hand and surged instantly to her feet. "I'm fine, thanks. I've got everything I need in my shell back there. I can pay for the night and be gone in an hour or so. I'll get keys from Irene, park at the house."

He came to his feet and dug his hands firmly into his pockets. "I'm not accepting your cash. Could never do that. Stay as long as you want."

She wavered, feeling awful about leaving him like this, about all the things she wanted—*needed*—to say, but couldn't. She ached with every fiber of her being to just hug him tight, bury her face into his chest, say sorry, tell him that she'd missed him, too. And in that instant Meg knew with a horrible, cold certainty that Jonah was right. There *was* something wrong with her, because she *couldn't* do it.

He nodded to her ring. "So, when's the big wedding, then?"

"I need to do this first."

"You mean write this book?"

"Yes."

His brow hooked up.

She changed the subject quickly. "And you—married, I see. Who?"

"Allison McMurray."

"Allison from my class?"

He nodded, his eyes shuttering. He was closing her off. She didn't know why it hurt that he'd married sweet, gentle Allison who'd tried so hard to befriend her at school, but it did. It was ridiculous. Sometimes the kid inside never died. She had no right to jealousy or any sense of proprietorship over Blake.

A big, rusted Dodge truck rumbled suddenly down the driveway and into the gravel lot in front of the office, a boat on a trailer in tow. It came to a stop and the truck doors swung open. Two older men outfitted in jeans with suspenders and flannel shirts clambered out.

"Yo. Sutton," one called out to Blake with a wave of his hand. The other positioned a ball cap onto his head.

"I . . . I should let you get to it," Meg said, watching them.

"Yeah. Later." And with that, he turned his back on her and walked off to meet the men. His stride was long, powerful. The movement rolled into his shoulders. A stubborn bull, like his dad. And as Meg watched, she felt torn. The shape of her world had just shifted, and she was no longer certain where her center lay.

———

"Hey, Sutton, any crab bait today?"

Blake approached his customers, two old-timers in their late sixties. "Harry, Frank, you guys are bright and early." He opened the shop door for them. The bell *chinkled* as the men entered and Blake followed. From his fridge he took a bag of fish heads. "How many you want?"

"That one bag is good."

Over the shoulder of Frank, who was peeling notes from his wallet, Blake watched Meg, long red hair blowing in the sea wind as she made her way back to her camper. A memory of that fateful day snaked into his mind, Sheriff Kovacs grilling him with a scary-ass intensity in his eyes.

Harry followed Blake's gaze. He frowned. "That looks just like—isn't that—"

"Meg Brogan, yeah." Blake took Frank's cash, put it in the till.

"What's *she* doing back?"

"Got some ghosts to slay, I think." Blake gave a soft snort. "Going to write a book about the Sherry Brogan murder."

The men paused, then exchanged a glance. A current passed between them.

"A book? What in the hell for?" said Harry.

"Cash in on a personal tragedy, is my bet," grumbled Frank, picking up his bag of fish heads, the dull, dead eyes peering through the cold plastic. "I seen her on TV. She's big shit now. Tara and Jack would turn in their graves if they knew she was going to drag all that old crap out. Won't look good for Shelter Bay, neither, being splashed all around bookstores all over the country as the place of a gruesome killing."

Defensiveness rose in Blake, but he kept his yap shut.

Frank started for the door. Harry wavered. "So, how's she going to do it, go talking to everyone who's still around, hauling out memory baggage from old closets?"

"Something like that."

"I can tell you one person who's gonna be really pissed. Sheriff Kovacs. That case ate him and his wife up whole. Changed the whole damn town. Never the same after that. Like an era gone."

"And now his boy is running for sheriff," Frank added, pushing open the door. "Her timing sucks."

Blake followed the men out. He handed them crab pots, watched them go load their boat. His father's contemporaries. Friends of the old sheriff.

Meg was backing her rig out. Her vehicle headed up the driveway and took a left onto the coast road. Guilt, hurt, a twinge of anger filled Blake. If he hadn't been so hung up on Meg all those years ago he might have made a better go of his marriage. He'd have a better relationship with his son. And now that he was finally on track, plans for the marina, could see his life here with Noah, here she was. Like a bad penny. Because his body still reacted to her like a teen on hormone overdrive. Or was it just knee-jerk muscle memories chasing down old neural channels before he had time to think them through? He turned to go down the gangway, telling himself to use his head next time he ran into her. If there was a next time.

He could have handled that conversation better, that was for sure. He'd been an ass. It was self-defense and he knew it. Because he *couldn't* want her. She was spoken for and sporting a big-ass diamond cluster to prove it.

And she was wrong about one thing. There were still secrets to keep.

———

"She's able to recall the smallest details from decades ago, but can get confused by the present." The director of the assisted living facility glanced up from the file on her desk and peered at Meg over small-rimmed glasses, as if examining something rather distasteful. And Meg supposed she was. In the eyes of everyone here she'd abandoned her aunt.

"When her short-term memory trips her up it can make her defensive. Irene sometimes thinks people are out to fox her, or that there's a conspiracy afoot."

Meg cleared her throat, feeling for all her thirty-six years and lifetime of experience like a kid in front of the school principal. "I . . . hadn't realized it was so far advanced."

"Her dementia is heading into what we call stage four—a CDR2—moderate impairment. At the moment she manages her own hygiene," the director said crisply. "And although she's fine with social activities, outings, chores, she's reached the stage where she needs to be accompanied when she does leave the facility. As she progresses into stage four, and it can happen quite rapidly, her spatial and time disorientation will increase, and it's at this point that our loved ones can get easily lost, and when short-term memory becomes seriously impaired. It'll be difficult for her to remember anything new, including people she's just met."

"Why did no one tell me?"

The woman, handsome, with soft silver hair swept back into a sleek chignon, regarded Meg across the expanse of her desk as a judge might stare down a petty criminal in the dock. "Irene asked that we withhold informing any relatives as long as we could, so as not to alarm you, or force you into returning prematurely." She cleared her throat. "But it's appropriate that you're here now— decisions will need to be made."

"So I can take her out?"

"As long as she's signed out by a responsible adult, she's free to leave." The director smiled thinly as she got to her feet. "I'll show you through."

Meg followed the woman and her loudly clacking heels down the overly warm corridor. The place smelled of antiseptic, and bacon and eggs and burned coffee being served for breakfast. Is this what it all came down to? A place like this? Irene had put her life on hold to care for her brother's child. And this is where Meg had left her aunt; *this* is how she'd thanked her. She swore internally, and vowed she was going to make this right. She *would* atone. One way or another, while Irene still had time.

Jonah's words dogged her into the bowels of the facility.

You haven't even been to see Irene since she went into that home. You haven't returned in eighteen years. You can't put roots down here, yet you can't go back, either. See? You have not put it behind you. This is not about your work. It's about your problem with intimacy, with letting people in. You want connection, yet you push people away . . .

Her skin prickled and a pearl of sweat slid slowly down between her breasts. The director knocked on room 117, opened the door, let Meg in.

"If you need to talk further—"

Meg nodded, her gaze fixed on the frail, stooped woman pacing in front of a window, scratching at her sleeve.

"Irene?" she said, stepping into the room. The door closed quietly behind her.

Her aunt spun around. Her jaw dropped.

"Tara?"

"I . . . no, it's me, Megan." She went forward.

Irene hesitated, confusion chasing through her features. Her hand touched the silvered hair at her temples.

"You . . . look just like her—your mother. My goodness. I . . . I didn't expect to see you, Megan. What . . . are you doing here?"

"I came to see you, of course." She kissed her aunt's cheek. Irene's skin was cool, papery, but her scent was familiar—lavender, lemongrass—and it brought a rush of memories.

Irene's gaze darted around the room in panic. "I . . . I should get some chairs in here. More chairs."

"The bed's just fine." Meg seated herself on the edge of the bed. "You've got a pretty view of the garden. I like the birdbath right outside."

Irene looked out the window, as if seeing the view anew.

Meg swallowed. *The long good-bye* is what Nancy Reagan called it. Today was a start. She still had time. And suddenly this was no longer just about the book, but so much more. It was about setting right all sorts of past wrongs. It was about growing up and beyond being the self-indulgent "victim" as Blake had so brutally called her this morning. And he'd had a right to do so.

Irene finally took the lone chair. She stared at Meg. "It's been so long," she said in a whisper. "When did I last talk to you, Megan, how many years ago?"

"I phoned," Meg said gently. "Remember? At least once or twice a month since you moved in here." She cleared her throat. "I've come to see how you're doing. And I'm going to fix up the house. Give it a paint job, spruce up the garden. Maybe you'd like to come and help? Or just watch? Sit in the garden, if the weather turns, while I try and work that darn mower." She smiled. "I see the gate is padlocked."

Irene frowned, her eyes going distant. Then her face lit up suddenly. "Ah, yes. Chained. Because of the vandals. There was graffiti. You're not going to sell it, are you?"

"Well, I am thinking of listing it—"

"Maybe you could move back in, Meg? I could come and stay."

"I . . . how about we talk about all that later." She hesitated. "I'm going to be in town for a while—we'll have plenty of time."

"You stopped visiting your dad, too. You never visited him in prison. You hurt your father, you know that?"

Shock rippled through Meg, and defensive walls slammed instantly up.

Well, he hurt me. He hurt all of us. He killed Mom.

"I did visit him."

"You . . ." Her brow furrowed, and she started scratching at her sleeve again. "You stopped going. That's it. Now I remember. I know it's a long drive from Seattle to Salem, but not once in the last five years did you see your father. He died without seeing you again, Meggie."

"I stopped going because he *refused* to see me the last two times that I did drive all the way out there. If I'd known he was sick—if someone had told me . . ."

Irene started to scratch her sleeve aggressively. A nervous tic, Meg noted, when her aunt was having trouble recalling something.

"That's right," Irene said. "Yes. Of course. He refused to let me tell you that he was ill. He wanted you to get on with your life, Meggie. That's why. He said the punishment should be his alone to bear, that you should not have to spend your life driving for miles upon miles to visit him in prison. You needed to move on."

A sharp surge of emotion rose up the back of her nose, catching Meg by surprise. Wind gusted outside and dry vine leaves ticked against the window. "I wish I *had* known," she said softly, holding Irene's eyes, once so dark, and bright, like her dad's. "I'm sorry."

"You were always our little Meggie. We only wanted the best for you."

Shit. This was sucking her back too deep.

"How is that man of yours?" Irene said, glancing at Meg's large engagement ring. "What was his name again?"

"Jonah. He's fine." Meg slapped her knees. "So! How about it—want to help me with the house? I'll need the keys for the padlock on the gate, and for the house, so I can get in, take a look-see what needs to be done. Then we can make a time for you to come out. Maybe we can go into town for lunch some day, tea? Shopping?"

Irene's face crumpled into a smile and her eyes gleamed with moisture. "I'd like that. I've got the keys somewhere in my dresser drawer." She got up, shuffled over to the dresser, opened the top drawer, and started rummaging around. Meg noticed a copy of her new hardcover atop the dresser. It was bookmarked and lying beside a silver-framed photo of her family taken a month before Sherry's murder. She got to her feet, picked up the frame. Complex emotions corded her stomach. She really did look like her mother. In this photo Tara Brogan was not much older than Meg was now. It brought the memory of her mother suddenly closer. It painted a new perspective around their family tragedy, and it made Meg wonder how she herself would have handled her own daughter's violent death, her husband going to prison for murdering the assailant in a vigilante rage. She sure as hell wouldn't have killed herself, leaving her youngest child an orphan, that's for sure. Meg set the frame down firmly, an old bitterness resurfacing at the back of her tongue.

Irene set a small, padded box on the dresser. "The keys should all be in here," she said, lifting the lid. "Ah, here they are." She handed Meg a fob with several keys attached. "I should also give you Tara's boxes, all her files."

Meg looked up from the keys. "What?"

Irene's mouth pulled to the side. She scratched hard at her arm. "It's all in the boxes, you know. What your mother was working on. I must let you have it all now. Maybe you can make sense of it all."

"What boxes? What are you talking about?"

She hurried over to her closet and yanked open the doors. "Up there, Meg. Top shelf. Two of them. Get them down, will you?"

Meg stared at her aunt. "What's in them?"

Frustration bit suddenly at Irene. "After the fire. I'm so sorry about the house fire, about leaving the candles burning like that. It's why I decided to come here, to the facility. I was worried it could happen again. Or worse."

"I know, I know. Go on."

Irene's hand moved rapid-fire along her sleeve, two hot spots forming high along her cheekbones. Meg placed her hand gently over her aunt's agitated one. "Tell me, Irene."

"The fire and water damage—we had to get in contractors to fix up the kitchen. Tommy's company came and did it. He did it for nothing, you know. There was that dividing wall between the kitchen and the living room, remember, the one with the book-shelves, where Sherry used to keep her goldfish?"

Don't be stupid, Meggie. They live in a perfect world. There are no predators in their water, like the poor wild fish have to deal with in the sea . . .

"I remember."

"Well, when they came to hack that drywall out, they removed the damaged books from the shelf and found there was a large fire safe at the back of one of the shelves. It had been hidden by those books, which I'd never moved. That was where your mother kept the file boxes, and her journal."

Meg felt blood rush from her head. Her breathing slowed.

"Journal?"

"Get it all down, will you?"

She did. Two file boxes. Dust layered the lids. Meg set them on the bed, opened them. Inside were folders, envelopes stuffed with papers, photographs, a leather-bound journal. Meg lifted out the top folder, flipped it open. Ice slid down her spine. She shot a glance at her aunt. "It's a transcript," Meg said. "Of the sheriff's interview with Tyson Mack."

Irene nodded.

Quickly, Meg flipped through more of the folders, her hands beginning to tremble. "Sherry's autopsy report," she whispered. "And a diary." Meg opened the first page of the leather-bound book. Her mother's handwriting filled the pages.

I visited with Lee Albies this evening, Ty Mack's defense counsel. We spoke well into the night. She's a remarkable woman. Believed passionately in her client. A startling defense she'd been mounting. She gave me copies of everything, and the more I read, the more I believe there was no doubt a jury would have acquitted Ty, at least on grounds of reasonable doubt...

Meg's knees buckled, and she sat slowly on the bed. "Who ... what does this all mean?"

"Your mother didn't believe it was your dad's fault, killing Tyson Mack. So, she started gathering all the information she could—"

"But Dad confessed. There was irrefutable evidence. He planned it. He *did* it. He killed Ty Mack in cold blood. Hunted him down in those woods. Shot him to death and beat his body to a pulp with bare fists, kicked in his ribs and face."

"Tara believed he was set up."

Meg stared, uncomprehending.

Irene seated herself on the chair. "My brother, Jack, he was a good man, Meggie, deep inside. A good, God-fearing man—"

"Yes, who literally believed in an eye for an eye, and had a problem bottling his rage if he touched booze, we know that."

"He was a man broken by the defilement of his baby girl, and there were people who knew why Jack didn't touch alcohol, knew that he was prone to hot passion. That he was capable of violence under the influence ... they knew why he'd been forced to leave the Portland police before coming here, and starting afresh ... " Her voice faded and her eyes went distant for a moment.

"Why, exactly, did my dad leave the Portland force?"

"Oh, Meggie, he'd gotten all heated up and physical while interrogating suspects on more than one occasion."

"*What?*"

"He was asked to leave, before things got public. Tara was convinced that someone who knew all about your father's past told him where to find Ty Mack that day. They said something to Jack that heated his blood—maybe they told him Ty Mack would walk free if he was charged, and it riled Jack enough to turn him to the bottle and make him buy those bullets."

Meg's heart thumped soft and fast against her ribs. Her mind reeled, things that had always puzzled her about her father's past slowly slotting into place.

"*Who?*" Meg said. "Who all in Shelter Bay knew this stuff about Dad?"

"It's all in there. In Tara's notes," Irene said. "I never knew about her journal, or those files. I had no idea what she was doing before she died . . . until the fire, until we found the safe." She rubbed her brow. "I never knew."

"You read her journal, you read all this and never called to tell me?"

"I didn't know what to believe, Meg. I can't even be certain that your mother was well in the head when she wrote that diary. And you'd put the past behind you."

CHAPTER 7

Blake dropped the orange sack full of squirming crab into the boiler. Steam roiled up into the cool winter air. Rain pecked outside the deck cover and pocked the waters of the bay. He set the timer. Frank and Harry were enjoying a lunchtime beer under the awning on the deck of Crabby Jack's. The gas fire pit sent flames spitting into the drizzle. A second table housed two intrepid Asian tourists who'd netted a good catch as well, and had opted to have Blake cook the crabs up, and show them how to clean the crustaceans.

He checked his timer, glanced at his watch. Noah would be home any moment.

While he waited for the crab to cook, he dialed his brother on his cell. A male voice answered.

"Geoff?" Blake said.

"It's Nate. Hang on—I'll get Geoff. He's in his studio."

Gulls screeched. Crows beaded the line up near the highway, watching for bits of discarded crab guts.

"Hey, bro, what's up?" came Geoff's voice. "Haven't heard from you in years." Then, a shift in tone, a deepening wariness. "Everything okay? Noah all right?"

The buzzer sounded and Blake pulled the net from the boiling water with his gloved hand. Steam clouded the air under the awning. Out of the corner of his eye he glimpsed the yellow of the school bus through the berry scrub up on the coast road. Emotions churned through him. He and his brother used to get off that bus daily. He hadn't spoken to Geoff in . . . how long now? Probably not since Geoff had returned for their father's funeral two and a half years ago. Theirs were not just philosophical differences, but lifestyle choices. His brother had quit Shelter Bay and the marina for the warmer climes of SoCal the month after Sherry's murder. He'd gone to study art and classics, leaving Blake to man the marina with their dad. The unease between all three of them was rooted in complex places.

"Meg Brogan is back in town," Blake said. "She's doing a book on the Sherry Brogan murder."

Silence hung for several beats.

"What're you saying?"

Blake waved to Noah, who appeared at the top of the driveway. Noah didn't return the salute. He scuffed his way down the drive. Damn. Something had happened again at school.

"She's going to be interviewing everyone, and she'll probably call you, too. Just a heads-up."

Another beat of silence. Blake carried the cooked crab over to the stainless steel cleaning station, phone pressed to his ear. Gray coastal drizzle kissed his skin.

"Listen, what happened on the spit that—"

"I won't lie to her, Geoff. Not by omission. Not this time. Not after—"

"You *didn't* lie. There was nothing to tell. It wouldn't have changed a damn thing."

"I know you were on the south beach, at the point that afternoon. I found the sack you dropped with your beachcombing shit. What happened? Why'd you leave your bag?"

"*Fuck it*, Blake . . . why can't you just let sleeping dogs lie? There's no point in dredging up anything else. It's not relevant, okay? Especially after all these years. We *know* who did the crime. And he paid for it one way or another."

"Or another."

"What, exactly, are you trying to say?"

"I'm saying that this might not be over. I'm saying Meg thinks she might be starting to remember something about the attack."

Silence.

A sick weight pressed into Blake's stomach. He waved the two Asian men to come over to the cleaning station, and said quietly, "Ty Mack was no hero, but the more I think about it now, the more I wonder if there was something else going on that day."

Geoff swore. "Mack was a sexual bully. When a woman turned him down, he went apeshit. That's what happened with Sherry. She went with him to the spit. He made an advance. She said no, and he cracked."

"He never did get a chance to stand trial. He maintained he left Sherry safe."

"His goddamn DNA, semen, his skin under her nails, his hair, witnesses—all the evidence was there. The only reason he *wasn't* charged and tried is because Jack Brogan didn't give Kovacs time to cross all his Ts and properly arrest him."

"Why won't you tell me what you saw out on the spit that day?"

"Because I didn't see a goddamn thing. I was messed up over Dad, that's all."

Noah reached the parking lot and crossed over toward the office door.

"Noah!"

He didn't look up. He shoved through the office door. It swung shut behind him. Blake cursed softly. The Asian men reached the cleaning station, all smiles, ready to learn how to dismember and disembowel their crab.

"I got to go," Blake said. "Just wanted to let you know that if she asks, I'm not holding anything back. I'll tell her you were there that day." He hung up, and tipped the cooked crab out of the bag. Keeping an eye on the window for Noah, worry rising inside him, he showed his guests how to peel and split the pinked, male Dungeness crab and use the hosepipe attached to the station to wash out the yellow and black innards, sluicing the gunk down the hole that led into a basin he'd dump later. Gulls whorled and wheeled and screamed above.

He rubbed his brow with the back of his rubber glove as the guys got started. *The choices we make, the secrets we keep for those we love, the ripple effect down the years, the prices we pay . . .*

He glanced out over the bay. Rain was coming down harder. The tide was rising. Nothing could hold back time or tide, or weather, or what was going to come out of this now . . .

———

Meg drew into the driveway of the home in which she'd grown up, and turned off the ignition. Mist fingered out from the woods and closed around the house.

It looked worse in full daylight. Spooky, with shattered windows boarded up, overgrown with weeds. Obscene graffiti. Dirt patches had commandeered the lawn that was once lush and green, her dad's pride. The birdbath listed to its side, brown with dead moss. Trees hemmed close to the house, branches brushing eaves and broken gutters as if the forest was coming down from the mountain to reclaim and consume the place. The old chestnut she once used to shimmy down from her bedroom window was now a brooding monster. She wondered if the remains of her tree house were still out back, overlooking the patio where her dad had been barbecuing that afternoon, waiting for her and Sherry to come home.

Anxiety trickled through her. She pulled up her rain hood, opened the truck door, and jumped down. Slowly, she approached the chained gate, keys in hand.

Looks like shit, huh, Meg? Remember that day? When you saw Ty pick me up . . .

She stilled. Trees rustled in a gust of wind. It was as if they were whispering at her with the sound of Sherry's voice. Meg glanced around, mouth going dry.

Sherry? Are you here? Are you going to speak to me, finally, after all these years?

Another gust, and trees bowed and swished. Bits of debris bombed down. Mist swirled around the house. A chill trickled down Meg's spine. She told herself this was ridiculous. She bent down and grasped the padlock firmly. It was cold, wet in her hand. She inserted the key, turned. Nothing. She jiggled it, tried again. It remained unyielding, encrusted with rust. She cursed and tried several other keys just to be sure she had the right one. Nothing worked. Rain beat down harder. She rammed the first key in again, frustration thrumming through her as she wrenched it. Nothing. Did she have some oil in her truck? She glanced up, then her heart kicked as a sheriff's cruiser slowed in front of her house, tires crackling on the wet street. The window rolled down.

"Well, well, if it isn't the famous Meg Brogan, our local resident done good, how in the hell are you, girl?"

She pushed damp hair back off her face, came forward to better see inside the cruiser.

"*Dave,* is that you?"

The door swung open. The deputy stepped out, unfolding to his full and impressive height in his tan uniform. He positioned his sheriff's Stetson against the rain, and a smile cut into his face.

It lit his warm brown eyes. Dave Kovacs was a massive echo of his father, Ike—sans the handlebar mustache. It was like staring at someone who'd stepped straight through a hole in time. Meg couldn't help but return his smile with a genuine rush of pleasure and a sense of relief just to have company right now.

"I could have sworn you were your dad for a moment. How are you? They haven't made you county sheriff yet?"

He gave her a kiss on the cheek, and she caught a whiff of Old Spice. An old-fashioned, conservative kinda guy—he even smelled like his dad.

"All the better for seeing you, Megan." His thumbs hooked into his duty belt and his attention went to the graffiti-covered house. "Nope, not yet. Just the chief deputy. But I've put my hat into the ring this time around."

"Good for you. So . . . you were just driving by? Or did you come to give me a warning about the eyesore here?" She jerked her head toward the house.

He smiled. "Yeah. It's a problem all round, vandals. Getting more and more of this with the vacant holiday homes, down on the beach especially. I heard you were back. Thought I'd come by."

She frowned, trying to read his eyes hidden by the shadow of his brim.

"I heard you're doing a book. On Sherry," he added.

"Ah," she said. "News travels fast."

"Not every day we get news like that in Shelter Bay. Here, let me help you with that lock." He took the keys from her and went up to the gate. He inserted the key, jiggled it a bit, then turned it firmly, his fingers stronger than hers. The padlock popped open. He dragged the chain through the gate, creaked it open wide and held the keys out to her.

Her cheeks went hot as she took them from him. "You make me feel like a girl."

He regarded her in silence, an inscrutable look entering his features. Her smile slowly faded. "What is it, Dave?"

"It's not a wise idea. The book."

"Why not?"

He gave a snort, glanced at the forest. "That old business cut the town apart. Messed up my dad. My mom . . . All of us." He turned and his eyes bored suddenly into her. "What's the point? Ty Mack's dead. Your dad—mom—are gone."

Her jaw tightened. She held his gaze in silence for several beats. Water dripped off the brim of his hat. Wind sighed again through the trees and brushed over her face, like a touch. A warning. Again, she felt Sherry.

"I need the truth, Dave." And it struck her right there. This really was more now. Not just a retelling. Not just interviews. Her mother had believed something deeper had happened, that her father might have been set up. And every minute more that Meg was in town, the sense that there was something urgent locked inside her memories intensified. Whatever it was had been festering in her head for twenty-two years, and she was going to flush it out. One way or another. She was going to do this. And it was not just for Jonah.

"Take my advice." Dave opened his car door. "Let it be." He paused. "And don't you go bugging my dad about an interview, d'you hear? He retired five years ago. His heart is not good. We'd like to keep him around a while longer. He's the grandfather to my kids now."

"I'm writing this story, Dave. Which means I do need to interview him."

"He won't do it."

"Why don't you let him tell me that himself."

Silence. The sound of traffic on the distant coast road reached them. And Meg felt the divide opening between them.

"Be careful, Meg."

"What's that supposed to mean?"

He held her gaze a second longer. "If those vandals come back, a woman out here on her own . . ." He shook his head. "You let me know, okay?"

She watched him get into his cruiser and drive off. Her heart thumped in her ears, Blake's words from this morning sifting into her mind.

. . . it's not going to go down well, your being here, doing this? No one is going to welcome it. Or you, because of it.

———

Geoff stepped onto the deck that looked out over the sea. Far below their stilted beach house a couple jogged along the sand with two dogs. Breakers rolled in white lines to the shore. The SoCal air was soft and rounded. He dug his hand deep into his pockets. He'd always known this thing might rise up to haunt him again. It woke him in a sweat at night. The dreams had been getting worse. And now? Now this. He inhaled and blew out a heavy breath of air.

What he craved with every molecule of his being was to come clean before his marriage, his new start in life. But in doing so he could lose everything. The irony was not lost on him.

Between a rock and a hard place. The saying was so overused it felt trite. Between the devil and the deep blue sea. Between Scylla and Charybdis . . .

"Everything okay?"

He tensed, spun around. Nate stood in the doorway, drafting pen in hand, sleeves rolled up. His smiled faded as he saw something in Geoff's face.

"What did your brother want?" Nate said.

"Just to catch up. I . . . I'm going home, I think."

Nate regarded him steadily for several beats, then said, "I could do with a break. Some wine? Out here on the deck?"

Geoff snorted and forced a smile. "Be great."

They sat side by side, overlooking the ocean, glasses of chilled Sonoma pinot grigio and a plate of organic cheeses between them. The light was odd. Coppery-purple, like before a storm. Streaks of rain formed along the horizon. They could see the cloud band moving toward land. Wind began to stir, but it was warm.

Geoff loved this place. He'd found freedom here for the first time in his life. He could be himself. But was he truly free if he couldn't take who he was, and go anywhere? Even home? Back into the past? Was he truly free as long as this thing continued to fester black inside him? He sipped his wine, thinking of something he'd read about criminals, how sometimes they just confessed because it was so cathartic. They *needed* to tell someone what they'd done. It was probably the idea behind the Catholic confessional. It cleared things off the chest so that believers could begin afresh again.

But how could he even begin to amend his past, come clean, without the risk of losing Nate? Without totally destroying someone else he'd once cared deeply for? That's why he'd run away in the first place. Avoidance.

And now this call, this tentacle from the past, sticky and tricky, and, yes, dangerous. Reaching into his life down here.

"So?" Nate said, finally. "Why go home now?"

He met Nate's eyes. They were a soft brown, turned down slightly at the corners, giving him a sad, but kind look. When he smiled, they turned liquid and mischievous. Gentle, was his Nate. Yet rock solid. Geoff's stomach churned in an oily roil of conflict.

"I'd like to tell my brother about us, about the wedding. In person. Invite him and Noah."

Nate's brows crooked up.

"I want to come out in my own hometown. I'm sick of god-damn half-truths, old deceptions. I . . . I just need to do this. Sort some things out in my life . . . before the wedding."

Find a way to wipe clean the slate so I can move peaceably, rightfully, into my new life . . .

Nate's eyes held his. "You sure?"

Geoff looked out over the ocean. "Yeah. I'm sure." He blew out another chestful of air. "Besides, the last time I saw Blake and Noah was for my dad's funeral. Noah was just six years old. And I was only there for the day—my nephew probably doesn't even know his uncle exists. I feel kind of shit about that, about Blake trying to run that decaying old marina, a single dad."

Nate nodded, but concern darkened his features. He sipped his wine in silence for a few moments. The distant susurration of the ocean carried up to them on the salt breeze. Wind suddenly ducked, swirled, and darted over the dune scrub, making it ruffle as if stroked by an invisible hand. The wind chimes on the deck *chinkled.* Geoff felt an eerie sense of sentience, of time, snaking in, shifting a paradigm, ever so slightly.

"Want me to come with you?"

He smiled. "Thank you but, no. I'll be fine. Honest. I need to do this on my own. I need to pave the way for my family to meet you."

Another intense silence as Nate held his eyes. In them Geoff saw a flicker of worry. Fear even. He broke the gaze, took a deep sip of wine, the sick oiliness in his stomach slithering toward his bowels—he could lose this. Nate. All of it. He could lose it by doing nothing, just sitting here waiting to see if Meg's memory returned, or if she managed to dig up the truth with the help of his brother's confession.

Going back to Shelter Bay he might stand a chance . . . he could try and stop Meg. He could try and convince Blake to keep his silence. Or, if shit hit the fan . . . he had no fucking idea what he'd do if shit hit the fan.

———

Meg entered Sherry's old room. Cobwebs wafted with currents of air made by her movement. Irene had kept this room permanently locked after she'd moved in to care for Meg, and stepping into it now was stepping back two decades in time. Sherry had been into purple. Purple and green walls. Lavender bedding. Jon Bon Jovi poster on the wall, pictures of track stars. Her Doc Martens still waited for her in the corner, never again to move with the rhythm of Sherry's feet.

Meg ran her finger softly along the rows of old CD cases. Thick with dust.

She stilled at the bed.

This bed where she'd found her mother on May first, twenty-one years ago—spring, supposedly a time for new beginnings. Tara had been on her back, mouth agape, a slime of yellowish vomit dribbling out of the corner of her mouth. Meg's stomach folded at the memory. She glanced at the bedside table where the pill container had been left. Empty.

Her mother had chosen this place, of all places, to take her life, while Meg, fourteen, had slept down the hall.

Emotion clawed at her throat. But her mouth tightened. She refused to give in to it. Refused to be the "victim" that Blake had called her. She was never a victim. He was full of crap. For a moment back at Irene's care facility she'd conceded the self-indulgence part—she'd seen where he might have drawn the analogy. But her so-called self-indulgence, her cutting everyone out of her life, had been an act of survival, not the act of a victim. It took courage. Not cowardice.

She yanked back the drapes. Dust motes exploded into the air and floated softly down around her. She sneezed and opened the window. Cold, fresh air flowed in.

Meg lowered herself onto the edge of Sherry's bed and, hunkered in her damp coat, her mother's journal in hand, she stared at the framed photograph of Sherry and Tommy Kessinger, taken on his dad's yacht. Eighteen and nineteen they'd been that summer, on the cusp of the rest of their lives. Laughing. Golden. Sun browned and lean limbed and filled with zest and promise.

Inhaling deeply, she pushed back a tangle of damp-frizzed hair, and opened the journal to the last entry. Surprise blossomed through her—it had been written April 30, the day before her mother committed suicide.

It's getting dark now, and from the back window I can already see the SUV parked at the end of the road again, beneath the broken streetlight, behind the cherry tree. I'm sure it's the same one. But it's hard to be sure in the dark and shadows. I called Ike Kovacs earlier. He said to lock the doors—he'd come around in the morning. I told him I thought I'd heard someone trying to break into the house three nights ago. He said it was probably a raccoon or a bear. They were really active right now. He said I needed to relax, that the medication I was taking for stress might be unsettling me. He was being kind. He surely meant to say paranoid, irrational, and I do feel overly anxious, my heart palpitates. My mouth is perpetually dry. But when I spoke to Dr. Armano about it, he said I was not sleeping enough. He gave me sleeping pills for the insomnia. Now I have pills for this and pills for that, and what next? The only thing that is going to put this right for me is to find the truth. Maybe then, finally, I will sleep.

I worry that I'm not giving Meg enough attention through all this, but I have only so much energy, and I want her to live her life. I'd love to talk to her about this, but she's too young. She took it so hard when Jack was arrested. Even harder when he was denied bail. And we still have his trial to face come December, which is why I **cannot** *rest. I need answers before then. Whatever I can find* **might** *help ameliorate his sentence.*

Oh, my dear Jack, I only wish you would talk to me and tell me who tipped you off to Ty's location, tell me who and what riled you so, and drove you to do this. Yes, I know that you bear the blame as yours, and yours only. And yes, possibly that person who told you where Ty Mack was hiding meant no harm, and yes, I know the knowledge won't get you out, but it could help lead me to the missing link, to a bad, bad man who still walks free, who could kill again. Who could rape and strangle another Shelter Bay daughter, while you live out your days in a small, square cell with no sight of the sun . . .

That was it. Where it ended. Her mother's last words, as if her pen had just run out of ink. What did this mean?

A bad, bad man who still walks free, who could kill again . . .

Had her mom come to believe Tyson Mack was actually innocent? And Sherry's killer was still out there? Had Tara Brogan closed her diary on this last entry, and locked the journal into her safe, replacing the books in front of it, then gone to bed? And what of the next day? What led to her overdose the next night? Because this sure as hell did *not* sound like a woman ready to give up and take her own life. It sounded like a wife and mother in love, on a fierce mission to help her husband. And she'd had a ticking-clock deadline to the December trial date.

Meg lurched to her feet, paced the room. It didn't make sense.

She held the journal tight against her chest. Her mother had *not* forgotten her—not in the way Meg had always believed. She'd been fighting for Sherry, Dad, the family. Truth.

She'd been doing the things I would have done, if I were in her position. Fighting for answers, not giving up . . .

And what of this SUV down the road, watching the house? Her mother's fears about someone trying to get in? Ike Kovacs brushing it off.

Her mother was not who Meg had believed her to be at all. Emotion stung Meg's eyes. She breathed in deep, controlling it. But in her gut a hot coal began to burn, a coalescing of will to get to the bottom of this. Shit. She was going to do this story come hell or high water now. She owed it to her mother. To Sherry. Dad. Herself.

Jaw tight, she marched downstairs and out to her truck. She got her laptop, and she carried the boxes inside. She put on more lamps, wiped the dust layer off the dining room table, and started laying the files out across the table between making calls to contractors about power washing and repainting the house walls, and replacing broken windows.

She was going to take this diary, all these files, transcripts, crime scene photos, and go through it with a fine-tooth comb, retracing every inch of her mother's steps.

And Dave Kovacs be damned. His father was right at the top of her list—she was going to grill retired Sheriff Ike Kovacs, gimpy heart or not.

CHAPTER 8

"Noah, would you like to tell your dad what you did yesterday?" said Ellie Sweet with a touchy-feely tone that made Blake's skin itch. She'd phoned and asked him and Noah to meet with her after school today. Blake was now seated beside Noah on a kid-size chair at a blue table in Miss Sweet's happy, shiny, yellow-walled classroom. He looked down at his pale son, his little head bent forward. He'd driven Noah to school himself this morning, and arrived to pick him up. Ellie Sweet eyed his kid over the top of her fashionable plastic-framed specs, and Blake felt himself siding instantly with his boy no matter what he might have done.

"It's okay, champ," he said gently. "You can tell me."

Noah glowered at some groove in the table.

"Noah?" he coaxed.

Silence.

A spark of irritation spat through Blake.

"You hit Alex with your backpack, didn't you, Noah?" Miss Sweet said.

Noah's mouth tightened. His knee started to jiggle.

"Is that right, champ?"

He cast a sideways glance up at his dad.

"Why'd you do that?" Blake said.

His son returned his attention to the table groove. His knee jiggled faster.

"I tell you what, how about you go wait in the truck for me. I want a word with Miss Sweet, alone."

Noah looked up sharply, a range of expressions chasing through his face, from fear, to anger, then hope. Blake's chest crunched.

"Go on," he said gently. "Here are the keys."

He waited until the door had closed behind his son.

Blake said to Miss Sweet, "There must have been some provocation. Noah is not an aggressive child. He's the opposite. Empathetic to a fault. So much so that I worry about him."

"No matter the reason, we cannot condone violence of any kind, Mr. Sutton. Our students need to understand that there are better avenues to resolve conflict—discussion. Arbitration. And this is not the first time we've had one of his classmates report a physical outburst from Noah."

"Did *you* see what happened?"

"No, but—"

"So, some kid snitches on him, and you take it at face value? Did you happen to notice that he also has a cut on his head? Maybe this boy hit him first. Why aren't we talking to this Alex kid and his parents, too?"

"Her."

"Excuse me?"

"Alex is a girl."

"He hit a *girl*?"

"You need to speak with your son, Mr. Sutton. I've already spoken to Ryan and Peggy Millar, Alex's parents. Possibly she did provoke Noah, but violence as a response is not tenable. We will not stand for another incident like this." She paused. "It'll be the principal you're speaking to next time. And the consequences . . . well, let's not go there, shall we." She smiled. Sweetly.

Blake cleared his throat, feeling a sudden and surprising affinity with his own father, and the struggles Bull had with Geoff. Noah was sensitive, artistic, like his uncle. Like his mom. He also harbored the dark and secret places of an imaginative introvert.

"Look, he's struggling with the loss of his mother—"

"I know." Ellie Sweet bowed her head slightly. "We understand. We understand that *both* of you might be having a rough time coping. But it's been a full year since Noah lost his mother, Mr. Sutton." She hesitated, color rising prettily into her cheeks. "Have you and Noah perhaps considered talking to a therapist? We could provide you with some recommendations that—"

Blake surged abruptly to his feet. "I'll speak to him. I'll handle it. Thank you."

He shoved out of the school doors, hot with adrenaline and burning with emotions he had yet to articulate. A fine Pacific Northwest rain kissed his face as he crossed the parking lot. He saw Noah's little shape in the passenger seat of his truck, and he clenched his jaw, turning all the fire inside him toward thoughts of Ryan Millar. He'd never liked that guy, not even in elementary school—never trusted him. Not one bit. He'd clobbered Ryan once or twice in his life, and had been clobbered back twice as hard.

Oh, the vagaries of a small-town life, he thought as he reached his vehicle. The old patterns of behavior, the family grudges just kept cycling back.

———

"Alex Millar must have said *something* to upset you, Noah. I understand that. But unless you tell me what it was, I don't know how to help you. And if that Millar kid goes and messes with your head again, and you lash out again, they're going to need to take action. If they kick you out of school, then what?"

"I don't care."

Blake's hands firmed on the wheel. Noah sat beside him, three boxes of fresh pizza stacked on his lap. Lucy stretched out on the backseat. He'd taken his son on his errand run after their school meeting, reluctant to leave him home alone. The bed of his pickup was loaded with the paint and the rest of the supplies he needed to continue his renovations on the Crabby Jack. It was getting dark. Rain beating down harder now, the pizza scent mingling with the smell of wet dog.

Blake drew up to a T-junction at the coast road, wipers clacking. He felt so goddamn alone right now. No manual for this shit. His thoughts turned again to his dad and Geoff, and how he himself had tried to protect his older brother against his father's machismo frustration with his artsy son who'd had zero taste for the marina life. Bull Sutton had been driven by old Victorian attitudes probably beaten into him by his own dad. He'd always been quick to resort to the physical, be it to reprimand, or fix something with his bare hands. Bull could have done with the softening touch of his wife, and in retrospect, Blake suspected his mom's death had been incredibly rough on his father.

But he'd have learned nothing from his own childhood if he hadn't learned that bullying his boy into line was not going to work. He needed to earn Noah's love. To do it he must stay calm, receptive, open. Kind. Patient. He inhaled deeply, fighting his urge to drive directly to Millar's garage.

He glanced at the three pizza boxes on Noah's lap, then at the clock on the dash. On impulse he turned left instead of right, heading up toward the southwestern subdivision that ran along the forest fringe.

"Where are we going?" Noah said, suddenly sitting up straighter. "You going to talk to me, now?"

But Noah turned his head to glare out the rain-streaked window.

Blake punched on the radio to fill the void. A music jingle sounded, and the program cut to the host.

. . . this is KCYJ-FM, your eyes and ears, the voice of the coast. And in today's town buzz, a little bird tells us that our own Shelter Bay celebrity, Meg Brogan, has returned to take up the gauntlet laid down on air several weeks ago by Seattle-based Evening Show *host Stamos Stathakis, who challenged her to write the Sherry Brogan story. Her arrival has rekindled an interest in the old murder, and the* Coast Gazette *tweeted this morning that its lead reporter is working up a feature on the old crime that once shattered this town . . .*

Shit. She was already stirring things up.

Noah looked at the radio, then up at his father, a subtle shift in his energy. "Are you going to tell me where we're going?" he said.

"You going to talk to me yet?"

Sullen, Noah turned away again.

Blake wheeled into the last street and drove along the row of houses that pushed up against the woods. "I'm going to see if an old friend is home." He hesitated, then thought it might be good for Noah. "She used to know your mother. They were in the same class at school."

Noah scratched at the sticker on top of the pizza box. "What's her name?"

"Meg Brogan."

Noah's eyes flicked up.

"She had a really rough time as a kid growing up here in Shelter Bay. She lost her mom, like you, when she was young." He slowed as they neared the Brogan house. "Her sister and father died, too."

"How did they all die?"

Bingo. He'd found a window in. Blake went for it, figuring a degree of honesty was the best policy in regards to a story that was clearly going to be at the top of the local news. He cleared his throat. "Her sister, Sherry . . . she was attacked by a bad guy—"

"A bad guy *killed* her?"

"Yup, then her dad, who was really angry, went after the bad guy. And—" *Shit, why did I start this* . . . "And he shot him."

"Dead?"

"Yup."

Noah stared at Blake, his mouth open, intrigue lighting his eyes. "Was that who they were talking about on the radio—Meg Brogan, and her sister, Sherry?"

Blake stole a glance at his son. Then he said, "Yes."

"And you knew Meg at school, too, as well as Mom?"

"I knew her most of my life. From when I was even younger than you."

"Did you go out with her?"

Where'd that question come from?

He cleared his throat. "I did. She was my very good friend. In lots of ways. She used to spend a lot of time at the marina with me and your uncle Geoff." Blake turned into the Brogan driveway. The gates that had been chained shut for so long stood open wide. The house brooded under heavy trees in the mist and rain. He stared at the lurid graffiti as he drove slowly in.

"What about Mom?"

"Meg was long before your mother, champ. Meg left Shelter Bay almost the day she graduated from school."

"Why?"

"To get on with the rest of her life."

He pulled in behind Meg's camper, along the side of the house that was mostly in darkness. The front living room windows were still boarded up. A rush of anxiety, and something darker, trickier, chased through Blake, as if taking a step with his son into the old

Brogan house might be crossing a point of no return. Was there such a thing, if a person had free will? He turned off the ignition.

Noah was staring at the side wall, which had been tagged with red spray paint. "Who wrote that stuff?"

"Vandals. The house has been standing empty for a long time. It happens."

Noah looked at him. A small link had re-formed between the two of them. Blake said a silent prayer of thanks, and took a deep breath. "You okay sharing some of that pizza, bud?"

———

TRANSCRIPT: Part I of recorded interview, TYSON MACK
Date: 8/12/1993
Duration: 41 minutes
Location: Chillmook County Sheriff's Office
Conducted: Sheriff Ike Kovacs and Detective Jim Ibsen
Present: Lee Albies, defense counsel

Meg scanned quickly through the transcript preamble, paused, and pulled the lamp closer to the document. It was prematurely dark inside the living room with the boarded-up windows. She read more slowly.

TM: I told you, I brought her home. Sherry was fine when I brought her home.

SK: Home? Like, to her door?

TM: Um, no. Almost home. I—

SK: You did, or didn't bring her home? Which is it now?

TM: I dropped her at the far end of the street, at the trailhead to the path that runs along the forest, behind the last row of houses on Forest Lane. She was fine. She was laughing.

JI: This is Detective Jim Ibsen, badge ID 439, entering the room.

SK: Why on the forest path? Why not outside her house?

TM: She didn't want her parents, her father, to see me with her.

SK: And why would that be?

TM: She . . . um . . .

SK: Because you have a bad rep with women, Mack, is that why? Because Jack Brogan knows your type?

LA: My client can't speak to Jack Brogan's state of mind.

TM: It's not like that—

LA: Ty, you don't have to answer that.

SK: What is it like, then?

LA: Ty—

TM: I dropped her off! She was fine. It was all consensual, fun. I went home. She was fine.

SK: We going to find your DNA on her, Mack? Under her nails? In those condoms? Did you strangle Sherry Brogan after you fucked her, or while you fucked her? We going to find your semen inside her body, Mack? That pretty girl Sherry all twisted and dead in the dunes. What did she say to upset you?

LA: Sheriff, that's enough. Unless you're going to charge him, we're outta here. Ty?

TM: I did *not* hurt Sherry. I'd never hurt a woman. We had sex, yeah. It was . . . energetic intercourse, so yeah, you will find my DNA. She wanted it. She went with me because that's what she wanted!

LA: Ty?

SK: And you know what a woman wants, do you, boy? Was it good sex, was she a good one, Mack? Got a little too rough, maybe? Got out of hand, maybe? You had to put her in her place? Did she say no at any time?

JI: Lee Albies and Tyson Mack are leaving the room.

SK: Cat got your tongue, boy?!

JI: Kovacs, easy. Give it time. We'll get him. We will.

Meg inhaled, and looked up from the transcript. She was losing track of time. She'd been reading all through the previous night, falling asleep only briefly atop the papers. Dirty mugs littered the table. The room smelled of stale coffee. From her mother's journal she'd deduced that her mom had secured most of these documents as copies from Tyson Mack's defense counsel, Lee Albies, a top Portland criminal lawyer who'd scaled back her law practice when she'd relocated to Chillmook County to begin her segue into retirement. In Chillmook she'd volunteered part-time with a public defender consortium.

She'd taken on Tyson Mack's case as part of a long-standing personal crusade against what she perceived as class prejudice in the justice system. Tyson Mack was disenfranchised and being made a scapegoat, in her opinion. He'd been the son of an illegal alien mother who was deported when he was three, after which he'd been "raised" by Keevan Mack, an alcoholic father with a history of aggression and an attempted sexual assault conviction under his own belt.

There was everything in these boxes from police interrogation transcripts to witness statements, Sherry's autopsy report, and crime scene photos—which Meg had not managed to psychologically brave up to yet, not after her first glimpse of a stark black-and-white image of her sister's naked body spread-eagled in mud. She'd placed those reports in a separate folder, which she'd work up to later.

Meg had also found that Lee Albies still had an address and phone number listed in Chillmook, the large town a few miles down the coast that gave the county its name. The old lawyer had just risen to the top of her interview list.

A vehicle sounded outside and a car door slammed. Meg's head jerked up, her pulse quickening. Lack of sleep, this reading material, too much coffee, was making her twitchy. She pushed back her chair and moved quickly to the window in the kitchen and peered out. A pickup, black, was parked behind her camper. Shit.

She glanced at the dining room table through the open-plan kitchen archway. The papers were spread out all over the place.

Knocking sounded on the door.

Anxiety speared through Meg. She hurried to the front door, hesitated. No peephole.

No one is going to welcome it. Or you, because of it . . .be careful, Meg . . .

She opened the door a crack.

"Blake?"

"Hey." A grin dimpled his rugged face. A familiar sense of kinship punched through Meg. It was instantly undercut by leeriness.

"What are you doing here? What do you want?"

His grin faded. "You look like shit, Meg—what's happening?"

Her hand went to her hair. It was swept up in a wild topknot, tendrils spiraling loose all over the place. She hadn't bothered with makeup, and was wearing the same clothes as yesterday, over the top of which she'd thrown one of her dad's oversize sweaters. She'd found it in his closet. Her mother had kept it all as it was, as though she'd been awaiting Jack Brogan's return from prison. And when Meg had seen the old sweater, the memories had crushed her. She'd taken it from the closet and buried her nose in it, inhaling the long-forgotten scent of her father, swallowed by memories of being a little girl in his arms, riding high on his shoulders, being tossed in the air, him building her tree house and tending to her scraped knees.

She drew the ends of the sweater tightly across her chest.

"I'm fine. Just busy."

Blake's gaze went over her shoulder, into the dark and dusty house.

"I've got new windows and the power-washer guys coming tomorrow," she said, trying to appear normal. "What are you doing here, Blake?"

Then around the side of the house appeared a young boy with pale blond hair, thin face, skinny arms loaded with pizza boxes. The scent of the food slammed her in the stomach. She hadn't eaten all day. Had she eaten yesterday? She needed to buy some food for the fridge—she was starving.

The boy stared up at Meg. Green eyes. "Hi," he said.

She brushed her hair back from her brow, self-conscious suddenly. "Hey," she said to the boy, then her gaze shot in question to Blake.

"What are you doing in the dark, Meg?" He pushed past her, into her house.

"Wait." She grabbed his arm.

He stilled.

"Just . . . wait here a minute, please." She scurried into the living room and began scooping up the whirlwind of papers. He didn't wait. He came in and stood in the archway, eyeing her as she tried to hurriedly plug all the documents back into their respective folders.

"Just one sec, okay?" She got everything back into the boxes, and opened the wall safe. He watched as she placed the boxes and journal in there and closed the door. She locked the safe.

"There." She forced a smile and dusted her hands off on her jeans, her heart beating unnaturally fast. The kid stood next to Blake, still holding the pizza boxes, still staring with his limpid green eyes.

"You okay?" Blake said.

"I'm fine."

"So, can we come in now? Thought you might be hungry." He gestured to the boy with the pizza boxes standing at his side.

"Sure." She flicked on all the lights she could find, and blinked against the sudden brightness, her eyes gritty and raw, feeling like a mole startled out into daylight.

"This is Noah. My son. Noah, this is Meg Brogan."

Meg froze. She turned slowly around. Her gaze lit on the kid. She stared, seeing him anew—why had her brain not jumped to this conclusion instantly? Why had her mind been resisting the obvious? He even looked like Allison, had her pale coloring. Her eyes lifted slowly, met Blake's. He was watching her intently.

"I . . . didn't know you had a son." She cleared her throat. "Good Lord. Hey, Noah—nice to meet you."

"Go put those in the kitchen, Noah," Blake said to his boy. The kid turned, and headed off into the kitchen.

"You look a wreck, Meg," he said softly, coming close. Into her living room, her space. Her heart beat harder, faster. She gave an embarrassed laugh, pushed more loose tendrils back off her brow.

"I . . . I guess I should have expected it, that you had children. I've been self-absorbed. I . . . is he the only one, or do you have more?"

"Just Noah," he said, his eyes holding hers, a strange sort of energy, visceral, rolling off him in waves.

She swallowed, her thumb beginning to absently fiddle with her engagement ring. "He looks like her, like Allison. Like I remember her looking. But he has your eyes."

"What were you hiding? Putting in the safe?"

Noah returned before she could answer. The kid regarded Meg intently. Her cheeks warmed and she pulled her sweater closer across her chest.

"You knew my mom," Noah said.

Meg shot another questioning glance at Blake. He offered no guidance. "I . . . yes, I did, indeed. Allison was in my class. I haven't seen her for a long time, though. Is she coming over tonight?"

"She's dead."

———

Meg sat opposite Blake at the dining room table, Noah to her right, munching his pizza. It was surreal, the three of them in this dusty, boarded-up house, eating by the glow of lamps. She glanced at Blake's wedding band again. And he noticed her doing it. He met her eyes in silence.

So, he was a widower. Why did she feel that changed everything? Why did she feel a wild kind of hope? She got up abruptly. "I'm going to make some tea."

In the kitchen, she put the kettle on, and stood staring out the kitchen window into the dark while she waited for the water to boil. Her own sorry reflection stared back, marred by worms of water wriggling down the pane. She glanced at her cell phone lying on the counter. It had beeped earlier. A message from Jonah to call him. She had not returned his call. Blake came in behind her, carrying plates. He set them in the sink.

"I left Noah watching TV. Hope you don't mind," he said.

"I'm surprised cable is still connected. I bet they've been debiting Irene's account since she left here. I must check."

"Dishwasher?" He held up the plates.

"It's broken." Yet another thing on the fix-it list.

He ran water into the sink.

"What happened to Allison?" she asked, dropping a tea bag into her mother's pot—Tara had always loved her tea. It was a habit she'd acquired from her Irish mother.

"Breast cancer. It's just over a year now that she's been gone."

"I had no idea," she said quietly.

"Of course you didn't." He squirted dish soap into the running water.

"I'm so sorry, Blake."

He didn't look at her. He scraped the leftovers off the plates, and put the dishes into the warm soapy suds. Meg watched the movement of his big hands. Capable, strong hands. Hands that had once touched her.

"He's gorgeous," she said softly. "He really does look just like her."

He snorted softly and placed a clean dish in the drying rack.

"First your dad, then Allison so soon after, it . . . it must be rough. You. Noah."

"We're coping. We got a plan." He cast her a glance, smiled, but she could see that it didn't quite reach into his eyes, or fan out those crinkles.

"Is that why you quit the army?"

"Yes."

He said no more. She weighed him, trying to read between the lines. And inside her belly a desire started to build, to know more, everything about him. But at the same time she felt she had no right to any part of his life. She was the one who'd left. She had her own plans with Jonah. None of them included Shelter Bay.

He finished washing the dishes, drained the water from the sink, and reached for a towel to dry his hands. Her stomach warmed as she watched the roll of muscle under the tanned skin of his forearms, the gold hair. It made her think of how he'd looked that last summer, working down on the dock without his shirt, how the hair on his chest had tapered into a delicious whorl between hard abs and vanished into the low-slung waistband of his shorts. He caught her watching, and for a second time he stilled. Electricity crackled in the silence between them. She swallowed.

"Kettle's boiling," he said.

She spun around quickly. Grateful for the distraction, she poured hot water over the tea bag.

"It was on the radio," he said, hanging up the towel. "That you're doing a book on Sherry." He paused. "Are you really sure you want to pursue this? Because it's already taking on a life of its own. Could get ugly."

Her mind shot to her mother's journal, the transcripts. "And why would it get ugly if no one has anything to hide?"

"I'm just saying, Meg. A lot of people just wanted to put this behind them. Not all of them could leave town."

Irritation flared right back up to the surface. "Is that why you really came by? To stop me from doing this?"

"Maybe I came to bring you some food. Look at yourself. You haven't even plugged your fridge back in. What have you been doing all the time, holed up here in the dark, in this vandalized house that needs a cleaning service? What's with all those papers in the safe?"

She moistened her lips, unsure suddenly of how much to share, how much to trust. Trust was an unfamiliar thing to her. She'd learned how to stop trusting the day her dad killed Tyson Mack and kicked his body to a bloody pulp. His gaze ticked to her diamond, then back to her eyes.

"You know what worries me," she said. "is the fact that so many people *do* seem to feel threatened by my doing this."

"Like who?"

She hesitated. "You, for some reason. Deputy Dave Kovacs. He came by earlier, yesterday—" It struck her suddenly how time, days were blurring. "He warned me off."

"Dave came by *here?*"

She nodded. "As I was moving back in. Like he'd been waiting for me to show up. He cautioned me not to go near his father, or mother. Apparently Ike has a heart condition, and getting his blood pressure up, as I apparently would, could kill him. Dave also let drop that it was an election year, and that he's running for sheriff."

Blake snorted. "Yeah. And he's running on his dad's law enforcement legacy. I can see why digging up an old case of his father's that resulted in the key suspect's death might threaten Dave right now." He hesitated, as if reading something deeper in her demeanor. "What are you *not* telling me, Meg?"

"I want to know why you seem threatened by this, as well. What's bothering *you?*"

He braced his hands on the sink and blew out a chestful of air. He stood like that, as if fighting himself for a moment, then he turned slowly back to face her.

"It's personal," he said softly, quietly. He reached up and moved a wisp of hair off her brow, hooking it behind her ear. His skin was rough. Warm. Meg's pulse raced.

"I'd gotten over you. I was working through things. And when I saw you again . . . I didn't feel like having my boat rocked again. I was being selfish." He paused, lowering his hand. But his eyes continued to bore into hers. His mouth was close. "You *can* trust me, you know?"

"Blake, I—"

A noise startled them. Both spun around.

Noah stood watching them from the archway. Blake cleared his throat and quickly stepped back from Meg. Her heart hammered.

"Hey, buddy, how long you been standing there? TV no good?"

The kid remained mute, hands fisting at his sides. He glowered at Meg.

"Noah," Blake said, going up to his son. "You okay?"

"My dad only married my mom because *you* went away!" Noah spat the words at Meg.

She reeled, shot a look at Blake. The color had drained from his face.

"And now she's gone." Noah's voice rose, going high, sharp. His eyes started to pool with tears. "And now my dad is stuck with me, the kid he never wanted in the first place!" Noah whirled to face his father, his neck muscles tight little cords. "And now *she's* back." He pointed at Meg. "What about Mom? What about me?"

"Noah, oh, Noah, come here—" Blake crouched down to gather his son in his arms. But the boy forcibly shoved him away.

"Get away from me. I don't want you, either!" He spun around and raced for the front door. Jerking it open wide, he slipped out into the wet, black night.

"Noah!" Blake called as he started after his son. He wavered at the door. "Meg, I'm sorry, I have no idea what's gotten into him. He's never done anything like this—"

"Go, go after him. He needs you."

The door shut with a click. She heard the truck door slam. Meg dragged both hands over her tangle of hair, her world spinning.

CHAPTER 9

Whakami Cove. 9:58 p.m.

Geoff drove his silver Wrangler Rubicon into the near-empty parking lot of the new Whakami Bay Beach Hotel. Mist was thick as he reached into the back of his Jeep for his duffel and slung it over his shoulder.

He entered the lobby. The place was so new it had a chemical smell. He approached the desk, rang the bell. A man came out from the office behind the reception desk.

"I have a reservation." He smiled. "Geoff Sutton."

The front desk clerk signed him in, handed over a key card, and gave directions to a room on the second floor. "Sea view," he said. Geoff smiled his thanks. But the smile died on his lips as he turned away from the clerk and swung his duffel back onto his shoulders. He doubted many of the rooms were occupied this time of year, hence the sea view. Nothing special there.

Not that anyone would be able to see much in this fog, he thought as he made for the elevator. But he had to admit, it was one thing he loved about this place, in winter, especially. The moodiness, the atmosphere of it. The Hitchcockian shadow play at night, the baleful moan of the foghorns. The way the weather had no regard for man nor beast.

Literature, classics, art, movies, photography, human moods, and the magic of story—these were his passions.

Upstairs in his room, he opened the drapes. As suspected, nothing but blackness—the halos of lamps vanishing into the fog along the sea walk. And his own reflection in the glass. He smoothed his goatee between his thumb and middle finger, a reflexive habit, and then he checked his watch. Not too late to call.

He inhaled deeply, bit the bullet. Dialed. His heart gave a kick of adrenaline when a male voice answered.

"Hey. It's me. Geoff Sutton."

Silence. Thick, palpable silence. Nerves bit into him. Perhaps this was a mistake.

Then came a low whisper. "Where the *fuck* did you get this number?"

"You're listed—"

"Don't call me on this landline. Ever." A quick hesitation. Then, "What do you want?"

"I need to talk. I'm in town. I'm staying at the Whakami hotel."

A soft, hot curse. "Is this because of Meg Brogan, because she's back, because of the story she's writing?"

"So you know that she's doing a book. Who told you?"

"It's still a small town. Everyone knows everything by osmosis. It's even been on the radio."

Geoff closed his eyes, pinched the bridge of his nose. "Look, Blake knows that I was on the spit that night, near the point where he found Meg. He saw me returning earlier in the evening, without my shit. He saw blood. But he covered for me—it was no one's business to know."

"What're you saying? Why are you even telling me this? I know that he covered for you."

"Because he won't keep his silence any longer. He said he'll tell Meg if she asks him to rehash that night from his point of view. And she will—Blake was the one who found her, saved her life. He's key to her story." Geoff wavered. "He suspects I'm hiding something."

"Shit."

Geoff inhaled, anxiety twisting deeper. Upsetting another person was never easy. "I need to talk to you. We need a plan."

"Not on this phone, understand?" The voice was barely audible now, the words coming fast. "I . . . I'll meet you. At seven a.m. There's a strip of beach down from the Whakami hotel. It's isolated, no one there in winter. There's a parking lot behind the dune grasses."

The phone clicked.

———

Henry Thibodeau set the receiver quietly back into its cradle. His bowels had turned to water. Outside, leafless branches backlit with streetlight looked like the gnarled hands of crones, and they *tick, tick, ticked* against his window. Shadows twisted in his dimly lit office. A dog barked down the street, and a siren wailed somewhere far along the coast road.

He palmed his hand over his thinning hair. Everything. He could lose absolutely everything. Wife. New baby on the way. The sudden realization of just how deep this would cut cloaked his shoulders with a heavy, cold dread. He'd dared believe they'd gotten through those years—that it was over. He'd even begun to believe that maybe it didn't actually happen, that it was some bizarre nightmarish imagining of youth, because if he didn't believe this, his life now would make no sense.

Fucking Geoff. Fuck fuck fuck.

He rubbed his face, trying to seek a way out. But no matter which way he sliced this, he couldn't see escape. Packing up his family and fleeing town was not an option. He couldn't even quit his job—he'd dreamed about it once upon a time, but he was basically a prisoner there. And now Geoff. Now this. Meg Brogan. Blake and his pathetic crisis of conscience.

Fuck!

It wasn't fair. *He* was the victim in all this. Somehow, Meg Brogan needed to be persuaded to stop this stupid shit. If she stopped, if she packed up her bags and went back to whatever rock she'd crawled out from under, Geoff might shut up. Blake would stay silent. Meg.

It boiled down to Meg.

He reached for the phone. But fear choked him for a moment, and it pulled up from the pit of his gut an almost forgotten bile-like festering hatred. Sweat dampened his armpits. Then he grabbed the receiver.

The call picked up on the second ring.

He just blurted it out straight. "Geoff Sutton is back." His hand tightened on the receiver.

"So what?"

"He's . . . here to talk to Blake because Blake knows that he was on the point that night, and will no longer cover for him. Blake will tell Meg if and when she asks him to recount that night."

A pause. The branches *tick-tick-ticked.* Sweat pearled on his brow, slid slowly down the side of his face.

"Why are you even telling me this?" came the voice.

Because this is on you, mate. Your fucking doing, you sick, twisted, controlling, evil shit. You're the one who needs to fix it.

He closed his eyes. "Because something is going to crack, and it's all going to come out. I can't control this."

"And *I* can?"

"If the Sherry Brogan case is reopened—"

A soft laugh. "Reopened? On what grounds? They got their man. And so what if people know Geoff was on the spit that night? It has nothing to do with me, Henge, old boy. I was never there. We both know that, don't we? And we know what the evidence will show if they take another look."

Another laugh. The phone went dead.

A scratch sounded outside his study door. Henry's heart lurched into his throat and he spun around, panting, receiver still in hand. He listened.

Nothing more sounded. Other than the noise of wind and branches. He set the receiver carefully back into its cradle, and edged toward the door on socked feet. He creaked it open, peered down the passage. Shadows blue and black moved softly against the wall. He made his way down the passage, stopped outside the baby's room. He put the light on. The baby mobile above the empty crib was turning slowly. The window had been left open a crack. He swallowed the new taste of fear in his mouth and securely closed the window. Quietly he went down the passage and opened his bedroom door.

She was asleep. Lori-Beth. His wife. Bathed in the soft glow from the night-light she insisted on plugging into the wall. She was like a child sometimes. Her wheelchair sat empty next to her bed.

He took a shower and washed the acrid smell of fear from his pores. He crawled in under the covers.

LB turned and moaned. She reached out her fingertips to touch his shoulder. "Everything okay?"

He rolled over, kissed her, and smoothed soft hair back from her brow. All he'd built, this family they were becoming, respectable in this community, well-off. Normal. It could all be gone in a flash. He'd fashioned himself into an all-American guy. A good accountant, and then vice president of a massively growing company based right here in Shelter Bay—handling top and tricky accounts. And yes, sometimes big business involved some sleight of financial hand. That's what corporations did. But as he lay back onto his pillow, the doubt demons laughed.

It's a house of cards, you Thibodeau fool, all fake, you're a prisoner in your own skin, you should have had the guts to flee Shelter Bay all those years ago, like Geoff . . .

Because now . . . now he was in so deep and so twisted, that no matter where he went, it could not end well.

"Who was on the phone?" LB murmured.

"Just a client."

"Everything okay?"

"Fine. All fine."

———

Lori-Beth Braden Thibodeau lay there, eyes wide in the dark, heart thudding as she listened to the wind. Her husband had begun to snore. Quietly she sat up. She manually moved and dropped her legs over the side of the bed, reached for her chair.

She wheeled down the hall, past baby Joy's room. She stopped outside her husband's study door, and listened to be sure he had not woken. She edged the door open, wheeled softly in. Neat as a pin inside. The big desk in front of the window had nary a stray piece of paper. The chair in front of it was positioned just so. The framed accounting accolades on the walls had been hung in plumb-straight lines. The windows of the gun cabinet that contained his neat rows of hunting rifles and pistols had not a smudge. Even the books on his shelves were arranged alphabetically.

LB picked up the phone, checked to see the last number Henry had called. She frowned. Then ice branched into her chest as she sensed something, someone, behind her. Slowly she turned, then gasped as a shape shadowed the doorway. Her hand shot to her throat.

"My God, Sally," she whispered. "You gave me a fright. What are you sneaking up on me like that for?"

Her sister pulled her fluffy white nightgown close over her chest. "I thought I heard something." She glanced at the receiver still in Lori-Beth's hand. "You look pale—are you all right?"

LB nodded and replaced the phone. "I . . . I . . . couldn't sleep."

"Me neither. Let me wheel you back."

"I can do it," LB snapped quietly, harshly. Then toned it down. Her older sister had come to stay, to be here to help when baby Joy came in the next week or so. "I don't want to wake Henry," LB said more gently, with a smile.

Her sister nodded, casting another glance back at the phone, then she followed LB out and closed the study door quietly. She watched Lori-Beth go to her room.

LB paused, looked back over her shoulders. Sally met her eyes. And it troubled her that Sally hadn't even asked what LB was doing in Henry's sacred study in the dark of the night.

———

Blake locked up the marina office and the house. It was around 11:30 p.m. when he walked past his son's room and paused. The door was closed, but a band of light showed beneath it.

He knocked.

Silence.

Blake tried the door handle. To his relief, it opened. Noah had not yet locked him out fully. His son was in his Spider-Man PJs. His face was red from crying and he was reading the book they'd up until now been reading together. Lucy lay on his feet.

Blake sat on the edge of his son's bed, but Noah did not look up. His son had given him the silent treatment all the way home from Meg's place, and had marched straight up to his room and slammed himself in the minute they'd arrived. A hollowness ballooned through Blake. The sense of emptiness, unhappiness, aloneness, inside their home tonight was stark.

"Please, Noah, tell me where you got that idea about me not wanting you?"

Noah's mouth tightened. A little blue vein swelled under the pale skin at his temple.

"It's not true. And if you heard someone say that, you must remember that people often say really odd things about others, and they're usually totally out of context . . . I wish you'd tell me where you heard that?"

Silence.

"It hurts me, too, you know. This is not just an attack on you. It's an affront to our family. To your mother's memory." He placed his hand on his boy's knee. "We're a team, champ. You need to tell me what you know and who said this, so I can fix it?"

Silence.

"Was it Alex Millar? Is that why you hit her?"

Noah's eyes pooled with moisture. A tear slipped down his cheek. He started to shake.

"Come here."

He gathered his son up into his arms. Noah resisted, tensing his body. But Blake was not going to give up. He'd never give up. He was going to win this one. He was going to learn his son. He held his boy until his little body stilled, until he felt the crying had stopped.

"Talk to me, please," he whispered into his boy's hair that smelled like hay, and sunshine and childhood. "Tell me what Alex said."

"She . . . she heard her mom and dad." Noah's words were muffled against Blake's shirt. "They . . . they said, 'poor little Noah, with that rough father raising him on his own at that crumble-down marina, when he never wanted the marriage in the first place. That kid is the only reason he married Allison. And if she hadn't of died he'd never have come home. He only quit the army to look after a kid he doesn't want.'"

Blake's heart slowed to a sickening thud. He looked up, at the ceiling, as if some heavenward being might yield him some help.

"Listen—" He took his son's hot, tear-stained face in his rough hands. "Look at me."

Slowly, Noah lifted his red-rimmed eyes. Blake's chest caved under a punch of emotion.

"I loved your mother. Very much. I love *you*. You *have* to believe this. There are as many ways to love people as there are people." His voice snared on some thickness in his throat. It took a second to compose himself. "And I want you to know something. I will do anything for you. I will kill dragons for you."

Silence.

Blake inhaled deeply. Being a fighter and a physical fixer of things was easy. But this? This tricky territory of a little boy's heart and mind . . . this was the stuff of challenges. This was the stuff that scared Blake. It was so easy to lose someone, to say the wrong thing.

"Then why didn't you live with us?" Noah said quietly.

"When you serve your country, you get sent away to fight, so that everyone back home can stay safe. In the army, you don't have control over things like that."

"Why did you go in the army?"

Blake hesitated, then told a version of the truth. "Because I wanted to serve, Noah. I wanted to help."

Noah looked away, picked at a thread on his duvet. "Why did we go to see her, anyway?" he muttered.

"What?"

"That woman. Meg."

Clearly, that was a mistake. "I wanted to introduce you to her, show her how proud I am of my boy."

More tears released down his cheeks. "I miss Mom."

"I know. I miss her, too." *I have so many regrets about your mother.* "And whatever the Millars said, Noah, it twists things. It's *not* true. I will go and speak to them about it."

His eyes flared wide in horror. "No. No you can't. Please."

"Why not?"

"Alex and Jamie will think I tattled. They'll call me a wuss."

"They call you that before?"

Noah glanced away. Anger stirred into Blake's blood. "Okay. I won't say anything. On one condition. That you keep sharing with me what happens at school, and with Alex and Jamie, okay?"

He nodded.

Blake leaned forward, kissed his boy on the head. "Now let's get tucked up and get some sleep."

But as he reached the door and was about to flick off the light, Noah said, "What about Meg?"

"What do you mean?"

"Did you want to marry her before Mom?"

"We were far too young to think about marriage back then, kiddo. Now, sleep."

"Do you want to marry her now?"

Blake's heart kicked. "Not even a question, champ. She's engaged to marry someone else. Someone very clever and very, very rich."

"So we won't go back there, to her house?"

Wham. The coup de grace. Blake regarded his son, the choices before him stark. "No, Noah," he said softly. "We won't."

"Promise."

He swallowed. "Promise."

Noah snuggled down into his duvet. Blake clicked off the light and stepped out into the hallway. He closed the door gently and ran his hand through his hair. Slowly he walked to the long window at the end of the upstairs hall. He shoved his hands deep into his pockets and watched the beam of the lighthouse in the dark and mist.

Out of the mouths of babes. And the sacrifices we make to keep them safe, and happy.

Because, *yes, Noah, I'd have her back in a heartbeat, but it's not gonna happen. She's taken. So it's you, me, and Lucy, kid. And I'd best listen to you and stay the hell away . . . because good things have never come from getting mixed up with Meg.*

CHAPTER 10

Whakami Bay. 7:00 a.m.

Geoff parked his Wrangler behind a line of gnarled shore pines, alongside the only other vehicle in the sand-strewn lot—a polished cherry-red MINI Cooper with two white racing stripes. A wry smile pulled at his mouth as he got out with two coffees in cardboard cups. He kicked his door shut and made his way up the small dune. Cold wind lifted his hair.

He crunched over to a log where a man sat huddled in a coat. The man did not turn around at the sound of his approach.

"Nice wheels," Geoff said as he reached the log.

The man looked up. Their eyes met. Geoff's heart crunched. He handed his old friend a cup.

Henry glanced warily at the offering, then took it. Geoff seated himself on the log, beside Henry. He noted the expensive designer coat, the softness around his bud's waist, and the roundedness in his shoulders. He took in the receding hairline, the silver flecks in Henge's once-dense black hair. Emotions stabbed through him. Affection. Sadness. A sense of poignancy over the lost passages of time. And something a little more sly. Love was a dark and oily thing.

"I'm getting married," Geoff said, taking a sip of his latte as he looked out toward the sea, the horizon beyond.

Henry's eyes flared to his. "I . . . congratulations. Who . . . is she?"

"He. Nate Fischer. An architect."

Henry stilled. He stared at Geoff for several long beats, then lowered his cup to his lap, cradling it in both hands. He closed his eyes, bent his head. His shoulders rolled inward. He was crying. Emotion whammed Geoff in the gut. He reached out, touched, just barely, Henry's hand.

Henry allowed it. Wind gusted, whipping up sharp specks of white sand. Spindrift blew off the waves rolling in the distance.

A tenderness between them hung, like a forgotten memory.

Henry swiped his eyes with the base of his thumb. "What do you really want back here, Geoff?" His voice was thick, defeated. "What do you want with me? You've got it all now."

Geoff removed his hand, took a large sip of his coffee. Inhaled deeply.

"I'm going to invite Blake and Noah to the wedding in person. I'm going to come out to them. I'm not going to hide from this, even here, back home." A pause. "I'd like you to come, too. To the wedding. It's in September."

Henry paled. He stared at the untouched coffee in his lap.

"I can't."

Geoff studied his friend's wedding ring. Questions crashed like the breakers through his mind.

"You can't do this, Geoff. You can't tell everyone in town."

"It doesn't need to impact you, Henge."

He nodded. But his skin had taken on a greenish tinge—he looked like he was going to throw up.

"And what you said about Blake telling Meg that you were on the point that night—what did you mean by making a plan?" He refused to meet Geoff's eyes.

"I'm going to the marina to see him today. I'll stay there a while, hopefully. I'll try to convince him it means nothing that I was there, and that keeping it from Meg will have no impact whatsoever on her story. I'll talk to Meg, too, try to dissuade her from digging up old hurts." Geoff paused. "But what worries me is that Blake said she was remembering things, that her memory might be returning."

Henry spun, faced Geoff square, eyes bright with anxiety. "If she does remember, or if this case is reopened for some weird reason, if they do learn that you were on the spit that night, they'll want to know what you saw. Or who you were with. If they know we were together—"

"Nothing. I saw nothing. And no one."

"Shit." Henry rubbed his brow. It was shiny with sweat, even in the chill wind. "Because it'll kill me, you know that, right? If it gets out that we . . . it'll finish me off, be the end of my marriage. My life . . . after all these years . . ."

He dropped his face into his hands, hunched over. Geoff placed the palm of his hand on Henry's back. Henry jerked upright. "Don't touch me, okay. Don't the *fuck* touch me." He was starting to shake.

"Listen," Geoff said, easing off. "I'll handle it. Whatever happens, whatever I say, it will have nothing to do with you. Trust me?"

Henry looked away.

"Henge, do you trust me?"

Slowly he nodded his head.

"The only problem, the only real problem, will be Meg's memory."

"And what if she does remember?"

Geoff looked up at the wild, gray sky full with scudding clouds. A gull wheeled. "Then we're screwed. Then we'll have to deal with it as it comes."

Henry jolted to his feet, took three strides away from the log, then stopped, spun back. "Are you *insane*? We don't deal with *it*—it deals with *us*. It'll be over. We're toast. What *is* it with you—you have a death wish? What is going on with you, Geoff? The only way to stop this is to stop Meg Brogan. Just . . . just—you've got to get her to give it up, leave town. She should never have come back."

"I'll talk to her. I'll get a sense of why she's doing this. I'll see how much she really might be starting to recall."

"And please, Geoff, just drop this thing about coming out, please."

"I need to. I'm getting married, and I want a clean, open start. I want to finally step out into the light and be myself. None of this hiding shit, anymore. It's been like a sickness my whole life."

"And what do you think it's done for me?" He held his hands out to his chubby sides, palms up. "Look at me. I don't even know my fucking self. I'm prisoner in my own skin."

Geoff nodded to the wedding band. "Who is she? You want to tell me about it?"

He slumped back down onto the log. "Lori-Beth Braden. Eight years now."

Geoff looked into his eyes, searching. "You're not happy."

"What the *fuck* is happy?" A pause. Then. "It's fine. I'm fine. I was, until now—you. We're expecting a baby. A daughter. In a week or two."

"Your own progeny. Wow. So . . . the physical part of the relationship is—"

Henry looked down, rubbed his knee, silent for a long time. A dark memory uncoiled like a smoke serpent between them. Neither wanted to go there, but Meg's arrival was forcing them to go there. It ground to the heart of everything.

"LB is a paraplegic," he said quietly. "We're adopting. From a young unwed teen. Her baby is due any day now."

"So, no sex?"

He moistened his lips and flicked Geoff a sideways glance, as if trying to decide whether Geoff even had a right to ask this question. "We tried. It wasn't working for either of us."

"A wife of convenience for the gay man," Geoff said softly. And a husband of convenience for the paraplegic. His heart ached for his friend, and in that moment he loved Nate more than he could articulate, for Nate had given Geoff the courage to be himself. Otherwise he might have ended up like Henry, living his life in an iron closet.

Very quietly, Geoff said, "Does LB know?"

"She might suspect. She's never let on, though. It's not in her interests." He cleared his throat. "Thing is, the birth mother is the teenage daughter of a devoutly religious family whose faith will not allow abortion. They're seeking a . . . couple with compatible values to adopt. We've signed a private adoption agreement based on some fundamental tenets, namely that we will raise our daughter in faith with . . . traditional . . . values." He looked up, eyes beseeching. "I know it's not something they can realistically go back on if they find out years later . . . about me. But if they learn before the baby is born, then that contract will be null and void. LB—we—will lose our daughter." He paused. "Geoff, I implore you, don't do this. If people in town put two and two together, and guess that we were close at school, I'm done. LB will *not* survive without that baby. Our marriage will not survive."

Compassion and pity unfurled through Geoff. He touched Henry's hand that rested on the log, just pinkie against pinkie. Henry swallowed. His face warmed. Geoff's pulse increased, and he felt himself stir.

Henry got up fast. He looked around, panicked. "I wish you well, Geoff, you and your architect," he said quickly, eyes frantically scanning up and down the beach, the parking lot behind them. "But I wish you hadn't come back. I'd rather you got the hell out of town, and stayed the hell away."

"And Meg? And what might be coming down the pike anyway?"

"I . . ." He rubbed his brow angrily, and his eyes were suddenly those of a desperate man. "Please . . . just leave. I'm a dead man, Geoff. You've fucking come home to kill me. You and Meg. Is that what you want?"

Geoff came to his feet. The wind was picking up, whipping sand into skin. Flumes of froth tore off the crests of waves. Geoff took his old lover's shoulders in his big hands. "Look at me. I'm going to do what I can, okay? That's the key reason I'm back. Trust me, Henge?"

Henry bit his lip, nodded.

———

The two men near the log on the rise of the dune hugged briefly, awkwardly—dark windblown silhouettes against a silvery sky. The driver of a silver SUV watched them from behind a row of dune shrubs at the back end of the parking lot. Before the men turned and made for their vehicles the driver pulled out of the lot, tires crunching quietly on sand and gravel.

———

Meg exited the GoodFood Mart loaded with bags and enough sustenance to last at least two weeks. In her truck she already had cleaning supplies, toilet paper, soap, stuff for minor repairs, fuel for the weed whacker. If it was going to be dry tomorrow, she might tackle some of the lawn and the weeds around the house.

She'd left the house at 8:00 a.m. when the contractors, cleaners, and window guys had arrived. She'd already been to a Realtors' office and spoken with an energetic young woman who said she'd come around and do an assessment of the property. Meg had momentarily wavered, thinking of Irene, but decided to go ahead and at least see what they might get for the house. It didn't mean she had to put it on the market right away. Plenty of time for that—she still had a book to write. Her plan for the rest of the day was to stash the perishables she'd just bought in her camper fridge, then maybe take Irene out for lunch, or afternoon tea. In the meanwhile, she had calls and appointments to make, which she could do from her camper.

The sky was bright, Front Street alive with banners snapping happily in the salt wind, and as she made her way back to the parking lot, Meg's thoughts turned to Blake and Noah—the bombshell the kid had dropped. Her heart ached for their loss. The notion of Blake struggling as a single dad stirred a deep compassion in Meg. With it came something hotter, trickier—she didn't trust her feelings around him. But it didn't matter, because she wasn't going near Blake, apart from an interview for the book, which she still needed to set up with him. Whatever had fueled Noah's outburst, it was clear that she was a problem for the kid. She needed to keep her distance—she'd messed up Blake's life enough in the past. And she had to keep focus on why she was writing this story.

As she passed The Mystery Bookstore, she hesitated at the sight of her books in the window. Her face smiled back at her from one of the jackets—a fake face, thought Meg. All sleek and sophisticated in a charcoal suit, ridiculously high heels. She was posing half perched on one of those tall bar stool–type chairs, arms crossed with self-importance. Barely the hint of a smile on her lips. The intent had been to project an image of approachability and "intelligence." Someone fit to tackle the gravitas that was true crime. Jonah liked that photo.

The door swung open. "Megan!"

Meg jumped as a woman bustled toward her, gray hair swept up in a chignon, red-rimmed glasses perched on the end of her nose. She wore a tweed skirt and a soft cream sweater, a demure strand of pearls.

"It's me, Rose Thibodeau! Remember? Your old English teacher from grade nine?"

Meg's jaw dropped. "Oh wow, hi, yes. Blake mentioned you owned the bookstore now." Meg set her bags down on the wooden bench under the store window, and gave Rose a hug.

"I was just looking at the display," she said. "Thank you so much for stocking my book."

"We have all your books in-store," Rose said with a smile that danced in her small blue eyes. "How are you, Megan?"

"I'm good. And you're looking wonderful. How's Mr. Tibbo?" Just the mention of her old elementary school principal's name sent Meg hurtling back through a wormhole in time.

"That's his shop next door." Rose motioned to a tiny door recessed into an alcove adjacent to The Mystery Bookstore. Above the door hung a wooden plaque that said SHELTER BAY STAMPS.

"I'm now a philatelist's widow," she said with a grin. "Albert travels the world in search of the elusive missing watermark, or rare collection. And when he's home, he's poring over his finds in the store."

"And Henry?"

"Henry married Lori-Beth Braden. They still live in town, and I'm so grateful for it. He's VP of Kessinger-Sproatt now. Tommy took over his dad's old company and has been growing it aggressively since. Best news of all is that Henry and LB are making us grandparents in a few days." A smile creased her face. The genuineness in this woman, the kindness in her eyes, it cracked something free in Meg. She felt welcome, and the sensation caught her by surprise.

"Congratulations—I'm so happy for you all," she said, affection warming her heart. That some lives had actually turned out well in Shelter Bay was good to know. It took the edge off her own fears about coming back here.

Wisps of Rose's hair blew free of her chignon as she touched Meg's forearm. "Would you do us a favor, Meg, could you come give us a talk—about the new book? I started a book club a few years ago. It's called the Armchair Sleuths and Philosophers Society." She flushed a little. "Several of us are wannabe scribes, too. And we love, love, love true crime. We're currently reading *Sins Not Forgotten*, and with you now writing the Sherry Brogan story—" Her flush deepened. "I mean, I . . . I heard on the news—"

"I'd love to," Meg said.

Rose clasped her hands together. "Oh, that would be so wonderful! We meet every second Friday afternoon at four, really informal. Coffee, pastries. Between ten to fifteen of us. Would this Friday work for you?"

"Nothing I'd like more."

"Thank you! And do bring Irene. I haven't seen her in a while. I . . . I've been meaning to visit her at Chestnut Place, but—"

"I'm sure she'd be delighted." Meg picked up her bags. "I'll see you Friday, then."

"This is so exciting, Megan, and so good to see you back home." *Home.*

She stood there a moment, in front of The Mystery Bookstore, loaded with bags, the sea wind rippling her hair, a yin-yang of feelings wheeling through her. It was like coming full circle, back to this little shop where she'd spent so much of her youth. Now here her book was, after she'd traveled so far, and she was giving a talk. Back home.

See? I knew it wouldn't be too hard. You read far too much into everything, Meggie. You need to lighten up.

Much easier to be you, Sherry.
I'm dead, Meg.

———

Lori-Beth folded the new, pale-yellow baby jumper and smoothed the soft fabric with the palm of her hand. She put it in the drawer, carefully, with the others. As she moved, currents of air stirred the unicorn mobile above the crib, and reflective strips made stars and rainbows dance around the walls.

Her haven. This room. All the planning. Her reason for being. So soon now she was terrified it might not actually happen. Her dream—a baby girl of their own. Atop the dresser was the last ultrasound image. She touched it gently with her fingertips. They had initially opted to keep it a surprise, the baby's sex, but then she couldn't stand it any longer. She was glad they knew. She'd been able to choose the soft pink and lavender pastel palette for the room. They planned to name her Joy.

Henry stepped into the room. He'd been working from home this morning.

"I'm off to the office." He had his briefcase. He kissed her on the cheek.

"Where'd you go so early this morning?"

"A walk."

"You never go for a walk in the morning."

He met her eyes. Something made her want to take back the question. But then he offered his easy smile. "I want to get back in shape," he said. "If we're going to be parents—I want be around for a long time, for Joy."

She said nothing.

Trepidation entered his soft brown eyes. "Are you all right, love? You look like you've seen a ghost."

"I heard on the radio that Meg Brogan is writing a book about the Sherry murder. She's back in town to talk to everyone."

"I know."

"Does that worry you?"

He moved hair back from her brow. "And why should it worry me? It's got nothing to do with us. I'll be back by six, okay?"

"I was in Meg's class. You and Sally were in Sherry's. It has everything to do with us. All of us. The whole town. There was before the murder, and then after. Everything changed."

After the murder Sally started to drink. After the murder she was driving drunk with me in the car, and caused the wreck that put me in this chair . . .

"Meg is not interested in us, honey. She'll want to talk to the key players. Not every single person who was at school with one or the other of the Brogan sisters is going to warrant a feature in her book."

"Not a whole bunch of us left in town, either. Kinda limits the pool."

Her husband's features changed. Tension shifted. The unicorn mobile tinkled, suddenly spinning the other way, sending the stars hurtling backward all around the room. Quietly, eyes lancing hers, he said, "What's really worrying you, LB?"

"It's . . . I . . . I just wish the baby would come. I just want her here, in my arms. It's . . . it's making me anxious." She took in the room. "We've been ready, planning for so long . . . I'm just scared."

"Scared of *what?*"

"That it won't happen. That something will go wrong."

"Nothing is going to go wrong, LB. Here, look at me." He hooked a knuckle under her chin. "Nothing. Understand?"

"There could be a last-minute medical issue. There—"

"Every parent-to-be deals with the exact same worries. It's normal. And the odds are stacked highly in our favor. Holly is young, healthy. Strong. All test results have been perfect. She's had all the requisite sonograms, the birth coaching, the nutrition. And you'll be there."

She swallowed.

"Why don't you go and visit Holly this afternoon—see how she and the baby are doing? It'll set your mind at ease."

She nodded.

"Want me to take you?"

"No. I can drive. Or, Sally can."

He kissed her on the mouth. "I'll be back for dinner."

She wheeled her chair to the window and watched her husband go down the path to his MINI Cooper, briefcase in hand. She thought of the strange phone calls last night, the snippets of Henry's side of the conversation she'd overheard. Henry's sneaking out in the morning. Dark thoughts serpentined through her mind, things she didn't want to even begin to entertain.

What would she do if her own husband somehow jeopardized her chance to be a mother? What else did she have in her life that took her beyond this chair? What, other than becoming a mother, could possibly give her the same purpose, meaning?

CHAPTER 11

Blake wheeled his truck into the marina driveway, Noah beside him in the passenger seat. He'd made a commitment to ferry his son to and from school instead of leaving him to catch the bus, at least until things normalized. Before picking up Noah today, he'd been unable to stop himself from swinging by Millar's garage and having a word with Ryan and Peggy Millar.

No one was going to fuck with his boy, least of all Ryan Millar.

Peggy had the grace to be embarrassed, and sorry that her kids had overheard something she'd said to her husband. She promised to have a word with Alex and Jamie, without revealing the fact Blake had been by. Or he'd be toast with Noah.

Ryan, however, had told him to piss off. Only a wuss kid hit girls. Blake had come within a hair's breadth of punching the bastard's teeth out himself. But he'd be nothing if he couldn't be an example to his son. So he'd backed off, but not without warning Millar he'd be eating dirt along with his words if he wasn't careful. Electricity still crackled through his blood from the encounter, his heart beating a rapid metronomic drum in his chest. What worried him more were the words Ryan had yelled after him as he'd stormed out of the garage.

And you better keep that Brogan woman of yours in check, too, or things could go to shit around here . . .

As they came down the driveway, he saw a silver Wrangler Rubicon, all shiny and contemporary-chunky, parked near the marina building. Cali plates. A man in a parka was walking along the dock. Dark hair. Skinny black jeans. Fashionable shoes, black coat. Artsy. Recognition slammed through him.

"Looks like we have company, Noah," he said quietly, putting the truck in park.

"Who?"

"Your uncle Geoff from California." Blake got out of the truck, wary. "Go take your stuff inside. I'll bring him in."

"Why can't I come?"

"Noah."

He stomped off.

Blake started down the gangway.

"Hey," he called out as he neared.

Geoff spun around. For a moment the Sutton men just stood there, taking each other in, the old sign up on the marina building still hesitantly flicking its faulty pink "B." *Bull's Marina.* Their dad gone. Yet the broken history hung between them all, and over this place.

Blake came forward, hugged his brother, emotion, conflict crashing through him. He stood back. "So, what brings you home? Meg? Her book?"

Your fear that I'm going to divulge your secret . . .

Geoff inhaled deeply, shoved his hands deep into his coat pockets, nodded toward the marina buildings. "Noah's grown."

His brother was looking fit, tanned, sporting a small goatee and fashionably cropped hair. He looked like he'd come into his own, which is more than Blake could say for himself. He turned and followed Geoff's gaze. Noah was watching them from inside the Crabby Jack windows, his little face like a pale ghost.

Geoff raised his arm high, waved.

Noah waved shyly back.

"I wanted to see him again. And you." Another deep, almost shaky breath. "Shit, I should just spit it out. I'm getting married. September. I'd like you both there, and I wanted to ask you in person."

"Whoa . . . *what?*"

A smile slowly curved Geoff's lips. "Yeah. Funky, huh."

"I . . . shit . . . *really?*" Blake couldn't help the smile that took over his face, the sudden flush of happiness through his heart. "Who?"

"Nate Fischer. My housemate. He's an architect, runs his own business from home. We've been living together five years now."

Blake lowered himself slowly onto a dock pylon. He stared up at his brother.

"The guy who answered the phone?"

Geoff nodded. Silence hung for several beats. Water chuckled under the dock.

"Why'd you never tell me?"

Geoff snorted, looked out over the ocean. "I figured you just knew. Dad did."

And Blake suddenly heard his father's voice, the gruff refrains of their youth . . .

I'm gonna teach you to hunt, use a gun like a man, Geoff . . .

Man up, for chrissakes, what d'you think you are, a fucking pansy?

And what're you going to do with an art degree? Become some fartsy-wuss who can't work for shit?

Blake's mind spiraled back yet further, to the storm-tossed night he'd found Geoff in the boathouse, bleeding from the head, his face sheet-white, his skin sheened in sweat.

The ways in which we deceive ourselves . . . the stories we tell others to hide from our own truths . . .

Perhaps he had always suspected, or even known this about Geoff. But back then, it was out of the realm of his experience, not something you spoke openly about. Only now did he see the full picture, the dark intent behind his father's physical and psychological abuse of his older brother. And sorrow rose in his throat. Remorse. Regret for not having wised up to this earlier. But he now also understood, on some level, why he'd always tried to stand between his father and Geoff. And why he'd so easily covered for Geoff that night of the murder.

"That day on the spit," Blake said quietly. "That's how this all ties back, doesn't it—and why you wouldn't, or won't, talk about it? You were meeting someone that day. That's why you didn't want anyone to know you were there."

Geoff nodded.

The dock creaked and moved suddenly beneath their feet. Both Geoff and Blake turned to see Noah coming toward them.

"We'll talk later," Blake said softly.

"Uncle Geoff?" Noah said, his green eyes wide.

Geoff dropped instantly to his haunches.

"Hey, buddy. You *do* remember me? Come here, let me give you a hug."

———

"Megan!"

She whirled around at the strident sound of a familiar voice.

Tommy Kessinger stood on the opposite sidewalk. Unmistakably him. All strapping six foot two of him. He covered the distance across the street quickly with a stride that still screamed star athlete. The football physique, the dense, sandy-blond hair, the broad shoulders, square jaw, electrical smile, it was all still there, just matured, which made him even more handsome, more real. He sort of stole Meg's breath.

"Tommy, my God, how *are* you?" she said, clutching her bags as he reached her sidewalk. "I was going to call you today."

"Good, I'm good. I heard you were back." He bent down and gave her a kiss on the cheek. "Welcome home, kid." Meg's heart crunched at the words, at the warmth in his smile. "Been hearing for years now about how famous you've become, and engaged, too, what did they call him—most eligible bachelor on the planet?"

She laughed, and it felt wonderfully free in the salt wind and sunshine.

"Here, let me help you with some of those." He relieved her of half her bags and gave her a long, measuring look. "You've come a long way from the black-haired punk waif, Meggie-Peg," he said, using Sherry's nickname for her. Hearing it was a punch to her chest, a reminder of how Tommy had almost been family, an older brother.

"I haven't sported the punk look since I was fourteen. And I'll concede, it wasn't one of my finer periods."

He chuckled heartily. "Where are you parked?"

"Next to the church."

He walked with her.

"So, how long have you been back in Shelter Bay, now?" Meg said. "I always expected to see you on the big screen, NFL superstar and all that."

He laughed. "Just over fifteen years now. I never quite got over that early injury in my career, then my dad asked me to help out with the construction company, so I quit school, learned on the job, and he handed over the reins in full about five years ago."

"Looks like you're doing well. I'm seeing the Kessinger-Sproatt logos everywhere. Even on the contractors' trucks in my driveway this morning."

"It's good."

"And Emma?" Meg said.

"We divorced years ago."

She stalled. "I had no idea."

"How could you have? You never came home. Never returned our calls."

"Tommy, I'm sorry. I—"

"Hey. No worries. I get what you were going through. It wasn't destined to work out with Emma and me. We'd bonded over the loss of Sherry. Married, had a daughter, Brooklyn—she's seventeen next week, can you believe it? But there was just too much baggage between us. Bottom line, I suppose, is that we never made a proper go of it because Sherry's ghost always lay between us." He smiled, a little ruefully, and they resumed walking.

"You remarry?"

He was silent for a moment. Meg glanced up at him.

"Deliah," he said. "I lost her in a boating accident. Three years ago now."

"I'm so sorry, Tom—"

He waved it away. "Nah. I don't want sympathy. She was the light of my life—we had good times, and no one can take away those memories."

"So . . . a widower, too. Wow."

"Actually, I married again. About eight months back." Tommy's features turned serious. "I can imagine what it must look like, Meg. I . . . I like the company of a woman, a partner in my life. It's part of who I am. But—" There was a bit of a catch to his voice. "I still miss her—Sherry." He glanced up at the sky for a moment, then met her gaze again. "Stupid, huh, those first relationships, how they kind of never let you go." Her mind kicked instantly to Blake. "And there you have it."

They reached the parking lot, and he raised his brows at the sight of her rig. "This yours?"

"My office," she explained, beeping the lock. She opened the back door, loaded her bags into the truck. He followed with the rest of them. "You heard that I'm going to write a book on Sherry's case?"

"I did."

"You okay with that?"

He smiled. "Would it stop you if I wasn't?"

"Probably not."

His smile deepened to a grin. "I didn't think so. I get why you might want to do it, Meg. Therapy in a way, I suppose."

She looked away for a moment. "I suppose, although I hate to admit it."

"Word is that you might be remembering things from the attack."

"I'm getting tiny bits more."

"Like what? A face?"

"It's more a sensation. Words that were yelled. A familiar voice, perhaps. I think that being here, going through it all again, could help tease something out. Would you honor me with an in-depth interview, Tom? Talk about Sherry. That day. How your life was with her before, and after."

He regarded her for several long beats. "Sure," he said, taking a card out of his pocket. "I'd be happy to. Here's my number. Call my assistant and she'll block me off a good chunk of private time. You can come around to the house. It'll be more conducive to talking there."

"Thank you so much. Everyone's been pretty hostile about the book thing."

"I'd like to talk about it. And it really is good to have you home, Meggie." He gave her another quick kiss and enveloped her in a hug. "Until later, then?"

"Gotcha."

She climbed up into the driver's seat, and was about to pull the door shut when he said, "I'm giving a big bash next Friday night, at the Whakami Bay Yacht Club. The new yacht basin is part of our development down there. It's Brooklyn's birthday, and we're using the occasion to kick off a fund-raiser for Dave Kovacs—he's thrown his hat into the ring for sheriff come the November elections. You remember Dave?"

"I ran into him the day I opened up my house. He told me to give up on the Sherry story, or else."

Tommy laughed. "I guess he thinks it might mess with his campaign. He'll be fine. This story—*our* story—has an end, if a poignant one. Dave's father fought for justice. So did your dad. In his way. The bad guy went down. We can spin this. Dave will come around. Everyone will be there Friday night, on stage, so to speak. From there you could arrange more interviews, just chat with people about the past?"

"I'd love to come."

She hesitated before closing the truck door. "It's good to see you, Tommy. To have someone on my side with the book."

He gave her a little salute, and again, she was thrust right back to childhood.

As she drove off, she glanced up into the rearview mirror. He was standing there on the sidewalk, hands in his pockets, just watching her drive away.

———

Blake and Geoff walked slowly up to the marina from the old boathouse cabin on the water. Blake had set his brother up in the cabin with fresh linen, firewood, and kerosene for the lanterns. The place was not wired for power. Lucy waddled behind the brothers. Smoke curled from the marina chimney up on the rise, and waves slapped gently along the shore. Down on the water the wind was turning icy as the day tilted toward dusk. Clouds scudded across the expanse of darkening sky.

"You sure you're okay to stay down here?" Blake said.

"I'd rather not get into your hair."

"You mean, rather not stay in the old house—too many bad memories?"

Geoff shrugged inside his coat. "Maybe I can do some work down here—the old logs, some sculpting."

"How long are you going to stay?"

"Don't know yet."

"What does it depend on?"

Geoff stroked his goatee. "Thought I might catch up with a few old friends now that I'm back. We'll see."

Blake cast a sideways glance at his sibling, a cool unease feathering into him. Or perhaps it was just the drop in temperature.

They reached the marina building, and Blake held the door open for his brother to enter the Crabby Jack space, which was still in the throes of renovation. Earlier, Geoff had helped him and Noah carry supplies in from the back of his truck, and the three of them had given the place one last coat of paint. It smelled strong, but looked clean and ready for the tables to move back in.

"You always did love this place, this bay," Geoff said, hands in pockets as he walked into the center of the room and turned in a slow circle.

Until Meg left me hollow. She took the heartbeat of the bay away. How can one be so fond of, so in tune with, so in love with a person? So crushed by rejection . . .

The thing about love, Blake mused, watching his brother, is that it came in so many colors, so many guises, and it could hold both small and enormous power. It could move one to do extraordinary things . . . like keep secrets against better judgment, just to keep someone safe.

"Hey, Dad." Noah appeared in the archway that led into the large open-plan kitchen. "The buzzer went."

"Thanks, bud—you set the table?"

"Yup," Noah said, eyeing his uncle with a kind of awe as he followed them into the kitchen. It made Blake smile inside as he opened the oven and took out the piping hot lasagna he'd made.

They sat at a table nestled into a small dining nook next to the old stone fireplace, in front of the big windows that looked out over the darkening bay. A wall of mist was beginning to menace in from the sea. The fire cracked and popped.

"So where is Meg staying?" Geoff said between mouthfuls.

"The old house."

"She never sold it?"

"Irene was living there, until recently. She has early stage dementia, set fire to part of the living room with candles she left burning. She's moved into Chestnut Place, that assisted living facility."

Geoff took a pull of his cold beer. "How is it—seeing her again?"

Blake stole a cautionary glance at Noah, who was tucking into his lasagna with unusual gusto. "She looks good. She's engaged. Some forensic shrink dude."

His brother held his eyes, unspoken words hanging between them.

"My dad told me you're an artist," Noah said, reaching for his juice.

"I am. A sculptor. Installations."

"You mean, like statues?"

"Sort of. Wood. Stone. Metal. Mostly really big projects now. I like to use stuff from nature. And old glass. Wire. Depends on the theme, the commission."

"Is your work in famous places?"

Geoff smiled. "You could say. I won a contract for the public art structure that now stands outside a big courthouse in San Diego, and a commission for installations along a mile-long sea walk, to name two of the projects I'm most proud of."

Noah stared at his uncle. "That's so cool." Blake felt a squeeze in his chest at his son's interest, at the light in his green eyes tonight. It drove home the importance of family. Of role models and mentors. Of openness, support. Things Bull Sutton had not been able to give his eldest son.

"I like art," Noah declared with pride. "It's my favorite subject at school."

"It is?" Geoff said, giving his nephew his full attention. "Have you got anything you can show me?"

"Some paintings."

"After dinner," said Blake, getting up to snag another two beers from the fridge. He placed one in front of his brother, popped the cap on his own, then stoked the fire.

"Say, I brought you something," Geoff said, digging in his pocket. He set a smooth, shiny, turquoise-green object in front of Noah. "California sea glass."

"Cool," said Noah, picking up the piece and holding it to the light. "What's sea glass?"

Geoff grinned. "Just a piece of broken glass, but washed smooth and shaped by the ocean and rocks and sand. That's the kind of thing I like to use in my art. And that particular piece," he said, "happens to be a good luck charm."

Noah's eyes flared up. "How do you know?"

"Feel it, rub your thumb over it."

Noah did.

"See how that feels? You can feel the magic, right? You can feel it in here." Geoff tapped his chest. His eyes twinkled in the firelight.

"I think so," Noah said, concentrating.

"Keep it in your pocket. When you feel troubled, you rub that sea glass."

Noah grinned. His legs swung back and forth under the table. And Blake wondered if it might be that simple, the answer to some troubles, a little bit of magic in the pocket. Belief.

He did the dishes while Noah showed his uncle his paintings. After Noah had bathed and was in his flannel PJs, Geoff read the bedtime story by the fire, with Lucy lying upside down and undignified on her mat in front of the hearth. Blake reclined in his father's old wingback, just listening and watching the two of them. He put his head back, closed his eyes, and thought, yes, this is what he wanted. The simple warmth of family once again filling this old marina, living by the rhythm of the seasons and tides. Perhaps he was just a simple man, a physical man, like his dad. A man who wanted to protect and cherish a small tribe of his own. It was no wonder Meg had left him, all those years ago. She'd had her sights set on a big-time glitzy career, a lover with a small fortune and the looks and charisma of James Bond. A shrink who analyzed monsters. Not vaguely in his league. If he could have seen this years ago, maybe he'd have given Allison a better chance. Regret washed through him, and he reached for his beer, taking a deep pull.

"Okay," Geoff said, closing the book with a flourish. "Bedtime. School day tomorrow. Installment number two tomorrow night—good enough?"

"Yeah!" said Noah. He bounded up the stairs to brush his teeth.

"Have a good day, kiddo, at school tomorrow," Geoff called after him.

"Will you be here when I get home?" Noah called from the upstairs landing. "For dinner again?"

"I don't know about dinner, kiddo. But I'll be around for a few days."

After Blake had tucked Noah into bed, he came back down-stairs and said, "Coffee? Nightcap?"

"Nightcap."

He poured two whiskeys and he sat by the fire with his brother, listening to the rattle of wind as it picked up.

"He's a damn fine kid," Geoff said after a while.

"I know."

"Not an easy time of it?"

"I'm learning my son," Blake said quietly. "I never really knew him. The tours in Iraq, then Afghanistan, I missed his birth. I missed out on so much of his growing. He's so much like his mother, too. It's good for him to see you, to connect with family." He paused. "Thanks, for coming, for spending some time."

A dark look shifted into Geoff's face. He broke eye contact. And something in Blake sank. The subtext, the real reasons he might be back, rose cool between them.

"He's a good artist." Geoff cleared his throat and infused his voice with an upbeat tempo. "Seriously. It's not just glib talk. I do some volunteer work with kids at a local community center, teach-ing art. From the drawings he showed me, Noah has inherent tal-ent. And an outlandish imagination. He could take this places."

"That's a talent he gets from you, I suspect. Or Allison. Or even his grandmother. Certainly not me." He downed the dregs of his whiskey and plunked the glass hard on the table beside him.

Geoff eyed him. "If I had to write a letter to my young father today, I'd say, acceptance is at the heart of love. Differences are what make the world a wonderful place. Be open, Blake, nurture him when he shows his passions. If you want to make your boy strong, this is how. Be the buttress roots. Support him. He'll sur-prise you with his strength."

Blake swallowed, embarrassed by the powerful emotion these words put into his chest. The fire crackled. He got quickly to his feet. "I need to call it a night. You want to stay by the fire a while, another drink?"

"This book on Sherry's murder, she's really set on it?" The elephant in the room loomed forward.

Blake stilled. "You know Meg, when she gets an idea between her teeth. She's like a dog with a bone."

"And you want to tell her I was on the spit that day?"

"If she asks me to run through it. What I remember."

"Blake, it has nothing to do with—"

"Doesn't it? Because someone else was there, too, the person you went to meet. This person was never questioned. This person could have seen something—"

"He *didn't*. Okay?"

Their gazes warred.

"What's the issue here? You think Tyson Mack didn't kill Sherry, or what?"

"No, it's just—"

"Just about the truth? Or is this about Meg, and you just not wanting to keep something from her? For what? Some weird crisis of conscience?"

Blake stared at his brother in silence.

"It's not going to win her back, Blake," Geoff said softly. "It's not going to change a damn thing, telling her I was on the spit. All that could happen is that she will go on a witch hunt, looking for the person I was with."

"And what is so wrong with that?"

"It would kill him."

Blake blinked. "He's still in town?"

"Yes. And he's living in an iron closet. His life is a facade. This would tear his marriage apart, destroy his life. Please, I beg you, just let him be."

"You loved him," Blake said quietly. "You still do."

"Those first loves . . ." Geoff cleared his throat. "I care about him. If Meg goes on a witch hunt . . . Please."

Blake walked over to the window and looked down at the water. He ran his hands over his hair.

"She's engaged, Blake. You have your own life with Noah here."

"I know."

"Let her write her story. Let her interview you, but leave me out of it. Leave what Dad did to me out of it. You honestly want to see our personal family issues in print all over the nation? Have her writing about us, about how Dad abused us, talking about it on national television?"

Blake's head began to pound.

"Don't let her get under your skin again." A pause. The flames spat, popped. Wind gusted and the building creaked. "She's not good for you. Please."

Blake turned, met his brother's eyes. He couldn't recall the last time Geoff ever begged him. For anything. Yet he couldn't shake the disquieting sense there was something more that lurked behind Geoff's words. That something else *had* happened that night on the spit.

"Maybe her memory will come back," Blake said.

Geoff held his stare. "Maybe. It still won't change anything."

"Are you sure?"

"Do I sound unsure?"

Yeah, you do. I've known you my whole life, bro, and I know when you're hiding something . . .

———

Noah tensed outside the door. He'd been listening. Like a super spy. But at the sound of his father's footfalls approaching, he ran quickly and softly on socked feet to the stairs. He hesitated, then scampered up, using hand over hand, crawling like a fast, giant tarantula. He raced to his room, closed the door, dived into his bed, and clicked off the lamp.

He lay there, listening to his dad's footsteps coming up the stairs. His dad's bedroom door closed. Noah's mind spun. He'd guessed they would talk about him. When adults suddenly said "go to bed," it was because they didn't want the kid to hear. It happened like that in his books all the time. And like a character in one of his books, Noah had crept back downstairs. He'd reached the door when they were talking about Meg doing the book.

And the secret Geoff didn't want his dad to tell her.

THE STRANGER AMONG US

By Meg Brogan

THE BROTHERS

You know her well . . . Very well . . .

Guilt twists through Blake as he watches the mist and storm swallow his dad's boat. Meg was wearing shorts, a skimpy T-shirt, Skechers. She's not dressed for this. He sees her in his mind's eye, lean, pale legs racing down the dock, a pennant of deep-red hair snapping behind her as she speeds her little tin boat across the bay. She wasn't wearing her life jacket, either. She never did wear one if she could help it—didn't think it was cool. Meg was fond of risk.

He casts his mind a little further back, and suddenly it strikes him. He remembers his brother's boat returning just after dusk, how his brother was shirtless, how he made straight for the boathouse cabin, how he didn't bother to securely moor his craft, and Blake had to do it for him when he noticed. A dark sensation coils in the pit of his belly. Geoff hasn't bothered to exit his cabin tonight, not even with all this commotion and the search going on.

Blake runs in his oversize gum boots down the twisting path, tripping over stones and sliding in mud, to the old boathouse where his older brother now lives. It's Geoff's hideout, where he does his "art."

Rain lashing his face, wind tearing at his slicker, Blake bashes the base of his fist against the peeling paint of the wood door. "Geoff! You in there?!"

Nothing.

"Geoff!"

He tries the handle. It's unlocked. He swings open the door and blows in with the wind and water. He freezes at the sight in front of him. Slowly, he pushes the door shut behind him.

It's hot inside. Too hot. A strong kerosene scent comes from the flickering, smoking lantern. But it's the strange smell of sweat, acrid, that assails, and startles him.

His brother sits in a chair at an old stripped-wood table. He's wearing jeans. Is barefoot. Shirtless. His back is to Blake, his head in his hands. His skin is sheened with sweat.

"Why . . . aren't you out helping?" Blake demands, suddenly unsure. His brother sits, unresponsive. Blake's attention zeroes in on a ball of fabric in the corner of the room, on the floor. It's the shirt Geoff was wearing this morning. The shirt is black with . . . blood? Fear trickles into him. "What's going on, Geoff?" he says quietly. "What happened?"

Silence.

"Geoff?"

"Fuck off."

But Blake stands his ground, rooted by an unspecified anxiety. Slowly Geoff turns around. What Blake sees in his older brother's eyes is not anger at his younger sibling for having entered his stupid sanctuary. It's something that guts him on a much deeper, more primal level. In his brother's eyes he sees fear. No, not just fear, a kind of bright, atavistic terror. Geoff's complexion is waxy white. A nasty gash has been slashed across his cheek-bone. There are scratches on his arm. Blake swallows, his eyes flicking between the soiled T-shirt, and his brother.

Silence swells. Wind moans and rattles at the doors and window, beseeching a way in. Surf crashes and thunders at the point. The foghorn is pleading. Air horns sound out on the bay, voices yelling on the water as volunteers search for the Brogan girls.

"Where've you been?" Blake's voice comes out hoarse. "You went to the spit—I saw you heading out there this morning."

Silence. Unreadable, unfathomable deep holes in his sibling's eyes.

"What happened on the spit?" he says quietly, coming forward.

Geoff looks slowly down at his hands, as if they somehow no longer belong to him, as if they've done things he doesn't comprehend. He looks back up at his brother and his eyes pool with moisture. Tears track down his cheeks.

Blake has to force his next words to form. "What happened? What did you do to your head? What happened on the spit—did you see the girls?" His questions come out in a rough wheeze, as if through a wind instrument constricted by a tension-tight reed.

"Nothing, dammit!" Geoff explodes from his chair. The chair crashes back onto the floor. His neck muscles cord blue. "I caught a branch with my face, now get the hell out of here!"

Inside his stomach Blake starts to shake. For the first time in his life he's afraid of his older brother in the way that he's sometimes afraid of his father. "It was Dad," he says hoarsely. "Wasn't it? I heard. Last night. I heard you guys fighting. He hit you again."

"Just fuck off, okay."

Blake goes to the door. Stops. "The Brogan girls are missing. Did you know that?"

"No. And I don't the fuck care."

"You didn't see them, on the spit?"

"What part of 'no' don't you get, you moron? Just fuck off, will you."

"Did you see anyone, anyone at all?"

His brother's eyes flare to Blake's. Electricity crackles from him in waves. He stinks. "No. No one."

But something about his brother's face deepens the fear in Blake.

"Where's your bag?"

Geoff turns away, rights the chair, and resumes his position at the table, face in hands, his back to Blake.

"I saw you go out with your sack this morning, the one you use to collect flotsam for your work."

Silence.

Blake turns and makes for the door, but swings back. "It was about you wanting to go to art school in the fall, that's why you fought, wasn't it?"

Silence.

"You're the one who's the moron—you should know better than to talk to him when he's had a few. You asshole." Blake reaches for the door handle, fighting compassion, bashing down his own unarticulated fear and mounting sense of urgency. It's always his brother who bears the brunt of their father's wrath. Geoff is Bull Sutton's punching bag. If Blake had to pinpoint the day the animosity started to fester between them, it was the day Geoff found their mom's seascapes stashed in the dusty old shed at the back end of their property, and he told his father he wanted to hang them in the house, because they were so beautiful.

"What are you going to do, Geoff?"

"Leave. Get out of this hellhole. Go to California."

"When?"

"I don't know. Tomorrow. Next month. As soon as I get my shit together."

Blake exits the boathouse. Heavy heart, thudding adrenaline. Anxiety churns through him. It'll be just him and his dad now. The sense of looming loss is profound. Tears mix with the water running down his face as he stomps up through the rain and enters the office. He fiddles with the radio channels, listening to the crackle and hiss of the calls out on the bay. Then he hears a snatch that thumps the wind out of him. They've found Sherry.

She's dead. Police have been called. The death sounds suspicious. Then there's an order to cut radio chatter on the subject.

Raw chill slices through him. *Meg? Where's Meg?* Frantically he scans through the other channels.

No sign of the other girl.

Blake can't stand it. His brain screams. Sweat pools under his arms, drenching his shirt. He paces, up and down, up and down, up and down, hitting his fist into his palm, the radio crackling, his mind racing. *What happened to Sherry? Where's Meg? What was Geoff doing on the spit today?* He explodes suddenly like a volcano—manning the fort be damned—he grabs his weather gear, a flashlight, headlamp, first aid kit, a portable radio of his own, and makes his way through the slashing rain down the gangway to his small boat.

He casts off the lines, motors into the storm wearing his tiny headlamp. Tossing like a little cork upon a boiling sea, he gooses his engine, setting his prow dead center of the incoming waves, slapping into the crests as they break and crash into whitecaps around him, spraying his face. He's watchful of the rebound surge coming off the dike that could hit him broadside. He keeps an eye on the backwash from the cliff side of the point. He knows the vagaries of the tidal currents in this bay, how they swirl when high tide pushes in, and he compensates, running his craft up the far left of the channel, knowing that even going full power into the surge, it will still carry him at least fifty yards over to the right, where he'll run into trouble against the rocks. Blake knows exactly where each painted cairn stands along the dike, marking where sailors have drowned. He has no intention of having his life marked by a cairn. Salt water driven by wind stings his face, leaks from his squinting eyes.

He aims for the flare of the lighthouse at the mouth, aims toward the boom of the waves against the riprap reef—the dangerous maw of the point and the south beach. He's a young Odysseus navigating between the treachery of a Scylla and Charybdis to rescue his red-headed little goddess. For he knows Meg's secret place. *Their* secret place. A small cave to which access is cut off at high tide. But if you know where to go, you can still get into the cave during high water, *if* you dive under and swim up inside the grotto, from where you can climb to higher ground and stay dry even at top watermark. If . . . just *if* Meggie ran into trouble, that's where she would go, that's where she might try to hide.

CHAPTER 12

Like the tides, the February fogs that rolled in off the Pacific had rhythms of their own. On this night, the crawling, creeping wall of wet stole into the Forest End subdivision around 1:00 a.m. It moved under streetlights in thick, soupy tatters, reaching, sifting into crevices, between trees, behind hedges, touching wet fingers to leaves, cars, dampening the road to a shining black. It trapped sound, light, and cast it sideways and bounced it back, a sentient presence trying to trick the innocent down the wrong alley.

The houses in Forest Lane, the last street that ran along the woods, were dark, the residents all asleep, save for one. The fog thickened as the clock ticked inexorably down toward 4:00 a.m., a time when the biorhythmic ebb of the human cycle dipped to its lowest, a time of night when it was most likely for a death to occur in the very old, or very ill. A time when temperatures fell to their lowest, just before dawn, and currents of air stirred across the earth, and it became easy for the grim reaper to reach through that fragile membrane that separates life from death, and crook a finger to softly summon a soul.

It was at this time a vehicle crept slowly up the dark street. Cutting lights, it came to a stop under the bare branches of an old cherry, just out of the sight line of the one lighted living room window in the street, yet the position still afforded a good view of the Brogan house.

A light burned softly downstairs. A lamp perhaps. The window had been replaced, but no blinds as yet. Drapes were drawn upstairs. The walls of the double-story had been cleansed of graffiti, scraped down, and sported a fresh coat of paint. A blank slate upon which to rewrite fate.

The vehicle door opened. Boots touched gravel, carefully, quietly. The door *snicked* shut. Gravel crunched as a hunched shape moved through mist. A black balaclava covered skin. Only eyes showed through the slits, and those eyes glinted black and wet in the gloam.

From directly across the street, Meg Brogan could be seen at a table, working by the light of a lamp and surrounded by papers, her hair piled into a tangled knot on top of her head, reading glasses slipping down her nose as she typed into a laptop. A mug sat beside her.

Wind gusted. Fog swirled in glee. Dead leaves clattered. A cat spooked with a meow into the street, stopped, as if taking note of the SUV beneath the cherry, then skittered under a hedge.

Meg got up from the table and stretched, arcing her spine slowly, and pressing her hands to the back of her hips. She picked up her mug and moved across the lighted window. For a moment, sight of her was lost.

But she returned with her mug again, steam coming from the top. Must have gone for a refill.

Several more minutes ticked by. She turned off one of the living room lamps, as if prepping for sleep, but she wavered, went back to her table, and slowly sat down to read more, as if something had snared her interest and would not allow her to go to bed.

The shadow moved across the street and slipped into Meg Brogan's driveway.

Seating herself at the table, a mug of tea at her side, Meg opened the file with the crime scene photos. Outside the night had grown cold and was choked with mist that pressed up against her new windows. The blinds she'd ordered had yet to arrive but her house was now spotless, and the exterior walls had been cleaned of graffiti and given a first coat of cream paint. Order was gradually being restored around her, and she was beginning to feel whole. More whole than . . . since she could remember.

But the first photo shut her down instantly. She closed her eyes, swallowed, and breathed deep.

Just another job. Treat it like all the others . . . you've looked at countless crime photos and postmortem reports . . . use the same tools you always use to distance yourself, intellectualize . . .

She reached over, clicked on her recorder. The little red light glowed. But her voice tightened in her throat as she stared at the image of her sister's body. Sherry's skin was paper-white under the harsh flash, stark against the black mud. Her head was wrenched sideways at an unnatural angle, her tongue, fat, protruding. Her legs were splayed, her crotch exposed, and there was black blood down her inner thighs. White lace panties were balled like a dirty wet rag near her left foot. Her shorts and blouse had been ripped and cast aside. A lone sandal stuck out of dead pine needles. Twigs matted her tangled hair. Her eyes were open wide and blank, and her skin glistened with rain. The glimmering essence that was her sister, gone. Meg's gaze lit upon the birthmark on Sherry's left breast, and a small noise escaped her mouth. Her own sound startled her. Blood beat in her head.

Focus.

The photographer had captured the small butterfly tattoo on Sherry's hip bone, one she'd kept hidden from Mom and Dad, now exposed to the world. No dignity in death. No secrets. No modesty. When you relinquished life, you relinquished your own story, the ability to tell it, shape it the way you wanted the world to see it.

The next photo showed discarded beer tins, used condoms in mud, and pine needles. All awash with rain and rising, muddy water.

"What happened, Sherry?" she whispered into her microphone. "I came looking for you late that afternoon. I beached my boat, pulled it up high so that the tide wouldn't steal it away, then I ran up the dune. A steep dune. Soft, white sand, which slipped out under my shoes. I used my hands, like I was crawling uphill. Then . . . I stopped. Why? . . ." Meg closed her eyes, her heart skipping faster. "A sound. I heard something that halted me in my tracks. A terrible sound. Part of my brain said it was one thing while another thought it had to be something else, and . . . then I heard it again. My muscles exploded as I forced my way through the scrub, and . . ."

Meg jabbed off her recorder and lurched to her feet. She paced, clenching and unclenching her hands, palms damp. From that point her memory was blank. She'd slammed right back up against that black hole again, but this was the farthest she had gone into it. And she felt a sense of several shapes moving, like shadow puppets, evil silhouettes, just beyond her mental reach. "How late was I, Sherry? Were you still alive? Were you struggling, calling for my help? What did I do? Who was there? What did I *see*, dammit—"

Wait. Stop! Don't run, Meggie, don't run!

Meg froze. She felt a shudder beneath her feet. The glasses in the kitchen cupboards rattled, and framed pictures on the wall slid askew. A vase crashed off the shelf, and her new windows vibrated. She stood dead still. It came again, another small tremor, the ground wobbling under her feet. She was about to run for a door frame when all went still. Meg waited another moment, then made quickly for her computer.

She pulled up the WorldEarthquakeWatchLive profile on her Twitter feed. And as she watched, one tweet after another slipped into the stream like some old-fashioned ticker tape—people reporting tremors all the way up the Oregon coast and into Washington State. Some even coming from BC north of the border. An earthquake had occurred fifteen miles off the Oregon coast, and according to the Live Earthquakes map, it had registered 5.7 on the Richter scale. The Pacific Tsunami Warning Center had not yet issued an advisory, but was on watch. Meg paced, clenching and unclenching her hands again, nerves biting.

It's like you're playing a joke on me, Sherry. That would be your style, wouldn't it? Let's rattle little Meggie-Peg's cage a bit, and see if we can spook her . . .

Meg forced herself to calm down, and she reseated herself at the table. Yet her world was oddly off-kilter now. It was as if looking at these photos of Sherry's defiled body had opened some fissure between tectonic plates in the Earth's crust, and a dark, inky evil was oozing out and creeping closer in the mist. Irritably, she clicked the television on, found the local weather channel. The reporters' voices and light invaded the room, dissipating the weird sensation, and distracting her a little from the harshness of the crime scene photos. If there was a tsunami warning coming, she'd hear it on this channel.

Meg slugged back the rest of her tea, and opened the postmortem report. She pressed the record button.

"As expected," Meg said into her recorder as she read, "the PM report obtained by my mother in March—seven months after Sherry's murder—details trauma from violent sexual intercourse, vaginal and anal tears, traces of semen that were later proved to have come from Tyson Mack. This is all consistent with Tyson Mack's assertions in police interview transcripts that sex with Sherry was 'energetic' and that his condom had ruptured." Meg cleared her throat. "Cause of death was asphyxiation. The report details petechial hemorrhaging in the conjunctival surfaces of the eyes, cloudy corneas, ligature marks around the neck. The internal examination revealed a fractured hyoid bone. All of this is consistent with the trauma clearly evident in the crime scene photos." Meg paused, and flipped over the page to the lab data sections. *What?*

She yanked the report closer.

Her sister's blood at the time of her death had contained between 5 and 25 mIU/ml hCG—human chorionic gonadotropin—a hormone that supported the development of an egg in a woman's ovary.

Sherry was pregnant?

Hurriedly, Meg scanned the document further. Her sister had been a few weeks pregnant when she was raped and strangled. She sat back in shock. Into her microphone she said, "Sherry was with child, barely. But according to this report, the DNA of the embryo did not match Tyson Mack's DNA profile, a copy of which my mother also has in her files. Neither was it a match to Tommy Kessinger's DNA profile—Tommy had voluntarily given a sample to assist with the investigation since he'd been intimate with Sherry prior to her murder."

Meg cleared her throat and continued speaking softly into the mic. "According to the report, several other used condoms had also been retrieved from the scene. The grove on the spit was a well-known make-out spot, so this would be expected. The DNA samples collected from these condoms were apparently in various stages of viability, due to weather exposure and the passage of time. There was also evidence of cross contamination. One of the condoms had traces of Sherry's DNA on it; however, the report notes that this condom had been found in a pool of muddy water into which Sherry had also bled." Meg turned the page.

"Two more DNA samples were retrieved, one from a beer can, and another from a tequila bottle. None of these DNA profiles was a paternal match to Sherry's embryo. However, hairs that had been found in Sherry's pubic hair were a match to one of the unidentified profiles—the semen taken from the condom found in the muddy pool that had contained Sherry's blood trace."

She paused, pulse quickening. Was it possible there could have been more than one perpetrator? Why had this angle not been explored more thoroughly? Meg quickly made a note to ask Ike Kovacs about this and the pregnancy when she interviewed him.

"My sister had been with another man at least several weeks prior to the attack, and she was carrying his baby. So, who in the hell was he? What could this mean in terms of Ty Mack's guilt?" She clicked off her recorder, feeling sick. She stood to ease the pain that was knotting low in her back. Arching her spine, she applied pressure with her hands to the back of her hips.

Who were you seeing, Sherry? Did you even know that you were pregnant by this man? And if so, did you tell him? What was his reaction? Anger? Pleasure? Confusion? Did you discuss options— keeping the baby, getting rid of it? Did he pressure you?

Meg snagged her mug and went into the kitchen to make more tea.

As she waited in the kitchen for the kettle to boil she stared absently at her reflection in the black window, and it struck her hard—her mother had been privy to all this. How had it made her feel? Had Tara Brogan first learned of her oldest daughter's pregnancy through this autopsy report that she'd acquired herself? If so, why had Sheriff Kovacs not told her mom as soon as he'd seen this? Meg hurried back to the living room.

She grabbed her mother's journal and flipped through to March, when her mom had secured this report. She found the entry she was looking for.

I got the autopsy report today. I'd never wanted to see it until now. I wasn't ready. The news of

Sherry's pregnancy near broke me. I drove to Ike's house in Chillmook that same night, shaking all the way. I could not believe he hadn't told me or Jack about the pregnancy, or the other DNA. I wanted to kill him. I could imagine how Jack felt, wanting to kill someone. Rage. It's an emotion I never thought deeply about until Jack murdered Ty Mack. It hijacks the logical part of your brain, and I could feel it happening to me as I drove, hands clamped to the wheel, vision narrowing. I had to keep telling myself—think, Tara. Focus. You're going to have an accident. You're not going to be of any help with Jack in prison. Meg needs a mother.

Meg stalled, and reread the sentence: *Meg needs a mother.* Shit. She sat back. Quietly she said into her mic, "Who *were* you, Mom? I wish you'd spoken to me. I might have been only fourteen, but if I'd known you were fighting, if I'd known . . . I could have perhaps helped, even if just being there for support—it could have made all the difference. It could have given *me* purpose. I've hated you for so long for giving up. For just abandoning me. But I didn't know you at all. These words in this journal are those of a strong, valiant, intelligent, caring, determined woman, and not a grief-soaked, helpless soul who could no longer face the world. I wish I knew what made you change your mind that day, and take your own life like that . . . it just doesn't make sense."

In her laptop she typed:

Question for Tommy and Emma: Did you know Sherry was pregnant? Did you know if she was seeing anyone else?

Meg returned her attention to her mother's journal.

When I got to the Kovacs', Ike told me that
the autopsy results, the pregnancy lab tests in
particular, came in after Tyson Mack had already
been shot dead by Jack. It had all happened so
fast. Tyson Mack was their prime suspect—they
were convinced of his guilt—but the DA advised
they'd need more evidence in order to secure
a solid conviction, so the police were holding off
formally charging him at that point while they
continued their investigation.

But if Jack had known about the pregnancy, or
the existence of the other condom with Sherry's
blood trace on it, as inconclusive as it was, he might
not have been so quick to the trigger. Because
to my mind, Sherry's pregnancy and the other DNA
put the possibility of another suspect, or more than
one, into the picture. And the baby gave possible
motive—perhaps the father was a violent man.

Ike explained to me that the other DNA was
worthless because of the high probability of cross
contamination along with the heavy use of the
grove as a make-out spot. The storm, he said, had
created challenges in the collection of evidence.
In his opinion it was unrelated to Sherry's assault,
anyway. Ty Mack was his man. He said he was simply
trying to soften things for us. He felt the news
of the pregnancy coming right after Ty Mack's
murder would have been too much for me and
Jack to bear on top of it all. And bringing it to
everyone's attention before Jack's trial could hurt
him in sentencing. It was better, he said, that a
jury believed one hundred percent that Jack

had killed an evil man, that there be no doubt as to Tyson Mack's guilt. Ike said the pregnancy did not change his conviction that Ty Mack raped, sodomized, and strangled Sherry, and he felt that when I was ready, if I wanted, I'd get the report myself, and be able to better deal with the information contained therein.

Ike was wrong.

*And now, my dear Jack, I wonder not only who tipped you off and might have used you as a loaded gun, but I wonder also if Ty Mack really was the one. Or if a man who made my baby girl pregnant could have killed her. And whether he still walks free out there. I don't know how I'm going to do it, but I **will** find out. And I **will** get Sherry's case reopened . . .*

A soft *whump* sounded outside. Meg's head jerked up. She braced for the start of another tremor, an aftershock maybe. Or perhaps the first was just a foreshock, a harbinger of some big tectonic subduction to come. Nothing moved. She glanced over her shoulder at the window. Wind? She listened, heart quickening slightly. She could make out a soft scratching sound, like branches rubbing against the outside wall of the house. Must be a breeze moving the trees. She made a mental note to call a garden service to trim back all the vegetation. It would be a fire hazard come summer anyway. She returned her attention to the journal. A thump. Her head shot up. It was followed by a strange scraping sound, then a metal clang. Fear struck a hatchet into her heart.

She stood up and reached to click the lamp off so she could see outside. But as she moved, a red laser dot danced over the wall. Her heart kicked. Slowly she turned. The dot moved onto her arm, and along her body, settling for a moment on her chest, then moving up to her face. She threw herself to the floor just as a sharp crack shattered the living room picture window. Glass clattered to the floor. The cold draft was instant. Another whizzing sounded as something thudded into the wall next to the safe. *Gunfire.*

Someone was shooting at her with a laser scope.

Meg scrabbled on all fours into the next room. It was in darkness. Carefully she peered up over the windowsill. Another crack exploded the glass over her head. She gasped, ducked, as shards rained down over her. Another bullet smashed the mirror on the far wall. Shit. Meg pressed her back against the wall. She fumbled in her sweater pocket for her cell phone. Glass tinkled upstairs. Hands shaking, she dialed 911.

"Chillmook County 911 dispatch, where is your emergency?"

"My house—58 Forest Lane, Forest End, Shelter Bay."

"What's the emergency, ma'am?"

"Someone is shooting at my house . . . someone's trying to kill me. Please. . . ." She gasped and dived as a bullet blasted the sill above her head. Her phone skittered across the room into the middle of the floor.

CHAPTER 13

Meg crawled into the small adjacent bathroom. High above the toilet was a tiny window. She stood on tiptoes and cautiously peeped out. Through the mist, under the soft lamp halo, she saw a shadowed figure running through trees. A car door slammed. Tires squealed. She saw the flare of red taillights at the end of the street.

Her heart hammered.

Her hands were shaking.

Sirens wailed down the twisting highway. She sank slowly down against the bathroom wall, huddling on the tile floor next to the toilet.

You should think about security, Meg . . . it's only a matter of time before one of the monsters you write about is going to come after you . . .

Tears filled her eyes. She ached, right at this moment, to feel Jonah's arms around her, have him stroke her hair, comfort her, and she detested herself for it. The sirens grew louder. She could hear them coming down her street. She crawled slowly out of the bathroom door, not wanting to get up into the line of fire again. Red and blue light strobed into her living room. Papers fluttered to the floor in the breeze from the gaping maw in the wall. Car doors slammed. Curt voices barked orders. She heard the words "all clear."

Booted feet sounded up her driveway. Then a pounding on her door. "Anyone inside? Hello? Police, open up!"

Meg got to her feet. Legs wobbly, she made her way to the door, opened it, and blinked into a flashlight. One deputy and an officer from the tiny Shelter Bay police force stood on her porch. Two cruisers were parked in the street, light bars on top pulsing. A third cruiser screeched to a stop on the far side of the street.

Then the tall, unmistakable form of Chief Deputy Dave Kovacs alighted from the third cruiser. He slammed his door and marched across her lawn, the throbbing lights casting him into huge, flickering, and garish relief.

"Are you all right, ma'am?" The Shelter Bay officer was talking to her. She couldn't seem to hear, to concentrate. She was fixated on Dave's strident approach, a part of her brain wondering what in the hell he was doing working a graveyard shift—didn't they use minions for that?

Another deputy came around the side of the house. "I think it's blood, sir," she said to Kovacs as he reached the porch.

"Blood?" Meg stepped out in her socked feet to see what she was talking about. "What's blood?" Then she saw—her freshly power-washed and painted walls had been defiled with hideous red paint that was dripping down the siding into the weeds. *Go Home Bitch. Fuck off, Bitch. Killer's daughter!! White trash. Gonna kill you, Bitch.* She stared. Her eyes burned. Giant shudders seized hold of her body. She wrapped her arms tightly over her stomach.

"Get some crime scene techs in here," Kovacs barked. The deputy went to make the call.

Meg went closer to see. Blood? How could it be blood?

"Please, step back—" An arm barred her. "Please, step inside, ma'am."

But she was fixated on the dripping letters. Someone had been right here, violating her house, her space, while she sat vulnerable and exposed in the big lighted picture window. They'd stalked her, toyed with her by dancing a laser sight over her face, her body.

They had me in their sights. They could have shot me, but didn't. This was designed to scare the shit out of me, and it has. But you don't know me, you bastards. No way in hell am I backing down now, game on, you A-holes—

"Meg. Meg!"

She jerked back as Kovacs touched her elbow gently. "Meg, you okay, want to come inside and tell me what happened?"

Papers—she needed to protect the files. She started back inside.

"Megan." Kovacs grabbed her arm in the hall. "Wait. Have you got shoes? The place is covered in glass."

She looked down at her socked feet. She'd left blood smears on the white floor tiles.

"You're cut," he said.

"I'm fine. Fine." She couldn't feel a thing. She rammed her feet into a pair of her dad's oversize slippers that her mother had kept by the door as if awaiting his return, and she hurried into the living room, started gathering up papers that had been scattered to the floor by wind from the open window. She stuffed them back into their folders, the folders into the boxes. Her movements were feverish, the cortisol slamming through her system giving her the shakes.

Dave's boots crunched over glass as he entered behind her. "What's all this in here?" He took in her papers, the file boxes. His eyes shot to the open wall safe between the bookshelves. "What papers are these?" He picked up her mother's journal from the table. She dropped her file box and lunged for it. "Leave that alone." She grabbed it from him. His eyes locked on hers.

"It's . . . it's personal. I'm sorry. I'm . . . a little worked up."

He cast a quick glance over his shoulder, then said, his voice low, "Want to tell me what's going on here? What happened tonight?"

"I was sitting here, in this chair, working at the table. No blinds."

She stuffed her mother's journal into her tote hanging on the back of a chair. She followed it with her laptop, voice recorder, and notebooks, and she slung the tote protectively across her body. Dave watched her every movement, eyes narrowing.

"I'd heard some noises earlier," she said. "But I thought it was another tremor, or wind. Then I saw a laser dot, like a laser from a hunting rifle scope. On the wall there."

He looked where she pointed: a small bullet hole marred the white drywall. "I turned sideways. The laser beam settled on my face. That's when I dived. Shots came through the window, and I scrambled into the other room, where I called 911. From the bathroom window I saw one figure, all in black, running toward an SUV parked down the road. A door slammed. Tires squealed, and it was gone just as I heard your sirens coming." She wiped the top of her lip with the back of her shaking hand. "I didn't get any plates."

"Color of the SUV?"

"I . . . didn't notice. Maybe silver—I can't be sure. It was dark down the street."

The female deputy appeared in the open-plan archway. "CSI guys are here, sir. Would you like me to take a statement from Ms. Brogan?"

"Give us a minute, Hoberman, I'll handle this." The woman hesitated.

"Yes, sir." She left.

Meg felt instantly threatened. This was not protocol, she'd swear on it. Kovacs wanted something from her, and he didn't want his team to know what.

"They could have killed me if they wanted to," she said. "They shot wide, into the wall up there." He glanced again at the wall, then looked toward the window, as if calculating trajectory.

"People are not happy with you doing that book," he said quietly.

Her jaw dropped. "And that gives them the right to shoot up my house, vandalize my walls, terrorize me?"

"I didn't say anything about rights. Just a fact."

A coal of anger ignited deep in her belly and began to burn hot. "And have you considered, Deputy, *why* someone might be going to such extremes to spook me into stopping? Have you considered that maybe someone has something to hide? That maybe, just maybe, *your* father screwed up the investigation, or covered something up, or provoked *my* father to kill Tyson Mack, because his case didn't stand a snowball's chance in hell of securing a conviction!"

A muscle twitched along his jaw. "What are you saying?"

She swiped perspiration off her brow with her sleeve. "I'm saying I'm going to interview your dad, like it or not. Because something is off here."

His gaze shot to the file boxes. "What's in there? Something to do with the case?"

"Nothing you can't access yourself."

"Sir." It was Hoberman again. "Found .22 shells out on the street. Crime scene tech wants to talk to you. It is blood. Not sure what kind. We'll need to get samples to the lab."

"I'll be right out," he said. Meg hefted one of her boxes off the table. Kovacs hesitated. "Where you going with those?"

"My truck. A hotel. Until you guys are done with this place. Then I'm going to fix it right back up and move right back in." She made a move toward the door with one box, but suddenly didn't want to leave the second box unattended.

"Sir?" The female deputy prompted Kovacs.

"Tell the tech I'll be right there, Hoberman," he snapped, then he turned to Meg, lowering his voice. "If there's something in there that pertains to the case, if you're obstructing justice in any—"

Yelling, arguing, sounded outside. "You can't go in there!" came a voice. "This is a crime scene!"

The front door burst open. And in blew Blake. Amped. Breathing hard. Hands fisted at his side. Meg's heart kicked.

"Jesus, Meg, what in the hell happened?" He came forward, took her shoulders in his big hands. "Are you okay?"

"Thank God you're here," she whispered. "Please, can you take these two boxes out to my truck? Keys are on the hook by the door. I . . . I need to get a bag of things, my toothbrush from upstairs."

Blake hesitated. His eyes shot to Kovacs. The chief deputy tilted his head slightly in acknowledgment, his mouth tight with irritation.

"Where are you going with your truck?" Blake said to Meg.

"Hotel. I . . . don't know. The Whakami Beach place. Until things are sorted here."

He held her gaze a moment, then scooped up one box, and balanced the other on top. "I'll be outside."

Meg turned to make for the stairs.

"Wait," Kovacs said.

"I'm just getting some personal effects."

"I need a statement."

"I gave you one. If you need anything more, here is my cell number." She yanked the notebook from her tote, scribbled down her number, ripped off the page, and thrust it at him. "Now, can I go upstairs?"

His gaze bored hot into hers. "I'm sending a female officer with you. Hoberman!"

Hoberman appeared.

"Go with Ms. Brogan. She's getting some personal belongings."

Meg gathered up her phone and stomped up the stairs, the female deputy in tow. What did Kovacs think she was going to do upstairs? Take some evidence? What the hell? This was her house.

Her stuff. His words from earlier curled through her mind, and in this new context, they took on more sinister meaning.

If those vandals come back, a woman out here on her own . . .

———

Blake stood on the porch waiting for Meg. A damp cold sank into his bones. The police lights throbbed eerily in the dense mist, a breeze beginning to stir. Kovacs was talking to a CSI taking samples of blood from the wall. He came over when he was done.

"What brings you out here at four a.m.?" Kovacs said. "Just driving around and saw police?"

"Geoff told me there was a shooting in Meg's street."

"Your *brother*? He's back?"

Blake regarded the cop, trying to get a read on him. He sensed hostility. Kovacs was a friend, but not a close one. He had a good several years on both Blake and Geoff and had moved in different circles, but he was one of the guys, one of Shelter Bay's old-timers. This animosity was unusual; then again, he'd never seen Kovacs working a case. This could be his cop face, a mask he wore for his underlings.

"Geoff arrived yesterday," Blake said cautiously, regretting his slip. "He's staying with me at the marina."

"Why's he back?"

"Why does anyone come home? Been a long while since his last visit. He wanted to catch up."

"After all these years?"

Blake shrugged.

"How did he know there was a shooting?"

"Radio."

"He was up, listening to the radio?"

Blake tensed. Telling Kovacs that Geoff had heard the report on his car radio as he'd pulled into the marina was just going to raise more questions about where his brother had been until the early hours of the morning. "You'll have to ask him yourself."

Kovacs turned and looked out over the lawn toward the street. The lights flickered eerily over the hard planes of his face. The brim of his Stetson hid his eyes. "It's a pretty quiet and isolated neighborhood up here. Not a thoroughfare."

A cool wariness unfurled through the tension already twisting Blake's stomach over his brother, and the timing of his arrival, and his concern over his secret, and Meg's digging into the past. Geoff had come home drunk, banged on his door, waking him to say there'd been shooting at Meg's house—apparently he'd heard on the radio the cops were there. He'd clearly been driving over the limit. Blake turned to face Kovacs.

"And you? Working the graveyard?"

"Short staffed. Flu's knocked half the department out."

Blake measured him. It made sense. It was an election year. Showing himself as one of the guys willing to do the grunt work as part of a team would be an astute political move.

Meg appeared with her bags. She was waxy-pale, her eyes huge, like dark holes in her head. Compassion, a fierce sense of protectiveness, chased into his blood, like an old neural memory, firing down and reawakening disused synapses. He'd always tried to protect Meg, whether she'd wanted it or not. And he knew this asshole gladiator drive in him was fueled by a deeper, baser, more primal need—he loved her. Be damned if he could kick the habit. And here it was, full flame again—a ferocious instinct when it came to this woman.

Meg shucked off her father's slippers and bent down to tug on her boots.

"You're hurt," he said, noting the pink imprints her socks left on the tiles. "You're bleeding."

"Must have been a bit of glass. It's fine." She stood up. He saw that she'd wrapped a handkerchief around her left hand. It, too, was spotted with blood. "You got my keys?" she said.

"They're in my truck."

She stared. "I—I need to get to the hotel. I need my keys."

"Come. I'm taking you home." He took her arm and one of her bags. It was heavy with her laptop and books.

"Blake, no. I need to—"

"Forget it. Either I'm taking you to the medical center, or I'm taking you home to get a look at those feet and that hand of yours myself. Medic, remember. And you need somewhere safe."

"I'll be perfectly safe at a hotel . . ." Her voice died as she caught sight of the lurid graffiti under a harsh klieg light. Her house looked like a set from some nightmare horror movie, drips of blood crawling down from the untidy letters into the dead flowerbed choked by weeds, a bed her mother had once tended with such care.

Go Home Bitch. Fuck off, Bitch. Killer's daughter!! White trash. Gonna kill you, Bitch.

"When . . . will you know what kind of blood it is?" she said to Kovacs, her voice hoarse.

"Lab should have results pretty soon."

"When can I wash it off?"

"I'll let you know when we're done."

Blake took her arm. "Thanks. If you need anything she'll be at the marina."

"Be careful, Meg," Kovacs called out behind them as they started down the path.

She stalled dead in her tracks, spun around fiercely. "That another threat, Deputy?"

"Just doing my job. Protecting the citizens of this county, making sure they stay out of harm's way."

She opened her mouth, but Blake pressured her arm. "Meg. Enough. Come."

He put her bags in the back of his truck, and opened the passenger door for her. She climbed in and sat staring at her defiled house with its shattered windows, illuminated with the CSI lights, the pulsing blue and red emergency lights, the dark forest hulking behind, mist swirling.

Blake's neck muscles were tight as he fired the ignition.

"It's just a house," she whispered. "Just a house."

"What?"

"Nothing."

"Meg?"

She looked at him. His chest torqued.

"It's *not* just a house, Meg. It's your family home. It's a vessel full of memories. They live in there. You have a *right* to feel violated, angry. No one has a right to do that."

"Jonah said I should get rid of it. That I was holding on to the ghosts—that I needed to let them go."

Irritation, and yeah, a spark of hot jealousy crackled through him. He geared his truck, reversed, and turned down the street, his beams cutting twin tunnels into the mist as he drove. "Guess that's why he's the shrink and I'm not. I don't have a problem with holding on to memories. You need to tell me what happened, Meg. What's with those boxes? What's gotten up Kovacs's nose?"

"Me. I've gotten up his nose. Me and Sherry's story."

He shot her a glance. She sat silent for several beats, fiddling with that ring of hers.

Frustration, desire to *do* something burned in him. "Megan, you *need* to tell me what's going on."

"It's personal stuff."

"Oh, don't give me that crap—"

"Blake, I don't want to involve you. You have a son who needs you. I . . . I've screwed up your life too much before. I . . . just need to do this on my own. I have my own life, a . . ." Her voice wavered. She rubbed her hands over her face. "Please. Just take me to the hotel."

"You have a fiancé? Is that what you're trying to say?" He dug in his pocket, handed Meg his cell phone. "Here. Call him. Tell him to come. And when he gets here I'll let you go to a damn hotel. In the meantime, you're coming home with me, where at least I can protect you."

"Oh jeeze, what, because you're now a trained soldier with a gun?"

"Damn right."

She stared.

"It's more than you'll get at the Whakami Bay hotel. Someone could have killed you tonight, Meg, and clearly the cops are not feeling terribly helpful toward you for some reason, and you have yet to explain why."

He turned into the marina driveway, and they bumped down the steep gravel track to the bay. Fog was more dense down on the water, a thick, tattered soup in the dark, bouncing back the lights of his truck, closing halos tightly around the lamps along the dock, as if trying to strangle them dead. The beam from the Shelter Head lighthouse arced through mist at the point. The horns sounded, mournful.

"Who's with Noah?" she said, noticing a light burning in the marina office.

"Geoff. He's sleeping on the sofa downstairs." It would be dawn soon. He had to think about Noah's breakfast, making his lunch, getting him to school.

She turned in her seat. "Blake . . . how did you know to come tonight?"

He inhaled deeply, turned off the ignition. He was in no mood to rehash the anomalies of his brother's story, and he had every mind to hammer it out with him later. "Geoff told me. Listen, Meg, before we go inside, I've got to know what's going on. And don't go telling me it's not my business, because it is. That selfish this-is-my-circus-my-monkeys, no-one-else-can-understand card is not going to work anymore. This is not just about you."

She stared. "Oh, that is so not fair."

He placed his hand over hers. Her skin was ice cold. She was shivering. "We need to get you warmed up, get a brandy into you to cut the edge off that adrenaline withdrawal that's going to kick in any moment. And I need to look at your feet, but first you're going to tell me about those file boxes."

She sucked in a chestful of air, and exhaled slowly. "My mother's," she said, finally. "They're full of transcripts—the police interrogations of Tyson Mack, Sherry's autopsy report, crime scene photos. My mom got most of it from Lee Albies, who was Ty Mack's pro bono legal counsel. Albies had started mounting her case in the event that Ty was charged."

"What was your mother doing with them?"

"She'd come to believe that someone had tipped my dad off to Tyson Mack's hiding place on purpose, knowing he would probably go and kill Ty. Someone wanted Ty dead, and the case dropped, and they used my dad like a loaded gun."

"Whatever gave her that idea?"

"My dad. He let slip to my mom on a visit that someone told him where Ty was hiding, but he would not reveal who, because he believed the blame was solely his to bear. So, my mom began her own investigation in the hopes of easing my dad's sentence when his case finally went to trial. Her journal details her progress, and it shows how she slowly came to think that maybe Ty Mack didn't do it." She paused, looked up. Her eyes gleamed in the dark. "I think my father might have gone to prison for killing an innocent man, Blake."

Blake's brain reeled as he listened to Meg recount how Irene had caused a fire, and how the safe was discovered when contractors ripped out the bookshelves to get at the subsequent water damage. She told him about the other DNA profiles that had been found in condoms left at the scene, as yet unidentified. And how one of those DNA profiles matched hairs found in Sherry's pubic hair. He heard about the pregnancy, and the mystery of the paternal DNA, which matched neither of the other two sets of unidentified DNA found on scene, nor Tommy Kessinger's DNA profile. And how Ike Kovacs sat on that information.

"None of this proves that Ty *didn't* do it," he said.

"But it does raise questions about reasonable doubt, ulterior motive, possible police tunnel vision."

He stared at the little light burning downstairs, thinking of Geoff. His being on the point that night. Meeting someone else. Someone whose identity remained a mystery. Him finding Geoff in the boathouse. How his brother had left town a few weeks after the murder, never to return. The flotsam sack he'd found near Meg, who'd been close to dead, lolling in those waves.

It all suddenly took on dark context. And it complicated his need for honesty with Meg right now because it butted hard against his reflex to protect his brother. Protecting Geoff was hardwired into him. And honestly, whatever secret Geoff was keeping, he did not—could not—have hurt Sherry.

"The other thing," Meg said, "after reading my mom's journal, and seeing how driven she was to get to the bottom of this, how she was working against a ticking-clock deadline for my dad's trial, I can't see how she could suddenly have committed suicide."

"What . . . exactly are you saying?"

"Her journal details fears about being followed, her house watched, someone trying to break in. She was scared. Scared enough to report it to Ike Kovacs. My mom felt someone might want to do her harm." She paused. "I think my mother might have been murdered, Blake. I think she was getting too close to the truth, and someone needed to silence her."

———

Lori-Beth wheeled herself in front of Henry's desk computer. She glanced nervously over her shoulder, then clicked it on. She'd never done this before. She never touched Henry's things in this office, and he knew it.

The monitor flared to life.

What was she looking for? Something, anything. Henry was scared. She could smell it on him, and it made her sick with nerves. He'd been acting weird, getting calls at strange hours that upset him, going out early in the morning. And tonight he'd said he was going to meet a business colleague for a drink. While waiting up and worrying about him, she'd heard about the Forest End shooting on the radio—their community was one of few that still had a human in the studio 24/7, following up on reports from police scanners. Henry had finally come home after 4:00 a.m. Drunk, reeking of booze. He'd passed out on their bed fully clothed. Something he never did.

She clicked open his web browser, and tried to open his history. His cache had been cleared.

Why? What did he have to hide? Her hands froze over the keyboard as she heard a car outside. A car door banged. Her heart raced. She couldn't move fast in this chair, so she sat still like a mouse in the dark, bathed by the soft glow from the monitor. The back door opened, closed. Panic kicked. She heard a door close down the passage, in the guest suite. Then all went silent. The antique clock on the wall *tick-tick-ticked*. She waited. Nothing.

Relief washed softly through her. Just Sally coming home. She must have gone to see that late-night movie at that artsy club she was talking about. Sally always had trouble sleeping.

She reached to click off the computer, but stopped as something caught her eye. An icon on his desktop.

———

"Meg, that's just crazy. Your mom's death was an overdose. They *were* her pills that she took. You were sleeping down the hall. No one else was there."

It was growing colder inside the truck cab with the engine off, but Blake wanted to have this out with Meg before running into Geoff, whom he'd left in the house with Noah.

"I don't know—I just can't believe she took her own life. Not after what she wrote right up until the night before she died. She didn't want to abandon me, Blake. She *cared* for me." Her voice caught, and Meg took a moment to corral her emotions. Compassion surged into Blake's chest. It came with an ache to hold her close, to comfort her. He exhaled heavily and ran his hands over his hair.

"In her own words, my mother was trying to protect me from all this. She loved me." Meg wavered, again trying to control her voice. "And I never knew. Her taking her own life just makes no sense now."

"This is big, Meg. Shit." He turned to her. "If, just *if,* Ty Mack didn't kill Sherry—*if* it's true that someone wanted Ty to go down as a scapegoat, and to use your dad to silence everything, it would mean that a very dangerous criminal could still be out there. And your poking around the case could threaten him. If, just *if* your mother did not take her own life . . . this is serious. You could be in serious danger." His gaze locked with hers. "You're staying here," he said firmly. "Until we figure this out. You're going to show me those documents, and I'm going to help you get to the bottom of this."

"The incident tonight, it could have just been someone trying to scare me off."

"And next time? When they see you didn't get the message?" Adrenaline thumped hot and silent in his blood. He was in full protective mode, an urge swelling in him to just wrap himself around her, keep her safe. *His* Meg. Like the old days. Except she wasn't his. She belonged to someone else.

"Are you going to call him?" he said quietly. "Jonah?"

She looked down and fiddled with her massive engagement ring. Several beats of silence hung. He watched her hands, her ring. He wanted to tell her it didn't suit her. Too big and flashy. If it were his choice to make, he'd pick out something completely different. More natural. Small but pure, an utterly perfect diamond with not a flaw in its facets. A blue white, maybe, that came from the far north of Canada. Clean. Enduring. Something that wouldn't get in the way of using your hands properly.

A ship sounded its horn out at sea. The soft flare of the light-house swept like a searchlight. Dawn was creeping nearer.

"I can't," she said finally.

His pulse blipped. But he waited for her to explain.

She looked up, met his eyes. "Jonah called it off."

Wham. His world wobbled dangerously on its axis. "What?"

She inhaled deeply. "It's why I came back to Shelter Bay. To prove I *could* do it—write Sherry's story, scrape away my own memories, rewrite them within a new context, a fresh understanding of the past. Put it all to bed properly, *'The End.'* So that I can move on."

"I don't understand."

"It's complicated."

"Try me."

She swallowed, looking suddenly small and scared and young, and he wanted to hold her, comfort her. So bad, with every fiber of his being, it made him hurt.

"You won't get it."

"Oh, fuck, Meg. What am I? Some physical brute who can't get a shrink's cerebral, touchy-feely crap? Give me some credit here. I know you better than anyone knows you." There. He'd said it. He'd slapped down his gauntlet. *I know you better than that tight-ass celebrity shrink . . . you were more mine than you'll ever be his . . .*

"I was having trouble committing. To everything. Including my old desk job at the *Times*. I just . . . couldn't stand being held down between four walls and a roof and a routine, and he thought it was because I have some PTSD thing going on. He wanted to set a wedding date, and . . . and I just couldn't do it, okay? So he called it off. And he's right. I can see now that he was right. I *needed* to come home. To fix things with Irene, the house, Tommy, Bull . . ." She looked up. The word hung.

You.

Emotion gleamed into her eyes. A tear caught light as it slid down her pale cheek. His stomach folded in on itself.

"I'm doing it for him, Blake. I'm writing Sherry's story to win him back. And now it's so much more."

Blake's throat tightened. His heart thunked, slow, thick, steady, as if trying to beat its way out of molasses.

She swiped the tear away angrily. "I just didn't expect this. I thought I knew what '*The End*' was. I don't."

And again, the subtext hung.

I don't know how to do this now . . . it's changed . . .

"Meg—" He touched her hand, and he fingered her ring, and it was like crossing a boundary, a point of no return, as if he'd decided on a cellular level before his brain was fully aware, that he was going to fight this guy. That he was going to see her take this ring off, of her own volition.

"I *can't* call him," she whispered. "Not until this is done."

"Do you want to?" he said, softly.

She was silent. Waves crunched out on the distant reef.

"I don't know."

His heart quickened. It was a gap, and he took it. Acting almost of its own accord, his hand reached up, and he gently cupped the side of her face. Every moral fiber of his being that told him, *no, don't do this; she's promised herself to someone else; she's vulnerable right now; this could get far too complicated; it could mess with your relationship with your son,* was being countermanded by another hot whisper in his head—*her engagement is off, she isn't calling him, doesn't want to, this is your window, this is your second chance to win her back . . .*

She leaned in toward him, her lids lowering, and desire gushed hot through his gut, kicking every residual thought clean out of his head and sending his blood south with a sweet, pulsing delirium as his lips met hers. Her mouth was cool, soft, firm, and she opened to him.

He slid his fingers up into the dense, soft waves at the nape of her neck. A moan slipped from her throat, and her hand touched his arm, moving up his biceps, along his shoulder, encircling his neck as she pulled him closer, and opened her mouth wider, moving suddenly faster, hungry, her tongue, slick, warm, mating, warring with his.

CHAPTER 14

Meg drowned into his kiss, into the rough sensation of Blake's stubble against her cheek, into the past, and present, and future, and nothing, drawing him closer, deeper. His body was hard, warm. His scent, his taste, filled her with a rush of the familiar and too long forgotten. It was a feeling so blinding and so right, like sliding into a shoe of perfect fit, into soul-warming comfort. His splayed hand slid firmly down her back as his lips forced her mouth open wider and his tongue sought hers. Something imploded deep inside her, cracking open a sweet, thick heat—a hunger that surged fierce up into her chest, firing her blood with driving need. A need to have him, all of him. Completely. She opened her mouth wider, her breath coming faster, faster, her nipples tightening and aching, tingling with desire to be touched, her consciousness spiraling into blackness. Down, down, down . . .

A banging sounded in a remote part of her brain. Then louder. He stilled his mouth on hers. His hand froze on her breast. She could feel the rapid beat of his heart in his chest. Knocking came again, against the driver's window.

She pulled back, shocked. At what had just happened. How she'd lost control. She stared at him, her breath coming ragged and raw. His eyes burned, dark and glittery, and desire etched the rugged planes of his features into hard shape. A kind of indefinable terror and confusion rose in her chest.

"Shit," Blake said as the banging sounded again, a dark shape looming behind the steamed-up glass.

"Who is it?"

"It's Geoff. Listen, Meg, I . . . " His eyes locked with hers. Words failed him. Her, too. Because, what now? What kind of threshold had she just crossed?

Blake swung open the truck door and stepped out. Air gushed in—wet, salty. Cold. Meg drew her coat close over her chest and got out of the truck, pain suddenly searing under her feet. She gasped, taking weight off her left foot, which hurt most, and she grabbed her tote from the front seat, shouldered it, then reached into the back for her bag of clothes. Wind was picking up. It whipped her hair around her face.

"What is it?" Blake said coolly to his brother. "Noah okay?"

"Fine. Still asleep. I saw the truck." Geoff came around the front. "Heya, Meg, long time." He gave her a big hug. He was lean and hard and smelled of booze as he kissed her cheek. He stepped back, his gaze flickering between Blake and Meg, a look on his face she couldn't read in the dark. The passage of years whispered in the mist around them. And he'd seen them kissing. This knowledge was now shared between the three of them and it put an uneasy feeling into Meg's chest.

It brought guilt.

It made her think of Jonah, of why she'd come here.

"Is everything okay?" Geoff said.

"It's fine," snapped Blake. "Just someone trying to spook her off."

Geoff glanced at his brother. "Because of the book?"

"Probably. Meg needs to get inside," Blake said abruptly, taking her arm.

"Wait—my file boxes. In the back."

"Here, I'll get them." Geoff reached for the back door.

"No." Blake's word was curt. The tone stopped Geoff dead in his tracks. A moment of tension pulsed between the two brothers. "Just . . . give us a bit of space," Blake said quietly as he opened the door himself, and reached in for the boxes. He piled one atop the other, hesitated, then said, "Where were you all night, before you heard about the shooting?"

"Told you. Couldn't sleep. Just taking a drive around town, a nostalgic look-see at all the old haunts."

"Did you go into Forest End?"

"I went everywhere."

Another moment of thick tension simmered between the brothers. Then Blake said, so quietly Meg almost missed it, "Shouldn't be driving over the limit."

"Says the saint to the sinner." Geoff stepped back with a slight stumble. He stared at Blake for a beat, then turned and headed off into the mist.

"Where's he going?" Meg said.

"Boathouse. He's staying down there. Come. Let's get you out of the cold."

"What was that all about?"

"I need to look at your foot," he said. "I can see you're feeling the pain now that the adrenaline is wearing off."

———

They entered through the office, and Blake led Meg into the back side of the marina that was the Sutton home. Coals still glowed in the hearth in the living room that looked out over the water. Lucy pushed herself up from her mat in front of the fire and wiggled a sleepy welcome. Blake set the file boxes in his study, and went directly over to stoke the embers, tossing in more logs, building flames to a crackling roar.

Meg crouched down to pet the Lab. Lucy licked her, and she hugged the dog, burying her face against fur. Assailed by a sudden sense of familiarity, of warmth, of hearth and home, she realized with a pang how much she missed having animals around. And it struck her just how exhausted she was, how much she wanted to give in, drop her guard, curl up and sleep somewhere safe. It seemed like she'd been awake for days, tight with tension ever since the *Evening Show* interview, since Jonah had broken up with her over a bottle of Burgundy from the slopes of the Saône River. Since she'd discovered her mother's earth-shattering journal and files. The attack tonight had come close to being the proverbial straw. That's why she'd been vulnerable to Blake. That's all it was. She just had to stay focused on why she'd come here, what she had to accomplish. On getting back to Seattle once it was all over.

But as she cuddled Lucy, Meg felt an eerie sense of being watched. She looked up.

Blake stood by the fire. He'd gone stone still, watching her, unblinking, iron poker in hand. An unreadable look in his eyes.

"Blake . . . what happened in the truck, it . . . it was a mistake."

He held her eyes in silence for a moment longer. "I don't think so, Meg." His voice was rough, thick. "Didn't feel like a mistake to me."

Meg swallowed at the rough intensity in his gaze.

"Come sit in this chair here by the fire," he said. "I'll get the first aid kit, bring you something warm to drink."

Meg allowed herself to slump back into a soft old wingback in front of the flames. Blake draped a blanket over her shoulders, and Lucy nuzzled her hand. Meg stroked her doggie head while the fire crackled. She shivered, unable to get warm. The cold seemed to have sunk down into her bones. But there was something more, deeper—the person she'd been in Seattle had begun to crack, and she wasn't sure what that meant, or if she even wanted to fight it.

Blake returned with a steaming glass mug and a red first aid bag.

"Hot toddy," he said, handing the mug to her. "Brandy, hot water, lemon, honey. Should do the trick." He smiled. It put dimples into his cheeks and a green light into his eyes. Her heart did a funny flip as she accepted the mug, sort of excited and terrified. She needed to try calling Jonah again, just to hear his voice. Orient herself.

Do you want to?

Or maybe not.

Because if Jonah knew she'd been attacked tonight, he'd be on a private plane and in Shelter Bay before morning, whether he'd broken off their engagement or not. All she would have proved to herself was that she couldn't do this without him.

Or was it because of Blake that she wasn't calling him? Was it because of what she'd felt when he'd kissed her? And still felt now?

Blake set an enamel bowl of hot water onto the stone ledge in front of the fireplace, and opened the kit containing cotton swabs, forceps, disinfectant, adhesive, and gauze bandages. Outside the wind was picking up, and she could hear the slap of small waves against the wooden dock as the tide surged into the bay. Sounds and rhythms of her youth, and they comforted her as she sipped and the brandy blossomed warmth through her chest.

Blake dragged an overstuffed ottoman in front of the fire and patted it. "Feet up."

It made her smile. She propped her feet up and he slid her boots off, then her socks. They were bloody. She took a deep gulp of her drink, put her head back, and just relaxed into the throb of pain rather than fight it. He pulled over a desk reading lamp, angled it, and set a pair of reading specs on the end of his nose.

She laughed. "How long have you been needing those?" she said.

He peered at her, mock stern, over the tops of his glasses. "Too long. Now, sit still."

He bathed her feet, dipping a cloth into water, wiping away blood, and wringing it out in the enamel basin. Blood pinked the water. In spite of the dull throb of pain, her eyelids grew heavy. "Gosh, how much brandy did you put in here?"

A half smile played over his mouth. His green eyes twinkled. "Enough." He squeezed the skin under her foot and she flinched. "You've got a fair-size shard of glass in here. It's going to sting a bit as I pull it out, ready?"

She nodded, and sucked air in sharply as he yanked it out. He plinked the splinter of glass into a bowl. "One or two more, okay?"

She felt blood flow as he removed pieces. He dabbed, wiped.

"How was it, being a medic?"

He grunted, concentrating. She studied him, seeing him anew in her relaxed and receptive state, without the energy to keep her walls up. Blake Sutton was a changed man. Matured. Stories in the lines of his face. The way he now had to wear glasses to see up close endeared him to her. Yet he still exuded an alpha physicality. It was his hallmark. It's how she always remembered him, even as a boy. He took up space unapologetically. He was a fighter—a gladiator. Kind. All about protecting tribe and family. His emotions were raw, you got what you saw, he said what he meant. No games. Whereas Jonah was sleek, sophisticated, cerebral. He played life like a game of chess. Calculating, second-guessing. Always wary and watchful. All about aesthetics. Meg liked to think in terms of mythology and archetypes when she crafted her books, and if she had to pin an archetype on Jonah, he'd definitely be the messiah. And part of her had always harbored a quiet suspicion that Jonah saw her as someone who needed to be saved.

Did you foresee what might happen to me if I came back here, Jonah? What chess move was this? Did you suspect that the facade I've been wearing for so many years in Seattle might start to crumble back in Shelter Bay? Do you really know me better than I know myself? Did you realize on some deep level that it really was over between us, or perhaps never truly was, and that at heart I'm a small-town, ocean girl who might want to write books in her cottage by the sea?

"What are you thinking?" he said without looking up.

"What makes you think I'm thinking anything?"

He looked up, angled his head, cocked a brow. "When is Meg Brogan ever *not* thinking about something?"

"I was wondering about Geoff. When did he arrive?"

"Yesterday."

"Ouch." She winced, reflexively jerking her foot back in pain. He held her steady, and dropped the forceps onto the plate. "Going to flush with disinfectant. It'll sting a bit."

And shit, it did. She scrunched her face, eyes watering as he rinsed the cuts with antiseptic. He repeated the process with the other foot, but that one had fewer wounds. He bound them both gently with gauze and then pulled on big, clean woolen socks he'd brought downstairs. The kind you make sock monkeys from and wear in construction boots. Warm and comforting.

"Hand?" he said, holding his palm out. She set her empty mug down, leaned forward, and placed her hand in his. He probed and prodded. "Just a few thin cuts—doesn't look like any glass left in here." He flushed out the tiny cuts, and wrapped a bandage around her left hand.

"You were lucky," he said, starting to pack up his stuff. "You could have hurt yourself badly on all that glass."

"Does he visit often, Geoff?"

"He came home once, when Dad died."

"And not for Allison's funeral?"

He shook his head.

"So why now?"

He snorted softly, came to his feet, enamel bowl in hand. "He's getting married."

"What—*who*?"

"I'm sure he'll want to tell you himself. I'm just going to clean up. Do you want to stay by the fire, or try to get some sleep in the guest room?"

"Fire," she said, leaning back and pulling the blanket over herself. She didn't relish the idea of being alone. It was warm down here. Comforting. He held her gaze a moment, then turned off the lamps apart from one. He busied himself cleaning up, and she felt herself drift on the distant sound of the waves. Wind was increasing, as it so often did over the bay just before sunrise, and a shutter banged somewhere. The buoys in the rafters outside began to thump gently against the wall.

"It'll be light soon," he said, startling her awake. "I'm going to shower, then make Noah's school lunch, get him up for breakfast, take him to school." He hesitated at the door. "You okay here?"

"Very," she whispered. Too comfy. Dangerously so.

He started to close the living room door behind him.

"Blake."

He stilled. Their eyes met.

"Thank you."

"Just promise me that you won't interview Ike alone, or do anything risky without me."

"Nothing risky."

He closed the door, leaving her with Lucy sleeping on the mat at the foot of the wingback. Exhausted, her brain thick with brandy, stress, nights without sleep, Meg slipped into deep slumber for the first time in weeks.

———

"Where did you go last night?"

Henry looked up from his mug of scalding coffee that he was sipping carefully at the table in the breakfast nook. His brain felt like cotton. LB's voice was hurting his head. But something inside him stilled when he saw the expression on her face. Her pupils were dilated. She looked crazed. Her hair wasn't right, either. Slowly he lowered his mug. "A client," he said. "For drinks. I told you."

"Where? Which bar? Whose house?"

He hesitated. Geoff had phoned him from a dive bar at the Blind Channel Motel just south of Whakami, a place that was dark and anonymous and old, home to sad, blue-collar drunks. He'd joined Geoff there against his better judgment, against his own damn will. He'd told himself it was just to discuss a solution to their Meg problem. And they had. And more.

"The Shelter Head Pub," he lied.

"You came home very late."

He said nothing. The fact that he was late, and drunk, had been obvious, and he'd rather not talk about it. It was a one-off. An old friend. And it was more than a hangover making him sick. It was what had begun to stir in him again. The way he felt false unto himself. Fragile. As if everything was a hair's breadth away from crumbling under him—his whole fucking, fake life.

"I'm talking to you, Henry."

He shoved up from the table, dumped his coffee in the sink. "I'm going to work early."

"Henry!" She wheeled her chair after him. He kept going, into his office to get his briefcase. She wheeled right in after him, her face reddening.

He turned, fury spearing hot into his chest. "For chrissakes, LB, give me some—" He stopped. Her face was wrong. Her silence, the tension around her was suddenly thick, dangerous.

"I saw."

"Saw what?"

"I saw what you have on your computer. I saw what you look at when you're in here late at night."

The blood drained from his head. He reached for the back of the chair.

"How . . . how *could* you, Henry? What *are* you!? I don't even know you. Is this who you are? I have no idea who in the hell I bloody married!"

———

Blake braced his hands on the bathroom basin and stared at his face in the mirror. The shower was boiling up steam, fogging his reflection. Meg's words, her very reason for having returned home, roiled through his mind.

I'm doing it for him. To win him back . . .

The irony—the sad, sick, twisted irony was not lost on him. In keeping Meg safe, in helping her to achieve her goal now, he was helping her win her fiancé back.

So why was he doing it? Was it self-interest? Hell yes. Because he saw a window to fight for a second chance. He'd felt it in her kiss—she *wanted* him. There *was* still something between them. And she was fighting it herself. She was flailing against the very walls she'd spent years erecting around herself to avoid hurt, and like a mythical maiden she was now locked up high in an impenetrable turret of her own making. And he was like the idiot knight at the base of the sheer stone walls, full of blustering bravado, thinking he could rescue her, and carry her off into the sunset. Offer her a life and ring that would suit her far better than the one she thought she wanted. Right here in Shelter Bay.

Conflict churned through him as steam obliterated his image in the mirror. It could never work. They had too much baggage. There was Noah. There was the information he'd kept from her and the cops all those years ago—it could cost him this fragile, newfound connection with Meg.

Shit. He could argue this every which way from Sunday, but no matter how he sliced it, there were big secrets in this town. Someone had attacked her house. Meg could be in danger. They all needed answers. He couldn't *not* help. And yeah, at the same time he was gunning to win her back now. His goal was to see her remove that ring from her finger of her own accord. That was also a game he couldn't *not* play. Meg was in his blood like the winds and the tide. And fate had brought both him and her, even Geoff, back full circle, to this marina, to this point in time. Surely for a reason? Surely for a second chance. And the trick would be to do it right this time. Yes, he could lose.

But, he *could* win.

He stepped into the steaming shower and let it scald his skin as he foamed up his hair and scrubbed his body.

As he was drying himself, he heard a knock on the door.

"Dad?"

He snagged a towel from the rack, hooked it around his waist, opened the door. Noah stood there in his PJs. His son's face was tight, hands balled at his sides. Lucy stood behind him, wagging her tail. Blake's heart dropped at the sight of the dog. He'd closed Lucy into the living room with Meg. If Lucy was out, it meant Noah had been in.

"Hey, champ. Good sleep?"

"Where's Uncle Geoff?" Noah demanded, unshed tears shining in his eyes. "*He* was supposed to be sleeping by the fire, not *her*. What's *she* doing downstairs? You promised!"

Noah's words walloped through Blake. His son was supposed to be his top priority right now, and he had promised him they wouldn't see Meg. Could he walk this tightrope? Balance both Meg and Noah? Did he honestly have any choice right now?

"Come here." Blake led Noah into his room. He sat on the edge of his bed in his towel, took his son's shoulders.

"I need to share something with you, Noah. But first I need to ask you a question."

His son eyed him, leery.

"If someone was in bad trouble, like, serious danger, would you help keep them safe, even if it meant making some sacrifices?"

Silence hung for a beat. He nodded.

"Even if it meant you didn't like that person very much?"

Noah hesitated, his gaze flickering to the door.

"Because that's what's happening here. Some really bad guys drove past Meg's house late last night and shot out all the windows with a hunting rifle. Now, you're the first to hear about this. It will probably be on the radio, and in the *Shelter Bay Chronicle*, and you could hear about it at school." Blake wavered, but opted to hold nothing back. The more honest and open he was with Noah, the more he gave his son some ownership of this thing, and the more Noah might buy in. Hide anything from him, and his kid was going to find out, especially in a small town like this. Look at what had already happened with Peggy Millar's comment to her husband over their dinner table one night—what was supposed to have been private had found its way into the school yard and hurt his boy.

"The bad guys also painted nasty words on her walls in an attempt to scare her out of town. And they painted those words in some kind of blood. Animal probably, but Chief Deputy Dave

Kovacs and his guys are figuring that out, and they *will* find out who those bad guys are, and punish them."

Noah's pupils darkened with interest. "Blood!?"

Blake nodded.

"Why?"

"Because she wants to write that story about her sister's murder all those years ago. And it looks like some people in town really, really don't want that to happen."

"Is she in *danger*?"

"She could be, Noah. That's why your uncle Geoff told me about the gunfire—he heard about it when he was out late last night. And that's why we brought Meg here, to the marina, where it's safe."

"*Is* it safe? Can't the bad guys come here?"

"We can make it safe. The fact that she's not alone will help. I don't think these bad guys have a whole lotta balls anyway, trying to scare a woman alone like that, and then running off into the dark."

"Wow," he said. "That's . . . cool."

Relief punched through Blake and he smiled.

"But what about the police?" Noah said, frowning. "Why don't they guard her in her *own* house?"

Blake cleared his throat. "It's a crime scene for a bit, until they've checked it all out. And the windows are all shot out, so it's cold, and it can't be locked. And the broken glass has to be cleaned out, and the blood washed off the walls. It needs more paint again. It could be a few days before that house is habitable again."

He looked uncertain.

"So—" Blake slapped his knees. "You okay if she stays in the spare room for a bit?"

Noah looked down at his bare feet. "I suppose." He glanced up slowly, met his dad's eyes. Blake ruffled his boy's hair.

"Thank you, bud. I love you, you know that?"

Noah lunged forward and threw his skinny little arms tight around Blake's neck. Emotion burned into Blake's eyes. He kissed Noah's hair and was again reminded how it smelled like sunshine. "Now, how about some breakfast? You go get changed, and I'll rustle up something downstairs. Eggs? Bacon?"

"Waffles!"

"You got it, bud. See you in five, downstairs."

Noah scuttled off, Lucy in tow.

Blake exhaled, dragged his hands over his damp hair. He was one hundred percent in with both feet now. Hell alone knew how this was going to play out. He dressed in jeans and a T-shirt, opened the small safe in the back of his bedroom closet, and removed his Glock 19 and a fifteen-round magazine. Inserting the magazine, he pulled the slide back, chambering a round. He hesitated, then took a spare magazine from the safe for good measure. From his drawer he removed a holster, which he threaded onto his leather belt, positioning the holster at the small of his back. He socked his pistol into the holster, and the spare ammunition into the adjacent pouch, before snagging a button-down shirt from his shelves, and punching his arms into the sleeves. He covered the holster with his shirt, and headed down to make waffles, his mind going back to the day he'd saved her life the first time. He'd do it again in a heartbeat, although he hoped it would not come down to needing a gun.

THE STRANGER AMONG US

By Meg Brogan

BLAKE

Black and oily is the sea, pocked with driving rain and veined with white foam. The closer Blake gets to the point, the more it heaves and seethes. Surf crashes against the man-made reef in a thunderous roar. He slows his little craft, waiting for a swell to crest, then he angles his prow and gooses the engine, riding the wave fast to a small wedge of sand between rocks. The wave breaks and boils around him. Water and foam fill his boat. But he keeps the engine gunning as long as he can before it floods and chokes, riding the angry froth. The lighthouse beam pans round, illuminating his path for a moment with stark white light. Rocks glisten black and surreal on either side of the sand. He hits the beach hard, and is tossed forward and flat onto his stomach, into the sloshing water at the bottom of his boat. He scrabbles quickly to his feet, boots squelching in water as he jumps out and strains to drag his boat up the beach, but the wave sucks back, and sucks hard, and his craft is weighted with water. It's too heavy. He lets it go, and the sea grabs it away with gleeful greed. He scrambles up the sand beyond its reach in his heavy gear, breath rasping in his chest, rain plastering hair to his head. He staggers up into a wild run, his small headlight poking a faint beam into the storm as he aims for the spot where he believes Meg might go to hide if she's in trouble. Given the news about Sherry, something awful must have happened.

"Meg!" he screams into the wind. It snatches his words, tosses them away. The tide is still pushing in, coming higher. Rain lashes at his face. "Meg!"

The lighthouse beam sweeps across the spit, high, refracting in cloud. He sees something. Down in the waves in a tiny cove. Something white that catches the light—shining fish-belly white. He freezes. A wave surges and the thing lolls like a dead seal. Except he knows—he knows with every fiber of his being. As much as he wants to find her, his mind recoils at this. No. Not like this. No, no, no.

The wind whines through rock formations as he nears. The foghorn answers. Blake breaks into a staggering run, down into the cove. He trips, smashes down, scrabbles back onto his feet. He drops down the twisty little path, and stumbles onto sand. He reaches the water and falls to his knees. "Meg?"

He rolls her body over. And his heart clean stops. Her clothes are torn, a breast exposed. White as a lily. Her face is alabaster, lips blue. A black, bloodless gash mars her brow. Her long hair is tangled with seaweed. A tiny crab scuttles over her face. Oh my God . . . Meg . . . Shit . . . Meg.

Focus.

He hooks his hands under her armpits, drags her limp body up the beach, sets her down gently on her back. He drops to his knees, angles her head back like he's been taught in first aid class. He opens her mouth and scoops around with his fingers, removing debris. His mind is telling him it's hopeless; his heart will not allow him to stop. A terrible kind of raw fear clutches and claws up in his chest, but he performs CPR. He keeps at it, counting the compressions, then touching his lips to her cold and life-less ones. More compressions. More breath. More compressions. More breath. And suddenly her body stiffens. Her back arcs violently and she gags.

A hatchet of hope strikes through his heart. Quickly he moves her head sideways, and she vomits a foaming slime. And again, and again, coughing, choking, convulsing. He gathers her upper body into his arms, tears streaming down his face. "Help! Oh, God. Somebody help! I found her! *Help!*"

But his words are snatched away. Blake's mind races. He shrugs out of his jacket, and wraps it around her. He shucks off his shirt, and balls it for a pillow. She's unresponsive to his actions. But she's breathing. She's alive.

Blake fumbles to open his kit belt. He frees the air horn, holds it high. He releases three short blasts, three long, three short. Waits a beat. Three short, three long, three short. Dot-dot-dot, dash-dash-dash, dot-dot-dot. SOS. The sailor's universal distress call. Then he unsheathes his radio, finds the channel he knows his dad and the searchers are using, keys the button. "Mayday. Mayday. Mayday. Anybody copy? It's Blake Sutton. Mayday. Mayday." Heart thumping, he releases the key, waits. Nothing. He keys again. "Mayday! Help! Anybody copy?"

He waits.

A crackle, then a voice. "This is Search Team Four. Copy."

Tears of relief flood him. With a shaking voice he replies, "Search Team Four, this is Blake Sutton. I found Meg Brogan. I found Meg." His voice chokes. "She's alive. Need help. Need medevac, stat. Do you copy?"

"Copy, Blake, what's your location?"

He gives it, then drops to his knees, cradling Meg's head, making sure she's breathing. "Hang in there, Meggie. Please. Please hang in. Help is coming."

And that's when he sees it. The sack. Up on the rocks.

CHAPTER 15

Drawn by the promise of coffee and a sweet pastry smell, Meg stepped into the kitchen. Noah sat on a stool at the counter eating a pile of syrup-soaked waffles. Blake was packing a school lunch. He glanced up sharply, and Meg saw his sudden worry at her appearance. She felt keenly that she was invading their space.

"Morning," she said to Noah, coming closer.

"Hi. I'm sorry about your house."

"Thank you." She shot a questioning glance at Blake. He looked good. Freshly showered. Shaved. Bronzed. The memory of his touch, his taste, surged unbidden into the warm kitchen. She felt her cheeks heat and she didn't want to think about it.

"I'm taking Noah to school," he said. "Geoff is still asleep in the cabin, but I can get him to come up to the house and stay here while you get some more sleep." He set a mug of steaming coffee on the counter in front of her.

"No. I mean, thank you, but I need to go fetch my camper and truck." She couldn't stay in this house with this boy and his dad. It was plain as day in this kitchen. Not while they were struggling through Noah's issues over his mother—Meg still hadn't asked Blake properly about that incident at her house the other night. And she needed to work.

"I've got an interview with Ty Mack's lawyer in Chillmook at noon. Could you possibly give me a ride to my house, on your way back from dropping Noah off?"

He hesitated, his coffee mug in hand. "You're not going anywhere alone."

"I doubt I'm going to be in danger in broad daylight, Blake. Or in talking to Ty's retired legal counsel."

"We had a deal. Nothing risky on your own."

"Lee Albies is not risky. Do I have time for a quick shower before we leave?" Noah was munching away, observing them both as one might watch a tennis match.

Blake set his mug on the counter. "I'm coming with you to meet the lawyer."

"Look, I really—"

"I want my own answers. I want to hear myself what she says. And if you interview Ike Kovacs, I want to be there, too." His eyes were narrowed, his posture unyielding. "And until they catch the shooter. Or shooters. Or until you have someone else with you,"— he paused—"you stay here nights."

"I'm not letting those vandals win. I refuse to be the victim you accused me of being."

"Don't twist my words, Meg." His gaze flickered to Noah, and he hesitated for an instant. "I was the one who found you half dead on the point that day. If the person who did that to you, to Sherry, is still out there—"

"Fine," she said crisply. "Time for a shower?"

"Five, ten minutes tops. Noah, please will you show Meg where the guest room is." He met her eyes. "It has a small bathroom en suite. Let Noah know if you need anything."

Eager to have a role, Noah scrambled off the kitchen stool. "This way, Meg," he called from the base of the stairs, before clattering up.

"Don't forget to brush your teeth!" Blake called after Noah.

Meg showered in haste, amped on adrenaline. She was thankful she'd had the presence of mind to pack a proper change of clothing and clean underwear, and she dressed quickly in jeans, T-shirt, and sweater. She eased socks over her feet, still tender, but Blake had done a good job of extracting the glass. She rewound the white bandage around her left hand. No time to dry her hair. She made a quick job of trying to run a comb through the tangles, but heard Blake's diesel truck engine rumbling to life outside.

She hurried downstairs, found her jacket, grabbed her tote with her laptop, camera, recorder, and notebook, yanked on her boots, and pushed out the office door, little bells *chinkling* in her wake.

The air was salty fresh. Cold. Sun had yet to crest over the ridge but the sky was clear, the bay still as glass. A silver Jeep Wrangler was parked in one of the camper sites near the railing above the water. California plates. She guessed it to be Geoff's. Noah was already inside his dad's truck, seated in back with Lucy. Blake held open the passenger door for her.

"Your hair's wet."

"It'll dry in the cab," she said, climbing up into the seat. "*If* we put the heater on." She smiled. He stilled, held her gaze. And she was suddenly conscious of the intimacy they'd shared in this cab not so many hours ago. She closed the door.

He geared the truck and they started up the gravel driveway. Geoff appeared up at the top of the drive in runner's gear, and he jogged down to meet them.

"Uncle Geoff!" Noah yelled.

Blake slowed, wound down the window. Leaned his elbow out.

"Thought you were still sleeping."

Hands on hips, breathing hard, Geoff grinned, his eyes light. "Been for a run. Does wonders to clear the head." He bent down, peered in at Meg, then Noah. "You guys taking Noah to school?"

"Yup. Catch you later?" Something in Blake's voice caused Geoff's smile to fade. He gave a small salute and resumed his jog down the driveway. But as they were about to crest the top of the driveway, a sheriff's cruiser swung into their path, and came to an abrupt stop, barring their exit.

Blake hit the brakes. "What the—"

The cruiser doors swung open. Out unfolded Kovacs and the female deputy, Hoberman.

"Great," Blake muttered under his breath, winding down his window again. He kept the engine running.

"Dave, hey, we're going to be late for school, what's up? You find who did it?"

Kovacs looked beyond the truck and raised his hand. "Geoff Sutton! Whoa. Got a minute?"

Geoff stalled, turned, hesitated, and came slowly back up the driveway. Hoberman, however, made her way down toward the Wrangler. She reached the Jeep, looked inside the windows.

"It was bovine blood," Kovacs said, waiting for Geoff to reach them, his thumbs hooked into his duty belt.

"Cow?" Meg said, leaning forward in her seat to hear.

Kovacs's gaze remained fixed on Geoff. "Sutton," he said as Geoff reached them.

"Dave, hey." He smiled, but his eyes were flat. "You look just like your dad these days—all business."

"That your Jeep?" He jerked his chin at the Wrangler. "With the California plates?"

"Yeah, why?"

"Can you tell me where you were around four a.m. this morning?"

Geoff glanced at Blake. Noah sat wide-eyed, his hand going to rest on Lucy, as if for comfort.

"I was driving around town. Taking a look-see at the old haunts."

"At four a.m.?"

"Yes. Nice and quiet. Feeling introspective. Been a while since I've been back."

"And this introspection took you into the Forest End subdivision, into the back street along the woods?"

Geoff regarded Kovacs. A beat of silence hung. "What is this about?"

"A witness puts a silver Jeep with Cali plates on the street outside Meg Brogan's house around the time she heard gunfire."

All eyes were on Geoff.

"Were you on the street, Mr. Sutton?"

"I drove around to see the old Brogan house. Yes, I was on the street. Briefly."

"Why?"

Geoff caught Meg's eyes. Her pulse quickened.

"I told you," Geoff said slowly, his face darkening, his eyes narrowing. "It's been a long while since I've been home, and I couldn't sleep, and I wanted to see all the old haunts. I drove all over town, not just to Forest End. I had the radio on and when I got back to the marina, I heard the reports of gunfire in Forest Lane."

"And you assumed the shooting was at the Brogan house."

"No. They *said* it was at the Brogan house. It's been the talk of the town for attracting graffiti and vandals, the radio announcer said. Everyone knows it. I woke Blake and told him, and he asked me to watch Noah while he went to see."

Kovacs eyed him. "Mr. Sutton, do you own a .22 rifle with laser scope?"

Blake swung open his door, and dropped down out of his truck. "Okay, Dave, you've overstepped here. I need you to move your vehicle, so I can get my son to school—"

"Yes, I do," Geoff said.

Blake spun to face his brother. "What?"

"The one Dad gave me—hunting rifle. A .22 with infrared sight."

"You brought it with you?" Kovacs said.

Meg's pulse beat faster. "What's happening?" Noah said, his voice rising. She reached in back, placed her hand on his knee. "It's okay. Dave Kovacs is just doing his job." The bastard. He was messing with them. There was no way Geoff had shot up her house and painted it with cow blood. Was there? Mistrust unfurled slowly in her belly. "Stay in here, Noah." She got out of the truck, marched around to where the men stood.

"I often take the rifle with me when I travel," Geoff said.

"You like to hunt when you travel?"

"Yes, I like to hunt. I like to eat clean, wild food. I'm not one for factory-farmed crap. How about you, Deputy? You hunt your meat, or do you just hunt lowlife humans?"

Blake clamped his arm on Geoff's, steadying him.

"Can I see the gun?" Kovacs said.

Geoff marched down to his truck where Hoberman stood. Meg and Blake hurried after them. Geoff fished in his pocket for keys, opened the back of his vehicle. He froze. What looked like a metal toolbox in the back had been forcibly wrenched open. Geoff lifted the lid. "It's gone," he whispered. "It's all gone."

He turned to Kovacs and Hoberman. "It's been stolen. The rifle and fly rods were in here. Someone's taken everything."

Meg swallowed, glanced at Blake. His face was tight.

Kovacs stepped forward. "I'd like you to come down to the station with me, Mr. Sutton."

"What for? I didn't do anything. This is ridiculous. Why on earth would I want to take potshots at Meg's house?"

Kovacs motioned to Hoberman. She stepped aside to place a call.

"We need to take in your vehicle, sir."

"Surely you need a warrant for that," Meg said.

"We're getting one. Mr. Sutton, can you come this way, please."

"Are you arresting me?"

"We'd prefer it if you came voluntarily, just to answer a few questions and to let us take some prints. For elimination purposes."

"Geoff, you don't have to," Meg said. "They need a—"

"It's fine." He held his palms up. "It's fine. I'll go. I have nothing to hide."

Kovacs motioned to Hoberman, who killed her call, presumably made to secure a warrant. She joined Kovacs. "Take him up," he said quietly.

"This way, please, sir." Hoberman touched Geoff's arm and led him up to the waiting cruiser. She opened the back door, and placed her hand on the back of Geoff's head, folding him in.

"Dad!" Noah yelled out of the window he'd wound down. "Uncle Geoff—where are they taking Uncle Geoff?"

"It's okay, Noah," Blake called, making his way back to the truck. "Geoff's just going to help the police sort out some confusion. It's going to be fine."

Meg made to join them, but Kovacs held her back, placing his hand on her forearm. She glared at him, then his hand. Slowly, he removed it.

"What was in those file boxes on the table last night?" he said. She glowered at him.

"Look, you're reading me wrong, Megan. I want answers to this thing, too, now. And I want them fast."

"Because otherwise it will mess with your campaign?"

"Like I said, don't get me wrong. I'm a cop. I'm a good cop. Something is off here. If it ties back to Sherry's case, I want to know about it."

"You'd reopen the case?"

Something flickered through his eyes, but they remained mostly hidden under the brim of his Stetson. "You're implying there's reason to reopen it?"

She swallowed. "I'm saying things might not be what they seemed."

"Because of what was in those files."

She said nothing.

"If there's something in there that—"

She took a step closer to him. "I'll tell you what," she said quietly, her eyes locked on his. "You get me an interview, on the record, with your father, and you can sit in and hear exactly what is in those files."

His mouth firmed into a grim line. She turned and marched back to the truck, climbed in, her heart thumping.

———

Noah got out of the truck, shouldered his backpack, and made for the school entrance. Meg watched him. He walked slowly. He walked alone. Others running and laughing around him. Small for his age. Delicate and pale against some of the other wild-haired boys who bounced around like big and boisterous puppies.

"What's going on with Geoff?" she said quietly to Blake, now that Noah was out of the truck.

"I'm not sure."

She glanced at him. "Why was he out last night?"

"You heard as much as I did—he's got his own dragons to slay here, Meg."

"Why now?"

The heat of irritation darted through his eyes. "I told you—he's getting married. He wanted to deliver the news in person. While he's here he's dealing with his own past."

"I feel like there's something you're not telling me."

He caught her eyes. "Nothing that isn't personal between me

and Geoff." He reached down, put the truck in gear. An uneasy feeling sank into her stomach. Blake erected subtle walls when it came to his brother. It made her realize just how much she wanted to trust him. Wholly. It worried her that she didn't. What ate even deeper was Geoff. It was strange seeing him again. It wasn't that she didn't like him—she'd always been fond of Geoff. But something felt off in her gut when she met his eyes, and she couldn't quite articulate it.

Blake pulled out of the school lot. Kids on foot and on bikes and skateboards were flooding down the sidewalks toward the school. They looked like colorful jelly beans in their winter jackets. One bounced a basketball. Meg's mind went back to Noah, walking alone. With the image came an acute memory of herself in high school and how she'd felt the day she'd finally returned after her sister's death. A teen with a murderer-father in prison. She'd felt fragile, unreal, like a thin specter of the kid she'd been before Sherry was killed. As if people could see right through her to the other side.

"You're having a rough time with Noah," she said.

He snorted.

She turned in her seat. "You want to tell me about the other night?"

"Not really."

His comment rankled. "You need to be careful with him," she said crisply.

His eyes flared to hers. "Like I don't *know* that?"

"Look, clearly this is personal for you, but I don't want to be part of the problem. Perhaps it's better if I—"

"What, Meg, if you what? Noah is more upset about his uncle being hauled off by the cops than he is with you being in the house right now. Until Kovacs arrests those guys, or until you get some . . . bodyguard to look after you, I'm it, okay? That's just the way it's going to be."

Her jaw tensed. Her blood pressure rose. She held her mouth, watched a mother pushing a baby in a stroller. The mother was yelling after two girls, sisters, she guessed, who were wheeling down the road ahead of her on bikes. Jonah's words from that day in the corn maze rustled through her mind.

Are you happy, Meg . . .

"You know when I was happy?" she said, staring at the sisters. "When I was Noah's age. I was happy at this same elementary school. I was happy in my own skin—when I was nine, ten, eleven, maybe even when I was twelve. I had the innocence of a child, yet I was old enough to take the boat out myself, ride my bike anywhere I wanted in town, not lock it up. I was free. Before the hormones kicked in, and all the girl-clique nastiness. And the inconvenient dawning that you're not pretty enough. Or popular enough. And with that awareness comes the self-restriction, self-consciousness. Self-hatred."

"You were always beautiful," he snapped. "That's just crap."

"But it's *real* crap. It's the stuff of bullying crap. It's the kind of crap that causes kids to kill themselves, be shamed on the Internet."

He glanced sharply at her. "What are you saying? Is this about Noah?"

"Kids should be happy, Blake."

He stared at her, almost crossing the center line before his attention shot back to the road and he corrected the truck.

"If I'm going to stay in your house you need to tell what was behind that bombshell Noah dropped the night we were having pizza. Tell me about Allison," she said.

He moistened his lips, took the turn that led to her subdivision a little too aggressively, hands tight on the wheel.

"Fine. What Noah said was true, if framed a little harshly. It was rebound sex with Allison. She got pregnant after what we both thought would be a one-night stand. Doesn't mean I don't love him." He took a deep breath. Exhaled.

"So that's why you married, because Noah was on the way?"

"I came back to see my dad for Christmas, during a stint between tours, after Iraq, and I guess I was looking for something I couldn't find once I got home. I missed what we had, Meg. You were gone. The place felt hollow. I was struggling. I ended up morose at the High Dive, that old bar down in Chillmook. Allison and some of her friends were there. We all got drunk. She'd just come off a nasty relationship and we commiserated. We ended up together that night, and the next I knew, our boy was on the way. So yeah, we decided to tie the knot for the kid. I stayed with the army, and she stayed here in Shelter Bay. She moved in with my dad at the marina. She and Bull kind of split the house in two."

"She didn't want to go live with you on base, or off?"

"No. She was not interested in the military-wife life. She hated the idea of living somewhere away from the sea and her family while I was deployed. Besides, I think Allison was relieved to have me gone for long tours, quite honestly. She had my name; Noah had my name. And I think she was seeing someone else very discreetly. She pretty much took over the running of the marina, and truly enjoyed it. Bull, of course, *loved* it, loved her. She cooked his meals. I didn't feel as though I was abandoning her. She was better off here than on some anonymous base. Noah had his granddad. And I convinced myself that I was doing something noble, serving our country. War. Medic. Helping soldiers hurt in battle. Brutal shit—but it was concrete. Guys got blown to bits and were bleeding out, and I could fix them enough to keep them breathing, to fly them out. Get them to hospitals, home. I could see, *feel*, that I made a difference."

"And it continued like that, until Bull died?"

He nodded. "Then came Allison's diagnosis. It was fast." His voice hitched. He swallowed, turned down her road. "I quit the army, came home to get to know my son. To try and make a family

with him." A soft snort. "Never thought I'd be a single dad raising a
son at the old marina." He was quiet for a long pause. "Funny how
history repeats itself. How it lies in wait. No matter how you try to
outfox it." He cast her a look. And the subtext hung: Now she, too,
was back here. Digging up the past and all the raw feelings and
complications associated with it.

"Oh shit," he said as they neared her house. "Cops are still here."

—

"It's not unusual for men to look at porn, LB."

"*That's* not porn." She wagged her hand at his computer, two
hot spots turning violently red on her cheekbones, her eyes shining bright and wild. "That's . . . sick. How *could* you? You're sick,
you know that? You're disgusting, a deviant. I can't believe that I
let you touch me."

"You don't."

"Oh, oh, so *that's* your excuse? Is *that* your justification? You
can't have sex with your poor paraplegic wife who can't get turned
on, so you must resort to that filth? Is this who you really are?"

His pulse thudded against his eardrums. A buzzing was starting in his head. Perspiration prickled his skin. He needed to get
out. Get away. He needed to get the hell away. He couldn't. He
couldn't run. He had nowhere to turn. Prisoner. Trapped.

"Is that why you married me, Henry? I'm some sort of place-
holder? A cover? Is that where you went the other night—to indulge
your sick inclinations? Those are *boys* in those photos and videos
on your computer. How old are they? Eleven? Twelve? What you've
got on there is criminal."

He took an abrupt step toward her. She cringed back into her
chair, suddenly silent and wide-eyed in shock. Scared.

"And you," he said, his voice low, very quiet. "Why did *you* marry *me*, LB? Because of my apparent low sex drive? Because I never *bothered* you with my needs? Because I was *safe*? Because, believe me, no other man was going to waste his virility, his youth, on someone like you, some needy woman with a host of weird insecurities, with a whacked-out spinster sister who hovers over you like some guilt-ridden raven because she happened to be driving drunk all those years ago and caused the wreck that put you in that chair, and now I have to tolerate her in my own house. She's always damn here, lurking and snooping about. I can't stand it!"

Blood drained from her face. Her knuckles whitened as her fingers clawed the armrests of her chair. She began to shake.

"You want that baby?" he said, eyes lancing hers. "Then you shut your mouth, understand? You don't tell a soul what you saw. Or you know as well as I do that Holly and her family will renege on their adoption deal."

She wheeled her chair closer to him, her eyes crazed. "No. Let *me* tell you what's going to happen, Henry. I'll keep quiet, and we'll get baby Joy. And then, when she's a little older, you will agree to a divorce, and you will get the hell out of our lives."

He stared at her, his meek Lori-Beth, all iron-willed in her desperation. "And how are you going to raise a child on your own?"

"I have Sally. You will pay child support."

"Get out of my office." He locked the door behind her. He paced. It was falling apart. It was all finally falling apart. And it could all be traced back to that day—that's when it all went wrong. Meg Brogan should never have come back. She was picking at the delicate threads that had bound into a tight and solid web over the years, and she was unraveling their lives, one by one. He had to do something. A half plan began to form in his mind.

He deleted all the files LB had found on his computer. He'd need to get rid of this system to be sure, but for now it was the best he could do. He set his briefcase on his desk, opened it, and then took his gun cabinet keys from the top left drawer of his desk. He went to his gun cabinet to get his pistol.

Shock washed through him—his cabinet was unlocked. He never left it unlocked. He flung open the doors, and his mouth turned dry.

His .22 hunting rifle and scope were missing.

———

Blake pulled up behind the cop cruiser parked on the street. Meg felt color drain from her face as she saw the blood-painted words in daylight.

Go Home Bitch. Fuck off, Bitch. Killer's daughter!! White trash. Gonna kill you, Bitch.

The blood leaking down her walls was stark, even more visceral in the bright light of day. Crime scene tape across her gate billowed slightly in a fresh breeze.

She grabbed her tote, flung open the truck door, dropped down to the road, and marched up to the cruiser parked in front, her hair drying into wild spirals and lifting in the wind.

A male deputy got out of the cruiser. "Ma'am, s'cuse me, you can't go in there."

"This is my house. I need to fix up this damage, repair the windows before the next storm front, or at least get the holes boarded up. When can I get back in?"

"I'm sorry, I can't say. We're not done yet with the scene, ma'am." His eyes were unreadable behind reflective shades. Blake came up to join them. He touched Meg's elbow, bringing her down.

"All we need is the truck and camper, okay?"

The deputy hesitated.

"It's not part of the scene," Meg snapped. "Kovacs was willing to let me take it last night."

"Hold on one second." The deputy got into his cruiser, made a call. When he got back out, he said, "You're clear to take the rig."

"Well, thank you. If you could remove the tape over the gate?" Meg said curtly, digging into her tote for her truck keys as she marched toward the gate. But as she reached it, her phone buzzed. She fumbled for it. "Meg Brogan."

"It's Dave Kovacs. You have thirty minutes?"

"Excuse me?"

"My father. He'll be ready for you in thirty minutes. He'll talk on the record." He gave the address for a house in Chillmook. "I'll be waiting outside."

"What about Geoff—what's happening with him?"

The call went dead.

Her gaze shot to Blake. "Ike Kovacs—he'll see me in half an hour." She fiddled for keys.

"What are you doing?"

"I'm going to see Ike—"

"We. *We* are going to see Ike. You're not doing this without me. Come. I'll drive."

"My camper."

He hesitated. "Okay, we'll back it out of the drive, park it on the street. We can pick it up on the way back, when we fetch Noah from school."

"I have an appointment at noon with Lee Albies, also in Chill-mook."

"We'll have time."

She wavered. She was being sucked into an undertow.

"Meg, we had a deal."

CHAPTER 16

Meg set her recorder on the coffee table, in the center. Ike Kovacs eyed it. Ruddy faced and corpulent under a shock of white hair, he was crammed into an overstuffed sofa beside his wife, Phyllis. The sofa was covered in a cabbage rose print that made the retired sheriff look comical, and uncomfortable. Blake sat in a chair to Meg's right. Dave, in uniform, leaned against the wall, almost out of her line of sight, crossing his arms over his chest, as if physically declaring his contempt.

Outside, clouds boiled puce over the sea. Nice view. Nice retirement house. Ike and his wife were clearly sunned out and happily weathered from their recent bonefishing trip in Florida. But tension lay thick, almost hostile, in the pretty living room. It sliced Meg. This family had once been so close to hers.

"I'm not the enemy, you know," she'd told Ike earlier, as he'd reluctantly welcomed them into the house.

"You're making yourself one by digging this up," Ike had retaliated. "Wouldn't have had your house attacked otherwise."

Meg took a sip from the water glass that had been placed in front of her by Phyllis. The others had mugs of coffee that sat untouched. She cleared her throat, leaned forward, and pressed the record button. Heat seemed to fill the room instantly. "I'm just going to start at the beginning," she said. "No judgment. Just questions."

Ike shifted, looking as though he'd been strapped against his will into the floral couch.

Meg spoke for the recorder. "Sheriff Kovacs, is it customary for a sheriff, essentially an administrative position, to personally take the investigative lead on a murder case?"

Ike's eyes flashed to Dave, his cheeks reddening with indignation. Meg waited. Ike cleared his throat. "What is this about? What are you insinuating?"

"It's a question that has been asked, and will be asked again about the case."

"No, it's not common. I took the lead because I was a damn good friend of your father's. Your family was good upstanding folk," Ike said. "Things like that—they're not supposed to happen to folk like the Brogans. Not in Shelter Bay. Not in Chillmook County. It was an affront, an attack on Jack and Tara. On everything that we all stood for and believed in."

"So it was personal."

"Hell yes, it was personal."

"It got you fired up."

"Megan"—Phyllis leaned forward, her brow creasing in distress—"is this really necessary?"

Ike's hand shot up, quieting his wife. "I have nothing to hide." His gaze bored into Meg's. "She'll see that I did everything in my power to charge Ty Mack and have him put away. I deeply regret that I was not able to do it before your father took the law into his own hands, Megan. I tried."

She took another sip of water, feeling Blake's attention keenly. She'd asked him to remain silent during the interview, but she could see him fidgeting.

"You were all members of the same church."

"What's *that* got to do with anything?" Phyllis said, her voice going high.

Again, Ike's hand shot up to still her. "You know that we all went to the same church, Megan, but your father's view on justice, an eye for an eye, was his interpretation, not mine."

She met his gaze. "You also attended the Oregon state police academy with him."

"When he was twenty. I was two years older. We graduated together. He was hired on by the Portland police. I started as a rookie right here, in Chillmook County. Been here ever since."

"Why did my dad leave the Portland police?"

Ike cursed softly under his breath. "You can find that out for yourself—got nothing to do with me, or Sherry's case."

"But you do know why?"

"Hell yes."

"Because he was a hothead? Because he lost his temper and got violent with a suspect on more than one occasion?"

"Some people have their hearts in the right place, but are not suited to law enforcement."

Meg rubbed her brow, making notes as questions rose in her mind. She looked up. "My dad was also drinking pretty heavily during his Portland period."

Ike's face darkened. "And it's why Jack stopped drinking when he came here. He knew it triggered his temper. He moved to the coast and started fresh here. Before Sherry was born."

"So you knew all this about him."

"Where in the hell are you going with this?"

"Who else knew this about my dad?"

"I don't know. A couple of people, I suppose."

"So if someone was aware of this propensity in my father, and riled him up by telling him that Ty Mack would likely be acquitted if he was in fact charged, based on the evidence in hand, and then told him where Ty, the man who raped and strangled his daughter, was hiding out in a cabin—"

"Whoa! Enough right there." Dave pushed off the wall, looming between Meg and his dad. "We had a deal. The file boxes."

"I'm getting there."

"Not with this line of questioning you're not."

She held his glare. "Okay. Okay, I'll move on." She cleared her throat. "My mother secured interrogation transcripts, copies of the autopsy report, and crime scene details from Ty Mack's defense counsel, Lee Albies."

Ike and Dave stiffened. Dave seated himself slowly on the small chair to Meg's left.

"She stored these files in boxes in a wall safe behind the bookshelf. It was discovered when my aunt, Irene Brogan, set fire to our living room." Meg took another sip of water. "From the evidence in those reports, my mother came to believe that Ty Mack might have been innocent."

Phyllis's hand flew to her mouth and her gaze shot to her husband. Ike stared unblinking at Meg. Not a muscle in his body moved. He didn't seem surprised. Rather he seemed coiled, guarded, ready to attack.

"According to the report, there were several other sources of unidentified DNA found on scene—"

"It was a make-out spot," Ike interjected. "The unidentified DNA was found in discarded condoms. There were also beer cans and a spirit bottle with DNA. This evidence was incidental to our case."

"Yet one of those unidentified DNA profiles also matched hair found in Sherry's pubic area, and it came from a condom that bore trace evidence of Sherry's blood."

"That condom was found in a muddy pool that Sherry had bled into," said Ike. "We could not rule out the strong possibility of cross contamination"

"And the hair evidence?"

"Same. High probability of cross contamination. We had our guy. His semen was all over Sherry. Her skin was under his nails." He leaned forward, breathing heavily. "Look, I'll be the first to admit the scene was not adequately secured. Mistakes were made. We had members unfamiliar with murder scene protocol arrive first. There was confusion with the search-and-rescue volunteers tramping all over the place, and the rain and gale-force winds severely hampered our efforts. Three times the uniforms tried to erect cover. Three times the storm tore the tent away."

"Cross contamination," Meg said quietly. "Yet, the existence of other DNA, a condom with Sherry's trace on it, could suggest another perpetrator, no?"

He glowered at her.

"Which in turn would likely hamper securing a murder conviction in court for Ty Mack, wouldn't it? Because in the eyes of the jury there could have been grounds for reasonable doubt."

"Which is exactly why we didn't charge Tyson Mack right away. Which is why we were continuing our investigation."

"But Tyson Mack remained the prime suspect."

"The only one. We knew he did it."

She let that hang a moment, turned the page in her notebook, looked up. "So, no other suspects? No other possible motive? No other avenue of investigation was pursued?"

"I told you. Tyson Mack was our guy. His DNA was on Sherry. He admitted to rough intercourse. She had his skin under her nails. He had scratches on his back, consistent with the skin under her nails. You yourself saw her climbing onto the back of Tyson Mack's bike. Emma Williams, Sherry's best friend, said Sherry called her to say that she was going with Mack to the spit."

"What about the pregnancy?"

Ike's face darkened. The room fell silent. Nothing moved. Tension swelled thick between them.

"Sherry was several weeks pregnant. You never told my parents."

"Ike?" Phyllis said, eyes wide. "Is this true?"

"It would have hurt them, Megan," he said softly, but a vein was swelling purple on his temple. His breathing had quickened. "It would have served no purpose other than hurt. Your father had already killed Ty. It could also have cost him at trial, too, if the pregnancy had been made public."

"It would have hurt his case, yes, because it would have raised serious questions about Ty Mack's guilt. It would have put another unidentified suspect into the picture—one you never found, or investigated—"

"Right. I'm done here." Ike made to get up.

"One more question. My mother wrote in her journal that she was being followed, and that our house was being watched." Meg spoke quickly. She was losing Ike's cooperation. "She detailed several instances, including someone trying to break into her house, and a vehicle following her too closely, trying to run her off the road, and a vehicle watching the house from down the street. She called you to report it, didn't she?"

Ike glanced at his wife, who'd paled. "It wasn't an official report," he said.

"But she did phone you the night before she died. She told you she was scared." Meg turned her page, making as if she was consulting her notes. "What did you say to her? Oh, right." Meg looked up. "You told her that her medication—medication she apparently overdosed on the next day—was making her paranoid?"

Ike's face turned beet red. He lunged to his feet, knocking over his untouched coffee. "You—" He pointed at her face. "You get out of my house. Now."

"Dad." Dave grabbed his father's arm. "Relax. You're working yourself up. You gotta keep your heart rate down."

Phyllis scrambled for a cloth to start mopping up the spill, her neat hair bun coming undone, silver strands spilling over her eyes. "Is it true, Ike? Did Tara call you for help?" she said, wet cloth in hand. "Is it true, Meg?"

"It's what my mother wrote in her journal the night before she died." Meg got to her feet. Blake took her cue and rose as well. Meg could see the fire in his eyes, the tension in his muscles, and she loved him for restraining himself because she knew how tough it was for an impulsive man like Blake.

She picked up her recorder, the red record light still glowing, and said, "Is it possible, Ike, that my mother did *not* take her own life?"

He went dead still. Sweat beaded his brow. His face was a disturbing shade of purple now. "What . . . on earth . . . do you mean?"

"I think my mother might have been getting too close to Sherry's real killer. I think someone might have wanted to silence her. Did you not consider looking into that possibility after my mom's death, *especially* since she reported her concerns to you?"

"Murder?" Phyllis said, her voice tight. "You think someone *murdered* Tara?"

"Get. The. Fuck. Out. Of. My. House." Ike turned, stormed toward the door. But he stalled in the doorway, and spun around, breathing heavily. "You wanna blame someone for feeding your dad's temper, for winding him into killer mode? You go visit that public defender bitch. If anyone is to blame for any of this, it's her."

"Ike!" Phyllis snapped.

"I'm done. I'm done here." He swung the door open wide. "Get out."

———

"Why did you sit on the fact she was pregnant?" Dave said to his father as Meg and Blake went down to their vehicle. He watched them from the window.

"You heard me. I was trying to protect that family. And *this* is the thanks I get? What's it going to be now? In a book? For the whole damn nation to read?"

"It's not right," Phyllis said. "None of this is right. You should have told Tara and Jack right away."

"What's not right is her writing that book. Jack was in prison. Tara was a wreck, grieving her daughter, coming to terms with the brutal murder of her beautiful child, her husband about to stand trial for killing the rapist. What good would it have done anyone at that point? I knew Tara would be able to get her hands on that report when she was ready, and she did."

"And look at what happened—now she's dead."

"This is not my fault, Phyllis. None of this is my fault. I did my best by that family. And whether Sherry was pregnant or not, Tyson Mack was my man. He did it. I have not one question of doubt in my mind."

"*This* is why you should have let one of your detectives take the lead," Phyllis snapped. "And the least you could have done is given Tara some protection."

He poured a stiff whiskey, took a deep pull, sunk into his chair, and cursed.

"You shouldn't be drinking that."

"Let me die in peace, woman—if I'm going to kick the bucket I'd rather do it drunk."

Dave said, "Do you have any idea who the father of her baby was?"

He looked up at his boy and held his eyes for several beats. "No."

"And it wasn't Tommy's, or Ty Mack's?"

"No."

Dave's gaze locked on his father's. Silence, tension, swelled.

"Dave was riding on your long-standing reputation in this county, Ike, and now—"

"Still a damn fine legacy," Ike snapped.

"Perception," Dave said quietly. "Politics is all about perception. And the story will now be all about Meg and the 'botched Sherry Brogan case.'" He dug his fingers into his duty belt and stood there awhile, watching Meg taking photos of his parents' house. Electricity crackled quiet and deep in his veins. He wanted to win the top job. But Meg Brogan was like a dog with a bone. It didn't help that Blake Sutton had her back. His thoughts turned to Geoff.

Meg was right about one thing—this case was off. And he had to fix it. Or lose the election.

———

"You've pretty much got it all summed up right," Lee Albies said, pouring tea. "I joined the Chillmook Criminal Defense Consortium as a volunteer when I retired from my practice in Portland. I believed in Ty Mack. He was a convenient scapegoat for a sheriff with tunnel vision, hell-bent on seeing justice done at any cost in a case he was taking far too personally, and with no oversight."

She seated herself opposite Meg and Blake, picked up her china teacup and saucer. She was a tanned and slender woman in her late seventies. Short, spiky silver hair, big red-framed glasses. An African gray parrot paced on a stand behind her, repeating the phrase "Hello my pretty. Hello my pretty. And how is my pretty today."

Lee sipped her Darjeeling with care, and gave an appreciative sigh. "It's my hobby horse, I'm afraid. I have a vehement hatred for prejudice in law. And in Ty's case, it was class, economic prejudice. In my view Ike Kovacs had blinders on when it came to Ty Mack, the dark half-breed from the wrong side of the tracks, so to speak, raping the golden girl of Shelter Point. The town homecoming queen."

"What made you so certain that Ty would be acquitted in the event he was charged and stood trial?" Meg said, checking that the red light on her recorder was still lit.

"While I was prepping in the event that Ty might be charged, and that we might go to trial, I used the services of a private investigator. He dug up a witness who was prepared to testify that Tyson Mack's bike was indeed at the Forest Lane trailhead at the time he claimed to have dropped Sherry Brogan off."

"A *witness*?"

She lifted a plate of cookies, held it out to Meg. "Want one?"

"No, thanks. What witness?"

The plate of cookies was offered to Blake. He shook his head, eyes riveted on Lee Albies.

"Her name was Ethel McCray. She was blind. She's deceased now." Albies set the plate carefully on the table, and met Meg's eyes. "Of course, had we gone to trial the prosecution would have moved quickly to discredit her on the grounds that she *was* blind, and old, and possibly confused, but I planned to show a jury how Ethel McCray could identify make and model of vehicles simply by the sound of an idling engine, and she clearly heard Ty's one-of-a-kind cruiser. There were voices, too, a male and a female, but their words were drowned out by the sound of the engine, according to Ethel."

"Did Ike Kovacs know about Ethel McCray?"

Albies nodded. "He brought her in to identify Ty out of a lineup, by voice. Which of course she couldn't do because the engine was too loud and she hadn't heard him properly. Kovacs dismissed her as unreliable in terms of his investigation." She leaned forward. "Now here's the kicker. There was also a vagrant living in his car in the state park. His name was Milo Sinovich, a vet. He's also deceased now, but he told my PI that he saw a red VW van parked behind trees near the trail that led to this infamous make-out spot where Sherry Brogan was strangled. The van was parked there *after*

Tyson Mack had allegedly dropped Sherry off. And it was there during the period the attack might have taken place." Albies took another sip of her Darjeeling. "Estimated time of death, you see, fell within a time frame that could match Ty's version of events."

"Did this Sinovich talk to the cops?"

"No. The police never approached him. He didn't go in and volunteer the information, either. He was living under the radar, and we were unable to convince him to make a statement, and he vanished shortly after we spoke to him." She took another sip of tea. "However, our blind witness said that after the bike left—she heard it going down the street—another vehicle drew up to the path where she was walking her beagle. It slowed, engine idling. There were sounds of arguing, angry, hushed voices, male and female. A scuffle, and, get this, the sound of a *sliding* door slamming shut." She sat back with a smug smile, and Meg could imagine this woman in court, working up to her coup de grace with relish, pacing her breaks of silence to build tension.

"And, Ethel McCray said the engine that drew up to the path that day was that of a VW van. Older model."

Meg's gaze flickered between Blake and Lee Albies. "Is that even possible? To identify a vehicle make like that?"

"We did a few test runs. This woman was ninety-eight percent accurate with the more obvious variations in engine sounds— vans, VWs, different bikes, buses, different sizes of diesel trucks. She'd been blind most of her life, and was always walking near traffic. She had a son, who, when he was little, would guide her on walks to and from school, and because it was his passion, he'd name all the makes and models of vehicles they heard along the way. And, the thing is, those older-model VW van engines do have quite a distinctive sound. Even I can tell one."

"Why don't I know of this blind woman, if she lived down my street?"

"She didn't live in Shelter Point. She and her beagle were stay-ing with her sister for a few months before moving into an assisted living facility."

Meg ran through several more admin-type questions, then said, "How did you find my mother's state of mind?"

Lee Albies was silent for a moment, then said, "Tara Brogan was a woman very much filled with the passion of living, and seek-ing out justice, getting answers before the December trial date looming. I spoke often with her. We grew close in a way. If you're asking whether I believe Tara took her own life, the answer is no."

Once the interview and tea were over Lee walked them out to Blake's truck. The sky was growing low and gray.

"You're so like her, you know," she said to Meg as they reached the truck. "Not just in looks, but in movement, too. It's almost uncanny."

A strange sensation spiraled through Meg. "Thank you," she said to Lee. "For helping my mother. For talking to me." Her voice caught. "For saying I am like her. I never really knew her. I thought she was someone else entirely."

Lee smiled, and it crumpled her face into pleasant wrinkles. "Do come back, even if just for a social visit. I was terribly shocked by Tara's death. And I'd love to know how all this turns out."

"I will." Meg almost hugged the woman, but held back. She climbed into the truck wishing she had.

Blake started the engine. But before Meg closed the door, she said, "Why was Ty Mack in that cabin, way up the mountain in the woods?"

"It was my grandfather's cabin," Albies said. "I moved Ty in there. Fevers in town were running high. I feared pitchforks and a witch hunt. I told the police where he was, in the interests of their investigation, and to show that Ty had no intention of skipping town, and was willing to be cooperative. But I told them the location on the condition they did not reveal it for his own safety." She paused. Her eyes narrowed sharply, and Meg saw the old defense lawyer at work again. "Clearly that confidence was breached. It was a criminal act, to my mind. And I do believe, as Tara did, that this information was revealed to Jack with the worst of intention. Jack was loaded up like a cannon, and pointed in the direction of Tyson Mack."

"Who?" Meg said. "Who do you think could have done it?"

"I don't know. I hope you find him."

As she closed the door, Albies said, "Be careful, Meg."

———

Blake glanced at Meg as he drove. Her mouth was tight and she looked pale.

"You okay?" he said.

Meg nodded. Then said, "No. I'm not." She rubbed her face. "I'm having trouble with the fact that all this information might have saved my father. And my mother. They could both be alive today."

He placed his hand on her knee, squeezed gently.

She turned away from him, looking out the window, as if to corral her emotion.

"This kind of writing comes with confrontation, hard questions, dealing with people who are in pain, but when it's your own story, it takes a different kind of toll." She swore softly. "I should have pressed Ike harder."

"You really think Ike might have told your dad where Ty Mack was hiding? You think it was Ike who set him up?"

"But *why*? It doesn't fit. He was my dad's friend. He wanted to solve this thing for our family. It's why he took the lead on Sherry's case against his better instincts in the first place. He knew from their mutual past just how volatile my father could be, so I don't believe he'd have told him where Ty was." She closed her eyes, put her head back.

Blake stole another sideways glance. His chest crunched. She looked vulnerable, and her hair was an untidy mass of curls. But he loved the look. Far more than those sleek and sophisticated photos he'd been seeing of her. She looked more his Meg than Jonah's Meg. It gave him a small and smug punch of satisfaction.

"What can I do to help?"

She cocked one eye open, smiled slightly. "You're helping more than you can know. Just being there. Feels good to be part of a team."

"What made you go into this true crime business anyway? Because of Sherry?"

She snorted. "You sound like Jonah. Or Stamos Stathakis. I just like the genre, the promise of justice at the end, of real heroes who save the day. Closure. And the story structure. The bonus is these stories are real."

He said nothing.

"You don't buy it?"

He shrugged.

"You think I've been seeking closure my whole life, and this is some perverted way of doing it?"

He snorted. "You know me. I don't think. I just act." He grinned at her, and she laughed. And it warmed his soul to be able to put light into her eyes like that.

She turned to look out the window again, then shot abruptly up in her seat. "Blake, wait. Stop! Back up, quick."

"What is it?" He glanced into the rearview mirror, checking traffic, then slowed, pulled over.

"Back up to that signboard over there." She twisted around in her seat, pointing.

He reversed.

"There!" She gestured at a board that hosted several commercial signs pointing inland, to the Chillmook dairy farming area. "That second logo down—Braden's Cattle. That was the same logo on the black van I saw at the gas station the night I arrived. The van Tyson Mack's uncle, Mason, was driving. I didn't recognize him—but the woman at Millar's Gas said it was Mason Mack. The way he looked at me, he knew who I was, and he was damned hostile about it."

"Braden's Cattle is a small, independent slaughterhouse," he said. "Used to be part of Braden Farms, until the family started subdividing."

"You thinking what I'm thinking?" she said.

"Access to bovine blood."

"And motive," she said, her eyes on fire. "And he knew I was in town. Do we have time? Before Noah?"

"Hell yeah," he said, swinging the wheel hard to the right.

CHAPTER 17

They drove slowly up to the gates of Braden Cattle. The small writing along the bottom of the sign on the gate said, *Family Run. Integrity, Quality.*

Meg exchanged a glance with Blake.

"You sure you want to go in?" he said.

"If Mason Mack works here, I want to speak with him. That was definitely the logo on the van he was driving that night."

"Doesn't mean he vandalized your house, just because he works here."

"Neither does it mean he didn't. If you think about the words on my wall, it fits that they might have been written by someone allied with Ty Mack, or Ty's family. At the very least, I might find out where I can get a hold of Ty's father, Keevan."

"You want to interview Keevan?"

"If he'll talk."

They entered the gates. The place seemed deserted. Blake drove around the back. There were two vans parked in the lot behind the main building. "That's it." Meg nodded toward the vehicles. "It looked just like one of those vans."

Meg and Blake got out.

"Hello! Anyone here?" he called into the door of the building.

A woman in her early forties exited the barn on their left. She was carrying a pail. "Can I help you?" she said, using her gloved hand to hold back blonde hair that blew in the chill breeze. "I'm Debra Braden. We're closed for a few days because of water damage. Had a breakdown with the plumbing system."

"Meg Brogan." Meg held out her hand. The woman set her pail down, took off her gloves, and shook Meg's hand, a furrow forming on her brow.

"And this is Blake Sutton." He leaned forward, shook Debra's hand.

The woman looked at Meg. "You're . . . Sherry Brogan's sister. You're the one who's come back to write the story of her murder. I heard about it on the radio."

"It's not the only reason I'm back," Meg said, forcing a friendly smile. "Did you know my sister?"

"I knew of her. I didn't go to school in Shelter Bay. I went to Chillmook Secondary. But who didn't know of Sherry and Tommy? My cousin, Sally Braden, was in Sherry's class. She was really messed up by the news of the murder. I think everyone was. Such a shock."

A bolt of recognition shot through Meg. "You're Lori-Beth Braden's cousin."

"Well, she's Thibodeau now. But yes. Small towns and all that," Debra said with a genuine smile. "What brings you guys out here?"

"I was wondering if Mason Mack worked for you guys."

"Oh, right," she said as the connection dawned on her. "Mason. Yeah. Both him and his brother, Keevan. Been here about seven years in all now." She frowned again. "This to do with the story, with Ty?"

"It is. I was hoping to interview them."

Debra raised her brows, looking dubious. "They pretty much keep to themselves. They live on site. Keevan provides security with his dog at nights." She turned, pointed to a dirt track. "We've got two staff bungalows up that road into the woods along the back of the property over there."

"Mind if we take a drive up?" Blake said.

"Suit yourself. They're not always the most welcoming, but they get the job done."

The road curved up into dense forest and led into a small clearing that housed two cabins about fifty yards apart. There was an old beater of a Toyota propped up on blocks outside. Coveralls on a wash line swayed in the breeze. Empty beer bottles filled a rusting container outside one of the cabin doors. Smoke curled from one of the chimneys. There was no one in sight.

Meg and Blake alighted from the truck and walked slowly into the clearing between the two cabins.

"Let's try that one, with the smoke. Someone must be home there," Blake said.

They knocked on the door. No answer. "Hello!" Blake called. Nothing but wind hushing through the pines as the forest stirred. Dark clouds were rolling in off the sea, blackening the sky to the west. Meg could feel the temperature dropping as the front closed in.

They walked around the back of the cabin.

A dog lunged on a chain.

Meg gasped, and jumped. Blake's arm shot out, holding her back. The dog, a German shepherd–Doberman cross, started to bark, mouth frothing as it jerked and clacked against the chain.

Meg started to retreat, but Blake clamped his hand firmly on her arm. Her gaze shot to him. His face was tight. His eyes sparking a warning. "Don't move," he whispered.

A click sounded. Then an unmistakable *kachunk.*

"Shotgun," he whispered.

"Where?"

"Can't see. But someone has us in his sights." He scanned the shadows in the encroaching forest, then took her arm. "Just move slowly. We're going back to the truck."

"Hold it right there." The voice was rough, bass. It came from behind them. "Turn around, now. Nice and easy."

Slowly they turned. Mason Mack. A shotgun aimed at Meg's heart.

"It's okay, Mason," she said quickly, and hated the nerves in her voice. "I . . . I'd just like to ask you some questions."

"Get the fuck off my property. Now."

"I only want—"

"Your family killed our boy. You come back here again, I'll repay the fucking favor. You start writing a bunch of shit about Ty, I might do it anyway."

Blake's hand moved to his side, and it struck Meg that he might have a gun.

"Easy, Mack," Blake said. "We're leaving. Just let her leave."

But Meg stood her ground. "So you know that I'm writing a book?"

"Who doesn't?"

"You're too stubborn for your own good," Blake hissed quietly at her. "Don't look, but there's another weapon trained on us from those trees on our right. We're outgunned and outnumbered. I suggest a careful retreat."

"I was hoping to give Tyson Mack a fair shake," she called out. "I think he might have been innocent."

Hesitation showed in Mack's posture.

"Do you know where I could get hold of Keevan Mack? I'd like to talk with him."

"Right here." The voice came from the trees. Keevan stepped out of the shadows, black hair ruffling in the wind. Sinewy, tanned. He looked like Ty. Just older, weathered. He had a rifle trained on them.

"Shit," she whispered.

"Now, unless you get off this property, I'm setting this dog loose, here." Keevan stepped closer to the growling animal. The man's eyes were deep blue under his thatch of brow. His features were hard, uncompromising. His threat felt real. Meg shifted closer to Blake.

"Easy and slow," Blake whispered. "Just take my cue."

"Did you do it?" she yelled suddenly at Keevan. "Did you shoot out my house with that rifle in your hands there? Did you paint that stuff on my walls?" Her voice was pitched with fear and she felt a mounting rage. Her body was wire stiff, vibrating.

"Megan," he growled. "Use your brain, for chrissakes."

Keevan inched closer to the dog. Mason took a few steps closer to Meg and Blake. Meg's heart began to jackhammer. Sweat dampened her chest, pooled under her arms.

"I didn't touch your house," Keevan growled through his teeth. "Wouldn't go near there. Don't want anything to do with scum like you. You just get the hell out of my sight, or I might just hunt you down like an animal, like your father hunted my boy after your whore sister seduced him. You Brogans killed my son. He was innocent. Not a bad hair on that boy's head."

Meg raised her hands, palms out. "It's okay, Keevan. I . . . I want to hear you out. I do—"

He raised the barrel of his rifle and fired a crack into the air. She screamed and jumped. The sound unleashed a frenzied frothing and barking in the dog.

Keevan bent down, slipped a collar around the dog, unleashed the chain. It barreled toward them.

Fuck.

"Don't run, Meg! Stand your ground!" Blake unsheathed his pistol, aimed it at the oncoming dog.

———

Henry left the house in his cherry-red MINI Cooper with its snappy white racing stripes. He'd called work to say he'd be late. He felt dulled inside. His briefcase lay neatly on the passenger seat beside him. The pistol inside was loaded, the weapon cocked. He'd brought spare rounds. He should have gotten help all those years ago, maybe seen a psychologist or something. Maybe he could have had a half-normal life if he'd been able to seek therapy for what he'd gone through. Maybe he could blame his predilection for violent porn on the past, on what had happened to him. Or maybe he couldn't.

You're sick, you know that? You're disgusting, a deviant . . .

His hands fisted around the wheel. He was going to work—*act normal. Appear as if nothing is wrong, even if it's all falling down about your ears, even if it's all finally coming to an end.* Emotion punched hard through him. His eyes blurred as he reached the T-junction.

A police cruiser turned in front of him. It went down his street, in the direction of his home. His heart started to stammer, and fear wet his skin. He watched the cruiser in his rearview mirror, indecision swirling through his brain. He pulled a sharp U-turn and followed the cop car, staying a fair distance back. It couldn't be going to his house, could it? They couldn't be coming for him. Not yet. Surely? He had to know.

The cruiser slowed and turned into his driveway.

Shit.

Henry tapped his brakes and quickly pulled into a parking space higher up the street, tucking tightly in behind a big Dodge Caravan. He kept the engine running as he watched two sheriff's deputies alight from the cruiser and make their way to his front door.

Shitshitshit. Sweat pearled along his brow, leaked down the side of his brow.

He waited there, watching for almost twenty minutes. Then suddenly his front door swung open. Out came Sally. She had her hands behind her back, head bent forward, hair hiding her face. The two deputies led her to the cruiser. One opened the rear door, and the other held the back of Sally's head as he guided her into the sedan and shut the door.

It pulled off.

Henry stared, dumbfounded. What the hell?

———

The dog stopped within inches of them, eyes wild, saliva glistening on incisors, foam frothing at its jowls as it growled and barked. Every impulse in Blake's body screamed to flee.

"Don't look in its eyes," he ordered Meg. "Get behind me. Right behind me. Hold on to my waist. We're backing away, slow. Very, very slow."

They began to inch away. He prayed she wouldn't trip. She'd be dead in an instant, that dog on her throat. His only hope was that this was the animal that Debra Braden had mentioned they used as security. Which might mean it was trained. The shock collar Keevan had slipped onto the animal's neck before unchaining it fueled that hope. It might mean the Macks had control over it. His only other hope was that the Macks *would* stop the dog short of killing them.

The dog followed them, step for step, darting closer, snapping, circling, growing bolder as they retreated. Blake's mouth turned bone dry. His truck felt a million miles away. The Macks did nothing, just watched.

"Call him off!" Blake yelled.

The men laughed.

His raised voice, the exchange, served only to further incense the dog. It lunged and grabbed Blake's jean leg, tore at it, growling low in its throat. Blake stilled, fighting every molecule in himself. He knew if he kicked, struggled, it would escalate the attack. He'd served with military K9 teams. He knew what could go wrong if the victim tried to fight back. And he kept his Glock aimed at the animal. A last resort, he thought. A very last resort. But he'd do it, to save Meg.

"I'll kill it," he yelled, eyes fixed on the animal. "Call it off or I shoot." He fired a round into the ground. Dirt exploded with sound. The dog yelped, backed off, then redoubled its charge. Blake aimed his pistol, tightening his finger around the trigger.

Keevan stepped forward suddenly and gave a sharp whistle. The dog hesitated. Keevan whistled again, and yelled, "Steel! Down!"

The animal jerked as it was shocked, giving another small yelp. It lay down, panting, eyes wild.

"Bastards," Meg hissed over his shoulder. "Fucking bastards." He could feel her whole body trembling behind his.

"Keep backing away," he whispered. "Get into the truck. Slowly. No sudden movements. Open the door for me."

"What about you?"

"Do it."

Meg slowly backed away, then turned and made carefully for the truck. Blake stood his ground, weapon trained on the attack animal, the bile of hatred rising in his throat. What kind of men did this to a dog?

He heard the doors open, and he cast a careful glance over his shoulder. Meg was safely inside. Slowly, he started moving.

He was almost at the truck when Keevan Mack released the dog with a sharp command and it barreled for him, low along the ground.

Blake turned and ran, breath rasping in his chest. He reached the truck. Meg had clambered over into the driver's seat on the far side and started the engine. He dived for the passenger seat as the animal's jaw clamped onto his boot. He shook it off as she started to drive, the door open. She bombed down the dirt road as he pulled himself fully inside and closed the door. His body was wet with sweat.

"Thank God you had the keys inside," she snapped. Her cheeks were red with anger. Her body was shaking. "They have no right to keep an animal like that. I'm going to report them. Phone Kovacs," she said, digging in her pocket, handing him her phone. "Tell him the Macks did it. They shot out my house, vandalized it."

He stared at her. She was unbelievable. Adrenaline was slamming so hard through him he thought his chest was going to burst. He sat back, her phone in hand, and he started to laugh. She shot him a look, her expression puzzled. "What in the hell's so funny?"

He laughed harder, wiping his eyes, and the relief felt good. Her lips curved into a slow smile, then she laughed, too.

At the bottom of the road, once they'd exited the Braden property, he said, "Stop. Stop right here."

Her smile died, and she slowed, drawing over onto the road shoulder.

He grabbed her behind the neck, pulled her close, and kissed her hard. She stiffened in shock, then softened almost instantly and turned hungrily, furiously toward him, breathing hard as her hands peeled back his shirt, buttons popping as her lips forced open his mouth, her tongue entering, seeking his, her teeth scouring his lips. He slid his hand under her T-shirt, into her bra, groaning as he found her nipple tight and hard. He felt her hands going down his waist, unbuckling his jeans, sliding into his pants. Her palm, her fingers, were soft, warm, as they cupped his balls, started massaging his cock. He tilted his hips, giving her access as his brain swirled into heady oblivion. She angled her head, coming up higher in the driver's seat, pushing him back into the passenger seat.

He fumbled wildly to undo her belt buckle.

A loud honking stirred logic, slowly, thickly, back into Meg's brain. She paused, her lips pressed against Blake's, her breathing ragged, her skin hot. She glanced slowly up.

"Uh, Blake," she murmured against his mouth, "I think we're blocking someone's driveway." A woman in a white SUV laid on her horn, long and loud, gesticulating angrily with her free hand.

Meg scrambled awkwardly off him, pulling her shirt closed. "You drive," she said, voice hoarse, her brain reeling, a wild panic beginning to lick around the edges of her mind. She tried to maneuver her body over Blake's as he wriggled under her into the driver's seat. He zipped up his pants and she hurriedly fastened her belt buckle and pulled on her seat belt. She waved a "sorry" to the impatient woman, and groped for her phone that had fallen on the floor. Her lips felt raw, swollen. She was breathing hard.

She'd been so fired up, and so swept into his laughter. And when she'd felt his mouth against hers . . . this couldn't happen again.

She keyed her phone, put it to her ear.

He pulled back onto the road. The woman in the SUV spat dirt up with her tires and she hit the gas and honked again as she turned aggressively in the opposite direction. Meg's heart thudded.

"Reminds me of the time we stole Mrs. Hargreave's apples from her prize tree," he said.

She shot him a look. Be damned if he wasn't still grinning, those dimples deep in his cheeks. His eyes danced with light as he met her gaze.

"Remember? You were just a little older than Noah. Me, around twelve. We bundled the apples into our T-shirts and bolted for the brick wall. She set her sausage dog on us."

The memory stirred through Meg, and she couldn't help the grin that stole over her face. "It bit your big toe."

"Moral of the story—never wear flip-flops when stealing apples." He changed lanes, turning onto the coast highway, heading back toward Shelter Bay. Rain began to fleck the windows. The sea was gunmetal gray, broody. "It was the only time I'd ever been bitten by a dog, and it was a sausage dog. How ignoble is that? At least this one was a Doberman."

Her call picked up. "Kovacs."

She jerked back to business. "Dave. It's me, Meg. I know who vandalized my house. It was the Mack brothers, had to be. They have access to bovine blood, and the wording of the graffiti fits someone angry with me, and my father as a killer."

Silence.

"You there, Dave?"

"Uh, yeah, Meg, can I call you back in a minute?" The line went dead.

———

Dave Kovacs killed Meg's call and continued to watch the interview with Sally Braden through the two-way glass.

"The .22 rifle we found in your vehicle belongs to your brother-in-law, Henry Thibodeau," the interrogator seated opposite Braden said. "Is that correct?"

She did not reply.

"Did you take it from his gun safe?"

Silence.

"We found traces of cattle blood in the back of your SUV, Sally."

Sally Braden looked down at the table, a fall of hair screening her profile from Dave's view.

"The GPS in your vehicle shows that you came from Braden Cattle farm in Chillmook, where you do the books for your cousin. The GPS shows that you drove directly to Forest End subdivision, and into Forest Lane. Was this where you were at four a.m. yesterday, Sally?"

Sally cleared her throat, shifted in her chair, but did not reply.

"We found someone who can place your vehicle there, Sally, parked under a cherry tree. A witness who had the presence of mind to recall your vehicle registration, which is how we found you."

Silence.

Frustration sparked through Dave. Unofficially, very quietly, after listening to Meg interview his dad, he'd reopened the old Sherry Brogan case. He wasn't sure what he might find, or whether he'd care for the answers if he did find anything. He trusted his dad. He believed his father had acted with the best intent, and out of a deep compassion for people he cared about. But for his own sake now, Dave needed to understand fully what had gone down all those years ago, and how it might come back to bite him during the election. And Sally Braden was a confounding addition to the puzzle. What had driven her to spook Meg like this? Was she capable of worse?

Sally had known Sherry Brogan fairly well—they'd been in the same class during their final year of school. Her younger sister, Lori-Beth, had been in Meg's grade. Sally had been driving drunk with Lori-Beth about six years after Sherry's murder, and had caused a five-car pileup in which her sister had been paralyzed from the waist down. Her family, a branch of the Bradens in Chillmook, had suffered financially as a result. The accident had killed Sally's plans for college. After serving her sentence for criminally negligent homicide, she'd gone straight to work at the family slaughterhouse. She had never married and spent most of her time visiting and caring for her sister, perhaps out of some terrible guilt.

The interviewer leaned forward. "Did you intend to harm Meg Brogan?"

Sally cleared her throat. "I want a lawyer."

Dave cursed, and left the room.

Meg climbed out of Blake's truck, irritated that Dave Kovacs had not called right back. She reached for her tote and slung it over her shoulder. "Thanks, Blake. I'll see you at the marina later."

"Sure you don't want me to come with you to see Emma?"

"She'll be far more candid with me alone."

He held her gaze, his expression intense. Heat rose in her cheeks as she thought of how close they'd come to having sex on the side of the road. "I'll be fine," she said.

But he waited in his truck until she'd climbed into her own rig, started the engine, and pulled into the road. He followed behind her all the way to the coast road intersection, and when she turned north toward town, he tooted his horn, and turned left, heading to the school to pick up Noah.

Meg drove about a mile before quickly pulling over onto the shoulder.

Engine running, she dialed Jonah. She needed desperately to hear his voice. Sure, he'd broken it off, but she'd also made it clear to him that she was working to win him back. She just needed to hear him speak, to get a sense of what he was thinking, because she was muddled as all hell now. Kissing Blake like that, just being with him, made her feel as though the ground she knew so well had been ripped right out from under her feet, and she was flailing in some other reality.

The call kicked to voice mail. She killed the call, chewed her lip, then dialed his city office.

"Lawson and Associates," came the crisp French-accented voice of his receptionist, Elise LeFevre. Meg could picture her sitting there in her sleek pencil skirt and white blouse, six languages and two degrees under her belt, an impeccable physique, flawless skin. Mani-pedi once a week. How Jonah had convinced her to answer telephones was still a mystery to Meg. Probably money. Or promise of work on the investigation side down the road.

"Elise, hi, is Jonah in?"

A moment's pause. "Megan?"

"Yeah."

"He's out of town. On a contract. You . . . you've tried his cell?"

Genius. "Yes, I've tried his cell, and there's no reply, which is why I'm trying here. Do you know where I can reach him?"

Meg heard the hesitation. She closed her eyes. So this really was it—she was now an outsider to Jonah's circles. Bitterness filled her mouth. "It's important I reach him, Elise."

"He's in Vancouver."

"Vancouver, Washington?"

"Canada. British Columbia."

Her brain raced. She thought of the news reports on television before she'd left home. Four running shoes, different sizes, three left, one right, none matching, had been found over a period of eight months along the beaches and river banks of the Seattle area. All containing the disarticulated remains of human feet. There had been similar finds in Canada, just north of the Washington border.

"Jan Mascioni's case?" she said.

"He's been asked to consult, yes. It's a cross-border joint task force now. I'm sorry, Meg, I don't know more. The best number to reach him on is his cell."

"Which hotel is he staying at?"

"I'm afraid I don't know."

Liar.

"Would you like me to get a message to him?" Elise said.

"No. Thanks." She hung up fast and sat there with her phone in her hands. A heavy, sad feeling of finality sank through her. Had she just not believed him before, when he'd said it was over? Was her hope so blind and stupid? She rested her head back, calling his face to mind. Those dark indigo eyes, chiseled planes. His sleek, muscular body. Gorgeous hands, she loved his hands so much. They could do the most amazing things. Emotion pooled under her lids.

I don't believe it. I don't fucking believe this. All this time, all these years, and I've never shed a tear. It's like I'm cracked open, and can't control anything anymore . . .

S'okay, Meggie-Peg. Mom always said it was healthy to have a good, solid cry. Salt water, she always said. Tears, sea, sweat. It fixes everything . . .

Meg tensed at the sound of Sherry's voice. It was in her head, had to be in her head. She didn't dare open her eyes and look over to the passenger seat, where she could *feel* Sherry's sudden presence. The air stirred and Meg caught a faint whiff of the perfume Sherry had loved in her final year. Happiness, it was called. And it smelled like sunshine and flowers, and summer. Slowly, Meg cracked an eye open. The seat of course was empty.

She snorted, and put her truck into gear.

I'll take you seriously, Sherry, when you tell me what happened that day . . . Let's go visit Emma then, shall we . . .

She pulled into the road, and glanced at the clock on the dash. She was going to be late for her appointment with Emma. She'd told Blake she wanted to do this one alone. She believed she'd get more out of Sherry's best friend just woman to woman.

Careful who you trust, Meggie. None of us were what we seemed back then . . . Everyone has secrets, even secrets from themselves. It's a marvel we can trust anyone at all . . .

CHAPTER 18

"Tell me to stop anytime you feel uncomfortable," Meg said as she pressed the on button of her digital recorder. It was positioned on Emma's round dining table. Meg had her notebook with questions in front of her.

Emma nodded. Dark-haired and pale complexioned, her beauty had worn around the edges. Life and time had not been so kind to Emma Williams Kessinger as it had been to others. Her home looked affluent, though. She lived in it with her daughter, who spent weekends with Tommy. Questions swirled in Meg's mind.

"You were Sherry's best friend," Meg said for the tape.

"We were tight. Very. It was terrible what happened, how it tore us all apart."

"You ended up marrying Tommy, my sister's boyfriend."

"The tragedy brought us close. Grief can do that. You share a bond through the person you both miss. In trying to work through it all, you take solace in each other. It was our way of healing, I guess."

"The fall after the murder you and Tommy parted ways for a while. You went to pursue pharmacology studies in Portland and Tommy went to Ohio State?"

"We both came home for Christmas, when our relationship developed further," she said. "And more so during spring break the following year. Tommy injured his knee just before that first spring break, and there were worries he'd never play football at the same level again. He was starting to second-guess his career options, studies, that kind of thing. And his dad was talking about grooming him to eventually take over Kessinger Construction."

"My father was in prison on remand during that period, awaiting trial," Meg said. "You visited my mom, I remember."

"Tommy and I both did."

Meg smiled ruefully. "I'm afraid I must have been an obstreperous kid at the time. I recall locking myself in my room when you guys came over, and turning music up loud in my headphones. Didn't want to hear about Sherry or the murder."

Emma cleared her throat. "It was a rough time."

Meg paused. "Did my mother ever express any doubt to you guys about Ty's guilt at that time?"

Emma made a moue, then shook her head. "No. I don't think so. I don't really recall."

Meg studied her for a moment, trying to get a read on the woman. "When did Tommy move back to Shelter Bay full time?"

"When he injured his knee again, and he learned the long-term prognosis was not good. That's when he quit school to work with his dad. I went back for another year, returning for vacations and every long weekend I could. We married the following December. Next thing we knew Brooklyn was on the way."

"Which is when you quit school and got a job at your mother's drugstore."

"As a clerk. Yeah. Could have been a pharmacist if I'd stayed at school . . ." Her voice faded. Something shuttered behind her eyes. "Look, it was never easy. Tommy loved Sherry passionately. His whole teenage life had been defined by his relationship with Sherry. *He* was defined by Sherry. They were the 'it' couple who everyone wanted to be, or be a part of. He continued to idolize her, and Sherry became a saint in death that I could never be in life. If she and Tommy had broken up through an argument, or even if they'd stayed together, over time he'd have come to see the warts and all. It became a trigger point. Things degenerated gradually. He'd stay out nights. Silly arguments." She paused. Her eyes seemed to go distant.

"What was the last straw with the marriage, Emma?"

She moistened her lips, as if casting her mind back, or perhaps deciding how honest to be. Then her gaze met Meg's cold and square. "I thought this interview was about Sherry," she said coolly. "Not me and Tommy. Our relationship."

Meg nodded. "It is about Sherry. I was trying to get a sense of my sister at the time. For example, if she was going out with Tommy, if they were this perfect 'it' couple, why was she two-timing him?"

"You mean, why did she go with Ty to the spit?"

"Yes."

"I . . . I don't know."

"She didn't say?"

"Other than telling me they were going to be intimate, no. Maybe she just wanted a last, crazy fling before heading off to Stanford."

"Was she seeing anyone else, apart from Ty?"

"What? No."

Meg hesitated. "Did you know Sherry was pregnant when she died?"

Emma's face paled. *"Pregnant?"*

"It was in the autopsy results."

Her mouth opened. Then closed. "Whose baby? *Tommy's?*"

"No. His DNA was not a match. And neither was Tyson Mack's. The paternity is unknown at this point. I was hoping you'd have a clue who the father might be."

"No. I . . . I had no idea." She got up, paced. Meg watched, thinking her sister would be this age. What might it be like to have Sherry around now?

"There was this guy one night at a beach party early in the summer," she said. "Tommy was away that weekend. Sherry got really drunk, and she was kissing this guy. She *might* have had sex with him that night. And if she did, there's a chance she wouldn't have even remembered it. She was completely out of it."

Meg's pulse quickened. "Who was he?"

"He was from Eugene, I think. On holiday with a bunch of guys. A postgrad thing. I don't know what his name was."

"So, you're saying that Sherry might not have known she was pregnant, if this man was the father?"

"If she did, she wouldn't have wanted to keep it, that's for sure. My guess is that if she did know, she'd have waited until she got down to California, and have gotten rid of it quietly over there. It was almost time for her to leave."

"You don't think, if she knew, that she'd have told the father?"

Emma stared out the window. "No."

Meg was besieged with the distinct impression Emma was hiding something. She'd interviewed so many people through the course of her work—criminals, murderers, victims, lawyers—she'd developed a gut detection for deception that was usually pretty spot-on.

"I thought Sherry and I shared everything," Emma said quietly, looking out into the gray, rain-soaked garden. "Guess not." She turned, reached for her box of cigarettes, tapped one out, lit it, then, as an afterthought, said, "Do you mind?"

"Your house."

She opened the window a crack, stood by it, an arm across her stomach, cigarette in her other hand hovering near her face.

"Why do you think Tommy kept my sister on a pedestal all

those years, if he'd learned after her murder that she willingly went with Ty Mack to the spit?"

She took a deep drag on her cigarette, blew smoke slowly out the window. Trees swooned in a building wind.

"Tommy refused to see it like that. A lot of others did, too. His take on the whole thing was, yeah, so Sherry went to the spit. She was being flirtatious, but she didn't want to have sex. Ty must have pressed her. She said no, and he forced it, brutally assaulting her to teach her a lesson for being a cock tease. Tommy blames Mack, not Sherry. She was always sorta flirtatious, but Tom believed it was in a completely innocent way. He liked that his girlfriend attracted the attention of other guys. Made him feel powerful. The alpha."

"How do *you* figure it played out?"

"Ty was a badass. Just look at the old pictures of him. He cultivated that image. He came from a shitty background, and I feel sorry for kids who grow up in homes like that, but not all those kids become killers and rapists like him. I don't know what pushed him over the edge that day. But I do know Sherry called to say she was going to do 'it' with him. Maybe she changed her mind." Another drag. "Did you know that Ty's father did time for attempted rape, when he was in his twenties? Apple never falls far from the tree." She exhaled smoke slowly.

Meg held Emma's eyes, an anger building low in her belly. This was the prejudice that Lee Albies had been talking about. This was the stereotyping and scapegoating she'd volunteered to fight against.

"Why?" Emma said suddenly. "You think he *didn't* do it?"

"There appears to be ground for reasonable doubt. I think if Ty Mack *had* been charged, and if the case *had* gone to trial, he would have been easily acquitted by a jury. He would have walked a free man."

She stared. "Because of the pregnancy?"

"In part. Plus other DNA on the scene. Witnesses."

"What witnesses?"

"Someone who corroborated Ty's claim that he dropped Sherry safely at that Forest End trail. Someone else who saw a vehicle parked on the spit that evening."

She stared. "And this is why you're doing this? Writing this book?"

"I started with the intention of just telling Sherry's story as we'd all understood it. But now I'm not so certain whose story it is. Or what *The End* is."

"Shit," she said quietly. "But who else could have done it?"

"That's what I'm trying to find out. If you think of anything, any ideas, will you call me?"

She nodded, but her eyes were unreadable.

Meg switched off her recorder. "Thanks, Emma. I really appreciate it."

"No worries. Hope it helped."

Meg packed her tote, checked her watch. Blake had suggested she bring Irene over to the marina for dinner. She had a few hours to spare before then. Perhaps she'd see if Tommy was available—she was burning to hear his side of the story now. Hooking her tote over her shoulder, she got to her feet, then stopped at a silver-framed photo on the dresser.

"This your daughter?"

"Brooklyn, yes."

"She's beautiful." Meg glanced up, and felt a strange pang in her chest, thinking of Sherry, and a baby that died with her. "She looks like a mix of both you and Tommy."

A wry smile twisted Emma's mouth. "Best parts of both of us, thank God. Her seventeenth birthday is coming up."

"I heard. Tommy invited me to the big bash. I'll see you there?"

Sharp heat flashed through her eyes. "No. Maybe."

Meg hesitated, uncomfortable. "It really did end badly?"

Emma snorted, stubbed out her cigarette in an ashtray on the table. "It's being around that new wife of his that makes me sick. Exact replica of Sherry, except a little more white-blonde than gold. And taller. Norwegian with an accent to match, and all of twenty-five years old. Not much older than Brooklyn. Not much older than Sherry when she died, either." She went to the front door, opened it.

Meg pulled on her boots and coat. "I heard about his second wife, Deliah," she prompted, deeply curious now. "That must have been tragic."

"Tragic," she echoed, no emotion to the word. "He got her business, though. Deliah had inherited Sproatt Renovations and Design from her father shortly before the accident."

The door closed behind Meg with a firm snick. She was grateful for the fresh air. As she walked back to her truck, she noticed Emma watching her from behind the drapes.

Sherry, Sherry . . . what were you doing that summer? Did any one of us really know you?

How does one know anyone, Meggie-Peg? By how they look? By what they do? Or say? Like I said, it's a marvel we trust at all . . .

Leaves skittered across her path in a sharp gust of wind. A fine mist of rain started to fall. In her truck, she called Tommy's assistant.

———

It was four in the afternoon when Lori-Beth Braden Thibodeau turned her SUV back into her driveway and maneuvered herself out of the driver's seat into her wheelchair in the pouring rain. She'd received a call from the midwife just after the cops had taken Sally that morning—Holly had gone into labor. She'd raced down to Chillmook at once. Alone. She'd not wanted to call Henry. Her most fervent hope was that baby Joy would arrive, and become hers before doom hit. And she was certain doom was going to hit now. In what form she did not know yet. But Holly's contractions had proved false. Braxton Hicks. Afterward, the midwife said it was a sign her body was getting ready. It should be soon now.

She wheeled into the kitchen to make a pot of coffee, wondering if she should take a hotel room in Chillmook so she could be close. Thinking about her baby, making plans—it kept her mind off the other things. It's all she wanted—all she was living for right now. And she'd do anything—everything—to make it happen.

She was sitting in the kitchen sipping her drink and eating a slice of toast when Sally walked in.

Her heart stopped. Carefully she set her mug down. Her sister's face was waxy and white, dark bags under her eyes.

"What happened?" Lori-Beth's voice came out hoarse.

Sally took a seat at the kitchen table, and rubbed her mouth.

"Did they charge you?"

She inhaled deeply. "No. Not yet. I got a lawyer. She's good."

"Did you do it, Sally? Did you vandalize Meg's house? Did you shoot out her windows?"

Sally's eyes locked with her sister's. And an indescribable kind of weight pressed down on Lori-Beth. This could not be happening. She was going to wake up. It would all be a dream.

"*Why?*" she whispered.

"I'd do anything for you, LB. Anything."

Lori-Beth stared, her brain folding in over itself. "What do you mean, 'for me'? Why would you terrorize Meg Brogan *for me*?"

Sally got up, poured a coffee, reseated herself. She reached across the table, took Lori-Beth's hands. Her eyes glittered with emotion. "I heard Henry on the phone. Twice. I—"

"You *eavesdropped* on my husband's phone calls?"

"LB, listen to me. Henry's been weird. I . . . I don't trust him. I've been watching him. For you—I have your interests at heart. The first call that night came from Geoff Sutton—"

"*Geoff?*"

Sally nodded. "Henry was totally strung out by it—he told Geoff never to call him again on the home number, and he arranged to meet him near Whakami Cove early the following morning. I followed him."

"So that's where he went. What happened?"

"They talked." Sally took a sip from her mug, hesitated, then said, "They hugged. Touched."

Lori-Beth stared at her sister. Inside her belly she started to shake. "So . . . so you know. What Henry is."

"I've suspected."

"How could *I* not know? For all these years. I . . . I only just found some stuff on his computer. I—"

"I've seen it."

"I don't believe you—you've been through his things? His private things?"

"I'd do anything for you, Lori-Beth."

Lori-Beth regarded her sister in stunned silence.

Who was this person? Who was her husband? Can we ever really know anyone at all?

She cleared her throat. "What does it mean, him seeing Geoff?"

"I don't know. But right after Geoff called that night, Henry phoned Tommy Kessinger."

"Tommy's his boss—he often phones Tom."

Sally leaned forward, cupping her mug in both hands. "Henry told Tommy that Geoff Sutton was back. He told Tommy that Blake Sutton knew Geoff was on the spit the night that Sherry Brogan was killed, and Blake covered for him all these years, but now he planned to tell Meg, for her book. His fear was that the Sherry Brogan case might be reopened."

"Why would he fear that?" Lori-Beth's voice was going tight, high, and she couldn't help it. "We all know who did it . . . right? It was Ty, right?" Sally said nothing. Fear speared deep into Lori-Beth's bowels. "What . . . what did Tommy say? Why was Henry even telling Tommy this?"

"He seemed to want Tommy to do something about it."

Lori-Beth closed her eyes. This was all too much. She didn't understand it, didn't want to try and unpick it for fear of what lurked, what terrible thing might have been done. "What," she said, very quietly, "was Tommy's response?"

"His words were 'It has nothing to do with me. I was never there. We both know that . . . And we know what the evidence will show if they take another look.'"

"What does that mean? What *evidence*?"

Sally took her sister's hands again. "I don't know, LB. I'm guessing it means they might find something to implicate Henry if the case is reopened."

"That doesn't make sense! Henry could *never* have hurt Sherry. Or raped her. He . . . he's not like that."

"I don't know what's going on, but it's made Henry scared. And it all started with Meg Brogan's return, her dragging the past up like that. Next thing Geoff is back in town, and everything's going to shit."

"So you thought spooking Meg off was the answer—is that what happened? You tried to scare her off? You think whatever is going on is *that* serious?"

"If Meg stopped her line of questioning, things could go back to normal. At least until you got the baby. I know how much she means to you. I *know* you won't cope if the adoption doesn't go through."

"You're mad, Sally," she whispered. "I can't believe you did that."

"And what wouldn't *you* do to bring baby Joy home safely? It was my chance," she said softly, her eyes gleaming. "My chance to give something back to you. For what I did."

———

"I heard about the vandalism—awful. I'm so sorry," Tommy said as he motioned for Meg to take a chair in his home office in front of the gas fireplace that flickered cozily. "Have the cops arrested anyone yet?"

"I don't know." Meg seated herself and set her tape recorder and notebook on the low coffee table between them. Tommy had been doing some work from home and had agreed to squeeze her into his busy schedule. Blake would be furious she was doing this alone, but this was Tommy. He was virtually family. And Meg had no doubt he'd be more forthright with her alone. She was also hot to talk to him after listening to Emma. She'd cracked open a dark window into Sherry's life, and Meg needed to probe further.

"Would you like some tea? Coffee? I can get Liske to bring some."

"I'm all tea-ed and coffee-ed out. The perils of interviewing," Meg said with a grin, but inside she felt walls go up at the mention of Liske. She'd met the latest wife at the door upon arrival. Emma was right. A Sherry clone, but sleeker and more platinum. Big blue eyes and a Nordic accent. Young. Very young to Tommy's forty years. It felt like a betrayal to Sherry's memory, although it shouldn't—Tommy had a right to his life after a sad divorce, and the loss of his second wife. "You ready?"

"Fire away." He leaned back into his armchair with a smile, an accomplished man at ease with himself.

She pressed the record button. "When was the very last time you saw Sherry?"

He moistened his lips. "It was the day before she was killed. We met in the village, went to the arcade, and then she came over to my place. We made out." He palmed his hand over his thatch of dark blond hair. "I'd have killed Ty Mack myself, you know. If your dad hadn't. I can see how it happened. I . . ." His voice faded, and he inhaled deeply.

"What did you and Sherry talk about that final day, Tom? What were her last words to you?"

"'See you tomorrow.'"

"And what do you believe happened the following afternoon?"

"Same thing everyone believes. She went to the spit with Tyson Mack, and—"

"Why do you think she went with him?"

His eyes flickered. "I don't know. A lark. Perhaps she wanted a ride on his bike."

Cover for me, Meg . . . tell Dad we went to see that movie . . .

"Did it make you angry? That she went with him?"

He blew out a puff of air. "Yeah, of course it made me mad. Because it got her killed. But that was Sherry—she was fun, spontaneous, flirtatious. But she never, ever crossed the line."

"Meaning?"

"Our relationship line."

Meg glanced up from her book, held his gaze. "So you didn't know that she was seeing other guys?"

"What do you mean?"

"You had no suspicion she was being unfaithful?"

"Meg, what are you driving at here?"

Meg paused. "She was a few weeks pregnant when she died."

Tommy did not blink. He did not move a muscle. It was as if he'd turned to stone. The clock on the wall ticked. He cleared his throat. When he spoke, his voice was thick.

"Pregnant?"

"The autopsy results revealed—"

"Whose baby? Mine?"

"No, Tom."

He surged to his feet. *"Whose?"*

"We don't know."

"Why . . . why didn't I know this? When did you find out? How?"

"My mom was conducting an investigation of her own. She'd secured a copy of the autopsy rep—"

"Why?" he demanded, blue eyes crackling, his cheeks coloring. "Why was Tara investigating? *What* was she investigating?"

Meg waited a few beats for him to settle. Then said, "I know it's hard, Tommy. It's hard on all of us. But it appears things were not quite what they seemed. My mom was beginning to believe that my father might have killed an innocent man."

He stared down at her. Slowly, he seated himself on the edge of his chair. "Tara thought Ty Mack was innocent?"

"She thought it was possible."

"Was this stuff, this autopsy report, in those file boxes that Irene discovered in that wall safe, after the fire?"

"Yes."

He glanced out the window, dragged his hand over his hair, and cursed softly. "I don't see how Tara could even begin to think that. All the evidence pointed to Ty."

"There seems to be some other evidence that was not properly accounted for, or investigated further."

"Like?"

"The pregnancy, for one. No one knows who the father is. It puts another potential suspect into the picture. It could give motive. If Sherry wanted to keep the baby, and he didn't, perhaps the father needed to keep it quiet for some reason, and she refused."

"It doesn't make sense. I . . . I just can't see Sherry doing that. I . . ."

"I know. Things, people, my sister—it appears nothing is what it seemed."

He dragged his hand down hard over his mouth, then gave a snort. "I don't know why it guts me like this. I mean, it's over. It was a long, long time ago. We've all moved on."

"It's a natural reaction, Tommy. It's a shock to think we don't actually have closure." She paused. "Even more of a shock is the realization that the real killer could still be out there."

His eyes flared to Meg. He stared. "Have you spoken to Kovacs about this?"

"Yes."

"And? Is he reopening an investigation?"

"Not yet."

"But you think he will."

"It's my intention to get there."

"Fuck." He surged to his feet again, paced. "I can't believe this. After all this time." He spun. "And you have all the records."

"My mother got most of the records from Ty's defense counsel."

"Fuck."

"Do you want to give it a break?"

"No. No, it's okay. I want to talk about this." He reseated himself. "I'm sorry, it's just a shock. I'm having trouble wrapping my head around it all. Go on."

Meg inhaled, nodded. Breaking his gaze she turned a page in a notebook. She felt hot. Uncomfortable. "Do you have *any* idea who Sherry could have been seeing, on the sly? Who might have made her pregnant?"

He shook his head. "I must have been totally naive, or self-important. I believed she was faithful."

"And that day she was killed, you were with Ryan Millar."

"Yeah. In his garage, tinkering with my wheels. I was there the whole day, until I got the call that Sherry was missing."

"And you never heard anything about a red VW van parked at the spit, near the trail to the make-out grove that evening?"

His eyes narrowed. "No. Why? Was there one?"

"A witness saw one, yes. Another witness identified the presence of an older-model VW van at the trailhead behind the houses in Forest Lane, around the time Tyson Mack said he dropped Sherry off. That second witness confirms that Ty's bike was there just seconds earlier."

"This is serious. This . . . this is evidence. Why was none of this used?"

"Police did not feel the witnesses were credible."

"But *you* do?"

"Ty Mack's defense counsel does. Lee Albies planned to prove it if they ever got their day in court. But Ty was killed. And Ike Kovacs closed the investigation. Tommy—one more question."

"Shoot." His voice was flat. His eyes were distant, as if he was reliving the whole, horrible period in time.

"You and Emma visited my mom on and off during the time my dad was awaiting trial."

"Yes, we needed to. We all needed to talk. It was a way of keeping Sherry alive a little longer for all of us."

"And how was my mom during these visits? Did you get a sense she was depressed?"

He nodded. "She was taking a lot of medication."

"She never told you about her suspicions that Ty might be innocent?"

"Never."

"Her suicide didn't come as a surprise?"

A sadness turned down the corners of his eyes. "No, Meg. It did not. Emma was studying pharmacology, and she'd seen the collection of pills that your mom was taking in the bathroom. She told me what they were for—anxiety, depression, insomnia. Tara was on a bad cocktail."

Meg's pulse beat faster. "Emma said this?"

He nodded.

She hesitated. "Your marriage with Emma was not good, I take it."

He snorted. "I hate to say it, but . . ." He glanced at the recorder. "Off the record?"

Meg reached over, hit the off button.

"Emma proved to be a passive-aggressive. A pathological liar. She lied to me. Everyone. Even the police. She told both me and the cops that Sherry had called her to say she was going to make out with Ty. That was a lie. Sherry was going to the spit with Ty to buy Ecstasy. Both Emma and Sherry were dabbling in 'e.' We'd all tried it. Ty had contacts. I think Ty must have made advances on Sherry when they were alone, and she said no, and that's when things went sideways. Emma did not tell the police the truth because she felt it would implicate her in the drug angle. And years later Emma let slip that she'd lied to me about what Sherry said on the phone, because she *wanted* me to believe Sherry was being unfaithful." He paused. "I came to realize Emma could do some very dark things to get what she wanted. And she wanted me. She wanted Sherry's guy. It turns out she'd coveted just about everything Sherry ever had."

Meg's mouth went dry. "But you just said, on the record, that maybe Sherry went with Ty for a 'lark,' a joyride on his bike. Now you're saying it was to buy 'e.'"

"I didn't want to implicate Emma. But . . . but this is looking serious now. Everyone needs to tell the truth now."

"And not back then?"

"Like I said, I didn't know about the lie until years later, when Emma let it slip during a fight."

Meg stared at him, her brain reeling.

"It wouldn't have changed anything, Meg. The evidence still all pointed to Ty Mack, no matter the reason Sherry went with him."

"But you do know for a fact she lied to the cops?"

"Unless she was lying again during our argument."

"Will you say this on record?"

"You can ask her yourself."

Meg held his eyes, a dark feeling rustling around the edges of her mind as she mentally ran through her interview with Emma, weighing Tommy's words against hers.

CHAPTER 19

"So, I picked up where Mom left off with her investigation," Meg said to Irene as she turned into the marina driveway, relieved to have her aunt with her this evening as a buffer between her and Blake. "I've been going through the files, reading her journal."

"Journal?" Irene said.

"Yes. Looks like Mom might have been on to something."

"What journal?"

Irene was not having such a great day, so Meg dropped it. When she'd arrived at Chestnut Place earlier to pick Irene up, her aunt had been focused solely on food, and what they were going to get to eat at the marina tonight. Meg was just happy to have this time with Irene. There were only so many growing seasons in a life—Jonah had said that. The lost time was something she'd never get back, but she had the present.

As she drew into the parking lot, Blake was getting out of his truck with Noah. The bed of his truck was loaded with construction supplies.

She pulled in alongside his vehicle.

Geoff's Jeep was parked at the far end of the camper sites. The cops must have returned it to him, and speedily so. Meg would have expected them to hold on to it longer if they'd wanted to properly examine it for trace evidence. Then again, it was just vandalism, not a murder. And this was not television. She knew well enough those kinds of CSI resources were not applied to minor crimes. Geoff was busy unloading grocery bags from his Jeep.

Blake opened the door for Noah, but he watched his brother intently. His body was wire tense.

"Would you take Noah inside?" he said quietly as Meg alighted from her truck. He nodded a hello to Irene, but his attention remained fixed on Geoff. "Make him a snack or something?"

"Sure," she said, following Blake's gaze. "Have the police cleared him, then?"

"I don't know what's going on," he said quietly. "Could you give us a minute, Meg, please?"

"Hey, Noah," Meg called. "How about a snack? Got anything good inside?"

Noah eyed her warily.

"This is my aunt, Irene." Meg smiled. "I think she's hungry, too."

"Sure," Noah said, scuffing his feet as he led them reluctantly toward the office door.

Meg and Irene followed Noah into the building. Through the window Meg saw Blake was waiting until they were properly inside. When the door swung shut behind them, he marched over to Geoff, like an angry bull.

Geoff rose to his full height as his brother approached. Words were exchanged, brother to brother, Geoff's dark hair and Blake's sandy blond darkening as a soft Pacific Northwest drizzle soaked them.

A dark sense of foreboding settled on Meg's shoulders.

———

"What happened at the station?" Blake demanded as he reached the Jeep.

Geoff's spine stiffened as he faced his brother square on. "They took my fingerprints, rehashed my movements during the night."

"And?"

"And what . . . they're not going to be a match. I didn't do it."

"Where's the rifle?"

"I don't know," he snapped, flinging open the back of his Jeep. "See for yourself. The lock has been jimmied. Rods in their cylinders were stolen as well as the rifle, and I don't know where it happened along my drive up. Could have been in California. Could have happened outside the Whakami hotel or down the beach, for all I know."

Blake met his brother's eyes. Mistrust swirled in with the mist. Who was Geoff Sutton, really? How far could he be trusted, this own flesh and blood of his, this brother for whom he'd always covered.

The secrets we keep for love . . . the lies we tell ourselves . . .

Geoff stepped closer to Blake. They stood toe-to-toe in the rain. Wind was starting to whip. It was getting dark, clouds boiling low. "Trust me, please," Geoff said. "I went to meet someone that day. It had nothing to do with Sherry, or what happened."

"Why did I find your sack—the one you used to gather flotsam—near Meg's unconscious body?"

"There are only a few spots you can put ashore on the point. That was one. That's where I went in with the boat. I must have dropped it there."

His gaze bored into his brother's. "I need to tell Meg."

"Has she asked?"

"Not yet. But I'm going to tell her before she does. Tonight." He paused. "I'm not going to lose her, Geoff. Not this time. Not because of this stupid secret."

"Give me one more day. Just one."

"Why one more day?"

He cursed, looked away, palmed his hand over his wet hair. "Because Meg will go looking for him. People will put two and two together about us. This man has not come out, and if he's outed, it *will* destroy his marriage. It . . . it'll kill him. Trust me. I . . . I need one more day to talk to him, allow him to prepare. To maybe tell his wife himself."

Wind gusted. The swell in the bay surged on the incoming tide.

"What is this truth worth, Blake, honestly? A man's life for Meg's book? *Especially* if our presence on that strip of land had *nothing* to do with what Meg is after. Think about it." He paused. "I wish you could just drop it entirely."

"The longer I leave it, the more gnarly it gets."

"It's not a big deal to sit on it. I keep telling you."

"It is a big deal. It's a trust deal. Meg has not trusted anyone since she was fourteen. I need her to trust me now."

———

The drop cloth, ladders, and scaffolding had been cleared out of the Crabby Jack cafe. The walls were gleaming white and freshly painted. Tables had been moved back in. On one of the tables near the glass doors that opened onto the deck was a giant puzzle-in-process that Noah had been working on. It fascinated Irene. And she was now sitting at the table happily working on the puzzle. Unsure of how to best handle her aunt, Meg had temporarily left her there with a promise to bring tea and cookies.

"You must have been really busy with your dad after school today," Meg said to Noah as she fetched mugs down from the kitchen cupboard. "The Crabby Jack is looking as though it could open for business any day now."

Noah perched on his stool, watching her in the kitchen. His vantage point also afforded him a peekaboo view of his dad and uncle Geoff through the side window. "Dad said he wants to open the cafe in the spring. I can help in there in the summer," he said, his attention going to the window. "What are they fighting about?" Noah said.

"Probably brother stuff. Oh, yesss! Nutella!" She held her find high in the air, like a trophy—the answer to all kid woes. And some adult ones, too. She could handle a dose herself about now, on fresh bread with a mug of hot tea. She filled the kettle. "Siblings do argue, Noah—it's totally normal. You like Nutella?"

Consternation creased his brow. He eyed the jar, nodded. Then his features crumpled and he looked up at Meg, an imploring look in his eyes, tears pooling. Her heart crunched. She set the kettle down quickly. "What's the matter, Noah?"

"My dad said I shouldn't eat junk when I come home."

She bent down, leaning her elbows on the counter, looking dead in his eyes, and she put her finger to her lips. "Shh. It's our little secret, then, 'kay?" she whispered. "Besides, what's he doing with chocolate spread in the cupboard anyway, if it's not for eating?"

A tear plopped. "That's what Mom used to say."

"Oh, hon, come here." She moved quickly around the counter and hugged the little body tightly against her own. And it stirred a deep power in her. A kind of energy. A drive. To help this little boy. And it struck Meg square and hard in the face. *This* is who she was. It cut to the heart of why she'd loved Sherry, tried to save her. Why she hadn't been able to bear her own failing to do so. She *needed* to protect, to save, to nurture the vulnerable. She'd kill to do it. And the realization was profound. She'd lost this part of herself. She'd left it behind in Shelter Point. And she was reconnecting with it in holding Blake's sad little boy. Allison's son. Regret washed through Meg. And love. For this boy's father. This place. The Sutton men. Home. Ocean and sky and rhythm and tide—it all overwhelmed her in the scent of this child against her body.

The feeling of his warmth, the sensation of his soft hair under her palm, the beat of his heart.

She blew out air as she rocked him, overwhelmed by the tidal wave of emotions.

She moved back, held his shoulders. "You going to be okay?"

He nodded. "Why're *you* crying?"

"Oh, God." She wiped her eyes, laughed. "Silly, huh?"

He stared, waiting in his innocence for an answer.

"'Cos I love you, Noah."

He frowned.

"I know. It seems odd. But here's the thing. You're kinda like family to me. You're part of this place, and part of your dad. And . . . my roots go deep here. It's . . . I think I need some Nutella." She smiled, and swiped at her tears. "Our secret, okay? No telling I was crying. I'm not a wimp. I don't cry."

A tentative smile tempted his lips. "My mom used to say it was good to cry sometimes."

"Yeah. My mom used to say that, too." Meg set the kettle boiling and went over to the hearth in the open-plan living room. "Can you show me how to fix this fire, Noah?"

He hopped down from his stool and the little man got busy handing her kindling first, then bigger logs. The fire grew to a crackling roar. Meg smiled inside as she watched him, awash with affection she didn't quite understand. But she was in no mood to fight it right now. No mood to fight herself any longer. Engaging him was her plan.

The kettle whistled and Meg made tea for herself and Irene, and poured a glass of milk for Noah.

"Can you take this mug and plate of cookies through to Irene?" she asked.

"Sure." He hesitated, his mouth pulling into a crooked moue. "Is she . . . okay?"

IN THE WANING LIGHT

Meg grinned. "Yup. She just forgets things. Sometimes her memory is worse than others. You need to go easy on her. It's called dementia, and it can happen when you get old. Ask her if she wants to join us in the kitchen, will you?"

Noah scuttled off with the tea and cookies while Meg slathered fresh bread with creamy Nutella, thinking she had not eaten this stuff since she left Shelter Bay.

Noah returned and hopped back onto his stool, a fresh energy in his eyes. "Irene said no, she wanted to work on the puzzle in peace." He sipped his milk, and took a voracious chomp of his chocolate-topped bread. He grinned.

"You got chocolate in your teeth," Meg said.

He chuckled. Meg took a bite of her own slice and bared her chocolate-coated teeth like a monkey.

Noah guffawed, collapsing and slapping his hand onto the counter. Then, tears of mirth glistening in his eyes, he took another bite, and made a monkey face back. Giggling, they settled into an easy truce, munching their snack and sipping their drinks as the fire crackled and popped. Lucy appeared from nowhere and flopped down onto her mat in front of the flames. Outside, the light and sky darkened. Wind began to press against the marina buildings, creaking moorings and bumping buoys. Rain streaked down the windows facing the sea.

Noah began to swing his little legs. "My mom used to sit with me after school."

"She sounds like a very special mom. You must miss her awfully."

He nodded, jaw stiffening. He looked down at his last bite of sandwich.

"Your dad misses her very much, too."

Slowly, he glanced up, met her eyes. Meg could see Blake's eyes in there, among Allison's coloring and features.

"He said that?"

"He did."

He stared at her a long while. Lucy groaned and rolled onto her back, lips falling back from her teeth in a grimace that belied her contentment.

"Your parents were lucky to share the years they did have together. And to have you."

"My dad wasn't here most of the time. He only quit the army after she died, and only because he had to look after me."

"That's the rough thing about the army," she said. "About serving your country. You're a hero—people all over the nation, and right here in Shelter Bay, can sleep safe in their houses because the enemies are being kept at bay. The borders and the night skies are being kept safe. They're heroes, all. But at the same time, those soldiers cannot fight and protect without being away from their own families, their own loved ones. They must spend birthdays and holidays away from home when they're on a tour. At Christmas they might have to hide in bunkers, under enemy attack, thirsty and hungry, and all they have is a turkey dinner in a dehydrated little ration packet."

He stared, wide-eyed.

"Sometimes they die, and never come home. But your father helped many of them return, even after they were injured, because he was a medic. Injured soldiers who'd been bombed apart or shot were rushed into his tent. Sometimes they were missing legs and arms. Your dad would sew them back together, stop the bleeding, stabilize them long enough for big helicopters to fly them over borders to better hospitals." She paused. "Many of those injured men and women might never have made it home to their own children, Noah, if your dad had not been there for them."

"Nobody told me."

"Maybe you were just too young at the time."

"Do you think my dad would tell me now, about some of his adventures? Like in the books he reads to me?"

"I'm one hundred percent sure he would. Especially if you ask him."

He popped the last bite of his sandwich into his mouth, and chewed, his little legs swinging again. It lightened Meg's heart. The kid was a teeter-totter of emotions. She glanced at the window, trying to see Blake and Geoff, but it was getting dark and they'd moved out of her line of sight.

"Do *you* miss your mom and dad?"

Surprise rippled through Meg. "Of course. And my sister."

"I'm sorry she was murdered."

Meg blinked. "It's never easy, Noah. Loss. But with love, and time, it starts to become a little more manageable, and you can see more of the bright things in life. You're very lucky to have a dad like you do, you know. A real hero. Who loves you with all his heart. I think he'd move mountains for you."

"And kill lions?"

She laughed, and it felt good; she wiped her eyes. "Yes, even lions."

"We're reading about lions. It's an adventure story in deepest Africa. Do you want to read some to me tonight?"

Sobering, she said, "Yes. I'd like that. I'd be honored."

"My granddad Bull used to read to me. I don't remember him that well, though. My dad said it's because I was too little."

"You know what I remember about your granddad? He had this crazy-silly crab hat. Like a stuffed crab. Red fleece, with googly eyes sewed on, and legs and claws that stuck out to the sides. He was this super tall, big macho guy with a deep gruff voice who could look scary sometimes, but he'd wear that funny crab hat all summer long, when the tourists came, and he'd joke with them and make them laugh as he boiled their catch, and showed them how to clean the crab. And only when it got dark and they all went home did he take that silly hat off. He even went scuba diving wearing that hat once. There used to be a photo around of him with his head sticking out of the water, wet crab hat, goggles, and snorkel."

"Where is the hat now?"

"I have no id—"

A noise made her glance up sharply. Lucy's tail thumped.

Blake loomed silent in the doorway, a strange look in his face.

"Blake?" Meg got quickly to her feet, feeling exposed. "How long have you been standing there?" she snapped.

He came over, kissed Noah on top of his head, ruffled his hair, but his eyes held hers. "Long enough."

———

"So! Who's for pizza? A little bird tells me that Noah loves pizza." Geoff entered the kitchen behind Blake, wet hair, a big grin on his face, his arms full of bags. He plunked grocery sacks down on the counter and shrugged out of his jacket. "Got some supplies on the way home." He hooked his jacket over the back of a chair, rubbed his hands, and out of the bags he pulled a six-pack of beer, and a bottle of white wine. "Cold." He wiggled his eyebrows. "Glass of pinot grigio, Meg?"

Meg laughed. "Would love one," she said. "Let me go see if I can pull Irene away from her puzzle."

As Meg stepped into the Crabby Jack dining area, her phone buzzed. She turned a light on for Irene, who smiled happily, and Meg stepped back, just outside the archway to answer her phone, but from where she could still see Irene.

"Meg Brogan."

"It's Dave, I'm sorry I didn't return your call right away."

Dave. Not Kovacs. Her pulse quickened—the new informality did not escape her. Something had changed. "Is this about Geoff, and my house?" she asked quietly, her gaze flicking toward the kitchen.

"In a manner. He's in the clear. We have a suspect."

Her hand tightened on the phone. "Who? Keevan Mack?"

"Sally Braden."

Meg's mind looped. "I . . . Sally? I don't understand."

"We haven't charged her yet—she's got herself a good lawyer, but we'll get there. I need to ask you some questions," Kovacs said. "Informally. Off the record."

Meg's walls went up. "I can't guarantee—"

"I've reopened the Sherry Brogan case. Unofficially, on the quiet. Put two of my guys on it. They're going through the files."

Her heart stopped, then kicked into a fast, erratic pattern. Irene glanced up.

"I found it, Meg! I found the missing piece I was looking for."

Meg forced a smile, and held up her hand, telling Irene to hang on a moment. She stepped further around the corner. "What made you reopen it?" she said quietly.

"My father's heart was in the right place. I trust him on that. He did what he believed was right. But you've raised some serious concerns that will need to be addressed if this book of yours comes out. I've been going through the case files myself." He hesitated. "I need this solved as much as you do. And yes, in part because of my campaign. If I nail this now, I can use it—I can show the electorate that even if it involves family, or comes at personal cost, I can still be objective, that I will serve the public, not myself. And, in part because, no matter what you might think, I do believe in justice. You work with me, we both win."

Meg blinked, suspicion curling through her. "You been drinking, Kovacs?"

He laughed, then turned serious. "Okay, so why do you think Sally Braden might have done this? What would make her in particular want to take such radical action to scare you off this story? What connection does she have to you, to Sherry, to your family, to Ty Mack? Is there *anything* you can think of?"

Meg closed her eyes, casting her mind back. "Only that Sally was in Sherry's graduating class. And she's related to Braden farms, where Mason and Keevan Mack now work."

"She works there, too. Part-time. Doing their books," he said.

"Maybe she's tight with, or seeing one of the Mack brothers? Although it seems unlikely—Sally must be, what? Around thirty-nine, forty? The Mack brothers are in their late sixties."

"I've seen stranger things. Attraction can be a tricky little bitch."

"The wording of the graffiti would make sense, though, if Sally was on their side in hating my family for killing Ty."

"Still, the motivation doesn't really play, does it? Why would a single woman with no priors, apart from a drunk driving accident in her early twenties, take her brother-in-law's rifle, get a bucket of blood, of all things, and go shoot up a house in a peaceful subdivision? Just to vent? Doesn't add up for me. She's hiding something. She knows something."

Meg rubbed her brow, excitement trilling quiet and hot through her blood. Finally, maybe they were getting somewhere.

"Think on it," he said. "Call me, please, if something strikes you."

She hesitated, deeply unsure about this swing in Kovacs. "Okay," she said. "But the information flows both ways."

"Understood. Within the framework of police legality, of course."

"And you'll give me an exclusive, on the record, no matter how this plays out?"

A beat of silence. "Fair enough."

Meg was about to kill the call when he said, "Oh. Your house—we're clear. It's all yours."

She hung up, went over to Irene. "How's the puzzle coming?" she said, pocketing her phone.

Irene grinned. "I like puzzles."

"I can see. But it's getting cool in here. How about you join us in the kitchen, by the fire? Geoff is making pizza from scratch."

Meg led Irene into the kitchen where Geoff was pounding dough into shape in a big bowl. His sleeves were rolled up and he wore an old denim bib apron with an orange crab appliquéd onto the front. Noah peered up over the counter like a little Kilroy cartoon, watching the dough.

Irene stalled when she saw Geoff. Confusion chased through her eyes. "That's Bull's apron," she said. "He always wears it for the annual crab boil." Her gaze darted around the kitchen, as if in search of Bull, but fearful of asking and perhaps highlighting her failing mind.

Geoff and Blake exchanged a look.

"Bull passed away, Irene," Blake said gently. "Remember? Two years ago."

Her brow creased and she started scratching her blouse. Meg quieted her hand. "How about something to drink?" she said. "Some wine, pop?"

"I also have orange juice and sparkling water," Blake offered.

"Orange juice would be lovely," Irene said. "Thank you."

"So how have you been keeping, Irene?" Geoff said, turning the dough onto a floured board. "It's been a long time."

She frowned, as if trying to recall when in fact she had last seen Geoff. "Yes, it has." She quickly changed the topic, as if trying to avoid potentially showcasing her mental shortcomings. "Can I help?"

"Sure," Geoff said with a grin. "You could chop the peppers, slice salami, mushrooms, olives." He dusted his floury hands on his apron and pulled the vegetables out from another bag. He set them at the far end of the counter for Irene along with a knife and board. Blake pulled up a stool for her and set a glass of juice in front of her.

"Noah," Geoff barked. "Music! We need music. Be the DJ, man?"

Noah leaped off his stool and turned on the old stereo in the corner. A bluesy jazz tune filled the room. Noah turned it up louder. Blake poured Meg a glass of chilled wine, and she sat sipping it at the counter. Geoff dragged over a small wooden crate, and gestured for Noah to come stand on top. "Here's the roller. Now, do it like this." He showed Noah how to beat down, and roll out the elasticky pizza dough.

"Looks like we'll be christening Crabby Jack's soon," Geoff said to his brother over Noah's head. "Are the contractors all done?"

"*We* are all done." Blake snagged his own beer from the counter, took a long pull. "Noah and I did most of the work ourselves over the winter, right, champ?"

Noah bobbed his head, a huge grin splitting his face as he rolled the dough. He had flour on his nose. Meg glanced at Blake. He met her eyes, and she could read in his face what he was thinking. This old marina was full of warmth and food, and wine and music and laughter. *Family.* And it had not been alive like this in a long, long time. He raised his bottle, tipped it toward her, and smiled. She returned his smile, but something tilted inside her. She felt a sense of foreboding. Of time running out.

The wind outside gusted, and the night pressed against the windows.

———

"He hasn't come home," Lori-Beth said into the phone. "And he's not answering his cell. I was hoping . . . that maybe he was with you? Working late on something at your home office?"

"I'm sorry, LB," Tommy said. "Henry did come into the office today, but he left after lunch."

"And you don't know where he went?"

"I'm sorry, no."

"Was he . . . did he seem okay?"

A beat of silence. "What do you mean?"

"He hasn't been feeling too well. He's been acting a bit strange. I was just worried."

Another pause. "I'll let you know if I hear from him." His voice was curt, as if she'd interrupted something important.

She hesitated, glanced at Sally, who was stirring soup at the stove. "When does one call the police for this sort of thing? Do you have to wait thirty-six hours or something, or is that just on television?"

"Police?" Tom said.

"To report him missing, if he doesn't come home."

"LB, listen to me, it'll be fine. It's not even late yet. Do *not* worry. I'll look for him. I'll call around, okay?"

"Okay," she said quietly.

"Sit tight. Do not involve the cops yet."

"Okay."

"Is there . . . something else you want to tell me?"

Lori-Beth twisted the chain with the crucifix around her neck. "Did he perhaps call you the other night, and mention something troubling him?"

Silence.

"Tom? You there?"

He cleared his throat. "Sorry, I was just trying to think back. I don't believe so—nothing that stands out immediately."

She debated whether to tell him. She was sick about Henry, what she'd found. What he was. She was also terrified of rocking the boat until Joy was safely hers. And what then? Maybe a facade of marriage was better than being a disabled single mother living with a spinster sister who was beginning to make her uneasy, too.

She inhaled deeply, conflict tightening her throat. "Henry took his SIG Sauer to work this morning. It's not in the cabinet."

———

They sat around the table in front of the big windows. The fire crackled, and the music had been turned down softly. They ate piping hot, bubbling, cheesy pizza and Irene made them laugh with her tales of the big Crabby Jack crab boils hosted annually by Bull way back when. She even had stories of boils when Blake and Geoff's mother was still alive. Noah hung on to every word until his eyelids began to droop.

"School day tomorrow, champ, last one before the weekend," Blake said. "You better go up and get ready for bed."

As Noah got up from the table, he bumped Geoff's dirty knife with a clatter to the ground.

"Oh, I'll get it," Meg said, reaching under the table.

"Wait, stop, Meggie," Geoff said. "It's easier for me from this end."

Ice shot through her veins. Her hand froze midreach.

Wait. Stop! Don't run, Meggie, don't run . . .

Time warped. Sound stretched like an old cassette tape that had been exposed to heat. A moan began to sound in her head. Like a foghorn. Her skin turned cold, her mouth dry. Her eyes locked with Geoff's as he bent down to reach for the knife under the table, too. A current crackled hot between them.

He got up, plunked the knife on his plate. Slowly, Meg sat upright. She stared, unseeing, at Geoff. In her mind she was running, tripping, screaming. Rain slashed at her face. Darkness all around. Wind tore at her hair, her wet clothes. Fierce. Someone coming after her. The bushes tore at her legs. She hooked her toe on a root, smashed into the ground. Pain exploded in her chest. Scrambling to her feet, stumbling, going down on all fours again, scrabbling back up to her feet, running. For her life. Heart pounding. No, not water running down her face. Blood. Sherry . . . Sherry was . . . Sherry . . . naked. Sprawled in the black mud . . . she could see her body . . .

Wait. Stop! Don't run, Meggie.

A hand grabbed her. She jerked away, screamed, tried to run harder, faster. But the hand clamped tight on her arm, fingers cutting into skin. The hand spun her around, her shirt ripping. She saw a face. A face she knew. Then he was gone. Blackness. The familiar blackness.

Meg stopped breathing.

Someone she knew had been the monster chasing her into the storm.

"Meg. Meg! Talk to me. What's wrong?" It was Blake, on his feet, holding her shoulders, trying to pull her back, worry bright in his eyes. Geoff was staring at her, a strange look on his face.

She tried to swallow. Her hands were pressed tight on the table. Couldn't swallow. Needed water. No, not water, drowning, she was drowning.

"Noah, upstairs, please," Blake snapped. "Get ready for bed. Geoff, can you take Irene into the kitchen to make some tea?"

Geoff got up quickly. "C'mon, my man, it's bedtime. Irene, can you help with tea?"

"What's wrong with Meg?" Noah wailed, refusing to leave his chair. "Is Meg okay?"

Irene, too, remained in her chair, eyes shining with worry.

"I . . . I'm fine," Meg said, voice hoarse. "Please, everyone relax." She struggled to take a deep breath, to steady her heart. Her eyes burned. "Just . . . some water."

"I'll get it." Irene burst up from her chair and scurried into the kitchen. Geoff slowly reseated himself, his gaze fixed on Meg, his features tight, eyes dark, energy simmering from him in waves.

Irene returned with ice water. Meg took the glass, sipped, her hand shaking. Blake steadied her arm as she wobbled the glass back to the table.

"Noah," he said quietly. "Bed. I'll come up to read in a sec."

His son got up, stared at Meg for a moment, then made slowly for the door, glancing over his shoulder before exiting.

"Meg—talk to me," Blake said, taking her hand, feeling her pulse.

She sucked in a huge breath of air, blew it out slowly. "I . . . I had some sort of flashback." She cleared her throat. "It's happened before, but it always stops just before I could see who was chasing me. It always starts the same way. Me running. Someone chasing. A male voice, yelling for me to 'wait, stop, Meggie, don't run.' This time, he grabbed me, ripping my shirt as he yanked me around, and—" She reached for the water glass, took a deep gulp. "I saw a face. It was white, luminous, wet with rain. Hair plastered to his head. I *knew* who it was."

"Who?" Geoff demanded. "*Who* did you see?"

Blake shot his brother a hot look.

"I don't know," Meg said. "I just felt a bolt of recognition. That terrible shock that someone you know is trying to hurt you. But his face blurred away before I could make out his features."

Silence swelled thick and electrical around the table. The candle flickered, and the fire cracked.

"Did you see anything else?" Blake asked quietly.

"I had a flash of Sherry. Her naked body. Like a black-and-white freeze-frame, as if illuminated by a bolt of lightning—the kind of stark image that burns into your retinas. She was lying on her back, spread-eagled in mud. I . . . had the sense I was fleeing from that image. And that there were several shapes around her wanting to come get me." Meg looked up from the glass of water that she'd been staring at.

"It must have been triggered by Geoff calling me Meggie. No one has called me that in years, not since I was twelve, really, when I asked everyone to stop. Sherry never listened, she always called me Meggie-Peg." She cleared her throat. "And that image of Sherry's body, it *had* to have come from the crime scene photos I've been looking at. I'm transposing things after going through all those files." She took another clumsy sip of water, coughed again, eyes watering. She dug in her pocket for a tissue, blew her nose.

"I know how these things work—you can insert your own images, create your own false memories." She tried to laugh, but it came out a cough. "I don't even know whether to trust my own mind, now."

CHAPTER 20

Blake felt as though a cold stone had dropped right through his stomach into his bowels. A dark thought, one he didn't want to—*couldn't*—even begin to entertain, prowled nevertheless along the edges of his brain. Geoff had always called Meg "Meggie." He'd left Shelter Bay still referring to her as Meggie.

The image of his brother in the boathouse that night twenty-two years ago shimmered into his mind. His skin turned cold. He tried to push it away as he read Noah his bedtime story, but it lurked like a hungry wolf in the shadows of his mind.

Geoff had offered to drive Irene back to Chestnut Place and Meg was resting in the big wingback in front of the fire. Blake tucked his son in, and clicked off the light. He went downstairs and reentered the living room. Meg looked up and smiled. Relief punched through his stomach.

Color had returned to her cheeks. She looked golden in front of his hearth, the flames giving her hair a coppery light. Lucy lay at her feet and the music was soft. The vignette stalled him for a moment. And a coal of need burned deep. He wanted her. All of her. Here in his home, in front of his hearth, until death do us part. He came slowly forward, his attention going involuntarily to the diamond cluster catching firelight on her hand. The reminder she still wanted someone else.

He drew up a chair and sat facing her across the low coffee table. There was a notepad and pen on the table. The top page of the pad was covered in writing and lines connecting names.

Before he could ask what she'd been writing, she sat up and leaned forward. "I've been waiting for a moment to tell you that Kovacs called earlier. Just before supper. He's reopened Sherry's case, on the quiet."

His heart kicked. With it came a small spark of irritation. "Why didn't you tell me at once?"

"I didn't want to involve Irene or Geoff, or Noah." She smiled. "I didn't want to break the spell," she said softly. "It was such a warm evening. It . . . I felt like we'd all come home somehow. Until my little flashback ruined everything. I'm sorry about that—this case is just messing with my mind."

Blake swallowed, his pulse quickening, that coal in his gut burning bigger and deeper. And suddenly everything felt fragile. It was here, the whispering of a dream between them, but if he reached out to grasp it too firmly, or early, it would vanish like gossamer in his hand.

"Tell me," he said quietly, "word for word. What did Kovacs say?"

She told him about Sally Braden's arrest, and how Kovacs asked if she could think of a motive for Sally to shoot out the house. "He said he wanted to work *with* me. That he wanted this solved as much as I did now. It makes sense, I suppose, him wanting to clear this up before the election. But I got a feeling that something was off. It was just such a turnabout." She watched the flames for a moment, absently fiddling with her engagement ring. "I don't know whether to trust him. Perhaps he was fishing."

"Sally?" Blake said. He gave a soft whistle. "Whoda thunk."

Meg jerked her chin toward her notepad. "I've been trying to come up with possible links between everyone. Sally was in Sherry's graduation class. Along with Tommy, Emma, Ryan Millar,

Geoff, and Henry, who is now her brother-in-law. Henry is married to Lori-Beth, who was in my class." She glanced at Blake. "Lori-Beth was friendly with Allison."

"I don't see how that's relevant."

"It's probably not. I'm just laying out the links." She gave a soft snort. "Goes to show how interconnected everyone can be in a small town, how things now could relate way back to childhood—grudges, first loves and allegiances, bullying, jealousies, perceived slights."

First loves.

He thought of himself, and Meg. His thoughts turned to Geoff, and he felt a sharp stab of guilt for not mentioning his brother's secret relationship from the past. This was the first occasion where the need to bring it up had fully presented itself. From here, it edged closer toward a lie by omission, and not a lie from the past. But one hanging silent between them right now.

One more day . . . it will destroy a man's marriage. It . . . it'll kill him. Trust me. I . . . I need one more day to talk to him, allow him to prepare . . .

His skin grew hot. Blake rubbed the stubble on his jaw. "Sally dotes on her sister," he said quietly. "Everything she does is for Lori-Beth. The scuttlebutt in town is that Sally never got over the fact she put Lori-Beth in that chair, and she's devoted her life to atone. Her way of surviving the guilt."

"You're suggesting she vandalized my house for Lori-Beth?"

"Makes no sense, I know. But if you're looking at what drives people, Lori-Beth drives Sally."

A slow smile curved over her mouth. "You sound like Jonah."

Cold instantly washed over his skin. He got up, went to fetch a bottle of whiskey and two gasses from the cabinet. He set the glasses on the table, poured a finger into each, and handed one to her. Their fingers brushed. Her diamonds winked. Something inscrutable entered her eyes.

"I'm sorry," she said.

He shrugged, reseating himself. He cupped his glass in his hands, warming and slowly swirling his drink as he stared at the fire. "It's not like I don't know that you're going back," he said quietly.

She didn't reply. He glanced up. And hope kicked gently at his heart again. He quickly changed the topic. "And there's the fact Sally works at Braden Cattle, where Mason and Keevan Mack work, and live. Where she likely got the blood."

"Blood is extreme," Meg said. "The use of blood makes me question her mental stability, if it *is* proved it was her. And shooting all the windows—there's real aggression there. Passion. Rage. Over something." She pushed hair back off her face, and the firelight caught the scar on her brow. He thought back to when she'd gotten the injury—the black gash against alabaster skin when he'd found her near dead in the waves. Geoff's sack. His brother's face at the dining table tonight when Meg had her flashback. That dark, unarticulated thing prowling at the fringes of his mind edged a little closer. He took a quick swig of his drink.

"I also went to see Tommy today."

His gaze shot to Meg. "What?"

"He had a cancelled appointment. Could squeeze me in."

He stared. "Meg, we had a deal. We do this together. That's why you're here, in my house."

Her gaze flickered. A spark of anger? Irritation? He slugged back his drink, poured another. He held the bottle up to her. She shook her head.

He plunked it down hard. "What did he say?"

"Blake, I wasn't in danger. And he would have been far less candid if you were hunkering there watching him."

"Hunkering. Is that what you think I've been doing?"

"Oh, for Pete's sake." She got up, and went to the window. Folding her arms tightly over her stomach, she stared beyond the black, beyond her own reflection. In the distance, the beam from the Shelter Head lighthouse washed the sky. Her red hair hung in a mad, curly tangle down her slender back, and all Blake wanted to do was sink his hands into that hair, fist it, pull her toward him, crush her sweet mouth under his, push her naked body down into his bed . . . He took a deep pull on his second scotch and cursed himself.

"What did Tommy say, Meg?"

She remained silent.

"Meg?"

She inhaled deeply, turned, and Blake's chest torqued. Her face was sad. Her eyes confused. She was fingering her ring.

"He told me that Emma was a passive-aggressive. A pathological liar. That she'd lied to the police in saying Sherry had gone to the spit to make out with Tyson Mack. Tommy claims Sherry was going to buy drugs with Ty, that Ty had contacts. That both Sherry and Emma were into Ecstasy."

Blake slowly lowered his glass.

"Tommy said Emma also lied to him in order to turn him against his own girlfriend. He claims Emma was trying to steal him from Sherry."

"You're kidding."

"Thing is, I *saw* Sherry get on that bike with Ty. I spoke with them. And whatever cues I was picking up from those two, I was one hundred percent convinced there was a sexual attraction between them, and that they were going to do 'it' at the grove on the spit." She paused, holding his eyes. "One of them—Tommy or Emma—is lying."

———

Blake unlocked the old shed near the water. Clouds slid fast and silent across the sky, giving glimpses of a pregnant moon. Everywhere, water dripped, trickled, plopped. The sound of the nearby creek was loud.

Unable to sleep, Blake had come down here. Geoff had not returned after taking Irene home. It was now almost 3:00 a.m., and he'd not answered his cell. Blake told himself Irene must have gotten home safely, or the people from Chestnut Place would have called—they had Meg's contact details, and the marina number. Geoff must have taken off somewhere afterward.

Fuck you, Geoff, why don't you come the hell home so I can have this out with you . . .

Dark thoughts snaked through his mind as he edged open the old, waterlogged door, holding his kerosene lantern high. Cobwebs shimmered, and shadows jumped and ducked. He stepped inside, the floorboards creaking under his weight. The interior was dank. He could smell mold.

Maybe Meg *was* transposing. Maybe his brother being on the spit, and his sack being found on the same beach, *was* a coincidence. Stranger things happened. Maybe Geoff's calling her Meggie had simply triggered an old flashback that meant nothing sinister around the dining table. Because no matter Geoff's movements on the spit that day, Blake could *not* believe that his brother had anything to do with killing Sherry.

He set the lantern on a wooden table, and opened an old mariner's chest. He found what he was looking for. It was bagged in plastic, faded, but still in one piece—it had been mothballed and the chest was lined with cedar, which was a natural repellent to insects. Emotion tugged at him and memories swirled as he removed his dad's old crab hat from the plastic. He gave a sad smile, thinking about Bull, about the stories Irene had regaled them with around the table. The big, annual crab boils, festive events that brought Shelter Bay locals together, fostered an old-fashioned sense of community. At night they'd all gather round the fire pit to tell war tales about the season just passed, each raconteur trying to outdo the other with stories of the most ridiculous tourist moments that year.

The months that ended in "er," Bull always used to say. Those were the good crabbing months: September, October, November. And December. When the waters turned cold and the crab grew fattest.

Blake dusted off the fading red crab hat. The googly eyes wobbled. He positioned it on his head, and went over to the rust-pocked mirror. In the quavering lantern light, past shimmered into present, and for a strange moment he saw his dad looking back at him from behind the rust stains. Shock rippled through him. The likeness, DNA, it lies in wait. Time comes full circle, but not quite. He grinned ruefully at himself, and he almost saw his dad smile. Almost heard Bull's gruff voice among the cobwebs of the shed, here among his mother's dusty, boxed paintings. And he wondered, could he re-create that sense of life, that vitality around the marina that had made him so happy as a boy.

Could he take the good parts of the past, of his parents, and move with those into the future? Leaving the bad bits behind. Not wasted, though, for he'd perhaps learned from the bad parts what he did *not* want for his own son. He'd perhaps learned how to be a better father than his own had been. Bull had terrible faults, a dark streak. He'd broken under the grief of loss. But he'd not been without love.

The googly crab eyes wiggled and the crab feet jiggled as he moved his head. Blake almost laughed at his image. His most fervent wish, suddenly, was that Geoff *was* telling him the truth. That he *could* trust him. And even if Meg did return to her life in Seattle, that he and Noah and Geoff could be a solid family. Geoff could bring Nate to visit. Noah could bring friends home. He'd build up this marina. And he resolved right there: Come November, when the Dungeness crabs were pink and fat and plentiful, Crabby Jack's would once again host a Shelter Bay community crab boil. He'd haul out this stupid hat to make people laugh, and they'd all talk about Bull and the boils of the good old days. And the marina and Crabby Jack's would once again rock with soul.

Blake started to close the mariner's chest, but he stopped as a cardboard box of photos in envelopes caught his eye. He reached for the top envelope, opened it, and extracted one of the photos. It was of Geoff and his friends around an old VW van, taken maybe twenty-three years ago—guys posed ridiculously in front of the vehicle. Blake recognized several from school days. Geoff stood atop the roof of the van, like a king—legs astride, arms crossed, chin tilted as if in pride. Henry Thibodeau crouched in front of the wheel. The words of Lee Albies curled through his mind.

. . . he told my PI that he saw a red VW van parked behind trees near the trail that led to this infamous make-out spot where Sherry Brogan was strangled . . .

Blake frowned. Who was the owner of this van? He reached for another photograph but stilled as he heard a noise outside, a clutter of rocks. Then came the snap of a twig, and a soft crunch of gravel. He became conscious of the pistol holstered at his back. Slowly, he replaced the box of photos and moved to the door. He listened. But all he could hear was the drip and plop of water. The distant rush of the swollen creek.

He reached for his weapon, and holding it ready, he flung open the door, waited. No more noise. He stepped out. Listened again. The world was all shadow and shimmer and shining with water in the moonlight. The light in Meg's dormer was off.

A scuffle sounded on the bank. He spun toward the sound, heart hammering. A shadow, bushes moved. He heard a rattle of stones. *Someone scuttling up the path.*

"Hey! Who's there?" He ran toward the bank.

A car door slammed up on the coast road.

"Hey!" he yelled, scrambling up the twisting trail that snaked through the scrub up to the road. He popped out on the road, breathing hard, as tires squealed and brake lights flared momentarily at the end of the road.

Silence descended. Just the waving fronds of conifers. A shadow of a nighthawk across the moon. The moon silver on the bay.

Mouth dry, he slid his Glock back into his holster and peered down through the scrub toward the marina. From up here, through the branches, he could see yellow light glowing in Meg's window now. She'd been roused.

As he took a step back toward the path, his foot kicked something soft. A black glove. He bent down to retrieve it and weighed it in his hand. Leather. Expensive. He scanned his surrounds again before making his way back down to lock the shed, moonlight showing his way.

———

Screaming rent the air. The kind of screams that gut the human in you. The kind that rise out of raw terror. A sound that bypasses the logic center of the brain and zings right into the nervous system. Meg raced *toward* the terrible sound, not away, even as her mind told her to flee. She scrambled wildly up the bank, hand over foot in avalanching white sand still hot from the sun's radiation throughout the day. As she neared the dune ridge where scrub grew thick and the shore pines marched in hunched shapes across the sky, wind hit hard off the sea. Rain began to bomb down. It was turning to dusk, a strange purplish-orange quality in the sky— the kind that comes from distant forest fires and crackles with the electricity of simmering storms. The screams died. She stalled, the sudden silence even more terrifying.

Moving more cautiously now, her breathing ragged, she crested the ridge. And froze. In the strange waning light she saw . . . a thing of horror . . . Sherry, white and naked, splayed against black loam like a broken doll. All Meg could see was the bare, white body. Noise roared in her head. Her vision narrowed. Trees seemed to close in around her. Wind, rain began to lash hair against her face. She knew there were others, in the shadows.

See them, Meg. Try to see them . . .

She tried to peer harder. And then another sound snapped her to action: "Get her! Fuck! . . . *Stop* her—get her, or we're all fucking dead!"

Meg turned and fled back down the dune, and into tussock that was land-mined with horse droppings. Twigs tore at her face. Saw grass sliced her legs.

She heard footfalls thudding behind. Heavy breathing. Louder.

"Meggie!"

She ran faster. Her toe caught under a root and her body slammed to the ground. For a second . . . *how many seconds?* . . . she couldn't move. Rain pummeled her back. The sky darkened. She heard him coming closer. With Herculean effort she managed to scramble back onto her feet. She made for the south point. She knew where to hide, how to dive into water and disappear under foam and froth, and come up in secret under rock, in a grotto where there was a cave. A cave Blake had shown her. All she had to do was reach the beach, the water.

A hand grabbed her arm. She screamed and jerked free, tearing her shirt across her breast. He gripped her again, and swung her around . . .

His face. She saw his face.

Meg screamed from the bottom of her lungs.

The noise jolted her awake. She was shaking. Sweat drenched her body and soaked into her nightgown. Her breaths came shallow and fast. She got up on one elbow and reached for the lamp, clicked it on. Light flared into the dark, chasing away shadows. And she heard it . . . a screech of tires.

Not a scream.

Tires squealing.

Up on the road.

She sat fully up in bed and wrapped her arms tightly around her knees. She rocked, trying to calm her breathing. Each time the nightmare haunted her, there was a tiny bit more. And this time she'd seen. A face.

Geoff Sutton's face.

It made no sense. She couldn't trust the image. Meg knew just how fallible memories could be. She'd been looking into Geoff's eyes under the dinner table as she'd flipped into a flashback. And now she'd inserted that image into her own memory. Her own daytime research, conjecture, experiences, were sliding into the nightmare of sleep.

She couldn't trust her own mind. But it nevertheless rattled her. Raised questions she didn't want to ask.

Knowing she'd never get back to sleep now, she got out of bed and took off her drenched nightgown. She dug a clean T-shirt out of her bag, pulled it over her head, and reached for her mother's journal. She climbed into bed and leaned back against the pillows, opening the diary to where she last left off.

Emma and Tommy are home for spring break, and they came by again today. It heartens me so to see them both. Beautiful, strong. Sherry's friends. It keeps my daughter's spirit alive for me. And it helps me refocus on small things, like making coffee for her friends. Emma brought cookies today. Her mother baked them. Emma told me it was unusual for her mom to bake—she spends so much time at the pharmacy—so I better enjoy them. It made me laugh. She's enjoying her studies so far, and plans

*to be a pharmacist like her mother, maybe even
take over the small business on Front Street one
day, if the big chains don't gobble it up first.*

*I told them both I was investigating, that I
was beginning to think Ty Mack might be innocent,
and that I was doing everything I could to learn
more, as fast as I could, before Jack's trial come
December. I asked if they had **any** idea who else
might have wanted to hurt Sherry, if they could
think for me . . .*

Meg stilled. She lunged for her digital recorder, found the file of the interview with Emma she was looking for, wound it forward, and pressed play.

"Did my mother ever express any doubt to you guys about Ty's guilt at that time?"

"No. I don't think so. I don't really recall . . ."

A blatant lie? Or had Emma truly forgotten? She rewound, hit play again. Emma's "no" was curt and swift. What did that mean? How does one forget something like that? Meg turned the page in the journal, read further.

*Emma is such a dear, sweet girl. When she went
into my bathroom she came out with a worried
look in her eyes, and she told me those pills I had
in there were powerful. That mix. Tranquilizers,
sleeping pills, anti-anxiety. She said her mom had
spoken about some of that medication in particular,
and how evidence was growing that it could
cause depression, and worse. There was a suicide
rate associated with those pills. She told me to
be careful, maybe speak to my doctor about slowly*

coming off them, and taking up yoga, or maybe joining a group to talk through things. Tommy was supportive. He seemed worried, too. I think Emma will be good at her job one day. I think of Sherry and how she was planning to be a doctor. And the loss again becomes unbearable . . .

Meg scanned through her digital recorder and located the file with Tommy's interview. She wound it forward, pressed play.

"She never told you about her suspicions that Ty might be innocent?"

"Never."

Frowning, Meg wound the conversation a little further forward, hit play.

"Her suicide didn't come as a surprise?"

"No, Meg. It did not. Emma was studying pharmacology, and she'd seen the collection of pills that your mom was taking in the bathroom. She told me what they were for—anxiety, depression, insomnia. Tara was on a bad cocktail . . ."

Meg sat back, the Tommy interview replaying through her mind in its entirety.

"Emma proved to be a passive-aggressive. A pathological liar. She lied to me. Everyone. Even the police . . ."

An icy thought twisted through her mind: Could Emma have tampered with those pills? Meg scrambled over her bedding to reach her laptop. She fired it up, and punched in the names of her mother's drugs. They came in capsule form. Capsules could be refilled, or tampered with. She inhaled, casting aside the idea—it was too extreme. Or was it? Because . . . *if* her mother had *not* taken her own life, someone else had. And the verdict had definitely been an overdose. Forcing someone to swallow an excess of pills would in all likelihood have left signs of a struggle, and raised flags in an autopsy. But what if capsules could be filled with increased levels of active ingredients? And the person who swallowed them had no idea how much medicine they were taking? And who better to do that than someone with some pharmacological knowledge and access. Was it even possible?

Meg made a note to call Emma. She had more questions now. She'd like to speak to Tommy again, too. Because her mother's journal clearly indicated she'd told both Tommy and Emma that she believed Ty Mack could have been innocent. Her hand stilled at the sound of a crash downstairs. Her mouth turned dry. She sat very still, listening, those screeching tires earlier suddenly taking on new context. She heard another noise, a scratching, then a soft thump.

Quickly, she grabbed her robe. Belting it across her waist she went to the door and inched it open. It was dark down the passage, moonlight glinting through a window at the far end. She walked quietly along to Blake's room, rapped at his door.

"Blake?" she whispered.

No reply.

She turned the handle, edging it open. "Blake?"

His bed was empty, his bedding a jumble. Her pulse quickened. Meg turned and hurried quietly to Noah's room and edged open his door. He was sleeping soundly. No Lucy in sight.

She started down the stairs, sliding her hand down the railing for balance, bare feet quiet. She reached the bottom of the stairs, rounded the corner, and screamed as something lunged at her. It was huge. Shadowed. With horns. Her brain folded in on itself, unable to make sense, and she turned to flee... *run, Meggie, run...*

The thing grabbed her, spun her around, and clamped a hand over her mouth. Moonlight caught his face.

Blake!?

"Shhhh," he whispered, breath warm against her ear. "You'll wake Noah." He released her mouth slowly. She could feel his heart thudding against her body. "What in the hell were you doing sneaking up on me like that?" he hissed.

She stared up at him, heart jackhammering against her ribs, and she started to laugh. "What on *earth* is that thing on your head?"

"Shh!"

She clamped her hand over her own mouth, *snorting* as she tried to stifle her own laughter bubbling through her. He yanked the thing off his head and tossed it onto the counter.

"It's my dad's crab hat," he said stiffly.

"It stinks." She giggled again—like the child she'd always been inside—at the way his hair now stood up in comic tufts. A smile began to play over his lips, but it faded as he watched her laugh. A predatory intensity entered his gaze. His pupils turned dark, large, and an electrical heat began to thrum off him in waves. Meg's laughter slowly quieted. She swallowed. Her heart stuttered as a molten, tingling heat leaked into her belly, and a gentle throb began in her groin, each delicious pulse matching the beat of blood through her veins.

He reached for her hands, and drew her to him, slowly, inexorably, giving her time to stop him, the question implicit in his pacing, in the darkening pools of his eyes. And when she didn't resist, he yanked her firmly against his solid frame, his other hand sliding down her hips and cupping her buttocks. He pulled her pelvis up against his groin as he forced his mouth down hard on hers. She felt his erection pressed between them.

Heat exploded logic from Meg's mind. She came up onto her toes, arching into him, opening her mouth under the crushing aggression of his hunger, her tongue tangling, fighting with his. He slid his hand into her robe, under her T-shirt, and down into the lace of her panties. He cupped her between her legs. His skin rough, hot. He moved the crotch fabric aside and she felt his fingers against bare skin. A groan slipped free from her mouth. He parted her with his fingers, touched her, and a wave of pleasure washed through her as her limbs began to shake.

"Upstairs," he murmured over her mouth, his finger going inside her. "Come with me upstairs." Her knees turned to water as she sagged against him, aching for him, all of him, inside, down deep. Hard. Desperate.

———

Geoff sat in his Jeep facing the ocean. He'd driven around to the state park lot on the spit after dropping Irene off at Chestnut Place. The moon shimmered silver on the swells and phosphorescence danced in the lines of surf that broke along the shore. He snagged his tequila bottle from the passenger seat, swigged, thinking of the look in Meg's eyes as he'd reached under the table for that knife. It was like she was seeing into him, into the past. It was only a matter of time.

Wind gusted off the sea, buffeting his Jeep, and he thought he could hear the screams again. He would never erase those screams from his mind. They'd scored into his soul like grooves gouged in vinyl, destined to replay, and replay the same old sound. He took another glug from the bottle, relishing the hot-acid burn down his throat, eyes watering as he swallowed. Wiping his mouth with the back of his sleeve, it struck him full. It was reaching the end. One way or another, it would all come back to that day. It would come out. There was no way in hell that genie could realistically be squeezed back into the bottle that Meg had opened.

Good or bad, maybe it was a relief. He rescrewed the cap onto his tequila, tossed the bottle back onto the seat, and pulled out his cell phone. He dialed Nate in spite of the hour.

"Hey." He wiped his nose. "It's me."

"Geoff? You okay?" Nate's voice was low with concern.

Geoff inhaled, feeling the warmth of booze flush his chest. "Yeah. Just . . . wanted to hear your voice."

"All going okay with your brother? You told him about the wedding?"

A sad smile crossed his face. "I should have told him years ago. He was totally fine, relieved almost. Happy for me—for us. I suspect Blake always knew on some level. He must have known. He . . . he was always good to me." His voice thickened.

"You sure you're okay?"

"Uh, yeah. Yeah, I'm fine."

"Time to come home," Nate said.

"Soon. Just need to . . . speak to a few more people. See you real soon."

He hung up, closed his eyes, put his head back. Maybe if Meg had stayed away, if her memory had remained properly buried, or she'd died, he could have skated through and still had it all in the end. Or maybe it would have festered out of him, yet, in some unspeakable way.

The primal screams. You never, ever forget screams like that. Perhaps the end started for him with the first scream.

But no matter how he angled it, he could not see a way out now. It was like a glass pane that had been smashed. The damage was done and the cracks were insidiously feathering out, and it was just a matter of time before the whole thing shattered and crumbled to the ground.

He dialed another number, but the call kicked straight to voice mail.

"Henge," he said softly, thickly, using his old friend's nickname as he left a message. "We need to talk."

CHAPTER 21

Sex with Blake was elemental and it was rough. It was slammed up against the wall, her legs wrapped around him, and it was back down on his bed with her on top of him rocking against his pelvis, milking him, panting, a trembling tension building in every fiber of her body as she clamped his wrists down above his head, and he bucked under her, up into her. He flipped her onto her back, and she tasted blood as his teeth raked and bit her lips, and she responded with equal ferocity. He kneed her thighs open wide, and thrust up into her, impaling her, forcing her to gasp and burn with each push to the hilt of his thick cock. She felt the wet heat of his mouth down her belly, at her groin, his tongue inside her. And she shattered like bridge cables that had held too taut for too many years, suddenly exploding in an almighty crash as rolling contractions seized her body and her mind.

It was tender, too, when he made love to her again, a little closer to dawn, in the silver moonlight that puddled onto the sheets. It was a coalescence of past and present, and it brought them up to the uncertain maw of the future. Meg felt as though she'd been shattered into a million pieces, and reassembled in a way that was more whole than before.

They lay there, naked and entangled, skin hot and damp, breathing fast and shallow in the pool of moonlight, wind making shadows of trees outside. And the world felt changed. Uncertain. It felt delicate, and beautiful, and raw, a thing to be taken and molded into a fresh shape, where possibilities were suddenly like shells scattered on the hard-packed shore, left by the ebbing tide.

Blake laced his fingers through Meg's, and inside, she smiled. "Why," she said softly, "were you wearing that hat?"

She turned her head on the pillow, met his eyes. Her heart squeezed.

"I went to look for it, in the old shed."

"In the middle of the night? What for?"

"Because of what you said to Noah about his grandfather. Because of how you and Irene, and Geoff, made me see tonight how this marina could become a home again." He sat up, leaned back against the headboard, his chest rising and falling, still trying to catch his breath. "Because I want to share some of the good memories of my dad with Noah." He glanced down at her.

There was something in the way he said "good memories" that made her ask, "You have some bad memories of Bull, ones you'd like to bury?"

He scrubbed his hand through his thatch of hair, making it messier than ever, which made Meg feel a hot spurt of affection, and also a sense of trepidation. Feelings that should be contradictory were braiding tightly together into one confusing thing.

"He was a violent man, Meg. He used to hit us."

Shock washed through her. She scooted up into a sitting position beside him, pulling the sheet up over her breasts. "He *beat* you?"

"Mostly Geoff. He had a lot of latent rage after my mom died. He couldn't accept Geoff for what he was."

Meg held his eyes. "Do you mean what I think you mean?"

"Geoff's gay."

Meg leaned her head back against the headboard, and inhaled deeply. "You know, I wondered."

"I think we all did, if not overtly. On some level I probably always knew."

"And the wedding?"

"It's why I wanted him to tell you himself. He's marrying a guy called Nate Fischer. Geoff came home to come out, to invite me and Noah."

"And Bull knew his son was gay, or suspected he was?"

"That's my guess, in retrospect. He was always telling Geoff to 'man up,' stop being an 'artsy wuss.'" Blake swallowed, and for a moment silence filled the room.

Meg's mind turned to her nightmare, Geoff's face, the unreliability of memory. How sometimes we could recall things that were never there, or refused to remember those that were.

"He struck a particularly violent blow early that morning you went missing, cutting open Geoff's cheek. I suspect my dad had been drinking well into the preceding night. It was the final blow Geoff would take. He left home before the month was out."

"I had no idea this was happening," Meg whispered.

"No one did."

"And you never reported Bull."

Blake snorted softly. "Our dad? Christ, no. There was shame. It was our own dark little secret. And perhaps I never understood it fully, because there was also still love."

"Classic abuse scenario," she said quietly.

"He didn't hurt me like he hurt my brother. And when Geoff left, it stopped."

"He was afraid of losing you, too."

"But he did. In the end." Blake trailed his fingers down her arm, his hand coming to a rest over hers, covering Jonah's ring. He looked down at her and a sad smile curved his mouth. "But that wasn't his fault. It was yours."

"I made mistakes, Blake. Bad ones." *And that was the biggest one of all—hurting you.*

"So, I got the old crab hat out." His smile deepened into something genuine and instantly her heart lifted in relief. "I plan to proudly wear it when I reinstate the big annual Crabby Jack boil come November, invite the whole community. Beach bonfire. Lanterns. Live band. Like the old days." He paused, holding her eyes. And the question rose between them: *Will you be there, Meg, come November?*

"I think we need to find you a new hat." She laughed, sidestepping, but it sounded hollow even to her own ears.

"Once you've done all your interviews," he said, "and once you've gotten all the documents you need, will you return to Seattle to write it, or will you write your book here?"

Meg looked away, her heartbeat suddenly erratic, a soft panic licking at her belly. "I don't know," she said quietly, honestly.

"You don't *need* to live anywhere in particular to do your job, do you?"

The tongues of panic flicked harder. She swallowed. "Only in that I need to travel to the location of each case I take on, to research."

"But the actual writing, I mean, you told me your office was a mobile camper."

Her exchange with Jonah curled into her mind:

"You could get a real office, you know, with foundations and walls and a roof."

"I like the mobility."

"You can't put down roots. It's just a matter of time before one of the monsters you write about will be released from prison. You should consider security. A proper house, a condo—"

"A job like yours, you could do it anywhere in the world."

Meg cleared her throat.

He laced his fingers back through hers and clasped her hand tight. Almost too tight. "You could do it here, you know, in a nice little marina cottage by the sea. I could convert the boathouse. You'd have a private dock, just the ocean and sky in front of your window."

Meg's heart jackhammered. She could suddenly see it, writing at an old, stripped-down Oregon pine table in front of a window that played out the moods of the bay. The moonlight on a clear night, the lighthouse and foghorns in the mist. The constant crunching sound of distant waves on the reef, the rattling of the February winds. A black potbellied stove for warmth in the winter months, a dog like Lucy at her feet. The knowledge that Blake and Noah, family, worked and played and lived close by. Big crab boils in the chill fall. Emotion pooled in her eyes. Inside she started to tremble.

A memory suddenly snared her. She was standing outside The Mystery Bookstore in the cold, looking in at a poster of an author holding up her new book. Next to the poster was a line of glossy new hardbacks, the titles bold and shiny in an embossed font—a new mystery tale lurking between those covers, a new adventure for one of Meg's favorite heroines, and there were only three days left until she got her allowance, and she could buy it. She'd stood there, in the cold wind, imagining that she'd like to be just like that author one day, even when she grew old. Like a Jessica Fletcher in that television show who rode around her small seaside town on her bike with a basket in front while in her cottage, murder she wrote.

Meg closed her eyes, leaning her head back against the headboard, almost afraid of the power of the image Blake had just conjured for her. The allure of it. She'd forgotten that day in front of The Mystery Bookstore, and she realized in this moment that no, Jonah was *not* right. She'd not turned to a life of crime writing in an effort to seek justice, or answers because of Sherry's murder and the attack she herself had endured. It went further back than that. It was rooted in happier times, and this revelation was epiphanic,

---

suddenly liberating. Her heart beat even faster. Was it possible? To make her life here, with Blake and Noah and Lucy?

"What are you thinking?"

She smiled and opened one eye. "Remembering," she said.

His face tightened. "The attack?"

"No," she whispered. "A good memory." Meg reached for her robe.

"Where you going?"

She smiled, kissed him. "Just the bathroom."

Inside the bathroom she rinsed and dried her face and stared into Blake's mirror. She didn't quite recognize the person who stared back. Her hair was a wild tangle, her lips swollen from his kisses. She had a lambency in her eyes that sometimes she noticed in other women who were incredibly alive and invariably in love.

As she moved a fall of hair back from her face, her diamond cluster caught light. She stilled, stared at it. Then without trying to articulate her actions, she fiddled it off her finger and slipped it onto the small silver chain around her neck.

—

Geoff shut his right eye and squinted through his left in an effort to bring his vision into focus and stay on the road. The tequila was kicking in harder than he'd anticipated. As he rounded the bend on a steep rise above the ocean, veering slightly over the yellow line, his headlights hit a MINI Cooper parked on the opposite shoulder of the road. White racing stripes bounced his beams. Shit. *Henry?* Geoff slowed, scrunching his left eye tighter as he pulled a squealing U-turn and drew up onto the gravel verge behind the MINI. He came to a stop, shut off the engine. Nothing moved or sounded apart from trees in wind. Fear stuck a dart in his heart.

Geoff got out of his car, and crunched over gravel to the MINI, his breath misting in front of his face. He rapped cautiously on the driver's window.

A face turned to him. White. Eyes in black shadow. Expressionless.

He hurried around to the passenger side, opened the door. A pistol lay on the seat, beside a black glove. Cocked. He cursed softly and picked up the gun and lone glove. He climbed in and shut the door.

"Henry?"

Henry turned to him.

"What's going on?" Geoff whispered.

"Lori-Beth knows. She knows what I am."

"Okay, okay," he said. "That's not the end of the world. Turn on the engine. Put the heat on. It's like a bloody refrigerator in here."

Henry acquiesced while Geoff clicked on the overhead light, unloaded and de-cocked the SIG. He opened the glove compartment and secured the pistol away.

"Why are you here, just up the road from the marina? What were you doing with that weapon?"

"You smell like alcohol."

"Yeah."

Henry held his gaze, engine purring, the interior finally starting to warm and mist up the windows.

"Sally knows, too. Not just about my sexual leanings. She knows something more. Bitch is always snooping around, listening. I swear she's been going through my computer. She took my rifle, shot out Meg's house."

Geoff's mind reeled. "What? *Sally* did it?"

"Cops arrested her this morning."

"She been charged?"

"Don't know. Haven't been home." Henry smacked the dash hard and abruptly, and turned to Geoff, eyes sparking in the dimness. "Don't you see? Sally *only* does things for LB. Always trying to protect her. If she did this, she wanted to scare Meg off, because Meg, in her mind, is a threat to LB. That's how the logic adds up. Pure math. And if she thinks LB is threatened by Meg's digging up the truth about an old murder, it means Sally knows something about *me*. Meg quits town, and it all goes away. And our facade of a marriage remains unbroken, and LB gets her damn baby."

"Did you go to the marina with this gun?"

Silence.

"You wanted to shoot Meg? What are you? Mad in the head?"

Henry dropped his face into his hands, rubbed.

Geoff turned in his seat to fully face his old friend. "You'd never get away with it, Henge. Believe me, it's crossed my mind. But you try some asshole move like that, and the cops will link you instantly to Meg's motives for being here. And if they dig that old evidence out of those case files, you're toast, man."

"I wish she'd just died that day," Henry whispered. "I wish Blake had never gone out there and found her. She should have died. What am I going to do? I can't go home . . ."

"You're going to drive to the Blind Channel Motel just south of Whakami Bay, where we had a drink the other night, that's what. You're going to check in and call LB and let her know you're safe and staying in the motel."

"No, I—"

"Do it. Or she'll call the cops. That's the last thing you want."

"And then what? We sit around and wait for the executioner anyway? You're not going to be immune, either, Geoff. You know what happens to guys like us in prison? Sitting around, doing nothing—it's a slow form of suicide."

Geoff rubbed his brow, his brain slurping with booze inside his skull. He needed to crash, get some sleep, but even in his tequila haze, he knew Henge was right. They couldn't stop this now, even *if* Meg could somehow be made to drop her investigation. Sally knew something. Possibly LB knew, too, through Sally. Blake knew he was on the spit. There was Meg's memory. Kovacs was snooping around . . . it had taken on a life of its own. They could either sit and wait for the slow-rolling ball of justice to hit them. Or . . .

"Wait for me at the motel," he said quietly.

Henry regarded him in silence. The heater pumped into the car. "When will you come?"

"Tomorrow night, late," Geoff said.

"What are you thinking?"

A slow smile curved his mouth. *"Thelma and Louise."*

———

Meg lay naked in his arms. Blake stared at the beams on the white ceiling. Outside, the sky was turning a pearlescent gray, heralding dawn. Tension increased in him. He wanted to hold on a while longer to this night. To Meg. He was afraid that come the harsh light of day it would all shatter into brightness, like a dream.

He glanced down at Meg. She was asleep, her skin pale against his. He gently moved hair from her cheek. He loved this red hair, this face, this person so much he thought he'd implode. And now that they'd come together, everything felt so fragile and so powerful. He felt the hint of a future, a vision too elusive, too delicate yet to reach out and grasp, for if he did, it might crumble to moondust in his fist. For so long he'd waited for this, dreamed of this.

And now?

She stirred and her lids fluttered open. She saw him watching her face and came up onto her elbow, her breasts alabaster in this light, nipples dark rose. He felt his cock stir. He traced his fingers gently, along her collarbone, shoulder—and his heart stopped. He couldn't breathe. Around her neck on a silver chain hung her engagement ring. His eyes shot to hers. She smiled. And adrenaline exploded in his blood. For a moment he was blind, and his brain was blank. She reached up, hooked her hand behind his neck, and drew him down to her.

As Blake's lips touched hers, she pulled the sheet off her body and rolled onto her back, pulling him on top of her. Her hands ran down the sides of his waist, and she opened her legs under him, arching up to him. He could feel the damp heat of her crotch as she tilted her hips, and guided him in. Red and black swirls drowned his vision and he sank himself deep into her body, and she gave a small gasp.

"Mmm," she said against his mouth as she began to rotate her hips, her inner muscles sucking and pulling at his erection, as she grew slicker and hotter and hotter.

"Need to take Noah to school . . . make breakfast."

"A quickie," she murmured, thrusting her hips harder, faster, taking him inside her to the hilt, her breaths becoming fast, short.

———

Noah rubbed his eyes as he stumbled along the passage to the bathroom. A noise in his dad's room stopped him in his tracks—heavy breathing, panting. His first reaction was fear. His dad was sick! He quickly went up to the door, was about to open it when he heard another sound—a woman's sound, like a moan coming up her throat. He froze. His gaze shot to the spare room door. It was ajar, and the bed he could see through the gap was empty. A hot feeling rushed into his chest, and a funny feeling slid into his tummy. It made him angry. Scared. It made his heart beat too fast. His eyes burned and he curled his fists into balls at his sides. He began to shake. He heard more breathing, a gasp, and his dad moaned.

He spun around, raced back to his room, and dived into his bed. He covered his head tight with a pillow, and rocked side to side to make it go away.

CHAPTER 22

The weather was turning, a strange color filtering into the sky. As Meg dressed, she felt a heavy, cold, electrical presence, as if a massive Pacific storm front was pressing in. Downstairs, her instincts were confirmed. The barometer showed a sudden and sharp drop in pressure. And the instant she walked into the kitchen she felt a crackling tension between Blake and Noah. Lucy was edgy, too. She was outside, down on the dock, barking incessantly at something only she could see. Meg was seized by a sense of urgency, of time slipping fast like fine sand through her fingers.

"Morning, Noah," she said as she came up to the counter. But the kid didn't even lift his head to acknowledge her. He picked sullenly at his cereal. Blake set a coffee on the counter in front of her and caught her eyes. He shook his head, as if saying "let him be." Meg motioned with her head, telling Blake she wanted a word in private.

Outside the kitchen, out of Noah's hearing, she said quietly, "I don't think I should go with you this morning. Take him to school alone."

He glanced away, clearly conflicted. "I can't leave you alone here."

"I've got Geoff for company."

"His Jeep is gone. Either he didn't come home last night, or he went out early."

"I'll be fine," she said, placing her arm on his. "I need to compile my notes, phone Emma, ask her some more questions."

"How about I take you to work in the town library, while I run some errands—you said you wanted to go through the *Shelter Bay Chronicle* archives, and at least you won't be alone. I'll pick you up before the book club meeting."

"Blake, Noah hasn't even acknowledged my presence this morning. You need time with him. I . . . I'm not good for him right now."

"You are. I saw you with him. He's confused, that's all. He likes you. My guess is he feels the mere act of liking you is betraying his mother's memory in some way. We'll work through it."

The depth and the reality of it hit her—trying to make a life, a family from disparate pieces.

"Listen, I didn't mention it because I didn't want to worry you, but there was someone outside last night, on the property. I gave chase up the path and flushed whoever it was up into the road. There was a car waiting. Tires squealed. I'm guessing it wasn't Sally Braden."

Her eyes flashed to his. She'd heard the squealing tires.

"Get your stuff. We'll be in the truck."

Noah remained mute all the way to school in spite of Blake trying to cheer him up with the prospect of his Friday art class after school. In the end, Blake gave up and punched on the radio to fill the brooding silence. Wind whipped dead leaves and rusted pine needles across the road. Meteorologists on the radio were discussing the possible convergence of two major storm fronts offshore around midnight. If the fronts did clash, it could result in what one meteorologist was calling a "perfect storm" that would bring massive swells and gale-force winds. People in low-lying shore areas were being advised to stay tuned for further weather alerts.

"I should get the sandbags out," Blake said to Meg as he turned into the school lot.

Noah slammed the door and disappeared with his backpack into the throng of kids. A different mood pervaded the students today as they hunkered against wind and flying debris beneath the strangely colored cloud.

As they drove to the library, Meg dialed Emma.

"It's Meg," she said, when Emma picked up. "I was hoping to follow up on our interview with a question or two."

"I'm in a rush to get ready for work," she said crisply.

"I'll be quick. My mom wrote in her journal that she told you and Tommy that she was doubting Ty Mack's guilt, and conducting her own investigation, yet you said she didn't mention it."

"For chrissakes, Meg, it was almost a quarter century ago. Maybe she did, but I really don't recall."

"It's a major detail to forget, Emma."

"Oh, really? As major as what you forgot?"

Meg closed her eyes, pulse quickening. "Touché. I'm sorry."

"Is that it?"

"Just one more." Meg hesitated, then bit the bullet. "Tommy said that you lied to the cops about why Sherry went to the spit. He claimed it was for drugs, not sex. He said you and Sherry both dabbled in 'e.'"

"Everyone did."

"Did you lie to Ike Kovacs, Emma?"

Dead air.

"Emma?"

"No," she said, her voice suddenly low, cool. "I did not. That *is* what Sherry said on the phone. She was going to make out with Ty Mack."

Meg believed this. It's what she'd felt when she'd watched her sister and Ty rumble off on that custom chrome cruiser.

Cover for me, Meggie . . .

"Tommy's full of shit, and he knows it. I phoned him right after Sherry called, and I told him what she'd said she was going to do with Ty, so whatever he's saying now is a flat-out lie. And I'm done talking about it—"

"Wait." Meg tensed. "You told Tommy *before* Sherry went to the spit? Why'd you do that?"

Emma cursed. Meg could hear her lighting a cigarette, blowing out smoke. "Because he was a thick-skulled, navel-gazing, son of a bitch, that's why. He refused to see that Sherry was not interested in him anymore. I . . . I just thought he should know. "

"Because *you* wanted Sherry's boyfriend," Meg said quietly.

"And lived to regret it," she said.

"Emma, did Ike Kovacs know this?"

"It was none of his business."

"So Tommy was right, you did lie, just not in the way he led me to believe?"

"If that's all—"

"Emma, wait, please. If Sherry was not interested in Tommy anymore, why was she still going out with him?"

The line went dead.

"Wow," Meg whispered, staring at her phone.

"What was that about?" Blake asked, turning into the library drop-off zone.

"She claims she gave Tommy the heads-up that Sherry was going with Ty Mack to the spit that day to have sex."

"You believe her?"

Meg ran her hand over her hair. "I don't know. Tommy said she was a passive-aggressive, a vindictive and pathological liar. It just seems the more we dig, the more twisted this becomes."

Blake drew to a stop outside the entrance to the Shelter Bay Public Library. "You going to be okay?"

"Yeah." Her eyes met his. And instantly what they had shared in bed this morning rose thick and hot between them—raw, powerful. Fragile.

He cupped the side of her face, traced the rough pad of his thumb quickly over her lips. "I'll be back to pick you up at lunch. We can grab a quick bite before we fetch Irene and head to the book club meeting. After that we can swing by the house to assess the damage, before getting ready for Tommy's fund-raiser. We can talk to him there."

"Blake, I really don't need you to come to the book club meet—"

"Hey, I'm coming. I *want* to hear what Shelter Bay's most famous writer has to say, whether she likes it or not." He held her face, grinned. "Wild horses couldn't keep me away." His eyes sobered. "I want to see what you do, Meg. I want to know you. All of you."

She hesitated, and he stole the moment, kissing her quickly and fully on the mouth. And he did not drive away until she was safely inside the library doors.

Through the window Meg watched his truck pulling out, and she felt a tightening, a kind of unarticulated claustrophobia. She put it down to the low pressure from the storm. But deep down, she knew it was more. It was about her fear of intimacy. And commitment.

——

The librarian showed Meg to a computer station. The place was almost empty at this hour. A few women perused the stacks or worked at tables. Meg guessed them to be moms who'd just dropped their kids off at school. And a grizzled gent, maybe in his early seventies, hunkered at a computer two tables down from the one where Meg was being seated.

"Over the last three summers our student volunteers have been working to digitize the entire archives of the *Shelter Bay Chronicle*," the librarian said as Meg draped her tote over the back of the chair and set her notebook and laptop on the desk. She seated herself at the monitor. The librarian leaned over to show her how to work the system.

"You can now narrow your searches of the archives to specific time windows, and you can also search the entire collection just by name, or phrase."

Meg thanked the librarian and quickly got to work perusing news reports and feature commentary around the time of Sherry's murder. She noted which stories she might like to quote in her book, and which news photos she might like to secure the rights for. She paused at a grainy black-and-white image of the early search party that had gone out to look for the Brogan sisters. Bull Sutton was among them. So was a young Dave Kovacs.

Meg chewed on the inside of her cheek, a faint memory whispering around the periphery of her mind as she stared at Dave's younger face. But she couldn't quite tease it out.

She came across a photo of herself. Young and freckled. School photo. Headline: "Youngest Brogan Still in Coma." Another photo showed Blake Sutton. "Teen Hero Saves Life." Meg's heart kicked into an erratic beat. She felt hot.

Focus. Just remain objective. Get the info. You can feel the emotions later, in the writing of it.

After combing through the key editorial pieces, Meg set a parameter of dates around the event, and one by one, she punched into the search field the names of the primary players. Sherry Brogan. Her own name. Blake's. Ike Kovacs. Jack and Tara Brogan. Emma Williams. Tommy Kessinger. Tommy's alibi, Ryan Millar. Tyson Mack. Lee Albies. Her goal was to see what allied snippets of information she might find about each person, unrelated to the case. It would help her flesh out a picture for readers of the lives these people were living before, and then after the murder. Who they were. What track meets they'd just won. What football games their teams had been playing. What the crab fishing was like that season. What other crimes they'd been working, or legal cases they might have been battling.

There were sports photos of Tommy with the Shelter Bay High football team in action. Meg made a note to secure one of these for her book. She also found a news pic of Sherry being crowned homecoming queen, posing with Emma in her court. And one of Sherry bending over to receive a gold medal for track around her neck. One step down on the podium, awaiting silver, was Emma.

Meg tapped her pen on the desk thinking—Emma, always the princess, never the queen. Emma, beautiful, smart and talented in her own right, but always in Sherry's shadow. Emma wanting what Sherry had, including her star quarterback boyfriend.

The old man sitting two computer stations down from Meg cleared his throat loudly in irritation at the noise of her pen. She stopped tapping, dropped the pen, and typed into the search box the next name on her list. Ryan Miller. Alibi for Tommy Kessinger on the day of the murder, August 11.

Meg came across a photo of Ryan, also in sports action. It showed him as a massive linebacker in a leaping tackle, his elbow covered in blood, his eyes squeezing tight, his features pugilistic as he tried to crush the opposing team member fleeing with the ball. Another showed Ryan with his teammates after a game. Handsome in a brutish way. She remembered him now, with Peggy. Bit of a bruiser.

She punched in "Millar's Garage." Up came a story and photo in the business section from twenty years ago. According to the piece, Millar's Garage, a well-known family operation in Shelter Bay, was closing its doors and moving to a new location. Apparently environmental studies had discovered the underground fuel storage tanks were leaking and an environmental upgrade had been ordered for the site. Remediation work to remove contaminated soil and fuel vapor from the site would take several years. The photo showed the old location where the Millars had lived in a house adjoining the property. In the driveway, around the side of the house, was a red VW van.

Meg's pulse kicked.

She tried to enlarge the photo on the screen. It might not mean a thing—old VW vans were common enough now, and were even more so twenty years ago. The Millar family ran a garage. They could have been working on the van. Yet, it was parked around the side of their residential property.

She thought of Lee Albies and her homeless witness who'd seen a red van parked on the spit the day Sherry died, but had never reported it to the police.

Ryan had made a sworn statement to the cops that he was with Tommy from 10:00 a.m. until 11:00 p.m., working in his father's garage. And this photo was taken two years after Sherry's murder. The question was: Had he or someone in that house owned the red van two years earlier?

Her phone buzzed. Meg jumped and scrabbled in her tote as the old man two desks down scowled. Text from Blake. He was waiting outside already—she'd completely lost track of time. Quickly she looked up Ryan Millar's garage phone number, jotted it down, gathered her things, and hurried out of the library, mentally running through what she might talk about at the bookstore.

———

They'd been too late to stop for lunch, so they grabbed sandwiches and ate them en route to fetch Irene at Chestnut Place. Between bites, Meg explained to Blake what she'd found in the archives, and she dialed Millar's Garage. She got through to the main number, and an assistant gave her Ryan's direct line. She punched the number into her phone.

"Millar."

"Ryan, hi, it's Meg Brogan. I was wondering if I could come around and—"

"You can fuck off, that's what. Digging up shit like this, you and Sutton."

Meg blinked and cast a glance at Blake, raising a brow. "Just one question via phone, then, if I might, Ryan." She quickly activated the record app on her phone.

"Did you ever own a red VW van?"

A beat of silence. *"What?"*

"Did you, or anyone in your family own a red Volkswagen van twenty to twenty-two years ago?"

"What in the hell is this about?"

"It's an easy yes or no."

"We've been through tons of vehicles over the last decades. Probably refurbished and resold a couple of Volkswagens."

"Were you with Tommy the entire day on August 11, the day of Sherry's murder? You didn't leave the gas station at all?"

"What *is* it with you? You want to make a shitload of money making shit up, is that it? I was with Tommy in my dad's garage working on his truck. All. Day. Got it?"

The phone went dead.

Meg whistled softly. "He's a bit of a rough one. He wouldn't commit to owning a red VW. But he didn't deny it, either."

"What do you think?" Blake said, delivering the last bite of his sandwich to his mouth and reaching for his coffee in the mug holder.

She glanced out the window. Trees were bending under the mounting wind. The radio was on low, the hosts chattering about the storms that were powering toward shore. Thunder grumbled.

Meg wondered if the weather would hold long enough for Tommy's fund-raising and birthday bash.

"Old VWs are common enough," she said. "And they were even more so back then—cheap and easy vehicles for kids to buy second-hand and make road trips down the coast in. Surfers loved them. The one parked at the spit might not have even been local. Could have been anyone traveling up or down the coast—no one saw plates."

Blake turned into the Chestnut Place property. "Millar always had a bit of a rep at school, among the guys."

"What kind of a rep?"

"Coming on strong, not just on the field, but off, and with girls. There was a girl with a black eye once. And there was a rumor he got a bit rough during sex. People sort of swept it under the carpet."

"A misogynist?"

Blake snorted as he drew to a stop at the entrance to Chestnut Place. "Wasn't in my lexicon back in the day. I just hated his guts. We had it out twice." A wry smile pulled his mouth. "Ryan got the upper hand both times. That was back then. He's gone soft around the gut now. Bet he couldn't run a mile these days."

"He's the father of the kid who Noah hit?"

"Yeah."

Meg grinned, and couldn't help saying it. "Good for Noah."

He laughed. "Oh, look, Irene's all ready and waiting."

And so she was, standing in the doorway, her purse held neatly in front of her. Meg's heart squeezed with affection as she opened the door and went to collect the woman who'd raised her.

CHAPTER 23

The Mystery Bookstore was warm and comforting inside, just as Meg remembered, her little Dickensian getaway from the chill winters of her youth. Memories rose rich inside her as she entered, stirred to life by the familiar scent of books both new and secondhand. Inside this place her imagination had run wild, and the old owner, long gone, had indulged her, allowing Meg to sit in an overstuffed chair, reading in the back corner of the store for hours. In this place she'd imagined herself as Little Nell in her curiosity shop of odds and ends, or Tiny Tim looking in through frosted glass panes. She'd been a princess on a dragon, and an Asian warrior on wild horses. She tried to unravel mysteries along with her favorite female sleuths, crashed into snowy mountains in her airplane, and held her breath as characters escaped man-eating tribes in the darkest of Indonesian jungles. And it struck her just how profoundly she'd been shaped by the stories she'd found between pages here. How, in so many ways, those stories had influenced her own writing today, and the tales she selected to tell.

Rose had the electric fireplace going, and chairs had been positioned in a semicircle around the armchair that was earmarked for her. Irene, of course, made a beeline for the cakes on the table, and while they waited for everyone to arrive, Meg and Blake perused the shelves, and the Shelter Bay memorabilia and old photos on the walls.

"Oh, look. I remember that day," Meg said, going closer to an old color photograph of children on a rope swing above a gorge. She grinned and pointed to a pale, knobby-kneed girl with wet red hair. "That must have been in the fourth grade, when we went for a class trip to swim up at the falls." Her pulse suddenly quickened. "And there's Mr. Thibodeau's old van."

"It's a red VW," Blake said, quietly. Meg shot him a look. His features were tight.

"Mr. Tibbo?" she said, her gaze going to Rose, who was rearranging the chairs and greeting her book club members. "How could Tibbo have had anything to do with Sherry? Besides, this was taken years before Sherry's murder. And what about the similar-looking van parked outside Ryan Millar's house?"

"That Millar house photo was taken two years after Sherry's murder, you said. Plus, as you mentioned, the van that the witness saw could have been a tourist van traveling the coast. We have nothing solid without plates." He scowled as he studied the photo closer, a distant look entering his eyes.

"What are you thinking, Blake?"

"Nothing. It's nothing." He turned away.

A dark feeling sank through Meg. Something in particular about this photo was worrying him. But before she could press, Rose came bustling over.

"I think they're all here," Rose said. But she looked fussed, her cheeks oddly flushed.

"Is something wrong?" Meg said, her gaze flicking to Blake, who was now leaning forward to more closely examine the photo with Mr. Tibbo's van.

"No, no. It's . . ." She absently worried the pearls at her neck. "It's just that Henry was supposed to bring Lori-Beth today. LB never skips a meeting. But Henry is missing."

"*Missing?*"

"Well, not *missing* missing. But I . . . I shouldn't even be worrying you with this, Meg. Come. Let's go meet the gang. They're all seated."

But Meg held back, thinking of LB's connection to Sally Braden. "No, tell me, Rose, please."

Rose heaved out a sigh. "It sounds like a marital tiff. Things have been a bit stressed with the new baby on the way, and last night Henry booked into a motel. Now LB can't locate him. It's probably all fine." She smiled, but it was strained. "These things happen over the course of one's married life. Now, let me introduce you."

The talk and reading went well. Meg operated from rote, and was glad for all the interviews and readings she'd done in the run-up to the launch of *Sins Not Forgotten*, because her mind was busy racing off in other directions.

But as she opened the floor for questions, the ground began to shake. Books toppled from shelves, and teacups on the table rattled.

Blake, who'd been sitting in a chair off to the side, surged to his feet. "Everyone outside," he barked, taking Meg's arm and then Irene's as a freestanding shelf toppled to the ground with a crash. He ushered everyone out.

By the time they were all gathered on the sidewalk, huddled against the icy wind, people from other stores down the road also outside and looking around in confusion, the tremor had stopped. A siren wailed in the distance, and a car alarm shrilled. While they waited to see if it was all safe before going back inside, Blake checked his phone for details of the quake while the others circled Meg and took the opportunity to pepper her with questions about the book, her writing habits, and how she tackled research.

"You don't look much like your publicity photo, dear," said a woman in her late sixties. "You're far more approachable-looking in person."

Meg laughed. The wind tossed hair over her face, and she held it back. "I don't feel much like that person in that photo right now, either," she said with a smile.

"We've all heard that you're writing a book on your sister's murder," the woman added. "Will you tackle a personal story in the same fashion as your others?"

"That's the plan."

"Some people are not too happy about your digging up those terrible memories again," said another woman, her tone not quite as amicable as the previous questioner. "It could be bad publicity for Shelter Bay."

"In my experience, the publicity that comes from true crime books, oddly, is positive for the various communities involved. It's also been cathartic for all involved, in the end."

"Are you ever afraid?" asked another club member. "That one of those bad guys will come after you when he gets out?"

"I suppose that concern always lurks in the mind of a true crime writer, but as my mentor Day Rigby always says, the question is not whether you *are* in danger, it's whether you choose to worry about it. It's like swimming in the sea where there are sharks. You know they're there, but your choice is whether you allow your fear of them to stop you from ever going in. Sure, you take precautions, and you don't swim when there's a sighting, but you also don't let it stop you from reaching your goal, or the shore on the other side."

"Do you believe in evil, Meg? As a force external to man?"

"Like the devil?"

"Yes. Or a force that can inhabit people. Turn them into monsters."

"It's an interesting question. Mostly I take the Jungian view that we create the idea of monsters in order to externalize the bad that potentially lurks within us all, and we call this monster a devil, or beast, so we can examine it objectively, without having to see the beast in our own eyes when we look into the mirror."

There were murmurs—some of dissent, others of agreement.

"Does writing these stories, interviewing all these criminals, listening to victims over and over again, make you jaded in the end?" a man in his forties asked.

"I think, in doing these stories, it has made me far more aware of victims' rights, and feelings. I've come to believe that the mass of humanity is generally good. For every conscienceless killer I research, I find several dozen heroes—detectives, prosecutors, witnesses who testify even when they are frightened. With the cases I've tackled, the heroes did win in the end. It gives me faith, because these heroes are real. And I think this is the appeal of the genre."

Once back inside the building, Rose suggested they wrap things up. She looked rattled, and had a store to clean up. Blake offered to stay and help, but Rose declined, saying her husband, Albert, was on the way with some heavy lifters.

Blake hesitated before leaving and said, "That old VW van of Albert's, in that photo on the wall, whatever happened to it?"

Rose, preoccupied with the mess in her store and the disruption of her book club meeting, looked momentarily confused. "Oh, yes, that van. We let Henry have it. It was on its last legs by the time we gave him the keys. He pretty much ran it into the ground during his last year of school." She frowned. "Why do you ask?"

"Just wondering."

As they exited the store with Irene, Meg and Blake exchanged a quick glance. Outside, a chill wind whipped in a new direction. Street banners snapped. Thunder grumbled in the distance.

"Henry?" she said. "I'm going to need to talk to him."

"Except, he's missing."

———

"That was fun," Irene said as they neared Chestnut Place. Meg had offered her aunt the front seat, but she'd said she preferred the back. "Even with the earth tremor. I remember tremors like that back in the seventies. They came one after the other over a period of a few days, and then there was a big one. Not big enough to bring down buildings, mind you, but it did leave cracks in walls, and low-lying properties along the bay and beachfront were flooded by a small tsunami surge."

"I'm glad you enjoyed it, Irene. It really was a pleasure to have you there."

"Rose always has nice cake." Irene smiled. "Your mother and father would have been proud, Meg. And I'm so happy for Rose that Henry and his wife are starting a family. Must make her and Al Tibbo so happy. Both came from big families themselves, you know." She sat silent a while as they ferried her home. "And there Rose had once worried that her son might be a homosexual."

Blake's eyes flashed up into the rearview mirror. Meg turned around in her seat.

"Henry?" Meg said.

Irene frowned. She began to scratch her arm. "Rose confided in me once . . . I *think*. Back when I was still working as a public health nurse." Her frown deepened. She scratched harder. "I'm probably not supposed to mention it. But it doesn't matter now, does it? Because Rose's fears were clearly unfounded with Henry being happily married for so long now. And a baby on the way."

"It's okay, Irene," Meg said, reaching into the back to still her aunt's hand.

Blake's shoulders tensed. His mind shot to the photo he'd found in the mariner's chest in the shed last night. Henry was in it. It must have been his VW van. He thought about Geoff meeting a mystery boyfriend on the spit the day that Sherry was killed. Was Henry the one? Had he gone to meet Geoff, and parked his red van on the spit where the old vet living in his car had seen it?

One more day . . .

Almost as soon as they drove out of the Chestnut Place gates after dropping Irene off, Meg turned in the passenger seat to face him. "What's worrying you—what are you thinking?"

Blake cleared the thickness from his throat. "I suppose it could have been Henry parked on the spit that day."

She rubbed her brow. "Yeah, or a tourist. Or Ryan Millar's van. Without any more information, or the van's registration, it doesn't actually *prove* anything."

Urgency pounded though Blake. He fisted the wheel. He had to get back to the marina, stat. He had to find Geoff, have it out with him. *This* was where it ended. Right here. This was the line in the sand.

The radio announcer was talking about a small earthquake epicentered several miles offshore. It had caused tremors up and down the coast, but no serious damage. There was the usual chatter about foreshocks and aftershocks and "big ones" and possible alerts from the tsunami watch center. Blake felt like the earth's crust himself— he was being shattered by his own thoughts, fears about his own brother. And what Geoff might have done. And what it could all do to his tentatively blossoming relationship with Meg now.

"Are you okay, Blake?"

He changed the subject. "We won't have long at Forest Lane if we're to pick Noah up from art class and still get to Tommy's function by six thirty. We'll just have a quick look, then run by the school, and then head straight back to the marina. I need to see that Geoff is there. So that he can watch Noah tonight."

"And I need to pick up some clothes, something to wear tonight. Unless I go in old jeans." She turned to look out the window. "Maybe my mom has something in her closet."

His stomach bottomed out. Meg sensed he was withholding something; it was written all over her body language. He could hear it in her voice. He cursed. She'd taken off that ring. He was so close, yet with every second now he could feel the ground pulling apart between them.

Tonight, he told himself, he'd tell her everything tonight, as soon as he'd had it out with Geoff. If Geoff was clean, he'd have done as he'd promised. He'd have spoken with Henry—if that's in fact who he'd been meeting that day—and he'd have warned Henry that he was going to reveal he was on the spit that night, meeting someone.

And if Geoff was clean, he should have no trouble then sharing all of this with Meg. And explaining the red van.

——

Meg stared, dumbfounded, at her house as Blake pulled into her driveway and drew to a stop. The windows had all been replaced. The blood graffiti had been washed off and the walls repainted.

"What the . . . ?" Meg flung open the door, and jumped down. Digging in her tote for her keys, she made rapidly for the front entrance.

She unlocked the door, stepped in. Blake followed. A clean lemony scent greeted them. The broken glass had been cleared away, the carpets vacuumed. Fresh flowers smiled from a vase on the dining table. Beneath the vase was an envelope.

Meg ripped it open, and glanced up at Blake. "It says, courtesy of Kessinger Restoration Services."

"Tommy's guys," Blake said.

"Why would he do this?"

"Well, you're the one who said he's practically family."

She eyed him. "If I didn't know better, Mr. Sutton, I'd say you were jealous."

His features tensed, and his eyes grew dark. She swallowed. He stepped forward, grabbed her shoulders, and kissed her hard, backing her up against the wall. "Maybe I am, Meggie Brogan," he murmured over her mouth, his hand sliding down her back, and cupping her buttocks. Heat arrowed instantly into her groin. She was turned on by his rough and sudden intensity. "Shall we christen these nice clean carpets?" he whispered, his mouth moving down her neck, down to the vee in her shirt. Her nipples contracted.

Meg felt herself melting, her legs turning to water. She laughed, a little breathless, seriously contemplating it, but she placed her palms flat against his chest and pushed him away, even as she still kissed him. "Noah. School. Will . . . be . . . late."

He pulled back, his chest rising and falling fast, his green eyes sparking. He lifted her left hand and gently thumbed her naked ring finger as his gaze locked with hers. Silence simmered. Her heart beat louder, faster.

"I love you, you know that, Meg Brogan?"

Blood drained from her head.

But before she could think, or respond, he was making for the door. "Get what you need. I'll be in the truck."

———

Meg ran upstairs, feeling she was suddenly pushed up against the edge of an abyss. Blake was serious. Dead serious. She'd felt it in the aggression of his kiss, the intensity in his eyes. Heard it in the catch in his voice.

I love you, you know that, Meg Brogan?

She had to commit, or cut it off with Blake right now. *This* was the point of no return. She'd already taken off her engagement ring. She was growing in love with the idea of staying here, not going back to Seattle. But at the same time all her fears of commitment and intimacy were starting to clang like fire alarms around the edge of her brain. It made her skin prickle.

Tension tickling, she rummaged quickly through her mom's closet. As she moved the clothes, the scent of her mother's perfume rose from the fabric. How was that even possible, after all this time? Was she just imagining it?

Look for that dress, Meggie-Peg. The red one.

A chill lifted the hairs at the nape of her neck at the sound of Sherry's voice. Meg stilled. Slowly she glanced over her shoulder, fully expecting to see Sherry sitting there on the bed. All she saw was her own reflection in the far mirror, and for a startling moment she thought it was her mom. Her pulse quickened. Memories were strange. Scents especially could trigger them so strongly that the resulting memory almost seemed to hold enough power to physically reconstruct a person long gone, make them shimmer in front of you like some holographic image.

She returned to the clothes, and found a red dress hanging neatly in a protective plastic laundry sleeve.

Yes, that one. Killer dress, Meggie, Just retro enough. Full circle . . . what do they say? . . . Fashion goes in twenty-year cycles . . . and you do need a killer look tonight. Tonight's the night, tonight will be the big one . . .

Meg heard Blake's diesel truck engine rumble to life. Had to get to Noah. Couldn't be late for the kid, not with the strange mood he was in. Meg grabbed the red dress from the closet, held it up in front of her, and turned quickly to the mirror.

See, Meggie-Peg. Killer. Now grab some shoes . . .

No. She had boots with a heel in her truck. Boots would be better in this weather.

At least take the fake fur, kiddo . . .

Meg scratched deeper into the closet and found her mom's fake fur coat, and smiled. She folded it all into a bag, and made for the stairs. Jonah would die if he saw her in this outfit. But she didn't give a hoot. In fact, the very idea of dressing up as a version of her mom lightened her heart. Sherry would have gotten a kick out of it. As she hurried through the living area, she stalled at the sound of Sherry's voice again.

Meggie, remember my goldfish? They lived on that shelf, in their perfect world . . .

Her gaze shot to where the fish tank used to be. Where the safe was now in full view.

No predators in their waters . . .

The safe door was shut. She went over and tugged on it. Locked. The combination must have been turned. She was sure she'd left the door open while Kovacs was standing here. One of Tommy's cleaners must have closed it. Not that it mattered—why should it? But something suddenly felt off about the cleanup job, and people inside her house.

Meg locked the front door and hurried out to the waiting truck. As she climbed in and shut the door, it struck her how wrong Sherry had been all those years ago.

Sometimes the predator lives right here, and he looks just like the rest of us . . .

———

"Who's going to stay with *me* if you're both going to the party?" Noah complained, testy, weepy, and tired as they pulled into the marina parking lot. He hadn't eaten his school lunch, and according to his teacher had not participated in his art class.

"Your uncle Geoff," Blake said.

"He's not here. Look. His car's gone."

"He will be. He promised." Blake's blood pressure rose. He tried to tamp down his temper, but he was frothing at the bit about Geoff not being here. The clock was ticking. He needed to know from Geoff if Henry had driven his red van to the spit that day. And he had to tell Meg.

"Other kids are going," whined Noah. "There'll be rides in the harbor on the whale-watching boat. For free. Every hour, even in the dark."

"Those kids are older. And the weather might not be good, Noah. I doubt it's going to happen." Blake swung open his door, refusing to look at Meg. He'd laid his heart bare, and he could see it had unnerved her. What did he expect? For her to say, *I love you, too, Blake Sutton*? He was grabbing too hard and fast, because he was shit scared it was all going to go to hell in a handbasket now.

"But they said!" Noah yelled.

"Come, out," Blake said, opening Noah's door.

Noah dropped out of the truck and stormed toward the house, his shoulders and chin set forward.

"You sure Geoff will be here?" Meg said gently, touching his arm.

"He promised."

"Blake, maybe you shouldn't come tonight. Maybe you should stay with Noah."

"Maybe you shouldn't go."

"What do you mean?"

"I don't know. I'm sorry. I don't want you to go alone, that's all." He raked his hand over his hair. Thunder cracked. A jagged fork of lightning speared down over the spit. Daylight was waning. Puce and black clouds boiled in. Water slapped against the shore with the growing tidal surge. Another smash of thunder sounded right above them and the heavens suddenly let loose. Marbles of rain bombed to the ground. Together they ran for cover. A curtain of water pummeled down onto the tin roof of the marina, and the sky turned black.

He held open the door for her.

"I won't be alone," she said, entering the marina office. "The place will be packed with people. And I don't plan to stay long. I basically want to talk with Kovacs, and maybe Ryan Miller, and I want to ask Tommy a few more questions in light of Emma's latest revelations. And thank him for the renos. I can't accept the freebie. I need to pay him back."

"Everyone's paying him back. He owns the whole damn town." He made for the kitchen.

She grabbed his arm. "Blake, what is it?"

"Nothing. I'm just frustrated with Noah. It was going so well."

"And then I came along."

He held her eyes. Thunder cracked again outside, and growled into the distant mountains. "And Geoff is pissing me off. He should be here." *And I love you. I want you. I don't want to lose you.* "And I don't feel it's safe for you to go alone. That's the bottom line. And if I don't go, you shouldn't go, either."

Her mouth tightened. "This is about what you said earlier, at the house, isn't it?"

His heart beat faster.

"It's because I haven't said anything in return, is that it?"

"You took off his ring, Meg. I thought—"

"Blake . . . just give me a little while, okay?"

"It was a mistake." He turned from her and went into the kitchen. *You asshole. She told you herself she had trouble committing. She told you how Dr. Shrink backed her into a corner by pressing for a marriage date, and look what happened—she ran to Shelter Bay, a place of last resort. Now you're trying to push her into the same kind of corner? Asshole . . .*

"Noah!" he barked up the stairwell. No answer. He grabbed his phone, called Geoff. It kicked to voice mail. He swore again. Meg entered the kitchen behind him.

"Blake?"

"Go get ready," he said curtly, not giving her his eyes. "Geoff will be here by the time you are. I need to go unload those sand-bags, just in case."

———

From the upstairs window, Meg watched Blake reverse his truck up to the garage. He began to haul sandbags out from the corner of the garage and toss them up into the bed of his truck. His move-ments were powerful and angry, unrestrained. Meg swallowed, and her eyes burned. She clasped her hand around the diamond ring at her neck.

Maybe I love you, too, Blake Sutton. Maybe I always have. Maybe this was something else Jonah was wrong about—perhaps, deep down, you were the real reason I could never commit.

As she watched Blake, she wondered about destiny. If some things were just written into the cosmos. If Sherry's murder had been like a weird blip in a time-space continuum that had bumped lives into the wrong groove, and she'd been meant to return here, to rectify the blip, rewrite the ending, and reset the clock.

Her thoughts circled back to what Blake had told her in bed, that his father had beat them. And as she watched Blake laboring with the sandbags, her heart torqued with compassion.

Oh, the secrets we keep. How we deceive ourselves, often in the name of love . . .

How had this shaped Geoff? What invisible scars did he now bear?

Wait. Stop! Don't run, Meggie, don't run!

Geoff's voice. Her pulse stuttered as Geoff's face suddenly loomed into her mind again, waxy white, shining with rain. This time she saw a cut on his cheek. Shit. She rubbed her arms. Had she just added that detail because of what Blake had told her?

He struck a particularly violent blow early that morning you went missing, cutting open Geoff's cheek . . .

Or *was* it real?

Thunder crashed, and lightning streaked down into the bay. She glanced at her watch. She needed to change, or she'd be late, and she suspected Tommy's event was not going to last long in this weather. Meg turned to make her way to her room, and gasped.

A small, white-faced figure stood silent in shadow at the end of the passage. Watching her. Like a little ghost child.

"Noah? Goodness, you gave me a fright. How long have you been standing there?"

He spun around and disappeared into his room. The door *snicked* shut.

She rapped on his door.

"Go away."

"Noah, can I talk to you, please?"

Silence.

Meg hesitated and then tried the handle. Locked. Even more uneasy now, Meg made her way to her room, shut the door, showered, and quickly slipped into the red dress. It was a little loose, but she preferred not being sausaged into clothes. She smoothed it down and stepped in front of the mirror. Her heart stuttered in surprise to see a faint memory of her mother looking back at her.

Meg applied makeup, darkening her eyes, making them stand out. Lips glossed, she slipped into her high-heeled boots and shrugged into the fake fur. A wry smile pulled at her mouth. Sherry would approve—retro chic. Going to do battle in the name of her mom.

She smoothed down her hair, slipped her recorder, camera, and notebook into an evening purse, and started down the stairs.

Noah had come out of his room and was in the kitchen, alone, eating bread and Nutella.

"Not waiting for your uncle Geoff to make dinner?"

"He's not here," Noah mumbled without looking up.

Meg frowned and glanced at the clock on the stove. Slowly Noah raised his eyes. His body went stone still. He stared at her in her evening outfit with makeup. A small blue vein swelled on his pale temple.

Blake came in from the office door, taking off his work gloves. He stalled as he saw Meg. He whistled softly.

Her cheeks heated.

He came slowly up to her, his gaze locked with hers. Then he brazenly ran his eyes over her, slow, steady, a wolf eating her alive. She swallowed.

"Well, look at you." Approval darkened his eyes.

She became conscious of Noah still transfixed. He began to kick the toe of his shoe against the cabinet. *Bang. Bang. Bang.*

"Noah," Blake said. "Please stop that."

He kicked faster. *Bangbangbangbangbang.*

"For Pete's sake, will you please stop that? You're going to damage the siding."

Noah's face turned bright red. His gaze remained locked on Meg. He kicked harder. Blake stepped forward as if to grab his son off the stool, then he pulled himself back. "Listen, I know you're—"

"You're a liar!" he spat at his dad. Then he turned to Meg. "My dad and Uncle Geoff are liars!"

"Noah," Blake said, his voice going low, "what are you talking about?"

"They know stuff about your sister's murder. Uncle Geoff was on the spit that night your sister was killed. I heard him and Dad talking. I was outside the door."

"What?" Meg's gaze shot to Blake. The panic and heat she saw in his face struck a blade clean through her heart.

"Dad and Uncle Geoff have been keeping the secret since that day. Uncle Geoff said if they told you, you'd go looking for the other person."

"What other person? Blake—what in the hell is he talking about?"

"Noah." Blake took his son's arm. "Please, I need you to go upstairs."

"No!" Meg snapped. "Just *no*. I want to hear this. I want to hear every damn word he says." She spun to Noah. "*What* other person?"

"Some guy whose marriage would be killed if you found him out." His voice was going quiet. His eyes were showing fear. "They . . . they said you'd go on a witch hunt for him because you're like a dog with a bone. Uncle Geoff said, 'let her just write her story, and leave that part out.'"

Every last drop of blood drained from Meg's head. She reached for the back of a chair to steady herself. She felt as though she'd been shot.

Thunder boomed overhead. The windows shuddered. The buoys outside thumped in mounting wind.

"What does he mean, Blake?" she said, very quietly.

"Meg, I was going to tell—"

She shot her hands up, palms out, backing away from him as though he might be a viper ready to strike.

Blake grabbed Noah's shirt and pulled him down off the stool, shaking. "Get out of here. Go upstairs. *Now.*"

Noah clattered up the stairs. Blake's eyes crackled. His neck muscles bulged. "Sit down, Meg." He pulled out a chair.

She glared at him. "I don't know you. I don't know you at all."

"Sit. Hear me out."

Slowly, she sat.

He yanked out a chair and sat opposite her. "Geoff was on the spit that day. He went to meet someone. When he came back that night, I saw his face was cut. He told me that my father had hit him early that morning, and I believed it, because I'd heard them arguing. Geoff didn't want to reveal himself to anyone that night, because he didn't want the shame of being an abused son. And he didn't want to say he'd gone to meet someone for fear of being outed as gay."

"The other person was . . . a lover?"

"A boyfriend."

"Who?"

"I think it was Henry. Because of what Irene said on the way home today. It just started to add up. And last night in the shed I found a photo of Geoff and some of his schoolmates in front of a red VW van. I was going to ask him whose van it was."

Dizziness swirled. "That's why you were upset after the bookstore. You learned Henry had taken ownership of his father's van, and then you heard Henry might have been gay, and you put two and two together, placing Henry and his red van on the spit because you already knew Geoff was there."

He nodded, dropped his face into his hands, scrubbed his skin hard.

"*Why*, Blake? Why did you keep this from me? I *trusted* you. We were doing this together."

"Meg, I know. I told Geoff I was going to tell you—"

"You sat on this for twenty-two years!"

"No. Not all of this. Only that Geoff was on the spit. I was just figuring out the other pieces at the same time you were."

"Bullshit. How can I put the whole picture together when you two are hiding pieces?"

"Calm down, please. Just listen. Back then we were all convinced that Ty Mack had done it, and it didn't feel like a big deal that Geoff was on the spit. I believed Geoff back then. And I didn't want my dad in the news as an abusive father, either. I didn't want to lose Bull. I didn't want to be sent to some foster home by social services. Geoff was leaving—I'd have had no one. I did *not* see it as a big issue."

"But it is *now*. And you've been working with me on this for days now. You were with me when Lee Albies told us about a red van."

"I didn't know Henry had a red van, Meg, not until Rose told us."

"You saw a photo in the shed."

He dragged his hands over his hair. "I didn't know it was his—I just told you. I was planning to ask Geoff about it. And when I saw that photo I had no idea Henry might be gay."

She stared at him, dumbfounded.

"Geoff begged me to hold off telling you for just one more day, so he could prepare his lover. He said it would destroy his marriage. And if that person is indeed Henry, Geoff is right, it *will* destroy that marriage. It'll kill a guy like Henry Thibodeau. He's been living in an iron closet all his life."

Meg got slowly to her feet. She looked down at Blake, bitterness filling her mouth. "I trusted you, Blake. The least you could have done is trusted me with this, too."

"Meg, I can see how this looks from your perspective now, in hindsight. But until today—"

"This information about at least two other people on the spit that night could have changed everything. Ike Kovacs would have interviewed them. He might have been forced to look more deeply at the other DNA evidence. He might have scoured the area more thoroughly for witnesses. He might have found that homeless vet who told Lee Albies he'd seen a red van. Then blind Ethel McCray's testimony about hearing a VW van might have been given more credence." She paused to catch her breath. "All of this could have painted reasonable doubt all over Tyson Mack. An innocent man might have lived. My father might still be alive, and so might my mother." She pointed at him. "You and Geoff helped kill my family."

"Meg, that's not fair. You're not thinking st—"

"Forget it. I'm done." She grabbed her purse from the table, and walked woodenly to the door. Deep inside, her blood started to boil. Part of her desperately wanted to believe Blake, to hear him out more fully, to pull apart his story and try to see when he knew what, and how it might have affected his decisions. But the other part, the old part, was slamming up walls. And it felt easy that way, to be hard. To be livid. To lock out the hurt and the pain of betrayal that was going to buckle her if she let it in.

Just finish the job. Do what you came to do. Then get the hell out of this place and its sick, twisted roots.

Blake surged to his feet and grabbed her arm, stopping her as she made for the door. She swung around, vibrating now, with anger, affront, and yes humiliation. "Don't," she said, her voice low, cool. "Do not touch me." Tears burned at the back of her eyes, but she refused to allow them. She was back in her old zone, and by hell she liked it here. Walls up high and safe.

"Where are you going?" he said, voice low, eyes narrowed.

"To the Whakami Bay Marina. For one helluva party."

"It's not safe."

"And *you* are?"

She turned, and yanked open the door. Wind gusted inside, clamoring the office bells. She stepped out into the stormy night.

"You lied, too, Meg!" he called after her, the wind snatching his words. "You lied to cover for Sherry that day. Do you think *she* might have lived if you'd told the truth right away? That everything might have turned out different? Do you shoulder no blame at all?"

"Damn you," she growled under her breath and ducked out from under the covered deck and stepped into the rain.

"I tried to protect my brother!" he yelled. "You tried to protect your sister; you always did. How are we so different?"

She spun around as something struck her like a mallet between the eyes. She marched back up to him and faced him square under the deck awning.

"You know what I dreamed last night, before you made love to me? I dreamed I saw the face of the person chasing me—the face that has been eluding me for the last twenty-two years. And it was Geoff's face. I dreamed it was *him* who attacked me that night, and left me for dead. I heard *his* voice yelling, *'Don't run, Meggie, don't run!'* And you know what? I wrote it off as my wild imagination, because how *could* it be Geoff? Now I'm wondering if it was true."

His face paled. He said nothing.

She started to shake inside. "How much do you trust your own brother, Blake Sutton? Who have you really been protecting all these years—a murderer? A rapist? Will Geoff's DNA match one of those two unidentified profiles? Because you know what I'm going to do? I'm going to tell Kovacs everything tonight."

"Meg—"

She refused to hear him out. She spun around and strode out into the rain. She climbed into her rig in her mother's red dress and fake fur, and she drove off, leaving him standing outside his tumbling-down marina.

CHAPTER 24

Blake watched her go. Hollow. Shaking. Bereft. Fucking hell. He'd been an idiot! Fucking Geoff. He raked both hands over his wet head, fighting a ferocious urge to hunt her down, bring her back right this instant. But the harder he pushed Meg right now, the further she'd run, and he knew it.

Her words about his brother floated up like a black, slippery oil to mingle with his own dark memories: The blood on Geoff's shirt. His flotsam bag found near Meg's body. The haunted look in his brother's face that night in the boathouse.

Was it possible?

Her dream didn't prove anything. They needed proof, or an admission, so fine, let her tell Kovacs. Let the chief deputy find Geoff and Henry, question them. At least there'd be a ton of cops at the fund-raiser for the sheriff.

Right now he had to deal with Noah. His kid was an exploding volcano. Triage. Thunder split the sky over the bay, and rain and wind redoubled its assault on his marina, ripping one of the buoys free from its moorings in the rafters. The orange buoy crashed into the crab boiler, and bombed across the gravel, where it smacked to a standstill against the garage wall.

Blake ducked back into his house, shed his wet gear, and stormed up the stairs. He hesitated outside Noah's door. Then he knocked quietly.

No answer.

He knocked louder.

"Go away!"

Blake closed his eyes, inhaled deeply. "Noah, I need to talk to you."

"Go away."

"Please, champ. I'm not mad at you. All you did was tell the truth. I understand what you were doing, and why, but I do need to talk to you. I want to see your face."

"Leave me alone."

Blake opened and closed his fists. He could hear tears in his boy's voice and it gutted him.

Thunder rumbled again, and the whole marina building seemed to groan and shift as it braced against the mounting wind. Blake hurried downstairs and put on the radio. He tensed as he heard the host announcing that a tsunami watch had been issued as a result of the tremor late this afternoon. Worst-case scenario was that the two fronts would collide offshore, a few miles out from Shelter Bay, shortly after midnight, creating an epic storm with gale-force onshore winds that would coincide with a pushing high tide, and possible tsunami. A sailors' nightmare come to life. He needed to start sandbagging.

And the more he thought about Geoff, and Henry, and them being secretive gay lovers, the less likely he could see them brutally raping Sherry. Something just didn't fit.

He turned his mind back to the conversation he and Meg had had after her flashback over dinner.

"I had a flash of Sherry. Her naked body . . . She was lying on her back, spread-eagled in mud. I . . . had the sense I was fleeing from

that image. And that there were several shapes around her wanting to come get me . . ."

Several shapes?

There was also the photo of the red van outside Ryan Millar's house. Ryan, who was Tommy's alibi. Ryan, who years later was rewarded with a fat vehicle maintenance contract from Kessinger-Sproatt. And there was the mystery father of Sherry's baby. Plus another two unidentified DNA profiles. Plus someone had possibly tipped off Jack Brogan. Who? Ike Kovacs? The sheriff who'd, against protocol, handled the investigation himself?

And what about Tara Brogan, who felt she was being followed? Geoff hadn't been in town during that period. And he'd been nowhere near Shelter Bay when Jack was tipped off, and again when Tara died.

And what of Emma, who'd allegedly lied to the police?

Anxiety speared through Blake, and worry for Meg's safety tonight reared afresh.

He grabbed his cell and hit the number for his emergency sitter, dragging his hand down hard over his mouth as the phone rang. He wasn't going to get through to Noah himself tonight. But he *could* keep his son safe while he went after Meg, once he'd sandbagged the Crabby Jack side of the marina building. He paced as the phone rang. Water lashed the windows. It was almost full dark outside now, clouds low and black. The foghorns sounded repeatedly.

"Hello," came a voice though his phone.

"Anna, this is Blake Sutton. Can you babysit on short notice?"

"How short, Mr. Sutton?"

"Right away short."

"I . . . Wait. Maybe. Can I call you back in a sec?"

"Please."

She hung up.

Blake shrugged into his slicker and grabbed his gloves and an oilskin ball cap before heading out to his truck, which he'd backed up to the deck area. He hauled himself up into the bed, and began offloading sandbags with a thud. He'd almost cleared the load when his cell rang. He ducked under the awning, and answered.

"It's Anna. My mom will bring me in about twenty minutes."

Relief washed through Blake as he pocketed his phone. He resumed hauling the offloaded bags one by one around to the front deck area of the Crabby Jack cafe, where he began stacking them into a wall. His muscles burned and sweat dripped under his gear. He welcomed the burn. The physical action, the sense of purpose, was keeping him sane while he waited for Anna. He heard a vehicle coming down the drive. Dropping the bag in hand, he hurried around the side of the building, fully expecting to see his sitter. Shock slammed as he recognized the silver Wrangler.

Geoff.

Blake marched toward the car like an angry ox. The door opened as Blake reached it. He leaned in and grabbed his brother's lapels, hauling him out. Rain slashed silver in the Jeep's headlights, the engine still running.

"Where in the hell have you been?"

"Jesus, easy, Blake." Geoff put his hands up in surrender. "I promised I'd be here to sit Noah, and here I am. Just a few minutes late."

"It was Henry, wasn't it? That's who you went to meet."

Geoff paled.

A gust slammed rain at them, but the brothers were focused solely on each other, oblivious to weather and plummeting temperatures. "It was Henry's red VW bus parked near where Sherry was murdered, wasn't it? Was it the same bus that picked her up at the Forest Lane trailhead right after Ty dropped her off safe?"

Blake was vibrating now, terrified by the look in his brother's eyes, the pallor of his complexion, the fact he wasn't denying *any* of this.

"It was *you*, Geoff. *You* ran after Meg that night, yelling for her to stop. She remembered. It was *you* who hurt her, you fuck!"

———

Wind tore at her umbrella as Meg marched along the paved walkway that led toward the brightly lit Whakami Bay Yacht Club and Convention Center. Rows of lanterns swung wildly between banners that declared: KOVACS FOR COUNTY SHERIFF! Music thumped from the building—a massive, modern affair with a pitched and angled roof and lights way up in steel rafters.

High-end yachts creaked along the boardwalk and swayed against moorings, halyards rattling on masts as wind and tide pushed into the harbor.

Electricity thrummed through Meg's veins as she neared the glass doors. She was driven by a tunnel-visioned focus, her mind closed to the rest of the world. Her goal was to get in there, find Kovacs.

The big automatic doors slid open, and a blast of wind yanked her umbrella inside out. A valet came running out. Taking her broken umbrella, the man ushered her inside and asked if she'd like to check her coat. She realized she was shivering uncontrollably, and declined.

"Later maybe." She forced a smile. "When I warm up a bit."

Meg entered the massive convention area. Clusters of blue-and-white helium balloons bobbed everywhere. Banners strung from steel and wood rafters declared KOVACS FOR CHILLMOOK COUNTY. People in evening gear milled in groups. A long bar had been set up to the far right, and a raised dais toward the back hosted a shining grand piano where a man in a black tuxedo tinkled the ivories while a woman in a curve-hugging sequined gown crooned a husky lounge song. According to the sandwich board at the entrance, BROOKLYN'S 17TH BIRTHDAY CLUB BASH WITH LIVE BAND was "happening" upstairs. It must be this bash that accounted for the thumping techno bass she'd heard outside.

Meg scanned the crowd in search of a familiar face. She spotted Tommy and Dave Kovacs almost instantly. Both wore suits and stood slightly taller than most of the crowd. They were conversing with a group up near the raised dais with the pianist.

She made a beeline for Kovacs.

Tommy glanced up, caught sight of her coming. He separated from the group and came to meet her. He smiled, touching his hand to her elbow. "Meg, thank you for coming."

Out of the corner of her eye she caught sight of Emma at the bar. Adrenaline kicked through her. "I thought she wasn't coming," Meg said.

Tommy followed her gaze.

"She wasn't. But now there she is. Ignore her. She's drunk. As usual. And you're wet. Here, let me take your coat."

"No. I need to see Kovacs." She started to push past him.

He frowned, and held on to her arm. "Meg, are you okay? You look feverish."

She drew her coat closer over her chest, still shivering.

"I'm fine. I just need to talk to Dave."

"Listen, relax—just give him a minute. See that gray-haired guy he's talking with? That's the mayor of Chillmook. And that woman with him is the CEO of the Chillmook County Newsmedia Group. The gentleman to her left is one of our campaign's top financial backers. Let me get you a drink."

Emma was watching them now, from across the room. Meg could see Ryan Millar further down the bar, also watching her.

The memory of Geoff chasing her suddenly slammed through her again. Her heart began to race, fear circling . . . *wait, Meggie . . . don't run . . .*

"Is Henry Thibodeau here?" she said.

Tommy's frown deepened. "No, he hasn't arrived yet. Meg"— he drew her aside slightly—"talk to me, what's going on?"

Gaze locked on Emma, she said, "My mom wrote in her journal that she told both you and Emma that she thought Ty Mack might be innocent, and that she was trying to find out who might have tipped my father off."

"If she did tell me, Meg, I really don't recall. Tara said a lot of things that didn't make sense at the time, and sometimes we just let her ramble."

She glanced up, met his eyes. Compassion softened his features. "Your mother was consumed by grief, Meg. She was also desperate. Her husband was awaiting trial for murder. She was grasping at anything. And the medication . . . who knows what she wrote in that book, or was thinking. I probably wouldn't read too much into it."

Anger sparked into her blood. "You're saying my mother was nuts?"

"I'm saying, just think about it all in context. Now, let me get you a drink." He started to lead her toward the bar. But Meg held her ground.

"Emma said she called you to alert you to the fact Sherry was going to the spit. Did she?"

"No. Why would she say that?" Realization dawned in his eyes. His mouth hardened. He glanced at his ex and uttered a soft curse. "Oh, I get it," he said quietly. "My jealous ex is not only bitter, she's turned vengeful. Why else would she even be here tonight, if not to try and embarrass me?" He met Meg's eyes. "Her vindictiveness started to get worse when I married Liske. She tried to turn Brooklyn against us, too, and I see what she's doing now. She's trying to pin motive on me—give me some reason to have hurt Sherry." He snorted softly. "And you and your book are the perfect tool for Emma. Because that's what this looks like. After all, they always go after the boyfriend first, don't they? But they cleared me, Meg. I volunteered a DNA sample. I had a solid alibi—"

He halted as Emma pushed off the bar and started to weave through the crowd toward them, glass in hand. Tommy raised his chin, nodded at Ryan across the room. Ryan started toward Emma.

"Ryan will take her home," he said. "It won't be the first time."

He always had a bit of a rep . . .

"Your alibi was Ryan," Meg said. "And in the police report you swore that you were with him from ten a.m. until eleven p.m. on the day of Sherry's murder."

His eyes narrowed. "Yes."

"You were with him the entire time?"

"It's in the statements."

"Did Ryan own a red VW van?"

"What?"

"Did he—yes or no?"

"Meg . . . what does this have to do with—"

"A witness, Tom. Someone saw a red VW van parked on the spit during the time Sherry was likely killed. And someone else places a VW van at the trailhead earlier, where Tyson Mack said he dropped my sister off safe."

Not a muscle moved. His eyes didn't flicker. The piano music stopped and something louder started, with percussion.

"Yes," he said, raising his voice over the increasing drum noise. "Ryan Millar owned a red VW van. But he bought it defunct from Henry Thibodeau the winter after Sherry was killed. He bought it to refurbish it."

Meg rubbed her brow. She felt feverish. Okay, that made sense. The news photo that she'd seen in the *Shelter Bay Chronicle* had been published two years later. So Henry had owned the red van at the time of the murder, and then offloaded it to Ryan. It was most likely Henry driving it, who'd gone to meet Geoff, as Blake had said.

"Who were these witnesses?" Tommy said, having to bend down and talk directly in her ear now. The music was going louder. "Are they still around now?"

Kovacs looked up, and saw them. He stilled, drink in hand, watching them. Out of the corner of her eye she saw Ryan trying to lead Emma toward the doors, and Emma was arguing with him. Tension, claustrophobia, tightened around Meg's throat. A rushing noise began in her head.

"I need to talk to Dave Kovacs now. I need to tell him what I've found out."

Tommy hesitated, then said, "Good, this is good. Because he's reopened the case on the quiet."

"*Kovacs* told you this?"

"He told me you were working with him."

A cold feeling snaked up her chest. So much for "on the quiet." She shot another look at Kovacs. He regarded them intently. Fear tightened in Meg's throat.

The drums thumped louder. Tommy winced at the noise, took her elbow. "Come, let's go talk somewhere quiet and private. My yacht is right outside the front entrance. I'll get Dave to join us." Tommy lifted his hand and made a motion to Kovacs. He nodded, making a sign that he'd come in two minutes.

Meg hesitated. Perhaps Kovacs was not the best person to be looking into Sherry's case right now, given his father's involvement and his political interest in the outcome. Her mind went to the photo she'd seen of him in the archives. And the sense she should be remembering something about him intensified. The buzzing grew louder in her head. She was sweating now, but still shivering.

"I also need to share some other information about Emma with you both," Tommy said in her ear as he started to escort her toward the doors.

Emma the princess, never the queen. Emma who got the silver track medals to Sherry's gold. Emma always in Sherry's shadow. Emma who lied to the cops. Emma who wanted, and got, Sherry's boyfriend. Emma the pharmacist who'd noted her mother's medication. Emma the bitter, vengeful divorcee.

"What about Emma?" She had to speak loud. It hurt her head. She needed air.

"A suspicion I've had. About those pills. Come. This way."

At the door one of the coat-check people handed him an umbrella. He popped it up as the doors slid open, and stepped outside. Meg inhaled the cool air deeply as she followed, but hesitated. Tommy held out his hand for her. "That's my motor yacht right over there, just behind the whale-watching boat." It was literally across from the doors.

She glanced back into the conference area. Kovacs was slowly making his way over, talking to people who came up to him. She'd hear Tommy out, but she made a decision right there—as soon as she had, she was calling the state police. She'd hand everything over to them, and tell them about Geoff and Henry.

Tommy held the umbrella over them both as he escorted her down the gangway and along the dock that led to his sleek, high-end motor yacht. She guessed it to be almost fifty feet in length. Lights were on inside. Bits of plastic, Styrofoam, wood, a bottle, seethed in inky scum around the hulls. The rain was turning thick and gelatinous.

Tommy helped her step onto the swim deck to climb aboard. Out of the corner of her eye Meg saw the figure of a woman running out of the convention center, heading their way. No umbrella. Behind her came two men who looked like Kovacs and Ryan Millar.

"It's Emma," she said.

Tommy shot a glance toward the center. "Don't worry. Dave and Ryan will handle her. This way." He guided her up the port steps to the aft deck, and he drew open a glass slider that led into the upper salon.

Thunder cracked. Meg winced. A lantern ripped free in the wind and cartwheeled down the dock with a thunking sound. The boardwalk and harbor lights flickered, and the boat tilted. She braced against the glass slider for balance.

"Don't worry," Tommy said. "The convention center is backed up by generators. If the power fails they will kick in." He smiled. His teeth glinted in the dark. "This harbor has been designed to withstand even the most super of a super tide and storms. We have almost a half mile of riprap leading out into the sea, and a secondary reef to guide swells away from the harbor mouth. We're keeping a close eye on the tsunami alert."

He turned on the lights in the upper salon. It was warm inside. Sofas were cream and sleek and looked leather. The coffee table was smoked glass. Tommy held his hand toward a recessed stairway. "It'll be cozier down in the lower salon."

Don't go down into the basement, Meggie-Peg . . . only heroines in stupid horror flicks go down into the basement . . .

Meg paused. Her mind raced. She believed one hundred percent it was Geoff who'd attacked her and left her for dead. And Henry and his red van were involved. But she was still missing a chunk of memory. How did it all tie together? She glanced up at Tommy's face.

I want to share something with you about Emma . . . about those pills . . .

"Meg! Stop!" a woman yelled outside. "Please. Don't go with him!"

Meg stepped quickly back out onto the aft deck. Emma called out to her as she teetered down the gangway and onto the dock.

Her stiletto heel caught between slats. She pitched forward, toward the edge, but Kovacs caught up from behind, and grabbed her arm, barely managing to halt her plunge into the frigid harbor water.

"Emma, you're drunk!" Tommy called out to her. She looked up, white-faced, her dark hair plastered to her cheeks, her dress clinging to her body.

"Sherry got everything! She always got everything!" she yelled at Meg as she struggled to shake off Kovacs. Ryan took Emma's other arm.

"Ryan's going to take you home now," called Tommy. "Dave, will you join us once you've got her into Ryan's car?"

Dave made a small salute.

Tommy touched Meg's elbow. "Come inside. I'm guessing she's worried about what I have to tell you. And if my suspicions are right, she has reason to be. Dave will join us as soon as he can. He's going to want to hear this, too."

Tommy again held out his hand, showing Meg the way down into the bowels of his boat.

———

Blake shook his brother like a rag, rage turning his vision red. "You going to tell me what happened? Are we going to find *your* DNA matches that unidentified profile? Did you hurt Sherry, too, strangle her? What the fuck *are* you?"

"Jesus, no. No, Blake. I did *not* hurt Sherry. For God's sake, you *have* to believe this."

"Make me."

Geoff swallowed. His gaze darted out toward the bay, as if seeking a way of escaping this.

Blake tightened his grip. "You—you have cost me everything—"

"Bull fucking shit," Geoff snapped suddenly. "You made your own choices—"

"To cover for you, because I loved you. My own brother. I *believed* in you."

"And I covered for Henry because I loved him!" He shoved Blake off him, fire flaring into his eyes.

"And what did Henry do that you needed to cover for him?"

Geoff turned to go back to his car. But Blake slammed his hands down on Geoff's shoulders and spun him around like a toy. "Oh, no you fucking don't. You're not going anywhere. Look at me. Did you hurt Meg?"

"She fell. She fell when I grabbed her. She hit her head. I . . . I didn't mean to hurt her."

Blake stared, his brain flipping over itself. He started to shake. "You didn't *mean* it?"

Geoff pushed his brother's hands off him and sank down onto an upended log. He dropped his face in his hands. Rain beat down on his hair, dripped through his fingers.

"Look at me!"

Geoff's shoulders shuddered. He was crying. Blake grabbed a fistful of wet hair, and, yanked his head up. "Look at me, you shit. Be a—"

"Be a what? Be a *man*? *Man* up? You going to hit me, too, now, like Dad?

"Oh, you sorry-ass loser. This has nothing to do with sexual preferences, or Dad, and you know it. You chased a terrified thirteen-year-old girl. You grabbed her and made her fall. Her head split open, and you did what? You *left* her there, lying unconscious on the beach, in the dark, with a storm, and the tide coming in?"

Geoff stared at him, his eyes hollow, haunted, water sheening down his face.

"You left her to die, you bastard. *You* tried to kill Meg Brogan. She'd be dead if I hadn't found her. That's attempted murder in my book. And now you and your 'secret' have cost me the only woman I ever truly loved. Why? Why on earth *Meggie*?"

Geoff shook his head.

"What did she see? Someone raping and strangling Sherry? What made you try to stop Meg from getting away?"

His brother said nothing. It was as though he'd gone numb. Dead. Frustration exploded through Blake and it was blinding. He hauled Geoff up from the log, and drew back his fist. "Tell me."

"Go on. Hit me. I dare you. While your own son is watching from that upstairs window behind you."

Blake froze. He shot a glance over his shoulder. Noah stood silhouetted in the lighted window. Geoff used the distraction, walloping Blake in the solar plexus. Wind blasted out of him, and he coughed, doubling over and stumbling to his knees. Geoff lunged for the open door of his still idling Jeep.

"Don't you dare!" Blake yelled.

But the door slammed shut. Tires spun, kicking gravel into Blake's face. He scrambled to his feet, but Geoff spun his Jeep around, and hit the gas. Blake drew his Glock, aimed, fired. Once. Twice. Again. Tires popped. The Jeep skidded sideways. Blake put another bullet into the bottom of the gas tank. Geoff wasn't going far now, and he knew it, because he hit the brakes, flung open the door, and ran for the marina's north gangway. Blake gave chase. Thunder cracked, and lightning flickered through cloud. His brother reached the dock, sprinted to the south end, and scrambled into the only boat Blake had left in the water for small emergencies. It had a single two-stroke engine mounted at the stern, a full tank of gas, a spotlight, bailing scoop, and nothing else.

Lightning forked into the bay as Geoff cast free the line and pushed away just as Blake reached him. He yanked the starter cord. The engine coughed to life. He gave it full throttle and powered out into the blackness of the storm.

Shit. Blake ran his hand down hard over his mouth, his chest thumping with adrenaline. Either his brother would make it out of the mouth by some miracle, or he'd drown trying. His secrets would die with him.

"Daddy! Daddy!"

Blake whirled around. Noah was running down the gangway toward him.

"What's happening!? Where's Uncle Geoff gone?" He was crying hysterically. "Why did you shoot at him? It's all my fault, isn't it?"

Blake crouched down. "Come here, bud."

Noah flung his arms tightly around Blake's neck and clung like a limpet. His body convulsed with sobs. "He's going to drown . . . in the storm. He'll drown in that boat."

"Noah, listen to me." He held his son back and looked into his pale, rain-streaked face. "I never want to hurt you. You've got to understand that. I'm sorry about Meg. Will you give me a chance to talk about it later, please?"

An almighty crack sounded, right above their heads. Forked lightning sparked down into the water, throwing everything into a momentary freeze-frame.

Noah nodded, panic bright in his eyes.

"Now, listen carefully. I'm going to get the big speedboat out of the garage and go after Geoff, get him back safe, okay? But I need your help. Your sitter—Anna—will be here any minute. I need you to go inside and wait for her. When you get inside, call 911. Tell them your dad needs help at Bull's Marina. Tell them your uncle is out in the bay, in trouble."

"Why . . . what did Uncle Geoff do?"

"Trouble with the sea, Noah. He could hurt himself. And if he does manage to make it out of the mouth, he might hurt someone else."

"Will he hurt Meg?"

"Not on my watch he won't."

"I don't want him to hurt Meg . . ." His lip wobbled and his body shook. "It's my fault."

"No. It's not. Now do it. Anna will be here. You dial 911. Stay on the line with the dispatcher. They'll send all kinds of help. Now *go*." Noah turned and ran on his skinny little legs. Blake's chest clenched tight. He surged to his feet and made for his truck; his goal was to reverse up to the garage, hook up the boat on the trailer, haul it down to the concrete slipway, back it in, and go find his brother. His big speedboat was equipped with twin two-hundred-horsepower engines, a prow like a blade, a deep, sharp, heavy keel to slice through the waves. And it had spotlights, life jackets, flares, and other emergency equipment. He'd gun Geoff down fast, *if* he was still afloat by the time he found him.

CHAPTER 25

As Meg was about to start down the stairs that led to the lower salon of Tommy's opulent motor yacht, a terrible scream rent the air. Both she and Tommy froze.

"Was that Emma?" she said, heart kicking.

It came again, shrill and piercing and rising and falling and unrelenting. A woman in terror. It froze Meg. Her mind hurtled back . . . screams, just like that. Sherry's screams. She'd run toward them that day, her young legs powering her toward a horror even as her brain recoiled and cried: *flee.* An inhuman power exploded through her blood, blinding her. She shoved past Tommy, clattering back up the stairs, through the upper salon, toward the doors, toward the screaming, toward the raw sound of terror.

"Meg! Stop, wait," Tommy called behind her.

Wait. Stop! Don't run, Meggie, don't run!

She made it out onto the aft deck, breathing hard. Rain lashed and the boat tilted. She grabbed the railing. Another scream. A hand grasped at her from behind. She jerked free and stumbled down onto the swim deck, almost slipping off as she hopped onto the dock and ran toward Emma. She was under the halo of a lamp, dress clinging like a rag to her thin body, face sheet-white as she clutched at her cheeks, her mouth an open black hole—she was the universal *Scream*, an Edvard Munch painting against the oily water and shimmering sleet. Ryan Millar was holding her back from the edge of the dock. Kovacs was down on his knees, bending over to reach for something in the water with a grappling hook. People were running over from the conference center.

"Emma," Meg said, breathless. "What's the matter?"

Emma released her cheek and pointed with a clawed hand into the black water.

Meg's gaze shot to the water.

A thing, like a large bloated bull seal, bobbed with the flotsam between the deck pilings and the hull of a yacht. It took a moment for Meg's brain to register it was a man. Floating facedown in a suit jacket that was puffed up with trapped air. His arms flopped limply at his sides with the loll of sea, his hands ghostly white.

Emma sank onto her knees.

A group of off-duty deputies reached them. Meg recognized Hoberman, in a dress. Kovacs barked for one of them to hold him steady so he could reach farther. Thunder clapped, and wind gusted, stinging them with sleet.

One of the male deputies held down Kovacs's ankles as he leaned farther, struggling to drag the corpse closer with his hook.

Kovacs managed to roll the body over. Someone panned a flashlight down. Meg took a step back in shock. A chalk-white face gaped up at them with cloudy open eyes, a black hole in the center of his forehead.

"Henry," said someone next to her. "Oh my God, it's Henry Thibodeau."

More flashlights bobbed in the darkness. Someone made a call. A cop cruiser pulled up with uniforms. People gathered up on the boardwalk, holding coats tightly against wind and sleet. More lanterns ripped free. One of the election posters tore from its post and tattered down the gangway to slap against the side of the wet dock.

Tommy helped the deputies pull Henry out. The men grunted

with effort as they flopped him onto his back like a dead shark onto the dock. Seaweed hung from his mouth. A hush fell among the onlookers as Kovacs was handed gloves, and a police photographer snapped photos. Kovacs opened the jacket, carefully removing a wallet. He checked the ID.

"He's been in the water a while," the chief deputy said, slowly coming to his feet. "Where's the ME?"

"On her way, sir," Hoberman said.

Kovacs stared at the flotsam frothing around the yacht's hull. "He wasn't killed here. He must have washed in with all that other crap."

Meg's mind whirled. Henry might have been the only person alive, apart from Blake, who knew Geoff was on the spit the day Sherry was murdered. Geoff, who'd suddenly returned home with a gun, after all these years, at the same time Meg had come home to tell Sherry's story.

Now Henry was dead. Silenced.

Fear kicked her heart. *Blake.* He could be in danger. Noah, too. Noah also now knew that Geoff had been on the spit.

She moved quickly aside from the small crowd to call Blake. Thunder smashed overhead and she ducked as the air seemed to implode around her. The lights along the dock flickered, then died. The conference center went black. Yelling started down the board-walk. Flashlight beams bounced against silver sleet.

"It's okay," someone called. "The generators will kick in."

Meg put her hand to one ear, trying to listen to her phone ring. Her call flipped to voice mail.

"Blake, it's Meg. I think Geoff shot Henry dead. He might come for you and Noah. Please, be careful. Stay away from him." She killed her call, and glanced at Kovacs. Her instinct to tell him about Geoff warred with her growing suspicions. She suddenly trusted no one.

Meg made for the gangway.

"Meg! Where are you going?" It was Tommy, but she kept going, faster, up the gangway, breaking into a run along the dark boardwalk toward the parking lot, urgency building in her chest. She had to get back to Bull's Marina. She had to tell Blake. She'd call the state cops from her truck on the way.

———

Geoff goosed his little engine, but the boat was like a cork, spinning atop the surging sea, unable to slice deep into the water with any weight and cut a straight path. He'd never seen the bay like this, a seething monster swelling and writhing beneath the skin of the surface, spitting up tongues of foaming water to drag down whatever dared traverse its face. Fog poured in from the open ocean, so dense he could barely see the flare of the lighthouse to guide him to the mouth and thundering point. Wind tricked him, too, lashing this way then that. His engine sputtered as water sloshed over the prow and chuckled over his boots. Sleet cut like ice across his face.

He'd dared to form a new dream after he'd found Henry sitting in his MINI Cooper on the side of the road. It had coalesced slowly over the night. By the time he woke this morning it was what he wanted at any cost.

Mexico.

Prison was no place for men like him and Henry. Until Blake had pieced it all together, they'd still had enough time to reach the border, cross over, vanish somewhere into the hot jungles of South America where law meant something different, find a sleepy seaside town, a new life, *if* they'd left before this blew.

Now it was blowing.

He might yet make it if he could navigate through the Shelter Bay mouth alive, hug the coastline, just beyond breaker range, head a few miles down the coast, and come in at the new Whakami

Bay harbor. Just a mile or so south of Whakami was the Blind
Channel Motel where Henry was waiting. Henry had his MINI
Cooper. They could drive it through the night, change cars in some
small town tomorrow. He had everything else in place. He'd spent
the day sorting out his papers and bank accounts electronically.
He'd purchased ammunition and a small pistol now holstered at
his side. He'd mailed an old-fashioned letter to Nate. His goal had
been to babysit Noah, as promised, so as not to alert anyone. Then,
once Blake and Meg had returned home, steal out into the night.

Blind adrenaline drove him toward the raging mouth now,
bridges burning behind him. Only forward. Live or die. Last chance.

You know what happens to guys like us in prison, Geoff . . .

A horn blasted through the thundering noise of wind and surf.
He tensed, looked over his shoulder, saw a white, angry row of
lights barreling fast toward him through the fog and sleet. Shit.
Blake must have launched the big speedboat. *Shitshitshit.* He tried
to juice his little engine further, but his moment of lost focus cost
him as a wave slammed him broadside, and he tipped. Geoff dived
for the opposite gunwale of the boat, trying to counterbalance with
his weight, but water poured in over the bow, and he started to go
down into the churning monster that sucked at the weight of his
sodden coat and jeans and boots as he flailed to stay atop the glistening surface.

———

Meg battled against the wind to hold her camper on the road while
she dialed 911 from her cell, her wipers fighting to slash arcs into
slush plastering her windshield. She cursed as yet again she got
no reception. Lights were out everywhere, even at intersections.
Traffic was building in a steady stream from the opposite direction
as people flooded onto the designated tsunami escape route. She

turned up her radio. So far it was only a voluntary evacuation to higher ground. According to the announcer, some residents along the waterfront had opted to stay and try to sandbag their properties. There was also warning that the two massive storm fronts had clashed offshore far earlier than anticipated, catching pleasure boaters and fishermen making for safe harbor by surprise. A Japanese tanker that had lost power earlier was now also adrift, and washing dangerously close to rocks off Cannon Beach.

And then she heard it: landlines were down, and many coastal areas were not receiving cell reception. She cursed as she neared the turnoff to the marina. No pink sign flickered above the building. Blackness down on the water. She turned into the driveway, her beams suddenly lighting on Geoff's Wrangler parked at an odd angle halfway up the driveway. Her heart stuttered. The driver's door was open, the tires flat. She hit her brakes, leaped out, and ran to the Jeep. A heavy smell of gas filled her nostrils. She peered inside the Jeep. It was packed with Geoff's gear, and shopping bags.

She stood back, fear closing her throat. Blake's truck was down by the water. In the glow of her headlights she could see a boat trailer behind it, in the slipway, ocean rising around it.

She hopped back into her rig and drove it down, parking it so that her beams illuminated the marina building. She left her lights on as she ran up to the office, and banged on the door.

"Hello! Blake . . . Anyone here!?"

Silence, apart from the *thump thump thump* of the buoys in the rafters as they blew in the gale. She sloshed through pooling water to the side window of Crabby Jack's, wind tearing at her coat. Water drenching her hair. She peered in, couldn't see a thing. She banged on the window. "It's Meg! Open up. Hello!"

The office door opened a crack. A tiny beam of light poked out at waist level.

She ran to the door.

Noah stared up at her, white-faced, his eyes holes. In his hand he held a little flashlight.

"Where's your dad?"

"It's my fault."

She crouched down. "What . . . *what* is your fault, Noah?"

He flung his arms around her neck and she picked him up. She carried him inside, kicking the door closed behind her. He was shaking like a leaf. Meg set him down. The building creaked and groaned like an ancient mariner's ship straining against the mounting storm. Sleet thundered on the tin roof.

"Where is your dad?"

"He . . . had a fight with Uncle Geoff. He shot out the tires—"

"*Who* did?"

"Daddy did. He had a gun." Noah started to cry.

"Noah . . . easy. Focus. Just tell me."

"Uncle Geoff took a boat, from the docks."

"The little one?"

He nodded. "Daddy took the big speedboat from the garage and went after him. He said Uncle Geoff might hurt himself. Or he might . . . hurt you. I . . . was scared. Hiding. He said to call 911 but the phones weren't working and the lights went out. And the sitter didn't come."

"Oh, Noah, come here." She hugged him but fear beat a hammer into her heart. "How long has he been gone?"

"I don't know. Since before the power went out."

"And your dad had a gun?"

He nodded.

"And Uncle Geoff—did he have a weapon?"

"I don't know." He started to cry all over again, deep, palsied shudders taking hold of his little body.

Meg's mind raced. No phones. No power . . . the two-way radio. She'd seen one in the living room.

"Got any more flashlights, Noah?" she said.

"In the kitchen drawer."

She felt in the drawer for a flashlight, clicked it on, panned it around the room, and found a gas lantern. She lit it and carried the shivering light into the living room. Noah followed. She found the radio, and clicked it on. She depressed the key, hoping that Blake kept it on the right channel and that it had enough battery juice.

"Mayday. Mayday. I need help—can anybody hear me? Mayday."

She released the key. Waited. Voices crackled through in snatches, people talking to each other, sounding terribly distant.

"Mayday! Mayday! Anybody?"

She released the key, sweat dampening her body.

A crackling hiss sound came through. Then a voice. "This is Coast Guard Auxiliary, state GPS position, please."

She had no flipping idea. "I'm at Bull's Marina," she said. "Shelter Bay. Two seamen are in trouble out on the bay."

Static crackled over the airwaves, chopping in and out. Then came the voice. "Copy. All resources tied up. Tanker adrift near Cannon Beach. Other craft all out on call. Will try to allocate resources. Meanwhile, please prepare for self-rescue. Copy?"

Silence.

Meg glanced at the black windows, sleet sliding down the panes. Panic flicked in her belly.

"Bull's Marina, do you copy?"

"I . . . yes. I copy. Thank you." She replaced the radio, hands trembling. What now? She tried her cell phone. Still no reception.

"Okay, Noah, here's what we're going to do—"

"We can't leave Dad!"

"We won't. We'll wait here at the marina until he returns, but we'll stay in my camper. It's warm in there. I have a gas heater, and a battery-powered radio—we can listen to the alerts. We have food and water and blankets and a small washroom. We'll park facing the road, so we can be ready at a moment's notice to drive to higher ground if we need to. I'll tie one of your father's spotlights to the rigging on the Crabby Jack deck outside, so he can see his way back, okay? We'll be here waiting to help him if he needs help." She swallowed, emotion suddenly thick in her throat.

Please, Blake, don't die with my last words on your mind . . . please, God, give me a chance to make this right . . .

"Now, take a flashlight upstairs and go pack a bag of clothes, and anything else you might need. And your favorite book, okay?" She glanced around suddenly. "Where's Lucy?"

"I don't know. She gets scared and hides when thunder comes."

"All right, up you go. Get your stuff. I'm going outside to lash that spotlight to the pole. Wait down here for me."

Meg found a headlamp in the office and positioned it on her head so she could work hands free. She took one of Blake's spotlights, turned it on, and ducked outside. Wind ripped at her coat. Icy slush beat at her face. She dragged a table over to the railing and climbed on top. Reaching high, she managed to hook the spotlight onto a crosspiece and bind it into place with rope she'd taken from the covered deck area. As she worked she thanked her dad for teaching her everything she'd ever need to know about mariner's knots.

When she climbed down from the table, water was lapping over the sandbags and slinking its way to the glass doors. Nothing she could do about that now.

Once she'd gotten Noah and his gear secured in her camper, she warmed soup for him at her small stove. He sat eating and shivering while the gas heater fought to warm the interior with its clunky fan. Meg's mind was going crazy searching for something she could do to help Blake. She would try the Coast Guard again later, but she knew they were inundated, and prioritizing. And they had her on the list. She'd keep checking her cell phone at intervals to see if reception had been returned. Short of that, all she could do was look after his boy and pray his dad would come home safe.

"I want Lucy," Noah said.

"I know, hon. I'm sure she'll be fine. Dogs are clever that way. She has her tags on her collar, right? We'll find her when all this clears up. I'm sure of it."

"I want my daddy."

She tried to swallow, nodded. "I know . . . I know. . . ." The camper rocked as a blast of wind slammed them. Slush drummed on the roof. She tucked Noah into a down sleeping bag, and got out her laptop. She would write—to keep her mind off what was happening. As a way of moving forward. This is why she was here in the first place.

Meg found some fingerless gloves and seated herself at her small camper table in front of her laptop. Blinds drawn against the storm, she tried not to think of Blake out at sea, or what might be happening with Geoff, and she began to type a draft opening to her book. Eventually Noah fell into a deep sleep.

Partway into the first chapter, she chewed on the inside of her cheek, then scrolled quickly to the top of her document, and typed in a title. *Stolen Innocence.*

She stared at the winking cursor. Thunder clapped and she flinched. Deleting the title, she retyped: *The Stranger Among Us.* But her hands froze as she heard an odd clunk outside the camper.

A scratching came at the camper door, and the handle moved. Her pulse quickened. She heard another clunk and felt a sense of motion, as if something had bumped her truck upon which the camper shell was secured. The door handle jiggled louder. But the door was locked. She stared at the handle as she reached quietly over to the drawer below the fridge. She slid it open. Mouth dry, she closed her fingers around the hilt of a carving knife. Thunder crashed, and her heart kicked. Slowly, she got to her feet, knife fisted in her hand. She reached for the blind over the table, edged it open a crack. Lightning streaked into the bay, and in the freeze-frame she saw glistening black water, silhouettes of gnarled shore pines bending into wind, and silvery slush. Debris cartwheeled across the parking lot. A rope snapped in the wind. But nothing more.

Carefully, she moved to the blind on the opposite side of her camper, and as she did, she got a whiff of smoke. Then stronger. *Fire.*

———

As he neared the thundering reef at the mouth of Shelter Bay, Blake's spotlights hit on a small, black shape, the size of a volleyball, bobbing in the foam, surging closer and closer to the crashing break against the riprap. He swung his boat around to better point his lights at it.

Geoff.

His craft must have gone down. Every instinct screamed at Blake to gun straight toward his drowning brother, but experience held him back until the next major surge began to push in. As the face of the wave swelled, veined with white foam, he waited a second longer, moving his engines in and out of gear to hold his boat in place. Then just before the wave began to crest, he gave full throttle and cut across the face, slowing slightly as he came upside Geoff's head. One hand on the wheel, an eye forward on the wave face, he reached over the side for his brother's hand. Geoff grasped for Blake's outreached hand, but slipped free. Blake reversed, then moved forward again, losing precious time as the lip of the wave began to curl in behind him. With the second attempt, Geoff's fingers locked fast around his wrist, and Blake clamped his brother's wrist in return, forming a strong chain. He opened throttle as he struggled to haul his brother up over the gunwale. Geoff clambered over the side and dropped into the bottom of the boat just as Blake cleared the breaking lip of the wave. His heart thumped in his throat. Geoff scrabbled to the stern and dragged himself onto the bench as the boat pitched and rocked in the swell. Blake quickly brought his craft around in the calm of the next wave trough, and started back for shore.

Only then, prow aimed for home, the swell and wind at his stern, did he dare tear his attention from navigating and look at his brother, hunched over, dripping, retching.

"You could have bloody killed us both!" Blake barked as he swung one of his spotlights around to illuminate his half-drowned sibling hunched at the back of the boat. Geoff's face was ghost-white. He was shivering uncontrollably, probably going hypothermic.

"Should have let me go," Geoff yelled back.

"*You* pulled yourself up into the boat." Wind snatched Blake's words, forcing him to holler.

Geoff looked at his hands. "I can't. I can't go back."

"What?"

"I can't go back!" he bellowed, reaching suddenly for the waistband of his jeans. He brought out a pistol.

Shock slammed through Blake. He slowed engines. "Whoa, Geoff, put that thing away."

He raised it slowly, aimed it at Blake.

"No . . . Oh no, don't do this, bro."

"I did it," he yelled. "*I* chased Meg. *I* left her to die." He put his head back, laughed. Loud and maniacal. "God . . . feels good to get it out. I didn't know how badly I needed to get it out."

Nausea washed into Blake's stomach. His mind turned black. This was his worst fear confirmed—that his own brother had done this. This was the rabid wolf that had been prowling around the fringes of his consciousness, the beast he'd not been able to allow in, the possibility he'd been unable to entertain fully.

Geoff's features hardened suddenly. He cocked the pistol.

"No, wait." Blake held a hand out, his other remaining fast on the wheel. He prayed that perhaps the gun wouldn't fire because it had gotten wet, but it had only been in water a short while, and the ammunition was probably still viable. "Geoff, please, let's do this the easy way—right way."

"Police? Prison? Is *that* the right way? You know what they do to people like me in prison, Blake?"

"Just tell me," he yelled. "*Why* did you chase Meg?"

"Because she saw—Meggie saw Henry fucking Sherry. Sherry screamed and screamed until Tommy smacked her in the face, held her down, squeezed her neck, choking her to death as he yelled at Henry to 'fuck the bitch—fuck her hard, prove you're a man.' He called her a traitorous whore . . . He knew she was going to the spit to screw Ty because Emma had phoned to tell him."

Out of the corner of his eye Blake saw another swell rising. His attention split in two as he reversed the engines, holding back for the right moment, blood pounding in his head.

"Tommy made Henry fetch him in his van from Millar's Garage. All premeditated—King Kessinger, the psychopathic, puppeteer bully ever since elementary school, jerking people's strings, making them all dance to his tune. And God forbid he ever targeted you . . ." Geoff's voice faded, a strange look overcoming his face. The swell driving at them started to curl at the lip. Sweat drenched Blake under his heavy weather gear. He goosed the two-hundred-horsepower engines as the breaking wave came at them, trying to ride ahead of the surf. In the relative calm of the next wave trough, he slowed, and gave full attention back to his brother.

"Please, Geoff, just put that gun away. We can work this out—"

Geoff responded by curling his finger through the trigger guard, and keeping the weapon trained on Blake. "Tommy saw me and Henry together once. It was like he'd hit the mafia blackmail jackpot. From that day, Henry was his main target, his lackey, because Henry was softer than me and ripe for it—Henry's dad was a school principal. A homophobe. His mom was a respected teacher. Tommy had a nose for this shit." He couched, and retched again, over the side of the boat. He wiped his mouth with the back of his wrist.

"Tommy threatened to tell everyone Henry was a fag, that he'd been caught with his pants down giving it to Geoff Sutton. Henry would have rather died, and Tommy knew it. He started small, making him do easy things first, building up slowly. Henry knew the stakes if he declined. So that day he picked Tommy up at Millar's garage and they went to find Ty and Sherry—watched them first, screwing each other like rabbits. It drove Tommy-the-narcissist insane with rage." Wind blasted the boat suddenly as they rounded the point. Worry sliced through Blake. From here he should be able to see the marina lights. But all was black, shrouded in fog. "What happened then?" he said, keeping his eye on a point in the distance where he expected to see the shore lights, his brain racing for a way to get that weapon away from Geoff.

"Tommy had Henry follow them, and when Ty dropped Sherry off, he forced her into the van. They took Sherry back to the spit, to the scene of her 'crime.' Tommy raped and sodomized her first, showing Henry 'how it was done like a man,' then he made Henry do it while he choked her to death."

"So, you didn't go to the spit to meet Henry?"

Geoff snorted, wiped water from his face. "Just my goddam luck I was there. I was collecting flotsam, and heard the screams. I came over the ridge almost the same time as Meggie on the opposite side of the grove. Couldn't believe what I was seeing. Henry with his pants down, sobbing as he fucked Sherry. I knew instantly what was going down, and it killed something in me. Meg took off like a frightened hare. Tommy yelled at me to stop her. I knew Henry would take the fall for this. I . . . I loved the bastard. I wasn't thinking . . . I didn't know what to do. It all happened so fast. I raced after Meggie, and when she reached the point, she fell, and I thought she was dead."

Blake reversed engines again, holding back until the right moment before gunning ahead of another wave, riding the swell further toward shore.

"What about Tommy's DNA?" he yelled.

"They used condoms. Tommy pocketed his. Henry dropped his. It'll match what's on file. The hairs, too."

"Whose baby was she carrying?"

"Fuck knows."

Blake's mind hurtled back to the night he found his brother in the shed. How complicit was he himself, for not having pushed his brother further, for not telling Kovacs that he'd seen Geoff heading out to the spit that morning? For not mentioning the flotsam sack he'd seen near Meg's unconscious body? What damage had their respective secrets wrought over the years? If he'd spoken up, would Jack and Tara Brogan still be alive?

"Jesus, Geoff. Why didn't you just tell the cops?"

"And send my friend to prison for raping a woman he never wanted to rape? For being a victim? I *loved* him. I hated what Tommy was doing to him, what he *let* Tommy do to him. I just wanted to get the hell out of this sick town."

"You made yourself accessory to murder."

Geoff coughed, retched again. "Almost got away with it, too." The boat lurched and he grabbed the gunwale with his free hand for balance. "Except little Meggie-Peg comes home after twenty-two years and all goes to hell in a handbasket." He launched suddenly to his feet, raised the pistol, aimed it dead at Blake's chest.

Blake's skin turned to ice. His mind catapulted through possible scenarios—he could spin the boat sharply, try and tilt Geoff over the side. Or keep him talking while waiting for the right wave to hit them broadside and capsize them. "And if you kill me—how far do you think you're going to get?"

Geoff abruptly flipped the gun around, stuck the muzzle in his mouth, and squeezed the trigger. The back of his head blew out.

Shock slammed through Blake.

For a nanosecond Geoff's body seemed to hang there. Then his legs buckled slowly under him. The boat rocked and his brother tipped backward over the stern. Blake heard an oddly innocent-sounding *splosh*.

The boat shuddered as propellers hit the body.

Bile lurched into Blake's throat.

———

Meg saw the flickering of flames through the small window that looked into the back of her truck cab. She lunged to unlock the door, then halted. Panic squeezed her brain. What if someone was trying to flush them out? She had to chance it.

"What's happening?" Noah sat up, confused and thick with sleep.

"Grab your jacket, get over here!" She twisted the door lock free, swung down the handle, pushed. But the door held fast. She shouldered it. Nothing happened. She rammed harder. But it was stuck dead. The scent of smoke thickened. It was seeping in from below the bed. Noah started to cough.

Someone had locked them in. They were trapped—human meat in a tin can about to explode.

Focus. Panic kills. Think. Logic . . .

Hands trembling, Meg yanked up the blind and struggled to slide open the window. It was stuck. She lunged for the opposite window, breaking nails as she scrabbled to open it. It had been jammed shut, too. Her gaze shot around the interior. Fire extinguisher. She snapped it free and rammed the back of it into the glass of the biggest window over the table. Cracks feathered through the glass. She rammed it twice more, and pieces crumbled outward. Rain, wind, slush blew in, saturating her face.

"Noah, over here." She smashed the extinguisher along the bottom rim of the window, eliminating sharp edges. Wrapping a blanket around Noah, she helped him onto the bench seat. "I'm going to lower you out, okay? When you hit the ground, run. As far as you can, up to the coast road before this blows. I will find you up there. Go!"

Rain drenched through her sweater as she helped Noah out. His feet hit gravel. He glanced up, white-faced, wide-eyed.

"Go! Run!"

He turned and raced away, a little form on skinny legs into the wet, black storm.

Meg struggled to squeeze herself sideways through the window. Her legs swung down, feet hitting gravel. She reached back inside to get the knife. But as she did, she felt a hard crack at the back of her skull. Her body juddered, went still. Pain exploded through her head and radiated down her spine, to her fingertips. Her vision blurred. She tried to turn around, to put a foot forward, to run, but her knees buckled and she slumped to the ground.

Another blow came sharp at her ribs. She felt a bone crack. Gasping for air, she tried to roll away, to get onto her hands and knees. To crawl. In the periphery of her mind she was aware of flames licking out of her truck, fed by the tearing wind. Smoke roiled, acrid, thickening. Slush beat down. Meg staggered up onto all fours. Her vision was blackening. She had to get away before the gas cylinders exploded. But as she moved one hand forward, someone yanked her up by the hair, spinning her around.

Lightning split the sky. And in that instant she saw.

Tommy.

His eyes met hers. And in that moment, suspended in time and pain, she felt herself sliding back into the dark of time. She was running up the hot, white sand dune, pulled by Sherry's screams. And as she crested the dune, she saw. Her sister's naked body spread-eagled in dirt. Her sister had gone quiet. Her head was at an odd angle. Eyes open. Henry was sobbing, pants down around his thighs. He was pulling his penis out of Sherry, and it was glistening, going limp. Tommy had his hands around Sherry's neck. He glanced up at Meg with wild eyes. Meg was trapped by those eyes, unable to move as someone came over the opposite ridge. Geoff.

"Get her!" Tommy screamed at Geoff. "Get her or we're all dead."

She spun around, and raced down the dune.

Meg was jerked back to the present by a sharp jolt of pain. Tommy was dragging her to his vehicle. And she knew. With bilious, oily certainty. She finally had *The End* of her story—and she'd never get to write it.

Because she was as good as dead.

Tommy opened the back door, but stilled as a high-pitched banshee-like scream sliced through the wind and sleet. Noah. He came barreling out of the blackness yelling as he swung a crowbar at Tommy, striking him across the hip. Tommy grunted in pain, stumbling forward as he dropped Meg to the ground. He lunged for Noah.

"Run ... Noah ... go ..." But Meg's words came out a hoarse whisper. "Please, God, go." Her vision spiraled inward to a small pinprick of light. Sounds stretched. She tried to reach up, grab Tommy's pant leg, stop him from going after Noah, but her fingers failed to find purchase, and her hand flopped limp to the ground.

My dear Noah, you should have stayed hidden. Instead you tried to save me. Now he's seen you ... now he'll kill you, too, because you've seen him ...

She heard Noah screaming, far away, in a distant tunnel. She couldn't see. She clawed the wet gravel, trying to drag her body toward the screams. She moved maybe an inch before an explosion slammed the air around her. Sound died. Pain swallowed her whole. She was floating, floating, falling. Into the blackness.

———

Blake's brain went numb. He stared at the bloodied froth on the black water under the glare of his spotlights. His fingers on the controls were icy. He couldn't seem to make them move. Couldn't make anything in his body move. All he could see in his mind's eye was the mutilated body of his brother sinking slowly down, down, down to the seabed that crawled with a live carpet of hungry Dungeness crab.

His boat drifted sideways, toward the rocks, as the image of Geoff's brain spraying out the back of his skull replayed and replayed in his head. The look in his brother's eyes at the last, dying moment. Him tipping backward, and over the gunwale. The sound as he hit the sea. The shudder of the boat as the props mashed into his brother's body. Acid burned in his stomach. He started to shake. His eyes started to burn. Water ran cold down his face.

A wave rose slowly up. He could feel his boat rising with it, tilting toward the starboard side, and panic struck, forcing him back to the present. He swallowed the vomit in the back of his throat, and opened the throttle. Revving the engine he brought his craft around just in time to run ahead of the wave before it broadsided him.

His heart punched against his rib cage. The tears came now, as he aimed for shore. For their marina home, his life unalterably changed.

His brother dead. His brother, who'd let a murderer walk free.

. . . the ways in which we deceive ourselves . . . what misguided action we take in the name of love . . .

Memories of Geoff, as a young boy, a brother, a friend, played through Blake's mind. He'd loved him. He'd tried to protect him. He'd failed him. On some level both he and his father had utterly failed Geoff.

And now it had cost Blake almost everything.

But as he refocused and steered for shore, Blake was hit with a new fear. Tommy. Meg at his party. His pulse started to race as new purpose formed—get back to the shore, call the cops, go find Meg . . .

The rain turned fully to snow, and through the fog and swirling flakes, he caught the glimmer of a light on shore. Just one. Burning like a candle in the ancient mariner's window to guide him in from the storm. Relief punched through him. But as he aimed for the light, he realized all else on land was dark, and it wasn't just from fog. No lights at all burned along the entire shoreline, save for that one. And as he aimed for it, an orange explosion rent the air. He gasped and jerked backward in shock as a giant ball of roiling flames laced with black mushroomed over his marina. Shock waves slammed across the water. Then another explosion boomed. A fireball began to crackle and roar on the shore, fueled by gale-force winds.

He could smell it. Fuel.

Dread fisted his heart as he raced for the marina. As he neared, his mind fought the horror that sank like lead into his blood.

Meg's camper. On fire.

CHAPTER 26

Meg came around gradually. Her brain was molasses. She felt herself rolling, pitching. Blood in her mouth. Pain—back of head, temple, scalp. Ribs. Trouble breathing. She tried to move. Shock sparked through her as she realized her ankles and wrists were bound tight.

Slowly, she tried to open her eyes. Light struck the back of her brain. She closed them again. Nausea churned in her stomach. Her clothes were wet. She could hear engines—feel the throb of big diesel machines. She heard the slap and rush of the sea, wind. Oh, God. She was at sea!

Her eyes flared open. She fought to pull her surroundings into focus. Paneling. Expensive yacht. She was in some kind of stateroom. On a bed. She tried to sit, but the boat pitched and she rolled with a thud to the floor. Pain crushed through her ribs and she coughed, spitting blood and saliva from her mouth. She could feel a tooth loose, bleeding gums.

Trying to orient herself spatially, Meg stared up at a small porthole, black water gushing past. She must be on a lower deck.

"Meg?" a voice whispered.

She turned her head. "Noah?" Her heart kicked. "Is that you?"

He clambered down from the big bed and placed his cool little hand on her face. "You're alive," he said.

Oh, God. Tommy had taken Noah. She'd put Noah's life in danger. But he was still alive. *Try to speak. Be strong now, for this child. You have to do this.* "Yup," she managed to say, and she spat out another gob of blood and spittle. "Help . . . me sit up, will you?"

He lifted her under her armpits as she tried to scoot up and lean against the base of the bed. She saw now that she was tightly bound with duct tape. Noah moved matted wet hair back from her face, which was sticky with blood. "He cut your head open."

She tried to nod. Pain was overwhelming. She moved her bound hands to her side and pressed against her left pocket. He'd taken her cell. "It's . . . it's going to be fine, Noah. . . are you okay, did he hurt you?"

"I hurt him first, with Dad's crowbar. Then I tried to run, but he caught me. I tried to kick and bite him but he was too strong."

"Where did he take us—are we on his motor yacht?"

"He took us to that big new marina in Whakami where the party was supposed to be. Everyone was gone. It was all dark."

Meg's heart sank. No one knew where they were. Blake was lost at sea. Or he'd been hurt by Geoff.

"I dropped my magic stone on the deck for Daddy to find," he said. "The one Uncle Geoff gave me, made of sea glass. I dropped it before that man carried me onto the boat."

Her mind folded in on itself. Poor kid. Anger began to coil low in her gut at the thought of what was happening to Noah. Her anger morphed fast into rage that surged up her chest. And it pumped into her blood. Her brain recoiled at the memory of Tommy holding her sister's neck while Henry raped her. She didn't understand—why Henry? It didn't seem to fit in her mind. But the look in Tommy's eyes when he'd seen her come over the ridge . . .

Get her! . . . Get her or we're all dead . . .

Stop, wait, Meggie . . . don't run . . .

380

That's why Geoff must have chased her. And there could be only one reason Tommy had come for her now. To silence her. And Noah, too, because he was a witness. He'd seen Tommy's face.

Even if no one was coming to help them, she could not, *would not* let Noah down. She'd rather die than let that bastard win. She'd kill him with her own bare hands, the smiling sociopathic shit.

"How . . . how long have we been on the boat?"

"I don't know."

"When did you stop hearing the foghorn?"

He thought. "Just a little while ago."

"Good, good, we can't be too far offshore. Is there anyone with him?"

"No."

"Did he speak?"

"No."

"Not even one word?"

He shook his head.

The boat pitched violently and, unbalanced, she rolled back onto the floor. Shit. She was weak. Lost a lot of blood. She retched again, spat out more blood.

Noah hurried into the bathroom, fetched a towel. He got down on his knees and wiped her mouth. Meg's heart nearly broke. She struggled back into a sitting position. Using her hands and butt, she edged herself over to the stateroom door. She leaned against it with her back, and slid up the door and onto her feet. She tried the handle with her bound hands. It wouldn't give.

"It's locked, Meg. I heard him lock it. I already tried it."

"Open the bloody door!" she screamed, bashing it with the backs of her bound hands. Blood ran afresh down her face. Down the back of her throat. She gagged.

And she felt Noah watching.

Focus. Stay calm. Panic *will* kill you.

She hopped to the queen bed, and balanced against the edge, trying to breathe through mucus and the blood in her throat, and she wondered if her nose was broken. Her whole head was a ball of pain. "We'll get out of here, Noah, we *will* get out of here."

"I want my dad."

"I know." Meg's heart sank again. A sense of defeat weighed heavy. She had no idea how to do this.

Meggie-Peg, you've never given up . . . C'mon, you came back to Shelter Bay. Do this for me. I'm waiting, kiddo. You're almost there . . . rescuer of little animals and the vulnerable . . . You're the Amazon inside, Meggie-Peg. If you die, you choose to die fighting. Do it for me. Dad. Mom. Noah. Blake, too. I know you hate him right now, but he needs you, too . . .

"Sherry?"

By God, she felt her sister now, really felt her presence here on Tommy's yacht. Talking inside her head. "You are here, aren't you?" she said out loud.

"Who are you talking to?" Noah said.

"My sister. She's going to help us."

"She's dead."

"Her ghost isn't. She's inside me. Ghosts don't die. You can scrub people and places out, but you cannot destroy the ghosts."

"Meg . . . I'm scared."

"Okay, Noah, we're going to try something. I saw a demonstration once, when I interviewed a former CIA operative. You know what that is?"

"No."

"A spy."

"Like a super spy?"

"Like a super spy."

She had his interest. This was good. She was keeping him

engaged. Making him feel as though he had some control over his fate. "This agent showed me how you could get out of duct tape." She got to her feet, wobbling with the roll and pitch of the waves. She showed Noah her wrists. "Like this."

She'd never tried it, still didn't quite believe it could work. Meg raised her arms well above her head, then in one quick movement, with all the force she could muster, swung them down hard to her sides. The duct tape split. She was free.

She stared, dazed that it had worked.

"Wow," he said.

A wry smile pulled across her mouth. It sparked adrenaline back into her. "Okay, now we look in all these drawers and closets for anything that might help cut the tape off my ankles."

She started by opening the cupboard closest to her. Noah got to work on the hatches that lined the side of the bed.

She found clothing, underwear. Tommy's and Liske's, she guessed. In a drawer at the bottom of the closet was a pouch of documents. She opened the pouch. It was stuffed with legal papers, bank account details, and a *Mexico passporte*.

Meg flipped open the passport cover.

A photo of Tommy stared back at her.

Under *Appellidos* was the surname "Sullivan." Under *Nombres* was the name "Jack Anthony." *Nacionalidad* was listed as "Mexicano."

Tommy Kessinger had a fake Mexican passport. Mexican bank accounts. He'd clearly planned this for years—a last-minute back-door escape hatch. Without his wife. And right now he obviously felt threatened enough to use it—the sign of a desperate man. Her wager was that he was heading down the coast, for the border. He'd likely get rid of them overboard along the way.

"How about this, Meg?" Noah held up a small pair of nail scissors he'd found in the storage locker next to the bed.

She got to work quickly, the small scissors making slow work of the fibrous duct tape. Finally free, she ripped it off her pants. No time to waste. They needed to find a way out of here.

She looked at the porthole again. Even if she could smash through that glass, the sea was riding over the windows. She'd flood the place, take down the boat. She got up, felt the door. It was solid, reinforced wood. And trying to break through it might bring him running.

She thought back to everything she'd ever known about the boats, and motor yachts she'd been in. Many had escape hatches on lower decks for emergencies, often cleverly designed to blend into paneling.

"Noah, open every cabinet you can find, feel along the edges of paneling for gaps, or levers. Some yachts have escape doors in really unusual places. Start on the starboard side, I'll start here." She pocketed the scissors and started fingering along grooves in the paneling. A wave of dizziness made her stumble. She sat on the bed a moment, trying to marshal her brain.

Think. Focus.

She'd seen the outside of Tommy's yacht. She knew the size and shape and the upstairs layout. The top deck had a salon and bridge area, with wet bar. Tommy had been about to lead her down into what he'd called the lower salon when she'd heard Emma scream. The lower salon must house the galley, because there'd been no galley on the main deck. So this master stateroom must be on the lowest deck, downstairs from the middle deck salon and galley. From the tapering shape of this stateroom, she guessed they were in the prow. The engine room must be on the other side of the locked door. But the small bathroom, to the right of the door, extended beyond. Which meant the back wall of the bathroom was also likely the wall of the engine room. She'd seen two motor yachts of a similar design that had emergency escape hatches leading from the head into the engine room.

She got up, went into the small bathroom area, and felt around the mirror. She started as she caught sight of her own reflection— hair wild and matted with blood, her face streaked with it. A gaping gash along her cheekbone. Don't think, don't look.

You look like a witch, Meggie-Peg . . .

Thanks a lot, Sherry. Help me out here, will you . . .

She opened the bathroom cabinet. Among the toiletries inside was a midsize can of hairspray. She slipped the can into her jacket pocket—anything for a weapon. And then she found it—riveted into the wall of the shower, a watertight escape hatch to the engine room, with an inset key handle. She flipped the handle out, twisted, and the vacuum door popped open with a suction sound. Noise from the big diesel engines drummed through the space and vibrated into her bones. Exhilaration burst through her chest as she peered into the dark hole.

"Noah." She stepped out of the head. "There was a flashlight in that hatch over there. Pass it to me. Quick."

Meg flicked it on and panned her beam around the interior of the engine room. Chrome and pipes gleamed. She could smell fuel, oil. At the back of the engine, a chrome ladder bolted into the side led up to what she guessed must be an access hatch that opened out into the aft deck area, right outside the glass sliders.

Anxiety laced into her initial bolt of exhilaration. She ran her flashlight beam over the walls, lighting upon a small fire ax clamped to the side, beside a fire extinguisher.

"Okay, Noah," she said, exiting the head. "Here's the plan. You're going to stay down here, where you're safe. Do not move. Do not come through that engine room, even if you hear bad things, understand?"

He paled. His mouth tightened and the blue vein on his brow swelled. But he nodded.

"I'm going to go through the engine room, and up out of the hatch. And I'm going to see if I can catch him by surprise."

"What are you going to do to him?"

"I don't know, Noah. But I *have* to stop him." *Or he will kill us both as soon as he gets far enough offshore.*

Tears pooled and slid soundlessly down his face. He started to shake. Meg held his shoulders steady, and kissed his forehead. "Have faith, Noah Sutton. We're going to get through this. Got it?"

He nodded.

And she slipped into the head and climbed through the hatch into the engine room. She moved past the droning engines, the smell of machinery and diesel strong in her nostrils. She unclamped the fire ax, and holding it in one hand, biting down on pain, she climbed the ladder, pausing to cling on as the boat yawed violently. At the top, she twisted the handle on the hatch, and pushed. It opened easily on hydraulic arms. The scent of sea and cold slammed into her instantly. Her heart kicked. Mouth dry, body wire tight, she climbed out of the hatch. Wind whipped her. She closed the hatch behind her for fear a wave would crash over the stern and douse the engines.

Shaking with cold, or fear, or adrenaline, she wasn't sure, she crouched on her haunches, balancing with one hand on the deck, the ax in the other. She peered through the glass sliders. A small row of lights burned in the cockpit area. Tommy sat in one of the two captain's chairs, hunched forward in concentration as he tried to navigate into the storm. Meg got up slowly, and reached for the door.

———

Blake used a spotlight to scan the gravel around the burning wreck. He worked in increasing circles. Smoke burned his nasal passages. His eyes watered. He held his jaw tight and his heart thumped slow and steady. He focused on keeping panic at bay. He used his military training now, his mind kicking back into an old zone, one he'd perfected in the war arena when he'd often been the only soldier who'd stood between the life and death of a blown-up comrade, when he'd sometimes had to amputate, sew body parts, stop bleeding, all under the rattle of enemy fire. When he'd had to calm the raw terror in the eyes of a fellow soldier in great pain.

He'd found the house empty. No Noah. No sign of a sitter. And the fact that Meg's rig was here at the marina meant she'd returned from Tommy's party. Either she was inside that burning wreck, or she'd been inside the house when it happened. Perhaps she'd let the sitter go when she'd arrived.

He stopped as something in his beam of light winked back from the slush-covered gravel. Dropping to his haunches, Blake picked up a diamond ring. On it hung a small, broken chain.

Meg's engagement ring.

His stomach folded over. He pocketed it, looked further. A clump of long, red hair caught his beam. He lifted it out of the slush, examining it closely. It had roots and bits of scalp attached, as if it had been pulled out. He lowered his beam back to the ground. Deep drag marks in dirt. He panned his light further up the driveway. Tire marks. Recent ones, in the slush, now starting to fill with wet snow. Prints. Big, and smaller ones—Noah's?

Blake surged to his feet, heart beating faster.

There was no cell reception. Phone lines were down. Power was out. Cops and the Coast Guard were inundated. He thought of his brother's confession, how Tommy Kessinger had masterminded this. He was the one man who truly stood to lose everything if the truth came out—the puppeteer. The man who'd killed Sherry. A manipulative, sociopathic bully who had a controlling interest in just about everyone's business in town. Including Dave Kovacs for sheriff now. Tommy was the man who needed most to silence Meg.

He had to act. Fast. Make a choice. It was a gamble, but he had to take it. If Tommy had taken Meg in a vehicle from this marina, where would he go? Where best to hide her? And get rid of her?

It struck him suddenly—Deliah Sproatt. Drowned at sea. Tommy's yacht. He ran for his truck, praying to God that it was the sitter who had taken Noah somewhere to higher ground, somewhere safe. Yet he feared the worst.

———

Counting on the noise of the storm to drown out her movements, Meg slowly slid open the glass slider. She entered through a crack, and shut it quietly behind her. On the glass coffee table she saw a lighter in an ashtray. She reached for it, slipped it into her pocket, and moved forward in a slow crouch.

The boat yawed, and her heart kicked. She grabbed onto the back of the leather sofa for balance. Terror rose into her heart along with pure white hatred as she looked at Tommy in his captain's chair, bathed by soft blue light from the instrument panel. Her palm grew sweaty around the handle of the ax. What was she actually going to do? Kill him? Hit him in the head with the blade of an ax? She didn't know if she could do this. Inside her belly she started to shake.

You're a fighter, Meggie-Peg. You've got to do this.

There has to be another way, Sherry.

He will kill you. He will kill Noah. Unless you stop him first. Think like a cop: don't necessarily aim to kill, but aim to stop—with whatever force required—the threat.

Think of what you saw him doing to me that day. How he raped and strangled me. Think of how he smiled at you, and kissed you when you came home, and how charming he is on the outside—a snake. A sick narcissist. All wonderful until you cross him, and then he turns deadly. Think of Ty Mack. Of Dad. And Mom. Think of Henry.

Meggie, think above all of Noah. That boy does not deserve this. It's not his battle. You cannot let him die, and Tommy will kill him if you don't do something while you still can . . . you'd both already be dead if you hadn't escaped the camper . . . there can be no doubting his intent . . .

Sweat prickled along her brow. She clutched the ax handle in both hands. Her heart jackhammered. Slowly she moved forward in a crouch. She entered the cockpit area, and raised the ax high, hesitating again, unable to do it, just kill a man in cold blood from behind. He spun suddenly around in his captain's chair. He held a gun at his waist, and it was aimed at her.

Meg gasped.

His finger curled around the trigger.

"Marvelous," he said, "how windows can function so perfectly as mirrors at night."

She swallowed, lowering the ax, her body trembling.

He raked his eyes over her. A slow smile curved his lips. "Wondered if you'd come around again. So much better to be present for one's own demise, don't you think?"

"You did it." Her voice came out hoarse. "You strangled Sherry. You raped and killed my sister. I remember. I saw."

He angled his head, as if assessing a strange animal.

"Say something!"

"What's to say? Sorry? She was a whore. She paid."

"My . . . my mother . . ." Her voice started to shake. Blood leaked afresh from her head wound—too much, she was losing too much. Must stop it. Getting weak.

"Tara was getting far too close. It was an easy matter to empty capsule powder into her tea. It's pretty tasteless, from what I learned from Emma's books. All I had to do, once she'd drunk her fill, was help sweet Tara Brogan up to her dead daughter's bedroom, and leave an empty pill container at the bedside. Nice touch, don't you think—Sherry's room? While little Meggie was all barricaded up in her own room down the hall, headphones on her ears."

The boat listed, and she stumbled sideways, reeling into the bar counter.

An alarm sounded on his control panel, and a radar beep began on his monitor. Worry darted through his eyes and he glanced quickly over his shoulder. Meg used his momentary distraction to swing the ax out to her right. She aimed for the side of his neck. But as she brought the ax down, he ducked sideways, and tried to roll out of his chair. The armrest stopped him from making it all the way, and her blade sliced into his upper right arm. He howled like an animal, his gun clattering to the floor. Bile lurched into Meg's throat. Eyes wild, he lunged for her, and backhanded her across the face with all his might. She was flung backward onto the floor. Her ax skittered across the wood.

The warning blips on his monitor sounded louder, faster. They were on a collision course with something. *Reef. Rocks.*

Tommy clamped his left hand over the bleeding wound on his upper right arm and leaned over the controls, trying to steer the boat away from whatever was making the radar scream. Waves were washing the boat sideways. She could hear surf. They had to be colliding with Hobart's Reef.

Meg struggled onto her feet. She closed her hand around the can of hairspray in her pocket and pulled it out. She reached for the gas lighter. Staggering forward, her vision blurring, she depressed the nozzle, releasing a hissing stream of spray. She flicked the lighter and the stream ignited with a whoosh.

She kept the nozzle depressed and lurched toward Tommy with her flaming torch. His hair and clothing caught fire instantly. He spun around, horror on his face, as he dived for the carpeted floor in the salon. He rolled, screaming. The smell of burning hair was acrid.

Meg stumbled toward the wall that held a fire extinguisher. Her half-formed goal was to use it to knock him out cold, then put out the flames before the whole boat caught fire. But the prow of the yacht smacked into something and the whole boat shuddered. It came to a groaning standstill, engines still growling. A wave crashed over the prow, rolling the yacht sideways. Alarms started clanging. Tommy pulled himself along the floor toward the sofa. Grabbing the blanket that hung over the back, he batted out the rest of the smoldering flames on his body. Another wave crashed over the front of the boat. The yacht listed further. They were banked on something. Tommy crawled to the glass slider, leaving a trail of blood. He staggered to his feet, opened the slider.

The boat groaned and yawed yet further. Meg slipped in blood and fell hard to the floor. Under the console she saw his gun. She crawled over, groped for it, rolled onto her side.

Tommy was outside on the aft deck, fighting to unclamp a fiberglass life-raft container. He got it free and wobbled with it in his arms toward the starboard gunwale. He threw it over. Lying on her side, Meg aimed, fired. Glass shattered. She struggled to sit up, and fired again. He jolted, his body going stiff. A soft explosion sounded as the life-raft case exploded open in the water, and the raft began to inflate. She tried to crawl closer, getting dizzy. But he went overboard. And was gone.

Meg tried to get to her feet, but her brain spun, and her vision turned black as she dropped back to the floor, and passed out.

When she came around again she had no idea how long she'd been gone. An hour? Half a minute? Fire was crackling up the blinds on the port side of the bridge. Must have caught them with her makeshift flamethrower. Extinguisher? Where was it? Still affixed to the wall. She pushed herself to her feet. Gasping in pain, she freed the extinguisher, pulled the pin, squeezed the trigger, and released a jet of white foam. She aimed it at the base of the flames. Another alarm began to clang. Coming from the lower decks. Engine room? A breach in the hull—taking on water?

Noah.

She had to get Noah. Meg dropped the extinguisher and made for the stairs, falling down into the lower deck salon. She lurched for the next set of steps. Everything was at an odd angle as the boat was going over. Water sloshed on the floor. The hull had been breached, seawater pouring in. Ice cold. She reached the stateroom door, tried to yank it open. It wouldn't give. No key in the lock. No mechanism to open it. Had Tommy taken the key? Banging sounded from the other side.

"Help. Meg! Please, help me!"

"Noah, wait! I'm coming." She staggered back up the listing stairs, using the rails to pull herself up, and she made her way through the glass sliders and onto the aft deck. She tugged open the engine hatch. Thick, black smoke billowed out. Her heart stopped, then kicked into an erratic stutter. Water must have short-circuited the electrics, causing the engines to catch fire. She shut the hatch. Oh, God. Noah was trapped. The boat was going down.

Meg fought her way back up to the salon, found her ax. She half slid, half fell down to the lower deck level. "Noah! Stand back!" she yelled, swinging her ax high. She struck it down into the door. Wood splintered. She yanked the ax out, tried again. And again. But she was not breaking through. The wood was reinforced. She began to sob, desperation rising as she struck yet again, the force of impact convulsing up her arms, into her brain, spearing pain across her ribs. Blood leaked down her face. She heard a crack, then a groan and crunch. The boat canted further sideways. Water sloshed higher around her ankles.

"Meg! Help! Water is coming in. I can smell smoke from the bathroom!"

"Noah, go close that hatch in the shower." She struck her ax down again.

———

Blake found Tommy's SUV with its vanity plates parked up on the Whakami Bay Harbor promenade—it had been driven right up the boardwalk. But his custom motor yacht was gone.

The harbor was dark, deserted; ripped lanterns blew across the open areas, and torn election posters plastered the docks. Yachts clanked and bashed each other angrily in the roiling water. Blake stood at the top of the gangway in the wind and driving snow.

The fact Tommy's vehicle was here, and the yacht gone, went partway to confirm his guess—he might have taken Meg and Noah out into the storm. He might even be fleeing for good himself.

Blake could stand here and do nothing. Or he could choose *one* course of action, and fast.

Panning his flashlight over the vacant mooring space, something on the dock bounced light back at him. He hurried down the gangway. Between two boards was a shiny piece of stone. He dropped to his haunches. With cold fingers, he fished it out, and his heart imploded when he saw what it was. The "magic" piece of sea glass Geoff had given Noah. He fisted it.

His boy had been here.

Whatever gods were watching over them were leaving him signs. He *had* to believe they were still alive.

Blake surged to his feet and his gaze lit on the whale-watching boat moored in front of the vacant space left by Tommy's yacht. Noah's words filled his brain.

There'll be rides in the harbor on the whale-watching boat. For free. Every hour, even in the dark . . .

It was a custom aluminum-hulled Zodiac. Highly stable on rough seas, yet light, with a capacity to offer passengers an exhilarating ride at extremely high speeds. Emotion slammed into his chest when he saw the key was in the ignition—all ready to take kids on trips around the harbor before the storm had broken, and someone had forgotten to secure the keys when it had.

Blake moved fast. He climbed into the rigid-hull inflatable, got behind the console, fired the ignition. Engines grumbled to throaty life, water frothing around him. He hit a switch and a row of spotlights speared to life, cutting through the darkness and turning the snow silver-white.

He cast off lines, maneuvered away from the dock, and gave gas, gunning for the channel and harbor mouth. His mind raced as wind sliced his face, and his boat slammed against waves with a rhythmic thud, force enough to damage kidneys if sustained at any great distance. His trump was speed. Tommy's boat was high-end, but heavy and slow. Where would a man running from the law in a motor yacht go?

Not north. And not straight out to sea—not enough fuel for that. And a bad move in this storm. He'd head south. The border. In order to sail south, a mariner would first need to round Hobart's Reef, a jagged circle of volcanic rock that speared through the sea several miles offshore. Once clear of Hobart's, he'd probably have to hang several miles clear of shore to avoid the rough storm water. If he didn't have too much of a lead, there was potential to close in on him in the vicinity of Hobart's, *if* there was any visibility.

Blake blasted his Zodiac through the fierce chop at the mouth, and headed for the big swells, the steel hull slicing into the face of the waves.

He could be wrong. But he could also be right. Hesitate, and he'd lose the two human beings who meant more to him than anything else in this world.

He opened the engines to full capacity.

All he had was speed over size, a small Glock at his back. And his sea smarts.

Several miles offshore, almost at Hobart's Reef, Blake's spotlights caught something orange through the fog and snow. Cortisol fired into his system. He slowed, and aimed his spotlights on the smallish object tossing upon veined swells. As he got closer, he saw it was an orange life raft with a tented cover. He came up alongside the raft, reversing engines to hold steady. The raft bumped against the side of his Zodiac and he grabbed for the rope.

Blake shined his flashlight into the tented opening. His breath caught.

Tommy Kessinger.

Lying on his back. His eyes open and lifeless. Blood pooled at the bottom of the life boat. Blake ran the light over his body. He appeared to have been burned. His upper right arm had been gashed open wide.

A quiet dread filled Blake as he panned his light into the storm, looking for a second raft. Nothing. Judging by the wind and swell direction, he figured this raft had to have drifted from Hobart's Reef. He let Tommy go, and goosed the engines again, aiming for the reef.

As he neared the booming sound of surf on rock, he caught snatches of another noise. He quieted the engines for a moment, trying to identify it, and then it hit him—the bleat of emergency air horn sirens. Terror struck his heart.

He pushed closer to the reef, and suddenly he saw, through the fog and snow, the white navigation light of a boat's stern. Tommy's yacht. It had come aground on the reef, and was listing danger-ously over onto its port side and taking on water. Worse, he could smell smoke. He pulled up at the stern, and swung a rope with a grappling hook to catch the railing.

———

Sobbing with distress, Meg raised her arms high and slammed the ax back into the door, splintering it only a little more. A grating metal groan sounded as the maw in the hull squashed open fur-ther, the whole boat starting to fold under the pressure of the sea.

More water gushed in. It was just a matter of time before the side of the boat buckled right in.

Noah screamed.

She stilled as she heard something else—another voice. Male. Calling her name. *No. It couldn't be. Not possible.*

"Meg!"

Blake? No, she had to be dreaming. Voices playing tricks in her head again. She was losing it. She was dying.

"Noah! Meg! Where are you?"

Energy exploded through her blood.

"Blake! Down here! Help!"

Blake slid down the stairs behind her, landing in water. It was up to their knees now, the yacht listing further. Smoke smelled strong.

"Noah . . . he's in there . . . fire in the engine room."

He grabbed the ax from her. "Go up to the top deck. Find life vests. Find the other raft, unclip it, make sure it has a line attached to the boat, and throw the case overboard. It will float. Let it run out with the swell as you pull the line in. When the line runs out, the case will release, and the raft will inflate. Wait up there for us." Blake started to hack ferociously at the door.

Up on the aft deck, Meg found the one remaining fiber-glass case containing an emergency raft. The fire was now roaring through the cockpit. Coughing, and with shaking hands, she unclamped the case and noted that the line was attached. She struggled to carry the case over to the gunwale. It was heavy, slippery, wet, awkward. She managed to maneuver it over the side, breathing hard, pain riding her body. It landed with a splosh near the bobbing whale boat that Blake had secured to the yacht. She yanked on the line, spooling it out of the case until it jerked, and the raft exploded from the case and started to inflate with a hiss. She located the life vests in a bench chest, and put one on.

Defying Blake's request, Meg went back into the boat, and made it down the stairs now flowing heavily with water.

Blake had hacked a hole big enough for Noah, and he was pulling his son through. Noah was sobbing. Blake took his son's shoulders and aimed him for the stairs. "Go up."

Meg held her hand out to Noah. As Noah reached for it, the hole in the side of the boat splintered open wide with an explosive crash. Sea gushed in, ice cold, buckling the hull inward. The wall of the head caved in, crushing onto Blake.

"Put this life jacket on!" Meg screamed, shoving a vest at Noah. "Get up the stairs!" She rushed to Blake's side and started pulling bits of plank and wood off him. "Give me your hand, Blake." He reached out to her, and she pulled. He screamed in pain. His eyes held hers. The look in them stopped her heart. Timbers creaked again. Smoke was growing thick.

"My hand, right hand is crushed." He gasped in pain as she tried to pull him free again. "Go. Get in the raft. Go."

"No, Blake! *No!*" Tears poured down her face. *"Please."* She yanked on his arm again. But he was stuck fast. She hooked her hands under his armpits, and pulled. He screamed, and then bit down on the pain as he tried to speak, his face tight, gray, eyes watering. "Meg. Leave. Please."

"I . . . I can't."

The yacht slipped sideways. There was another crunching sound from the engine room. Alarms still clanged. Water sloshed higher. She ripped away another piece of bathroom. And saw. His hand was crushed between the caved-in paneling and cabinetry. Bleeding badly. Her eyes flared to his.

"Meg, no time. If you don't get out now, Noah will drown on his own."

Her gaze shot to the stairs—they were caving in.

"Do it. Please. Go. Save my boy. Get him home safe. Look after him."

Her whole body shook. She couldn't move. The yacht groaned, tilted further. Water came to her waist. Her teeth chattered. Her mind couldn't work.

"If you stand there, you *will* kill Noah. Hurry."

"I . . . can't." She grabbed his arm, and yanked again. He screamed. She stopped. She was shaking like a leaf.

"Go, Meggie."

The yacht slipped further, she could feel it going now.

Desperation burned in his eyes. "*Please,* do not let me die for nothing. Do not kill my son."

She held his gaze. The years they'd shared as kids, friends, as soul mates, lovers; the pain and happiness and loss and betrayal, and joy—all of it, she felt it all now. Swelling between them. And it killed her inside. Because she knew with utter certainty that he was the one she wanted in her life. Always had, on some level. And now he was going. She cupped his face, his rugged face. It was white with pain.

"Please," he whispered, tears pooling in his green eyes. "My boy."

She swallowed. Kissed his cold mouth. "I love you, Blake Sutton."

He nodded. Smiled. "Finally, she says it," he whispered.

And Meg felt her heart cleave in two.

Tears streaming down her face, she made it back up to the aft deck, where she found Noah shivering in his life vest and clutching onto the gunwale as the boat yawed onto its side. Slipping across the wet deck, she reached for the raft line and fought against the push and pull of the sea to drag the inflatable right up to the side of the yacht.

"Give me your hand," she said to Noah.

"Where's my dad?"

"He wants you to get into the raft, Noah."

He stared at her, refusing to move. "Not without him."

She grasped his hand. "Now. Do it. For him." Holding Noah's hand, she guided him down onto the water-covered swim deck, and into the raft. Meg hesitated, trying to hold on to hope a moment longer. But the yacht's stern started to sink, and she knew if she didn't get off now, she could be sucked down in the powerful vortex made by the sinking craft.

She jumped into the raft, and cut the line free with the tool affixed to the rope. They went spinning into the dark, driven by wind and swell. Her mind spun into darkness, too, her brain going utterly numb. Blank. She couldn't even feel the physical pain of her injuries any longer. Part of her was dead inside. On some level she knew she was in severe shock. Her body was shutting down.

"Dad! Where's my dad!?" Noah screamed as the lights of the yacht were swallowed by fog and darkness. "He's not coming, is he? Where is he!?"

Functioning on autopilot, Meg closed and secured the flap, cocooning them in tightly against the weather. And in silence, she took Noah in her arms, held tight. So tight. For a while she couldn't speak at all. All she could see were Blake's eyes as they'd held hers in the last moments. The rawness. The depth of pain. And love.

Please. Save my son . . . don't let me die for nothing . . .

She cleared her throat. "I'm so sorry, Noah." Her voice choked on a sob. She stroked his wet hair. "I'm so sorry."

CHAPTER 27

Meg's eyes flickered open, her lids thick, swollen. Medical smell. Drip next to her bed. A machine making a soft, regular beep. Monitors. She turned her head slowly on her pillow. Pain, maybe medication, dulled her brain. A heaviness swamped her body. She blinked as a face came into focus at her bedside. She tried to squint at it.

A hand reached for hers. A warm hand. A smile split the face with a row of teeth. Those deep indigo-blue eyes—she knew those eyes.

"Jonah?" Her voice was a reedy whisper.

"Shh. Don't talk."

Images slammed through her—the scent of smoke, the feel of ice water. She tried to sit up. *"Noah?"*

Jonah restrained her shoulder gently. "He's fine. Meg. He's in better shape physically than you. The Coast Guard pulled you both out the night before last. He's been checked out, treated. Cops have spoken with him. He's seen a critical-incident counselor, and she'll visit with him regularly for a while now. He's with Irene now, in the waiting room. I came as soon as I heard."

"Blake?"

A pause.

She closed her eyes, a dull cold filling her.

"I'm sorry, Meg. The yacht went down. No sign of it. Some debris was found down the coast that could match, but there's a lot of debris out there from the storm. The Coast Guard has been plucking people and bodies out all the way down the coast. The fronts came in way faster than anticipated, and with the surge . . ." He reached out, and with his handkerchief, he wiped tears from her face. Gentle.

"Maybe . . . maybe he took another life raft?" she whispered.

"There were only two."

"It was a reef—the yacht hit a reef. Did they look properly? Maybe they were searching in the wrong place. It was dark—"

"Noah told them that the yacht struck something. That there was breaking water around. They searched around Hobart's Reef. There was some diesel spill and fire debris."

"What about the whale boat?"

"They haven't found that. If the yacht went down, it was heavy; it could have pulled a tethered Zodiac down with it, perhaps. Or it could have broken free. It could have gone miles down the coast in that wind." He took her hand that had once worn his ring, and clasped it gently.

"I shouldn't have left him. His hand was crushed, stuck." Tears overwhelmed her. She couldn't speak for a few minutes. "He . . . he told me to save his son."

He moved hair back from her brow. "You did, Meg."

"Tommy?"

"They found his body in the life raft. There'll be an autopsy, but it appears he died from gunshot wounds and blood loss from injury."

"I shot him. I cut him with an ax."

He smoothed her brow.

"I killed him."

"Let's wait to talk to the police. Let them make that decision. Don't leap to any conclusions."

"I killed him and I'm glad."

"Meg—"

"I remember, Jonah," she whispered, her eyes closed. She was unable to take in light or look at the world. "I remember what happened that day twenty-two years ago on the spit. I saw Henry, Tommy, raping Sherry. Geoff . . . chased me." Her voice failed her again. She fell silent as she marshaled control. "I can see it, but I don't understand it—Henry. Geoff . . ."

She opened her eyes. "Geoff?"

"Don't know what happened to him, yet."

"His car . . . was at the marina. Blake followed him out into the bay. He left . . . Noah." She struggled to sit up again, but Jonah once more gently restrained her. "Shh, easy, or Nurse Ratched will be back." He smiled. "Believe me, you'll be wanting to delay that." He paused. "He's an amazing kid, you know. Stoic."

"Takes after his father," she whispered, an unbearable crushing weight on her chest . . . *gone. Blake gone.*

"Noah told them how his father came down and got him out. What you did."

She tried to sit up.

"Meg, stop fighting. You have got to rest. You have fractured ribs. Fractured arm." She realized suddenly her right arm was in a cast. "You've suffered a concussion. You have twenty-four stitches on your brow, and staples in your skull. You scared us for a moment there."

She lay silent, trying to process.

"What day is it?"

"Tuesday."

"I want Noah."

"First Dave Kovacs needs a word." Jonah went to the door, motioned for Dave.

He came in. Hat in his hands. Big and broken looking. "Meg."

"I got him," she said. "It was never Ty. It was Tommy. I remember everything."

He drew up a chair. Jonah slipped out. There was a look in Dave's eyes that made her tense.

"I have something to tell you, Meg." He inhaled. "It was my baby. Sherry was carrying our baby."

She stared, her world spinning weirdly. Out of focus. She struggled to absorb his words, the look on his face. "Sherry's baby was yours?"

He nodded.

It came to her then. That day in the alley—*that* was what she'd been trying to pinpoint when she'd seen a picture of the young Dave in the *Shelter Bay Chronicle* archives. She'd seen them early that summer—Dave and Sherry together. Dave touching her sister's face in the alleyway behind The Mystery Bookstore.

"We had a brief affair. She was . . . it was a mistake. All round. I . . . I have no excuses. I was newly married, and I don't even really know how it happened. She was flirtatious. Sexy. She came on to me." He cleared his throat. "In retrospect, I think she just needed something. Love. Escape."

"Did you know? That she was pregnant?"

He shook his head. "When you came to interview my father that day . . . it was a shock." He leaned forward, the plastic chair creaking under his muscular bulk. "I told my dad about me and Sherry, after the murder. In full disclosure, I told him that I'd been seeing her on and off. Just physical. Although he put that information under his hat, he did factor it into his investigation, Meg. And he didn't believe it impacted his judgment, or his belief in

Ty's guilt. I also felt that our affair bore no relevance on the crime. But I did *not* know about the pregnancy. My father kept that from me, from everyone, it seems. I think he suspected it was mine, and that he kept it as quiet as he could to protect me and my marriage."

"So many little secrets," Meg whispered, the scant energy she had left draining from her body. "So many consequences as people tried to protect those they loved, and they all intersected over the years . . ."

"I told my wife last night," he said. "It was a long time ago, and we're working through it now. I've withdrawn from the sheriff's race."

"Oh, Dave—"

"Not the time. Maybe next run. I've also handed the Sherry case to the state police. They've already matched Henry Thibodeau's DNA to one of the profiles on file. It was his hair on Sherry's body."

"It came from the condom with Sherry's blood trace on it?"

He nodded.

"Did Tommy shoot him?"

"That's still under investigation. But it sounds like he's a key suspect—Lori-Beth texted Tommy her husband's location after Henry called to tell her that he'd checked into the Blind Channel Motel. According to Tommy's wife, Liske, he left the house in the dark right after that text came through, saying he had a problem at a job site. And someone saw his vanity plates near the motel that night."

"Who told my dad where Tyson Mack was hiding? Tommy?"

"That's the assumption right now. Ryan Millar had a close friend who worked admin in the sheriff's office. She'd seen the report on Ty. They have him in for questioning. The belief is he told Tommy, and Tommy, the 'bereaved' almost-son-in-law, riled Jack Brogan up over drinks at the Otter and Goose, after which he went to buy a gun."

"Ryan lied. About the alibi."

"He's confessed to that, yes. Tommy has been looking after him in business ever since. He wasn't directly involved in Sherry's murder, but he's complicit, of course. He clearly knew why he was covering for Tommy, but whether he had prior knowledge of Tommy's intent that day is still in question. His legal counsel is seeking a plea bargain in exchange for more information." He paused. "It's over, Meg. It's over."

Closure. The End.

And what was it worth? So she could emotionally die, finally, and begin again? It was not worth the loss of Blake Sutton.

"I want to see Noah."

———

Noah placed his little hand in Meg's. His skin was cool. Their eyes locked. She tried to open her mouth but the emotion was suddenly too huge. It was a tsunami inside her, and it choked her words, and tears streamed, and she started to shake. She fought to hold it all at bay, but couldn't. While Kovacs had gone to fetch Noah, she'd formulated in her mind how calm she would be for him. What she would say. She would be the strong one. Noah was sensitive. He needed her help.

But it was the child who comforted her now. "It's okay, Meg," he said, his green eyes holding hers. His father's eyes. As if Blake were talking to her through him from the other side, through his boy, and she couldn't bear the gaping maw of loss.

"I . . . I loved him," she whispered. "I loved your father, and I'm going to be there for you, Noah." She sniffed. "We're going to finish fixing up Crabby Jack's for him. We . . . we'll have a grand opening in spring . . . We'll have that big crab boil in November, like he wanted. We'll invite everyone. The whole town . . ." She struggled to find her voice. Sniffed again. Tried to smile. "You can wear your granddad's crab hat . . . with . . . with the . . . googly eyes. We'll do it for your dad."

"Crabby Jack's got flooded," he said quietly.

She gripped his hand. Tight. "That's okay. We'll fix it. We will."

Please. Save my boy . . . look after him.

I will, Blake, by God I will . . . I will be there for him . . .

———

The next few days were gray, cold. Geoff's remains were found. Baby Joy was born, and the adoption contract declared null and void. Lori-Beth was left bereft, with only Henry's shell-shocked parents, Rose and Albert, to comfort her. She'd had a falling-out with her sister, Sally, who had been charged for her attack on Meg's house, and was now awaiting trial.

Brooklyn was devastated by the loss of her father, and was reeling in the face of the revelations of the horrific legacy Tommy Kessinger had left. Emma confessed that Tommy had been physically abusive throughout their relationship, but she'd stayed mum because he'd threatened to take Brooklyn away from her if she ever spoke out. She told police Sherry had been scared of him, and had been trying to break off their relationship prior to going with Ty to the spit. An investigation was reopened into the death of Tara Brogan, and Deliah Sproatt Kessinger.

Noah was meanwhile put into temporary foster care, but while Meg was still in the hospital, Jonah helped her start the process of filing for immediate guardianship. Her resolve was to adopt him, and she held Blake's last words like a mantra to her chest.

Please . . . Save my boy. . . Do not let me die for nothing . . .

Those words would guide her forward now. And when the day came that she was released from the hospital, she got news that a judge had granted her temporary guardianship of Noah Sutton. It was a first step.

"Are you certain that you're ready to do this, Meg?" Jonah asked as he drove her from the hospital to pick up Noah from foster care. She heard the deeper question in his words. She saw the concern in his features. And more.

She nodded.

"You're still in a state of shock, you know. These are big decisions."

"I know." She was scared. She knew that half of her was numb, that on some level she had shut down. But when they pulled up at the foster house, and the door opened, and little Noah ran out to meet them, his face white, his body thin, she dropped to her knees and hugged him tightly against her body, and she knew it was the right thing. The only thing.

Jonah helped her and Noah move into the old Brogan house on Forest Lane while Meg made plans to address the water damage on the ground floor of the marina building and finish off the renovations.

She and Noah visited the marina together, a quiet pilgrimage. They spoke about his dad, and Uncle Geoff, and how they'd restore Crabby Jack's together. Jonah was right, Noah was stoic. A tower of tiny strength in his sensitive shell.

"I worry he's bottling it all in," Meg told Jonah the night after they'd been to the marina, once she'd tucked Noah into bed. She hadn't read to him. Rather, she'd told him a story about how his dad had caught a big salmon once when they were little, and it had swum away with his rod. Her plan was to tell Noah a story about his dad's youth every night, as long as she had tales to tell. Then she'd learn more about what Blake had done in the army, and share those stories, too.

"All you can do is be there for him, Meg."

"What about you, Jonah?"

"I'm here for you. As long as you need someone."

"I mean, what about work, Seattle? The foot case."

He held her gaze in silence for several beats. Meg could see in his eyes that he knew what she was asking. The future. Long-term plans. His ring was gone. She didn't know where. She'd lost it sometime during the attack.

She'd told him that she'd taken it off, and why.

She'd told him that she'd fallen in love with Blake. That she probably always had been.

"I think the more important question is what about you," he said. "You're going to stay." It wasn't a question, yet it was. And he followed it quickly with "Because I want you back in my life, Meg. I want to try again."

She looked away. At the fire he'd built in her parents' hearth. So handsome, so smart. She was desperately fond of him. It would be so easy to slip back into a relationship as a way to assuage her grief, but then she'd have learned nothing. "I need to stay," she said quietly, and turned to meet his gaze.

"Noah?" he said.

"For me." Her words hung. The fire crackled. This old home was warm again. Messy with kids' things. There would be school again soon. Life. Irene was staying with them now. Meg was interviewing homecare nurses for a more long-term arrangement. She wanted Irene to live with her and Noah until the last possible moment. Her dad's sister had cared for her, and now it was her turn.

"You were right, Jonah, but not in the ways I at first thought. I did need to come back and rewrite the past within new context. Not only did it reveal the truth of what happened to Sherry, it showed me who I was, who I always had been, at the core. How, for all these years, I've been trying to run from my true self, mold myself into a woman I thought I should be, that you wanted me to be, but always, underneath, lay this struggle to reconcile those disparate halves. And this is who I am."

He appraised her in silence for several moments, then reached up, curled a lock of her hair around his finger. He smiled, a sad and poignant look filtering into his eyes. "Meggie Brogan, with the wild red hair, who belongs by the sea," he whispered. "Who'll write her books in a romantic cottage overlooking the waters of Shelter Bay on the Oregon coast. Who'll run crab boats with her lover's son. Be a community stalwart and famous for her annual crab boils on the marina." He paused, his eyes darkening, glimmering. "Who'll travel for her research and dress up for her interviews, but retreat to this place that is her home, and where her roots go down deep."

Tears filled her eyes. His smile faded. "Who learned, once again, how to find the sweet, sad release that comes from tears, and from opening her heart." A pause. "I love you, Meg, I always will." He came slowly to his feet.

"Where are you going?"

"To pack. I need to let you get on with it. But know one thing, I'm a phone call away. And I'm the best goddamn forensic shrink consultant you're going to find when you need one again."

CHAPTER 28

A week later, on a cold but clear Sunday morning, Meg and Noah were scrubbing and mopping the Crabby Jack floors clean of sea gunk, Meg doing her best with her right hand in a cast.

"When will we move back in here?" Noah asked.

"Soon, I hope," she said. "I'm putting my old house on the market next week now that it's all fixed up." That dream Blake had painted for her, writing by the sea in a renovated boathouse, had seized hold of her. "Irene would love it, too, I think." She smiled, wiping her brow with the back of her wrist. "And she has a nurse to help her now, so she'll be safe."

He started to cry. Finally releasing. Meg dropped her mop and held him while he sobbed. Finally, she could offer succor. Grief. She understood it. It was her old friend. She knew its tricky paths. How it could come and go, and surprise you in unexpected ways.

"I miss him," he said, his voice muffled by her jacket.

"I know. Me too." She stroked his hair.

"We should have waited for him. Maybe he'd have come out."

Meg closed her eyes. She'd been through this so many times herself—the questions. Was there something else she could have done? Was there a better way to have softened the blow with Noah?

Save my boy. Look after him . . . please, do not let me die for nothing . . .

She kissed his towhead, inhaling his scent—like sunshine and hay. "We'll make this work, Noah. I'm not going to lie to you, ever, and the first truth I will tell you is that it doesn't get easier over time. It just gets different. And it's never the same for anyone. Each one of us grieves in their own way, and the hurt can sneak up on you at funny times. But I think you already learned that, when you lost your mom. I think that's why it was so hard when I came into your and your dad's lives."

He was silent a while. Then he nodded, and looked up slowly. "You told me on the yacht that you can't destroy the ghosts. You can kill people, but their ghosts will always stay alive inside you."

"What I meant was—"

"Will Dad talk to me? Like Sherry talks to you?"

Tears flooded into Meg's eyes. For a moment she couldn't speak. "I . . . I don't know," she whispered. "It's different for everyone. When I was little I used to go down to the beach and sit and wait for Sherry's spirit to come to me, and . . . sometimes I think she did." Meg paused. "Why don't we do that—go across to the spit later, and find a warm place in the dunes, and just sit there and listen to the waves, and think about the people we love who are not with us anymore? Would you like that?"

"Yes," he said, looking away from her and picking up his scrubbing brush.

A memory stirred through her, Jonah's words in the corn maze. *Are you happy? . . . What do you want out of life—children?*

Happiness was a strange thing. Perhaps in her sadness she was content in her new role here now, with Noah. And Irene. With this town, and her writing, and the books that lay ahead. And she was struck suddenly by the disparate ways in which people could become family.

She'd always wanted a child, but never could have anticipated a family would become hers in this way. She reached for her mop, and as she did, something outside the window caught her eye. Her heart kicked.

"Noah!" she whispered urgently. "Look, over there." She pointed. He stilled, glanced up.

"*Lucy!*" He dropped his scrubbing brush, scrambled out of the office door, raced along the gravel. He fell to his knees, and hugged his black Lab, who was all skin and bone. Meg ran out after him. Lucy wagged her tail.

"Lucy." He sobbed, burying his face in her dusty fur. "Lucy, you came home!"

Meg joined him in the puppy pile, stroking Lucy.

"She's so thin," he said, surging to his feet, fire crackling fiercely back into his green eyes. "We need to feed her, get her some water. Come, Lucy, want some food, girl? Come." Lucy followed Noah into the building.

Meg stood, watching the boy and dog go. Her heart ached. She was about to follow them when she heard the sound of a vehicle approaching down the gravel drive. She started and spun around.

State police. Her chest went tight. An officer got out. She went up to meet him, drawing her jacket close against the cold. The breeze ruffled his hair. He took off his shades.

And she knew. She just knew. They'd found his body.

"You found him?" she whispered.

"We did, ma'am."

Her knees crumpled out from under her.

The cop led her over to a wooden stump under the covered deck area, and helped her sit. Noah came up to the window. She made a motion with her hand, telling him to wait inside for a minute.

"He was found three days ago."

"*Three?*" she whispered. "Where?"

"Ma'am, he's alive."

Shock gripped her like a vise. "What?"

"He's alive. He just came around. Until now they didn't know who he was."

Meg's world pitched like a boat at sea. "I . . . I don't understand."

"He was found among rocks with several other bodies from a small pleasure craft that washed ashore several miles south of Whakami. He was unconscious, had no ID on his person. It was assumed he was one of the pleasure-boat crew. Coast Guard and law-enforcement personnel have been working hard to match up bodies with missing persons and boats since the storm. They were looking in the wrong direction with him, until he came around after surgery."

"Surgery?"

"He's badly injured, ma'am."

"But he's alive, he's talking?"

The officer opened his mouth, but she lurched to her feet. "Noah! Get out here, Noah!"

"Wait." The cop's hand clamped on her arm. "He lost his right hand," he said quietly, as Noah flung open the door. "He lost a lot of blood. Head injury. Back injury. Broken femur. It's going to be a long road."

"Where is he?!"

Noah came up, Lucy in tow.

"They're airlifting him to Chillmook General. There's a surgical team on standby. He needs further amputation."

"Noah . . . Noah, come here." Tears streamed down her face. Her brain spun so dizzyingly she thought she might throw up, so wildly she couldn't even begin to articulate her thoughts or emotions, or absorb the cop's words. She was acting on gut drive. All she wanted to do was to see him, to prove it with her own eyes. To touch him. "He's alive! Your dad—they say he's alive. He . . . He made it. He's going to make it."

"He didn't drown?"

"No, Noah—" Her voice caught on a sob as she crouched down and gripped his shoulders. "They found him. He's badly injured, but he . . . he's *going* to make it. He *will*."

Noah just stared, eyes wide. His father's eyes. Then as comprehension appeared to dawn in his face, emotion started to gleam. A tear slid down his cheek.

The cop said, "I can take you to the hospital now."

They piled into the cruiser, Lucy too. Meg clutched Noah's hand tight. So tight. Her whole body was tight. Scared. Thrilled. Terrified.

———

The surgeon came forward in scrubs to meet them.

"You the family?"

"Me and Noah." She held his hand tight.

He gestured to a group of chairs nearby and seated himself. Meg tensed. She and Noah sat. The state police officer had offered to stay outside with Lucy. Meg's focus narrowed only on this man in his green scrubs now, this man who'd operated on Blake.

The cop had taken her aside prior to entering the hospital, and told her that Blake had used an ax—the fire ax—to chop off his own hand. Blake Sutton, an army vet, a trained medic accustomed to operating under impossible circumstance, a medic who'd done countless emergency amputations on others, had used his free hand to fashion a tourniquet with wiring and tubing he'd pulled from the wall as he was going down. He'd used the ax she'd been hacking through the door with to chop off his own hand. *That* was how badly he wanted to live. *That* was how badly he wanted to see his son again. That was what he'd told doctors when he came around after they'd operated on his hand. He'd stuck his bleeding stump into fire and coals on the boat, and seared off the veins. And he'd managed to climb back into the whale boat with his cooked, smoking stump, and he made it some distance before passing out. The rest, he'd told the team, he couldn't remember.

An expert group of doctors, led by this surgeon seated in front of Meg now, had gone in again to amputate more.

"He's going to pull through," the doctor said, his clear brown eyes earnest. "All things considered."

"Meaning?"

"There's always a risk of infection. We took off a clear margin." He held her eyes. "His presence of mind, under duress, the pain he must have endured—the human will to live is phenomenal. His military training, operating under stress and extreme circumstances, attack, could only have helped."

"He's stubborn," she whispered, glancing at Noah. "Blake Sutton doesn't give up. Neither does his boy. Right, Noah?"

Noah nodded in somber silence.

The surgeon talked a bit about the future, prosthetics, but Noah interrupted.

"Can we see my dad now?"

The surgeon nodded. "But go easy on the big guy." He smiled. It crinkled his eyes. "It's going to take a while."

When they walked in, Blake believed he'd died and gone to heaven, and this was a vision come to him. Noah and Meg. Alive. In one piece. Meg's arm in a cast. Her free hand holding his son's.

"Daddy?" Noah whispered.

"Come here, champ."

Noah rushed forward. With his good arm, Blake grabbed his boy, and just held him. Tears filled his eyes, and spilled from the corners. Meg bent over, kissed them away, kissed his mouth. "They say you're one stubborn brute," she whispered, holding his eyes. "That you refused to die."

He gave a weak smile. "I wanted that second chance, Meg," he whispered. "I was not letting it go, not this time. Those last words you said to me . . . they made me fight. They saved me."

She swiped emotion from her eyes, and his chest crunched. So much to say, and no words would come to him. It was all just there. The two people he cared about most in the world.

"We're fixing the marina, Dad. We're fixing Crabby Jack's. The water got in, but we went to look, and we're cleaning up, and we can do it, Dad. We can. We can still get it ready for a grand spring opening."

Blake's eyes swam. "God, I love you, champ." His eyes locked with his son's. "And you know what—you're going to be my right-hand man, right?"

He saw Meg's gaze go to the tented structure over his right hand. And her mouth tightened.

"Small mercies, huh," he said to her. "Good thing I'm left-handed."

She clasped his left hand, lacing her fingers tightly through his.

"I found something," he said. "Your engagement ring. It was in the gravel outside the burning camper. I put it in my pocket. It was still there when they rescued me."

Her mouth puckered in a surge of emotion. She cupped the side of his face gently. "Jonah will be happy, I'm sure, to get it back," she whispered.

And with those words he knew. She'd stay. At least for a while. At least long enough for him to work to convince her to make it permanent. He closed his eyes, and offered a silent prayer to the powers that had delivered him back to his family. Because that's how he was going to think of them now. His family.

The nurse came in. "I think we need to give your father a rest," she said, placing her hand on Noah's shoulder. "Is that okay? You can come back later." She looked at Meg. "He'll need to build his strength slowly."

"Meg," he whispered. "Thank you. For saving him."

She held his gaze for several long beats, the nurse waiting with Noah at the door. She bent down and brushed her mouth softly over his dry, chapped lips. "He saved me." She whispered. "You both did. In more ways than you will ever know. I really do love you, Blake Sutton." She paused. "I always have, and I believe I always will."

———

It was late March when Meg took an evening walk with Blake and Noah. They made their way slowly along the ocean side of the spit, along the miles of white beach, dune grasses bending in wind that lifted spumes of spindrift from the waves. Blake was using his cane, slowly rebuilding his strength by gradually increasing distances, his femur healing nicely in spite of the many pins. There'd been other medical visits, and measurements for a prosthesis, which would be fitted soon.

Noah was still seeing his counselor. He seemed to be coping, and happy enough, although Meg knew it was hard to tell with kids sometimes. He ran ahead of them now, chasing Lucy, who was scattering the sandpipers that scuttled along the foam scallops left by waves on hard-packed sand.

Meg thought back to herself at that age, racing along these beaches, sunburned and salt-stung with skinned knees and adventure in her heart. Those were good summers, before Sherry's murder.

. . . full of watermelons and sunblock and backyard barbecues, of purple blackberry smiles, of sea salt tingling on sun-warmed skin, of burning knees skinned raw in pursuit of tree houses and yet higher boughs. Of brightly painted buoys, and crab pots, and driftwood art. Of fresh local cheese from Chillmook farms, and the briny scent of pink crabs being boiled fresh from the bay.

A summer to be lived, full throttle, with the ferocity of youth. And skateboard wind in your hair . . .

Those were the words she'd decided to open her book with, and they were the kinds of summers she hoped would become Noah's now. He stopped suddenly up ahead, and dropped to his knees. As Meg and Blake neared they saw he was watching tiny fish trapped in a tidal pool left by the high tide.

Noah looked up as they approached. "They'll die in here! We need to get them back to the sea."

Up along the high-tide line of flotsam, Blake found an old bucket. He brought it down to the tidal pool, and he and Meg sat up a little higher on the warm sand, leaning against a log as they watched Noah catch fish, and scurry down to the ocean to release them into the wild water. The sun began to set and the world turned gold.

"Do you remember Sherry's goldfish?" Meg said quietly.

Blake smiled, and his eyes turned light green. "Yeah. I remember how they used to upset you, trapped behind the glass like that."

She watched Noah running down to the waves with another bucket load, Lucy cavorting after him. "She used to say they were trapped in a perfect world, no predators in their water. But I always thought they'd be happier in the wild."

"I guess we never know where the danger will come from," he said, eyes on his son. "Sometimes it's close to home. Or even right in the home. All we can do is our best to protect our children, the ones we love." He took her hand in his, laced his fingers through hers, met her eyes. "And hope for luck."

She smiled ruefully. "Sherry's spirit stopped talking to me, you know. Once Tommy was dead. Didn't even say good-bye. Typical Sherry."

He laughed. "But you did right by her. You must feel that?"

She nodded.

He looked away. "Wish I could say the same about Geoff."

Meg squeezed his hand.

"He did some terrible things, but I'll be damned if I don't miss the idea of having him around." He paused. "That night he arrived at the marina, after all those years, and he and Noah and I had dinner, and he gave Noah that stone, and encouraged him with his art . . ." His voice caught, and he took a moment to corral his emotion. "I dared dream we might all be a family again, that he'd bring Nate . . ." His voice died.

Meg leaned over and kissed him on the lips. His mouth was warm, the stubble on his jaw rough. He was thinner and a little pale yet, but he was all Blake. "We can still be family," she whispered.

His eyes glimmered, and he nodded. Then he grinned, and it put the dimples back into his cheeks. "I'll have to meet this Jonah some day, and thank him for sending you home."

———

Charles Dickens once said that "Home" is simply a name, a word, but it's a strong one; stronger than any magician ever spoke, or spirit ever answered to, in the strongest conjuration. And when I saw Blake again after we thought he'd died, as I held his son's hand in that hospital room, I finally understood how, sometimes, "Home" is not a place. It's a person . . .

Meg looked up from her table on the Crabby Jack deck where she was writing. It was April. Noah was under the covered deck around the side of the building, helping his dad lower a sack of fat writhing crabs into boiling water. Steam roiled into the cool salt air. Lucy was down on the dock, chasing gulls. Blake and Noah had put the small boats back into the water and they clunked together, nudging each other playfully, as if in anticipation of the warmth, and the tourists. Irene sat knitting near the gas fire pit, a rug over her knees. Her nurse was inside, prepping lunch.

Spring. New beginnings.

Meg returned her attention to writing.

> In all my other books, before I even started, I knew exactly who the perpetrator was. Don't pick an unsolved case, Day Rigby, my mentor, always said. It was a cardinal rule in true crime—you had to know the ending. You had to know who your villain was, that he'd been captured, charged, tried, and convicted. That justice had been served. That the natural order of things had been restored.
>
> But we knew now who the stranger among us had been, how close to us he had lived. And what he'd done in the waning light of that late summer day, just before the storm.
>
> Sherry got her justice. We got our second chance. It came through a twist in the helix of time, as if we'd all been brought back on stage by Fate to replay, and rewrite, what had gone wrong in our lives that day. The vellum has been scraped down of lies and secrets, like the sand is scraped clean by the tide. We have closure. We can begin again.

Meg smiled. And typed:

THE END, a new one.

ACKNOWLEDGMENTS

It was a trip down the moody Oregon coast in a camper with my husband and black Lab, and some excellent crabbing at a special little marina on majestic Nehalem Bay, that eventually became the inspiration for Meg and Blake's story. A special thank-you must thus go to Kelly and Janice Laviolette, who run Kelly's Brighton Marina. I have no doubt we'll be back!

Thank you also to JoVon Sotak for taking a chance on this story, to editors Kelli Martin and Charlotte Herscher for helping shepherd it into being, to copyeditor Scott Calamar for his feedback, Rick Edmisten for proofreading, Jason Blackburn for the cover design, and to the rest of the behind-the-scenes team at Amazon Publishing. It could not have happened without any one of you.

And as always, a deep debt of gratitude to my husband, Paul, aka my patron of the arts, who supports my writing habit in so many ways.

ABOUT THE AUTHOR

Loreth Anne White is a multipublished author of award-winning romantic suspense, thriller, and mystery. A double RITA finalist, she has won the Romantic Times Reviewers' Choice Award, the National Readers' Choice Award, the Readers' Crown, and is a Booksellers Best Award finalist, a double Daphne Du Maurier finalist, and a multiple CataRomance Reviewers' choice winner.

Loreth hails from South Africa but now lives with her family in a ski resort in the moody Coast Mountains of North America's Pacific Northwest. It's a place of vast, wild, and often dangerous mountains, larger-than-life characters, epic adventure, and romance—the perfect place to escape reality. It's no wonder it was here that she was inspired to abandon her sixteen-year newspaper career to escape into a world of romantic fiction filled with dangerous men and adventurous women.

When she's not writing, you will find her open-water distance swimming, skiing, biking, hiking, or running the trails with her Black Dog, and generally trying to avoid the bears—albeit not successfully. In the summer she will often be on the road, searching out remote camping/fly-fishing spots with her husband or participating in tracking and air scent courses with her Black Beast. She calls this work, because it's when the best ideas come.

Loreth loves to hear from readers. You can contact her through her website at www.lorethannewhite.com, or you can find her on Facebook or Twitter.